CRISIS

THE OMEGA SUPERHERO BOOK 5

DARIUS BRASHER

Special thanks to Flint L. Miller, a higher level supporter of my Patreon fiction writing campaign. Your support is much appreciated!

No plan survives first contact with the enemy.

— Prussian Field Marshal Helmuth Karl
Bernhard Graf von Moltke

Everybody has a plan until they get punched in the mouth.

— Mike Tyson

SERIES RECAP

SPOILER ALERT

The following is a recap of the events of the previous four books in the Omega Superhero series. If you haven't read the prior books and don't want to be spoiled by this summary, stop reading now.

Theodore Conley is a 17-year-old college student and naive farm boy when he unexpectedly develops telekinetic powers. At his father's insistence, Theo reluctantly registers his Metahuman powers with the federal government in compliance with the U.S. Hero Act of 1945. The government determines Theo is an Omega-level Meta, meaning he has the potential to be one of the most powerful Metahumans in the world.

Theo doesn't want to learn to use his powers or to become a superhero by getting a Hero's license. He just wants to return to his normal life.

Iceburn, a Metahuman supervillain known as a Rogue, sets fire to Theo's family home in an attempt to kill Theo. Theo tries to fight Iceburn, but he is no match for the experienced Rogue. Iceburn escapes, but not before killing Theo's father.

Now an orphan, Theo realizes he must learn to use his powers if he has any hope of tracking Iceburn down and killing him in revenge. Theo enrolls in Hero Academy, the country's only superhero school. During his time at the Academy, Theo learns Iceburn is a high-priced assassin, which begs the question of who wants Theo dead and why.

Upon graduating the Academy, Theo adopts the code name Kinetic. He becomes one of Amazing Man's sidekicks and continues his Hero training. Amazing Man's other side-kicks are Isaac Geere (code-named Myth) and Neha Thakore (code-named Smoke). Neha, whom Theo falls in love with, is the daughter of notorious Rogue Doctor Alchemy.

Theo finds and defeats Iceburn. Instead of killing him, Theo turns him over to the authorities. Iceburn refuses to reveal who hired him to assassinate Theo.

Now interested in becoming a Hero, Theo must pass the Hero Trials. During them, Theo saves the life of Hacker, who has the power to control computers by touching them. In exchange for Theo saving her life, Hacker reprograms the computer supervising a rigged duel between Theo and Isaac to make the duel fair. While doing so, Hacker discovers that the person behind the multiple attempts on Theo's life is a robotic Hero named Mechano. Mechano is one of the Sentinels, the world's premiere superhero team.

Theo passes the Trials and receives his Hero license. He moves to Astor City, Maryland, where the Sentinels are headquartered. With the help of a Hero and private eye named Truman Lord, Theo uncovers why Mechano and his fellow Sentinels Seer and Millennium are trying to kill him.

Theo is the vessel for the Omega spirit, a mysterious

entity that has helped protect humanity from threats since the dawn of man. The Omega spirit occupied Theo after the murder of its previous vessel, Avatar. Mechano, Seer and Millennium knew a world-threatening crisis was looming, and they believed Theo was too young and inexperienced to be the vessel for the Omega spirit during such a trying time. The three Sentinels offer to train Theo further to get him ready for the crisis, but Theo refuses. The Sentinels also want Theo to give them a powerful artifact known as the Omega weapon, but Theo doesn't know where it is.

Theo finds the Omega weapon in The Mountain, Avatar's secret lair. When Theo touches the Omega weapon, his body absorbs it and it augments his powers. Theo changes his code name from Kinetic to Omega and fashions the Omega weapon into a new superhero suit. Adopting The Mountain as his own lair, Theo secretly imprisons in it a Rogue named Mad Dog who murdered one of his friends.

Meanwhile, Mechano, Seer and Millennium kidnap Neha and demand Theo surrender the Omega weapon in exchange for her. Theo instead tricks them and escapes their clutches with Neha. Unbeknownst to Theo, the Sentinels planted a bomb on Neha in a final effort to kill him. Theo survives the explosion, but Neha does not.

Enraged, Theo destroys Mechano and incapacitates Seer and Millennium. Millennium mysteriously disappears.

Blaming himself for the deaths of Neha and his father, Theo vows no one else will die because of him. He throws himself into crime-fighting obsessively to prepare for the looming crisis the three Sentinels warned him about.

Theo is captured by the Revengers, a team of Rogues led by Doctor Alchemy which includes Iceburn and Mad Dog. After Doctor Alchemy tortures him, Theo manages to escape. He, Isaac, and a former Sentinel named Ninja defeat

Doctor Alchemy. Theo takes custody of the Philosopher's Stone, the magical book that is the source of Doctor Alchemy's powers. He hides it in The Mountain.

Theo learns from the Revengers capturing him that he should not try to face the coming crisis alone. He, Isaac and Ninja form a new team of Heroes in anticipation of the crisis.

The adventure continues . . .

PROLOGUE

SIXTH CENTURY BRITAIN

"You cannot deny my destiny," the Ancient One swore. "You can only postpone it." The ominous words echoed off Stonehenge's tall stones and sent a chill up King Arthur's spine.

Merlin spoke the last words of his spell, raising his long wooden staff high. Each of the dozens of rocks composing Stonehenge flashed, then dimmed again. Something milky-white leaked from the bottom of each of the prehistoric structure's stones, as if the stones were squeezed bladders of milk instead of solid rock.

The white substance glowed with a power that charged the air and made Arthur's skin prickle. It ran silently on the ground in dozens of rivulets toward the boulder in the dead center of Stonehenge on which the Ancient One's powerful body was chained with enchanted iron. As Merlin had instructed, Arthur and his men had positioned the boulder there. It was the only rock not a permanent part of this ancient structure.

The rivulets ran up the boulder, defying gravity. Like iron filings drawn to a magnet, the rivulets were drawn to the bound form of the Ancient One. They swirled over him. Soon the white substance coated the Ancient One like he had been dipped in it.

The Ancient One's enchained body glowed like a harvest moon. Arthur squinted, forcing himself to not look away from the glare. After the bitter war he and his comrades had waged against their powerful foe, Arthur was not about to miss this capstone of their victory.

The Ancient One's bound body spasmed. His head was thrown back, and he wailed in pain mixed with frustration. His glowing body fragmented into pieces, like a hot coal struck by a hammer. The glowing pieces then blew away, as if caught in a strong breeze.

Like sparks from a hearth, the pieces ascended, floating beyond the confines of Stonehenge's roofless structure. They disappeared into the cloudy night sky.

Soon there was nothing left of the Ancient One. The heavy iron chains that had bound him clanged against the face of the rock they were wrapped around, empty as the Ancient One's soul.

Merlin's heavy robes rustled as he lowered his staff, its tip glowing like an ember. It and the torches a few of Arthur's knights held were the only illumination within the gapped stone structure, though outside flickered countless campfires and torches from the tattered remnants of Arthur's army.

"It is done," the wizard intoned.

"Did you kill him?" rumbled Bodo. The dark-skinned Carthaginian eyed the old wizard suspiciously. His hand lingered near his sheathed sword's hilt, and he looked like he itched to draw it. The tall African seemed almost as wary of Merlin as he had been of the Ancient One. Bodo had doubtless heard the rumors circulating among Arthur's men that Merlin was half-demon. Men tended to fear what they did not understand. Merlin had taught Arthur that lesson when Arthur had been but a smooth-faced boy, and a lifetime of experience had confirmed its truth.

"No," Merlin answered Bodo. Merlin stroked his long white beard with his free hand. It was an unconscious habit that manifested when the wizard was troubled. "Would that I could kill him. Even in defeat, the Ancient One is too powerful for that. Aided by the mystic power of Stonehenge, I have instead imprisoned him in another realm. A noncorporeal one. The threat is abated. Despite his bravado, the Ancient One will trouble us no longer."

The armored men assembled within Stonehenge muttered amongst themselves at this news, though more in relief than in triumph. Their victory over the Ancient One had been dearly won. Everyone present had lost family, friends, and comrades in the struggle. They all were covered with blood and gore, and all but Arthur were wounded. Arthur had been grievously injured during the battle as well, but his wounds had almost immediately closed, healed, and disappeared, as if they had never occurred. Fortunately, none of those wounds had been catastrophic; Arthur's body was resilient, not invulnerable. Legend said that Arthur's sword scabbard was magical and prevented him from bleeding to death. As was often the case with legends, the legend was wrong.

If only my healing abilities extended beyond the mere flesh, Arthur thought. Though physically whole, he was sick at heart. Countless subjects, comrades, and friends had died in this final clash between Arthur's forces and the Ancient One's. Thousands of wounded, dead and dying littered the plain on which Stonehenge rested, the battle having ended less than an hour ago. The ground outside the confines of Stonehenge's rock slabs was slick with blood. Arthur's men were busy sorting the living from the dead out there. Between the countless flickering torches, the moans and cries of pain, the stench of death, and bodies and body parts littering the ground like a grotesque red tapestry, it was as if Britain had plunged straight into hell.

If it had not been for formidable foreign allies answering Arthur's call for help against the foe who threatened them all, the battle surely would have had a different ending. If Britain had fallen to the Ancient One, the rest of the world would've quickly followed. Even with the help of Arthur's allies, it had been a close call—the Ancient One and his forces had nearly prevailed.

A high price had been paid for their victory, however. Most of Arthur's foreign allies had fallen either today or in prior battles, many at the hands of the Ancient One himself. Only Bodo and the dusky woman from the Far East who now stared at Arthur with mysterious eyes had survived.

"Now that the enemy is vanquished, I must return home," Hua Trinh Khiêm said in her heavily accented voice. Her armor was made of a thick brown leather; a short sword hung from one hip, and a dagger from the other. The slight woman shyly smiled up at Arthur, erasing the grim look that usually hid her brown face's beauty. "Before I go, will you show me again? The trick with your sword?"

"The king is not a court jester," Sir Lancelot growled. The valiant knight did not approve of Khiêm and made no effort to hide it. Women who wore armor, fought battles, and did not defer to men defied his sense of how things ought to be.

"It's all right," Arthur assured Lancelot. "Our comrade

has more than earned a few royal japes and capers." Lancelot's snort of disgust made clear he did not consider the almond-eyed woman a comrade, regardless of all she had done in the long war against the Ancient One.

Ignoring his knight's disapproval, Arthur drew Excalibur from its supposedly magical scabbard with a smooth, practiced motion. Excalibur was a well-wrought, well-balanced sword, suited for royalty. According to legend, a sorceress known as the Lady of the Lake had given it to Arthur. That legend was also wrong, but mostly because it did not go far enough. As fantastic as the Lady of the Lake story was, the sword's true origins were even more fantastical. It was a weapon that had taken many forms and had many wielders throughout the ages. Arthur was but its latest custodian.

Arthur stepped toward the stone that had once bound the Ancient One. Excalibur began to glow, eclipsing the torchlight in intensity. Arthur thrust the sword forward, toward the huge boulder.

The sword slid into the boulder like it was soft cheese instead of solid rock.

Once the glowing sword had sunk into the boulder to the weapon's crossguard, Arthur let go of it. Like a torch plunged into a bucket of water, the sword immediately stopped glowing.

Arthur paused a moment for dramatic effect, then gripped the sword again. It resumed glowing. Arthur pulled the sword out of the stone as easily as he had thrust the weapon into it.

Khiêm clapped her hands with delight. Her face, normally dour, looked the way Arthur imagined it looked when she'd been a carefree child. "I'll never tire of seeing that," the Asian woman said as Arthur sheathed Excalibur.

Then Khiêm's somber mien returned. She clasped her

hands together and bowed deeply toward Arthur. Arthur hesitated for a beat, then returned Khiêm's gesture of respect. Arthur's knights all gasped, then Lancelot and a few others muttered angrily. They did not approve of the king of Britain bowing to anyone, much less to a foreigner. Especially when that foreigner was a woman.

Khiêm straightened, then turned and bowed toward Bodo. Instead of returning the bow, the big African swept the small woman off her feet and enveloped her in an affectionate bear hug. Irritation flashed on Khiêm's face, but she tolerated the embrace. The reserved woman did not like to be touched. It was a testament to how much she respected Bodo that his embrace was not answered with a dagger in his belly.

Khiêm took a couple of steps back once Bodo set her down. Her entire body burst into blue flames, as if she had been covered in pitch and ignited. Khiêm's fiery form crouched, then jumped. With a sizzling sound, she shot past Stonehenge's confines and into the air. In seconds she was so high up, she could be mistaken as the sole star in the overcast night sky. Then, like a shooting star, she streaked off into the distance.

Arthur turned his attention to Bodo once he lost sight of Khiêm. "You're welcome to stay," he told the large man. "There's a seat awaiting you at the Round Table." Arthur would have made the same offer to Khiêm, but he knew his knights would not have stood for it. If a leader gets too far in front of his followers, he soon finds that he has lost them.

"Thanks, but no thanks," Bodo said. "I have my own lands to protect back home. I've been gone too long. I shudder to think what's happened in my absence." Bodo's face split into a wide grin. "Besides, if I don't return, who will my wives henpeck?"

Arthur and Bodo clasped each other by the forearm and shook.

"Farewell General Bodo, son of Adad," Arthur said, using the formal Carthaginian form of address he had learned from his brave friend.

"Farewell King Arthur, son of Uther. I'd say this has been fun, but that would be an overstatement. Instead, I'll simply say this has been . . . interesting."

Bodo shot Merlin another wary look. Then there was a small *pop*, and Arthur found himself clasping thin air. Bodo had disappeared. The only indication he had ever been there was thin tendrils of rapidly dissipating smoke.

Arthur ordered his knights to supervise the tending of the wounded and the burying of the dead. The battle-scarred knights filed out of Stonehenge's confines.

Soon, Arthur and Merlin were alone. Together, they silently stared at the boulder on which the Ancient One had been bound. Both were lost in thought.

Arthur was the first to break the silence. "How long will your spell keep him imprisoned?" the king asked.

"Eh?" The wizard looked startled. "Why do you ask? Why don't you think he's gone forever?"

"Because I've known you too long, old friend. 'The Ancient One will trouble us no longer,' you said." Arthur remembered how Merlin had stroked his beard when he said that, a sure sign the wizard was worried. "The way you said it made me think he's gone for now, but not for good. Not to mention the Ancient One's own words: 'You cannot deny my destiny. You can only postpone it.' He is many things, but an idle blusterer is not one of them. So again I ask: How long?"

"My king is as perceptive as he is brave."

"My court magician is as evasive as he is unkempt."

Arthur reached over to teasingly tug Merlin's unruly beard, just as he had countless times as a mischievous boy. Merlin swatted Arthur's hand away. Arthur laughed, but immediately sobered. It seemed a blasphemy to laugh when countless men were dead and injured outside. "If you think I'll let you avoid answering the question, you're wrong. How long?"

"I'm avoiding the question because you'll like the answer as little as I do." The old wizard leaned heavily on his staff as he stroked his beard. His veiny, liver-spotted hand shook a little. Though Merlin had been alive for centuries, he usually seemed far younger than he was. Today he looked his age. "I am the most powerful sorcerer in the world. Perhaps the most powerful sorcerer to ever walk the earth. However, not even I could have banished the Ancient One without the assistance of Stonehenge's magic. As you know, Stonehenge is situated at the center of a network of ley lines, making it a powerful energy vortex. It's why I advised you to lure the Ancient One and his army here." Legend said that Merlin himself had arranged the stones of Stonehenge after stealing them from a race of giants in Ireland. Merlin had previously assured Arthur that, as old as Merlin was, Stonehenge had been here centuries before Merlin's birth. Not even Merlin knew who had built the ancient structure, or for what reason.

"My spell will hold the Ancient One for a while," Merlin said. "But not forever. Decades? Certainly. Centuries? Probably. Millennia?" Merlin shook his head, his rheumy eyes troubled. "I fear not. And, while he is imprisoned, he will grow stronger. The world's greatest champions barely defeated him today. Surely the world of tomorrow will fall before him when he is even more formidable. I fear the Ancient One will be unstoppable then. I fear he spoke truly. I fear we have merely delayed the inevitable."

Arthur let that sink in.

"Perhaps," the king finally said thoughtfully. "Or perhaps the horse will sing."

Merlin's white bushy eyebrows knit together in a puzzled frown. "What?"

"Have you forgotten the Herodotus you taught me? The Greek historian tells the tale of a thief who snuck into the imperial stables in the dead of night to steal the emperor's prize white stallion. He was caught and thrown into the dungeon.

"The next morning," Arthur said, "the thief was dragged before the emperor and his court. The irate ruler sentenced the thief to death, with the execution to take place immediately.

"'I accept Your Imperial Majesty's sentence,' the thief said hastily as the executioner approached with his gleaming ax, 'for I'm ashamed to admit I'm guilty of the crime I am accused of. However, I was a voice teacher before I fell on hard times and turned to a life of crime. As restitution for my crime, if Your Majesty will spare my life for a year and a day, I swear to teach your beloved stallion to sing.'

"The assembled court burst into laughter at the thief's ridiculous proposal. The emperor was intrigued, though. He suspected the thief could not teach his horse to sing, but what did the emperor have to lose? If the thief were lying, he would get the punishment he richly deserved soon enough. If the thief were telling the truth, though, the emperor would own the only singing horse in the world, which would increase the horse's value a thousandfold and the emperor's prestige immeasurably.

"And so, the emperor stayed the thief's execution for a

year and a day. When the thief was returned to the dungeon, he told his cellmates what had happened.

"'You're a fool!' his cellmates cried. 'It's impossible to teach a horse to sing. Why did you tell the emperor you could?'

"'Am I really a fool?' the thief responded smugly. 'Much can happen in a year and a day. The horse could die, and the emperor might let me off the hook for doing my best to try to teach the animal to sing. Or the emperor could die, and my death penalty might be commuted by his successor. Or I could die, making the whole thing moot.

"'Or maybe, just maybe,' the thief said, 'I'll teach that horse to sing.'"

Arthur let out a long breath. "We've done all we can to protect the world from the Ancient One. We've done our best, and our best is all God demands of us. Now it's the future's turn. Maybe the Ancient One will be unstoppable centuries from now as you say. Like the thief's cellmates thought about tutoring a horse, defeating a more powerful version of the Ancient One seems impossible to us."

Arthur felt his jaw tighten grimly. He put his hand on his mentor's shoulder.

"But every generation has its heroes," King Arthur said. "Perhaps, countless years from now, one of them will teach a horse to sing."

1

The same strange dream had recurred off and on for months.

That night, it returned.

I stood on a grassy promontory overlooking a narrow beach. I saw for miles in every direction. No one else was around. I was as alone in my dreams as I felt in the real world.

I wore only the shorts and t-shirt I had gone to bed in. A gentle breeze ruffled my hair; the tang of seawater filled my nostrils. The colors around me were otherworldly vivid, as if I were in a television show and someone had fiddled with the contrast and color controls. The grass beneath my bare feet was radioactive green; the sand far below the promontory was milky-white; the water that lapped the beach was sapphire blue; the sky was as blue as indigo dye; and the bright sun seemed dotted with countless volcanoes, erupting yellowish-red plumes of fire that danced and writhed like a squid's tentacles.

The indigo sky was clear and cloudless, except for far off in the distance over the oddly colored ocean. There, dark clouds gathered, lit up from time to time by jagged streaks of white, yellow and pink lightning.

The strange sun was directly overhead. High noon. Unfortunately, like a dummy, I didn't have my spurs on and had left my six-shooters in my other shorts. Some Gary Cooper I was. Not that there was an enemy here to square off against, anyway.

Thunder rumbled faintly from the distant dark clouds. A bad storm was brewing. I glanced at the dark clouds, then immediately averted my eyes. As usual, it was hard to look at the clouds. Something about them disturbed me on a visceral level, like they were somehow deeply and darkly wrong.

I knew from having this dream before that it was a lucid one, meaning I could consciously act instead of merely passively watching events play out. I could stand here and look at the water while avoiding looking at the storm clouds until I woke if I wanted.

Instead, already bored with standing in one spot, I began walking. In the real world I could use my telekinesis to fly. In this dreamworld, I didn't have Metahuman powers and was confined to the ground. I was also confined to the edge of the promontory I walked along. Even if I spun 180 degrees, the world around me somehow flipped so that the grass was always to my right and the cliff was to my left. It was bizarre, but no one ever said dreams were logical. I couldn't move very far to the right, toward where the grass extended out forever like a never-ending green scroll. I didn't test if I could move far to the left, off the edge of the promontory's cliff. Since I couldn't fly in this dreamworld, maybe I'd fall to my death on the rocks below. They say if you die in a dream, you die in real life. That probably wasn't true. How would anyone know? But why take a chance? My life was dangerous enough without going out of my way to tempt fate.

I walked for a while. Due to the peculiar way time and distance distort in dreams, I could have walked only a few hundred feet or for hundreds of miles. The grass, the promontory, the beach, the water, the approaching storm . . . everything stayed the same as I traveled, as if I were stuck in a loop.

Abruptly, off in the distance, I spotted something different. Something I had never seen in one of these dreams before.

I kept walking. The object got bigger and bigger as I got closer and closer to it.

No, not an object. A person.

A girl.

I stopped in front of her and looked down. She blinked up at me somberly. She was a cute little Asian child, no older than four or five. Her straight black hair was slightly below shoulder-length. A single thin pigtail secured by a plastic pink barrette sloped down from the top of her head. She wore black cropped pants, pink ballet flats, and a beige short-sleeved, white-dotted shirt out of which poked thin brown arms. The shirt had a bunny rabbit sewn onto its front.

Unlike the rest of the dreamworld, the little girl wasn't absurdly colored. She looked like a normal child I might see walking hand in hand with her mother in the Astor City Mall. Since the girl looked vaguely familiar, maybe I actually had seen the girl at the mall or someplace similar. Perhaps my subconscious had tucked the girl's face into my memory and re-created her here.

"Well, you're new," I said aloud.

"I was just thinking the same thing about you, buster," the girl retorted. "You're not who I was expecting."

Her speaking startled me. This was the first time I had heard a voice other than my own in one of these weird recurring dreams. "You can talk."

"Of course I can talk," she sniffed, flicking her ponytail with a tiny hand. "I'm not a potted plant."

The girl had the high-pitched, squeaky voice of an anime character. Though she had a child's voice and appearance, the girl's diction and attitude were anything but childlike. My weird dream had just gotten weirder. "How old are you?" I asked.

The girl's face scrunched up in thought. "I'm eighty-seven and three-quarters years old," she concluded.

I smiled down at her indulgently. "Really? You don't look a day over sixty-six and a half. You must have quite the moisturizing regime."

She rolled her eyes. "Everyone's a comedian," she muttered.

"What's your name?"

"That's not important right now. There's not much time."

"Mine's Theo."

"Duh! I know. Theodore Conley, the licensed Hero known as Omega. Champion of the right, defender of the weak, scourge of the wicked, vessel of the Omega spirit, wearer of the speedo of power. Aka the artist formerly known as Kinetic. I have all your albums." The girl rolled her eyes again.

"That's quite a name you have, by the way," she added. "Theodore is from a Greek word meaning 'God-given.' Conley is from a Gaelic word meaning 'Hero.'"

The girl paused, smacking her lips distastefully, like she tasted something rotten. "'God-given hero.' Oh brother!

What a name to saddle a kid with. Mighty big name to live up to. I hope you're game. If not, we're all screwed."

The girl shook her head and let out a long breath. "Oh well. Names are irrelevant to character. Calling a rose a turd or a turd a rose doesn't change how either smell. How do you smell, I wonder? Let's take a nice, long whiff, shall we?"

The girl slowly walked around me in a circle, tugging her pigtail absentmindedly. She eyed me critically, as if she were in the market for a used car and suspected I was a lemon. It was hard to not laugh at the somber look on her tiny face.

"You said before I was not who you were expecting," I said. "Who were you expecting?"

"It's 'Whom were you expecting?'" the girl corrected as she continued to circle me, looking even less pleased than before. "Sloppy language is indicative of sloppy thinking, and sloppy thinking is indicative of a loser. What the world needs now is a winner, not a loser. Alas, the turd smell grows stronger." The girl wrinkled her nose and waved a hand in front of it. "Just goes to show that 'She who smelt it dealt it' isn't always true. To answer your ungrammatical question, I expected someone older. Someone more experienced. Not a country mouse wrestling with the ways of the big, bad city. I'd hoped for Avatar, but the big oaf had to go and be seduced by some femme fatale. Tale as old as time, I know, but I thought Avatar wasn't a stereotypical male ruled by his gonads."

The girl suddenly stopped pacing. She grinned, her mien abruptly age-appropriate. "Or I should say, 'Tail as old as time'? T-A-I-L. It's a homonym. Tail got Avatar killed. Get it?"

"Oh, I get it alright." First my mind had manifested this

child, now it had her making bawdy puns. My subconscious was weird.

The girl's grin evaporated, replaced by a deep frown. She resumed pacing around me. "Humph! No, you don't get it. Not really. But I'll fix that soon enough. I'll get you as ready as I possibly can. The rest'll be up to you."

Finally, the girl stopped pacing and stood in front of me with her hands on her hips. "I guess you'll have to do," she decided. "You're not perfect, but one must work with the tools one has despite their flaws."

"I have no idea what you're talking about."

"I know. But you'll find out."

Thunder rumbled, louder than before, deep-throated and ominous. The girl eyed the distant clouds nervously.

"It's just a little thunder," I assured her. "A storm. There's nothing to be afraid of."

The girl's face was even grimmer than before. She glared at the storm clouds like she was willing them to go away.

"It's not a storm," she said.

"What is it then?"

"It's not even an it. It's a he. Lilu. The Adversary. The Ancient One. The Destroyer. Hellscape. He's had a bunch of different names and forms down through the ages. Some cultures call him the Devil, though of course he isn't. The Devil's game is seduction, not violence."

"That sounds like magic and fairytales," I scoffed. "Plus, the Devil's not real."

The girl gave me a knowing look. "Don't thumb your nose at magic and fairytales. There's nothing so dangerous as confident ignorance. And as for there being no Devil . . . well, don't go and bet your life on it, tenderfoot. You have much to learn. 'The universe is not only queerer than we suppose, but queerer than we *can* suppose.'"

"John Burdon Haldane," I said immediately, supplying the name of the British-Indian scientist the girl had quoted.

The girl's face softened, looking somewhat impressed. "Maybe there's hope for the country mouse after all. *Maybe*. Don't let me saying so go to your head."

She faced the storm clouds again and glowered at them. "Regardless of what other people call him, I call him Progenitor. Because he is the father of us all." Looking disgusted, she stuck her tongue out and blew a raspberry at the clouds. "Ugh! A shame you can't pick your family. Imagine, having him for a father. Right now, Progenitor is my problem. He'll be yours soon enough. I'll help you get ready."

Thunder rumbled again, louder this time. I forced myself to look at the dark clouds in the distance. It seemed like they were closer than they had been when the dream first started.

"But later," the girl said in a clipped voice, suddenly all business. "Right now I must turn my full attention back to Progenitor. He gets restless when I'm not totally focused on him. Time for me to head back to the salt mines. We'll talk later."

I shook my head in bemusement. "You sure are one strange figment of my imagination."

The girl spun around and stared up at me. Her eyes widened with sudden recognition and then pity, like I was a toddler she had just realized was learning disabled. "Oh you sweet summer child. We've been singing from two different hymn sheets this whole time. This is not a dream, dear boy. I wish it were."

"Of course it's a dream. Why else don't my powers work? Why else would a child look four-years-old but sound a hundred and four? How else do you know my real name and code name? I'm having this conversation with my subconscious. I'm asleep in the mansion. I know because crawling into bed and going to sleep are the last things I remember doing."

"Yes, you're asleep. But no, this is not a dream."

"Yes, it is," I insisted.

The girl's face screwed up with irritation. She stomped her foot. "No, it's not."

I couldn't believe I was arguing with an imaginary child. "Yes, it is."

The girl sprang off the ground like a missile, making me take a startled step back. Hovering above me, she balled the collar of my t-shirt up in a tiny fist and yanked me close, pulling me up on my tiptoes. She was stronger than she looked.

"Now you listen and listen good, buster," she snarled right in my face, her slanted eyes blazing with an inner fire. Her breath smelled like cinnamon and strawberries. "This is not a dream you . . . you . . . lunkhead! The sooner you get that through your thick skull, the sooner we can move on to more substantive matters." Her face left mine and she looked straight up into the absurdly blue sky like she was appealing to a higher power. "Morons! The universe has given me morons to work with."

A particularly bright bolt of pink lightning lit up the storm clouds marring the horizon. The girl's eyes shifted to the clouds anxiously, then back to me.

Speaking quickly like someone late for an appointment, she said, "I don't have time to go round and round the mulberry bush with you about this. I'll prove this is real. Hold still. This is gonna hurt. But you asked for it."

The girl slammed her free hand against my forehead.

It felt like a cattle brand searing my head.

I screamed.

2

_____

I bolted upright. My head throbbed painfully, my chest heaved, and I was drenched with sweat.

It was as dark here as it had been bright on the promontory. Confused, I had no idea where I was. It took a moment for my mental fog to lift.

A little moonlight trickled in through the tall window on my left, helping me get my bearings. I knew this room as well as my tongue knew the inside of my mouth. I was sitting in bed in my bedroom in our Hero team's Astor City, Maryland mansion. I was alone. Unlike in the dream, my hands burned and waves of power that were visible only to me radiated from them. The sight and the tingly feeling were as familiar and welcome as a mother's kiss. My hands had burned like this ever since my Metahuman powers manifested when I was seventeen, over six years ago. My hands were how I channeled and focused my power.

The digital clock next to my bed read 3:12 a.m. The alarm was set to go off at 4:30 a.m. I had gone to sleep a little over an hour ago. Thanks to the Omega suit being part of me, I did not need much sleep. I usually only got a few hours a night.

I'd gone to sleep, dreamed, and then woke up. To use the words of the Asian girl, it was a tale as old as time. What I had told her seemed correct: she and everything else I'd witnessed had been merely a dream.

Why then, did my head hurt like it had been stabbed by a hot poker?

In the superhero business, one could never be too careful. Better safe than sorry.

Triggering my powers, I sent out invisible and silent telekinetic pulses all around me, like a submarine using sonar to navigate in the murky depths of the sea. The gentle pulses bounced off everything and returned to me, giving me a 360-degree visual in my mind's eye of what was happening in the mansion. I called it my telekinetic touch.

Everything was as it should be. All the other Heroes in the mansion were asleep except me. Even Blur, whose augmented metabolism made him as much of a night owl as I was. 'Twas months before Christmas, when all through the house, not a creature was stirring, not even Mighty Mouse.

"You there, Minerva?" I said.

"Of course, Mister Chairman," came a sexy female voice from hidden speakers in the walls. "You're up late."

"There's no rest for the wicked. And knock it off with the 'Mister Chairman' nonsense. It makes me sound like Mao Zedong. Have any of the mansion's alarms been tripped?"

"No. You would have been alerted if they had been."

"Run a full spectrum security scan on the mansion, paying particular attention to my bedroom and the surrounding area. Anything unusual?"

"Working." There was a dull flash of green light in my

room, so low that I would have assumed it was my imagination had I not been expecting it.

Minerva said, "It's three thirteen in the morning and all's well. Though your heart rate is elevated. Are you jumping at shadows again?"

"Sometimes they jump back, so you can't be too careful. Thanks."

"Don't mention it, Mister Ch—uh, Theo. Want me to sing baby a lullaby to calm him down?"

"Maybe next time."

"That's what you always say. I don't think you like my singing voice."

"Now that you mention it, your singing reminds me of when tomcats used to get into fights back on the farm."

"I ought to come up there and spank baby instead. Sweet dreams, you tone-deaf philistine."

"That's Chairman Philistine to you."

"First don't call you chairman, now call you chairman. Sheesh! Make up your mind." Minerva fell quiet. She was the artificially intelligent supercomputer who helped run the mansion and our superhero team, named after the Roman goddess of wisdom and strategy. Her software matrix was designed by Hacker—one of the Heroes I went through the Trials with—and her hardware was inspired by notes and technical specifications left behind by Mechano, the robotic Sentinel I destroyed for killing my friend Neha Thakore. My teammate Isaac Geere—aka the Hero Myth— had supervised the UWant Technology programmers who coded Minerva's personality. Isaac had inserted a lot of his own personality into Minerva, and it showed. Talking to her was the next best thing to talking to him, especially these days when he barely spoke to me.

Isaac had carefully selected Minerva's warm, breathy

contralto voice. "It makes her sound like she has a big rack," he had said about the vocal choice at the time.

"Why can't you be satisfied with just your fiancée having a big rack?" I had asked.

"I thought I saw you staring at her. Stop drooling over Sylvia's chest, you boob-obsessed creep." That exchange had taken place months ago, back when Isaac still joked around with me. Now he pretty much only spoke to me when he had to for team-related business.

It was sad I had a warmer relationship with a computer than I did with my five human teammates. I shook my head ruefully at the thought, and instantly regretted it. The motion did my aching head no favors. Thankfully, though, the pain was subsiding. The dream girl had said touching me would hurt. Apparently, through the power of suggestion, my mind had made my head actually hurt. It was crazy how suggestible we humans were. It was why hypnosis worked.

Despite my psychosomatic pain, thanks to Minerva's confirmation of my own telekinetic scan, I was one hundred percent certain I had been dreaming and was not the victim of some sort of attack.

That was the good news. The bad news was, despite being tired, I was wide awake due to getting amped up by the dream. Might as well rise and shine. The early bird got the worm. Which was great if you were the bird, but sucked if you were the early worm who got gobbled up. The worm should've slept in. Maybe the secret to a successful life was figuring out if you were the bird or the worm and acting accordingly.

I slid out of bed and stretched. My back and shoulders went snap, crackle, and pop. Aches and pains, the Hero's breakfast of champions. My body's Rice Krispies impersonation was Ninja's doing. My teammate had tossed me like a salad in the mansion's Peril Room yesterday during a training exercise. Like Isaac, Ninja also wasn't happy with me; the master martial artist hadn't held back yesterday like she usually did. In the holographic scenario, Ninja had kidnapped a six-year-old and had stashed her in a crowded apartment building. My job had been to find the girl and subdue Ninja, all without using my powers. Finding the girl hadn't been too hard. Subduing Ninja had gone less well. As my aching body reminded me.

Those aches and the throbbing of my forehead weren't soothed by awakening in this blasted bedroom. Despite living in the mansion for months, I still wasn't used to it. Frankly, I didn't *want* to get used to it. It was why the room was almost as spartan and undecorated as the day I had moved in; I resisted thinking of this place as home. Even with the lack of clutter, I had still somehow managed to misplace the book I'd been reading a couple of days ago. I smiled wryly to myself. Maybe Tempus Fugit stole it, though legend said the fictitious Rogue group targeted items far more valuable than a used science book. If the imaginary Metahuman gang could make heads or tails out of the quantum mechanics the book described, I hoped they brought it back and explained it to me.

The bulk of my belongings were still in the penthouse apartment I owned near downtown. If I got fed up with the mansion, I could easily return to that apartment. I had been talked into living in the mansion and my rational mind understood the arguments for living here, but all that didn't mean I had to like it. It was why I had chosen this room, the smallest the sprawling mansion offered, instead of one of its palatial bedrooms the size of Nebraska.

I stumbled into my cramped bathroom, feeling achy and

out of sorts, wondering if I would feel like this all the time when I got old. Maybe I'd get lucky and a supervillain would put me out of my misery before then. Every dark cloud had a silver lining.

I flicked on the lights with my powers, squinting and bending my head to shield my eyes from the sudden glare. My eyes fell on my legs. My right leg was hairless and slightly discolored from where Doctor Alchemy had peeled it like a carrot. Good thing I had no aspirations to become a leg model.

I ran some cold water and, again using my powers, splashed it on my face. It helped. The throbbing of my head almost disappeared, thank goodness.

I grabbed a washcloth with my powers and dried my face. The towel scrubbed me as if by magic. Since leg model was out of the question, maybe I'd become a professional car washer instead. I could wash fleets of vehicles without ever physically picking up a towel or using a water hose. Customers would think it was a miracle. I could just see my business sign now: *Theo's Holy Water Car Wash—We'll Wash The Hell Out Of Your Car*.

When I pulled the towel away, that's when I saw it in the mirror over the sink.

A child's small handprint was burned into the center of my head like a brand.

3

The door opened and light spilled into the dark space like acid, burning my eyes. Hissing softly, the patient table slid me out of the gloom of the coffin-like scanning machine. It was similar to a magnetic resonance imaging machine, but far more sophisticated. It was cutting-edge technology that looked like it belonged in the sick bay of the starship Enterprise.

My eyes adjusted somewhat to the light and the technology in the mansion's underground infirmary came into sharper focus.

No, not cutting-edge technology—make that bleeding-edge technology. There was stuff here that made the Mayo Clinic look like it still treated people with leeches and mercury. Most of the tech had been designed by Mechano himself. As much as I hated the homicidal Hero, I couldn't deny his evil genius.

I lay on the patient table in nothing but boxers, squinting against the bright overhead lights. I'd heard enough about near-death experiences—and had more than my fair share—to figure that, as long as I didn't walk toward the light, maybe I'd survive.

"Give it to me straight, doc," I said. "I can take it. Will the patient live?"

Doctor Agrawal frowned in concentration as he examined the holographic readout shimmering in front of him. He waved a hand through it, and it disappeared like a popped soap bubble. More Mechano tech.

Agrawal's bespectacled eyes met mine. "You'll likely outlive me, especially if I don't eat more vegetables," he said. He spoke English with an American accent, sounding more like a Midwest radio announcer than the New Delhi native that he was. He was a short, portly Indian man who somehow managed to look like a doctor even when he didn't have his white lab coat on. Like now—he wore jeans and a dress shirt buttoned all the way to his neck. "I can't find a blessed thing wrong with you."

"Why, then, does his forehead look like a kindergartener's art project?" Shay asked. She wore red silk pajamas that were loose on her lithe body. If it weren't for her black Ninja mask that left only her eyes exposed, she could be mistaken for an exceptionally fit middle-aged woman who had gotten out of bed to tend to her sick child. My Omega mask covered my face too, leaving only my weirdly tattooed forehead exposed. Shay and I had not shared our secret identities with Agrawal despite the fact he had been in our employ for months, he had been thoroughly vetted, and the doctor-patient privilege applied. Better safe than sorry. Agrawal could not reveal what he didn't know. We Heroes on the team had dangerous enemies who would stop at nothing to discover who we were behind our masks. Shay, Isaac and I knew each other's secret identities and those of Blur, Flare, and Slab, but none of those

Heroes nor any of the mansion's support staff knew the identities of we three core members of the team. Minerva knew everyone's secret identities, but you couldn't get a computer to spill its secrets by threats or blackmail or violence.

Agrawal shrugged at Shay's question about the hand-print on my head. "If it weren't for the fact Omega is mentally sound—well, as mentally sound as anyone can be who runs around in public in a fluorescent onesie—I would say it's a case of Munchausen syndrome. Munchausen syndrome is—"

"A disorder where an illness or injury is feigned to attract attention," Shay interrupted. "We know. You're talking to educated people. You can dispense with the vocabulary lesson."

"I forgot I was dealing with not only people who run around in onesies," Agrawal said, "but more specifically, polymaths who run around in onesies. Physician, heal thyself. Since you know so much about medicine, Ninja, why do you bother employing me?"

"For the sparkling conversation," Shay said. She made a dismissive motion with her hand. "Omega draws ample attention without needing to fake an injury to get more. Let's operate from the dubious assumption he's of sound mind and dispense with the notion he inflicted the injury on himself."

"Dubious assumption?" I repeated. Lying here, I felt like a slab of spoiled meat a butcher and his customer were discussing the demerits of. "I'm not deaf, you know."

"Though I wish you were a mute." Shay pressed a cool finger to my lips. "*Shhh*. The adults are talking." I wanted to bite her finger but restrained myself; she'd likely take it as proof I really was crazy. "If Omega's injury is not the result

27

of a psychological disorder, doctor, then what is it the result of?"

Agrawal shrugged. "Your guess is as good as mine."

"That's the sort of insightful, fact-laden medical diagnosis you want to hear from the doctor you pay a hefty six-figure salary to," Shay said dryly.

"You want facts? Here are the facts. I've run every conceivable test and a few I invented just for this occasion. There's no evidence of blunt force trauma, no evidence of an energy discharge, no evidence of psionic energy, no evidence of anything whatsoever except some lingering inflammation—the apparent source of the pain Omega reported—and that mark on Omega's forehead. If I didn't know Omega did not normally sport the mark, I would say it was a vascular anomaly."

"Vascular anomaly?" Shay repeated. "In English, please."

"Ah, so polymaths aren't all-knowing after all." Agrawal grinned, exposing tobacco-stained teeth. How a doctor could smoke knowing all its risks was beyond me. Regardless of his bad habits, while Agrawal was no Metahuman healer like Doctor Hippocrates, he was more than competent. "A vascular anomaly is a birthmark or growth composed of blood vessels that have developed incorrectly. Like the port-wine stain on Mikhail Gorbachev's forehead."

"The ballet dancer?" I asked.

Agrawal looked at Shay in surprise. "I'm reasonably certain he's making a rather bad Mikhail Baryshnikov joke to imply he's far younger than us old geezers who lived through the Cold War," she explained. "That or they don't make us polymaths like they used to."

Agrawal shook his head and continued. "Unlike a birthmark, Omega's mark is rapidly fading. It's noticeably lighter than it was when he came in here an hour ago. If it continues to fade at this rate, it should be gone before the day ends. Omega says the pain has already disappeared. Though I couldn't even guess as to how much the rapid healing is attributable to the peculiar nature of the wound versus how much is attributable to Omega's faster than normal healing thanks to the Omega suit within him."

Shivering, I sat up on the patient table. I felt like one big goose bump. Why was every hospital room always as cold as an ice box? Maybe to discourage Munchausen syndrome sufferers. "The dream I described. Could my own mind have produced this mark and the pain that went with it?"

"The mind is a complex and wondrous thing," Agrawal said. "We've barely begun to plumb its depths. Take the placebo effect, for example. If you ingest an ineffectual sugar pill but believe it will shrink a tumor on your arm, more likely than not that tumor will shrink. Or the reverse can happen. If you blindfold a group of people and tell them you're rubbing their arms with poison ivy, most of the people's arms will react with redness, itching, and boils when all you really rubbed them with was a harmless shrub. The power of the placebo effect is well documented. And yet we have no idea how or why it works. It's entirely possible your dream girl telling you that touching your head would cause pain would result in this mark on your head. The medical literature—"

"Here's the CliffsNotes version of the answer to Omega's question," Shay interrupted. "You don't know."

Agrawal grinned again. "You're not paying me the big bucks for the CliffsNotes version. I thought you were paying me per word. Omega, you're fine and it's my expert medical opinion you will continue to be fine. Barring the intervention of one of those Rogues you're so fond of fighting. Here's my prescription: take two aspirin and call me tomorrow morning. Better yet, have an apple a day and don't call me at all so I can get some beauty sleep. You folks constantly waking me at ungodly hours to patch up your battle wounds has me sleep-deprived enough as it is."

Yawning and scratching his belly, the brown-skinned doctor walked toward the infirmary's exit. Shay called out after him: "You and Mrs. Agrawal are back together. I'm glad to see you've reconciled."

Doctor Agrawal, thunderstruck, stopped short. It took him a moment to find his voice. "I hadn't told anyone that we had separated, much less that we had gotten back together. How in the world did you know?"

"Lots of things," Shay said. "Though your damp hair and the smell of soap and shampoo say you've recently showered, there's still a hint on you of the Gypsy Water perfume your wife favors, indicating you were recently deep in her embrace. There's a fresh hickey where your neck meets your shoulder which you're trying to conceal by buttoning your shirt collar. Normally you leave the top two buttons open. And, you're wearing your wedding ring again after not having it on the last few weeks." Shay shrugged. "Like I said, lots of things." Shay's observational skills and deductive abilities were not her superpower, but she had honed them to the point where they seemed like they were.

Shaking his head and muttering more about polymaths under his breath, the doctor left the infirmary, leaving me and Shay alone. "Minerva, secure the room," I said.

"Sure thing, toots," came the AI's voice from the infirmary's speakers. A pause, then, "Room secure. Your privacy is assured. I see that you're half-naked. Are you and Shay about to do the nasty?"

"Maybe. So no peeking."

"Aw, nuts! You're no fun." Minerva's speaker switched off with two clicks, indicating she was no longer listening.

Now that I was certain we wouldn't be interrupted, I let the Omega mask sink into my face and disappear. "What do you think?" I asked Shay. "Do you think it was just a dream?"

Shay surveyed my nearly naked body with an odd look in her narrow dark eyes. She tossed my shirt and pants at me. "Put some clothes on first, then we'll talk about it. You're distracting."

"I'm distracting? My goodness." I made of big show of leering at her. "Maybe we'll do the nasty after all. Could it be that, behind the Ninja mask and hard warrior exterior, beats the warm heart of a soft woman?

"If you don't stop being such a wise guy and put some clothes on, your warm heart will be cut out of your chest and beating on that soft hospital bed over there."

I shrugged. "It's just as well. You're too old for me anyway. I'm not into Cold War GILFs."

An unsheathed stiletto appeared in Shay's hand as if by magic. Before then, I would have sworn she was unarmed. She began counting down from ten.

I laughed and pulled my clothes back on. Truth be told, I was gratified. Before my powers manifested, nothing about my body was distracting to women. Repulsive, yes; distracting, no. Years of weight training, rigorous exercise, and eating like a college football player hoping to go pro had done wonders. I certainly wasn't the jaw-dropping physical specimen Avatar had been, but I was far from the bag of bones I had been when I entered Hero Academy.

Shay's knife disappeared back into whatever sleight of hand black hole she had pulled it out of. She had a big future as a stage magician if she ever got tired of the Hero hustle. She unwound the fabric of her mask, letting down her black hair and exposing her high cheekbone Japanese face. Her face was unlined despite her age and all the things she had been through in her long Heroic career. Maybe the girl in my dream didn't have a moisturizing regime, but I knew for a fact Shay did. Plus, as Isaac—a black man—had once said about himself and Shay, "Black don't crack, and Asian don't raisin."

Shay said, "To answer your question, there's no trace of unexpected technological or Metahuman activity, either in your body, the mansion, or the surrounding area. All evidence points to what you experienced as being just a dream."

Shay's doubtful tone belied her words. "However . . ." I said, urging her to finish her thought.

"However, I've been a Hero a long time. You develop instincts after a while. I trust them." She shook her head. "This was not just a dream."

I sighed. "That's what I think, too."

"Did you recognize the girl?"

"No. Young, Asian, black-haired, cute."

"That narrows things down considerably. There are almost fifty Asian countries. Considering that, there are probably only five or six of us black-haired Asian females in the entire world. We've practically got the girl's fingerprints and DNA. Did you describe her to Minerva and run a search through her databases?"

I banged my palm against my head. It wasn't tender anymore; as the doctor had said, the pain was completely gone. "Since I just fell off the turnip truck, I didn't even think of that. I'll do it now."

"There's no need for sarcasm."

"I could say the same to you, Sarcasm Lass." I shook my

head. "As you say, there's more than just a few Asians who match my description. Minerva laughed at me when I asked her to run a search for my description of the girl."

"Can you at least narrow down the girl's ethnicity? Thai, Chinese, Burmese, Japanese, Korean, Cambodian, Laotian, something else?"

I hesitated, afraid to answer. Shay was almost as angry with me as Isaac, she was just less vocal about it than he. The fact she had come down to the infirmary to check on me but Isaac hadn't testified to that. Despite things being normal between the two of us on the surface, Shay's anger was always an undercurrent to all our conversations, like that of a wife who had discovered her husband had cheated on her but she pretended like everything was normal for the sake of the kids. I didn't want to add to the ever-present anger by insulting her.

"Let me guess," Shay said when I didn't respond. "You can't tell one Asian ethnicity from another."

"I didn't say that."

"Your silence and face did. Maybe you'd have picked up on the girl's distinguishing characteristics if you'd taken more seriously my attempts to sharpen your observation skills." My observation skills were sharp enough to notice that Shay didn't have bra and panties on under her pajamas. I was tempted to point it out and credit Shay's observational tutelage, but thought better of it. I hadn't forgotten about that knife. "Though I'm one to talk—half the time I can't tell you gaijin from one another. You should keep that mark on your head so I can pick you out of a lineup."

"Very amusing. You should do standup."

"Since all we Asians look alike to you, how do you know I don't?"

Ignoring that, I said, "I also did a search on the names

the girl mentioned. The Adversary, Destroyer, Ancient One, and Hellscape. Minerva dug up nothing helpful. Plenty cultures have references to such entities in their history. Lilu, the other name the girl used, isn't the name of a single person according to Minerva's databases. Rather, it's the name for demons in ancient Sumerian mythology who woke sleeping women and had sex with them. Legend says that Gilgamesh was descended from a Lilu. The Gilgamesh who is the mythological protagonist of the *Epic of Gilgamesh*, I mean, not the armored nutjob using that name we fought a few months ago."

"I gathered as much. Didn't Seer tell you Gilgamesh was a Metahuman and one of your predecessors as a carrier of the Omega spirit?"

"Yeah. But she and Mechano lied so much, it's hard to figure out when they were telling the truth and when they were full of it." Considering Shay's keen observational skills, I still didn't understand how she hadn't sussed out the shady stuff Mechano, Millennium and Seer had been up to right under her nose when they were Sentinels together. Even veteran Heroes like Shay, it seemed, had blind spots.

"Maybe," I added, "if it really wasn't a dream or some sort of trick or strange attack, we should take the girl's warning at face value. She said, 'Right now, Progenitor is my problem. He'll be yours soon enough.'" I shivered, and not just because the infirmary was cold. The storm clouds from the dream lingered in my mind like the memory of a gruesome crime scene. "I got the strangest feeling of foreboding when I looked at those dark clouds gathering. Could it be this is the crisis Mechano, Seer, and Millennium warned me about?" It had been years since those Sentinels told me that. As nothing like that world-threatening crisis had yet occurred, over the years I'd tried to talk myself into believing those accomplished liars had been lying about the crisis too.

Shay shrugged. "To quote the good doctor, your guess is as good as mine. Unfortunately, we can't simply ask my former teammates. You destroyed Mechano, Doctor Alchemy killed Seer, and Millennium is an uncommunicative vegetable thanks to Grimoire. I still wonder how she managed that. Millennium was Omega-level, after all, and the most powerful of us Sentinels. Or at least he was after Avatar was murdered."

"Beats me. If I ever meet Grimoire, I'll ask." I too was very curious about the mysterious Hero Grimoire. She had somehow managed to find Millennium after so many other Heroes had tried and failed. Myself included. Despite the fact Grimoire was a media darling in nearby Washington, D.C., the city she apparently operated out of, no other Hero seemed to know much about her. I had even contacted Ghost himself to find out more about Grimoire and how she found and defeated Millennium, but the Heroes' Guild's chief investigator had been extremely tight-lipped about the subject. If I hadn't known better, I would describe Ghost's curt answers to my questions about Grimoire as evasive and not entirely truthful. But that of course couldn't be the case. Ghost was as straight of an arrow as anyone who ever donned a cape.

My mind moved away from Grimoire and returned to thoughts of the strange dream. Somehow, deep down in my core, I always knew the disgraced Sentinels hadn't been lying about the looming crisis despite efforts to convince myself otherwise. What if what the girl in the dream alluded to was that crisis?

Excitement mixed with dread rose within me at the prospect. I tried to tamp the feeling down and view the situation dispassionately. Hard experience had taught me that running off half-cocked was a disaster in the making. Like when Isaac and I broke into Mad Dog's apartment in an attempt to stop him from abusing my friend Hannah Kim, leading to him murdering her.

Shay said, "Since you appear unharmed and it seems like there's nothing more we can do about the dream, for now, we must shelve the subject. If you have the dream again, we'll revisit the issue."

"I've had the same dream for months, though this is the first time the girl's made an appearance. She said she needed to prepare me for something. I've the feeling it's not a question of if I see her again, but when."

"Excuse the interruption," Minerva interjected. "Chairman Philistine, you wanted me to remind you to get ready. Preparations still need to be made."

I groaned, and not because of how Minerva had addressed me. I reluctantly got off the patient table.

I was dreading what I had to do almost as much as the crisis the Sentinels had predicted.

4

I floated high in the air with explosions thundering around me. I was almost as blind as a bat, unable to see the surrounding pandemonium other than the occasional dull flash from a too close explosion. I felt the detonations in my bones. My every instinct shrieked at me to fly far away.

I hovered in the center of an over 200-feet-long balloon about the size of the Goodyear Blimp. The balloon had been manufactured to look like me in my Omega suit. Featuring a dark blue costume glinting like armor, a matching mask, a snow-white omega symbol on its chest, and white gauntlets and long cape, the balloon was how I was currently dressed writ large. Packets of bubble gum bobbed in the air around me like floating butterflies, making the inside of the balloon smell like a candy store. My powers, not helium, held the balloon and the gum aloft.

A particularly powerful explosion made my teeth rattle. I was the Mini-Me to a polyester doppelganger filled with a truckload of gum while what seemed like the War of 1812 raged around us. *And the rocket's red glare, the bombs bursting in air, gave proof through the night that Omega was still there.* Unbelievable. Mama hadn't said there would be days like this. And if she had, I wouldn't have believed her.

"This is humiliating," I complained. "I feel like a human piñata."

"This is no picnic for us either," crackled Shay's voice through the bone-conduction communicator plugged into my ear. "I can think of a hundred things I'd rather be doing than participating in this circus. Like getting a root canal from Doctor Alchemy without anesthesia."

"We wouldn't have to put on this dog and pony show if it weren't for you, Theo," Isaac interjected. "So how about zipping your lip before I come up there and zip it for you?"

"Sheesh, you don't need to jump down my—"

But Isaac couldn't hear me anymore. Two quick beeps of my earpiece indicated he had logged out of the executive channel we three used when we didn't want the rest of the team to hear us.

I sighed in resignation. "How long do you suppose he'll stay pissed at me?" I asked Shay.

"A while. I wouldn't hold my breath if I were you. He's as stubborn as you are."

"I'm not stubborn."

"Sure you're not. You're ever flexible Theo, the Human Pretzel. That's what the rest of the team calls you when you're not around. That plopping sound you hear is my voice dripping with sarcasm. Now hush. Momma's busy."

I hushed. Though I couldn't see with my eyes due to the material around me blocking my view, I still sensed what was going on around me thanks to my telekinetic touch. Between it and the team's pre-event rehearsals, what was happening below and around me played out like a movie in my mind's eye.

Well over a thousand feet below, Slab single-handedly hauled a massive metal ramp into place in front of the sprawling four-story white mansion that once housed the Sentinels but now was our team's headquarters. Living in the mansion was like living in the White House: it was simultaneously an office building, house, museum, security complex, terrorist target, and tourist attraction.

The ramp weighed tons, and the ground shuddered when Slab set the vaguely L-shaped structure down. It glinted under the spotlights shining on it. Cameras projected the ramp and Slab moving it onto two massive screens. The assembled crowd watched Slab's feat of strength on the huge screens with *oohs* and *aahs*. There were a few thousand people down there, all carefully screened to weed out security risks and people who disliked Heroes in general and me in particular. Millions more were watching the event live online and on television. Or so I'd been told. My last name was Conley, not Nielsen.

Once the ramp was in place, the fireworks display Flare generated with her powers came to an explosive climax, turning dusk into red, white and blue-tinged day. Our team operated primarily in the United States, and the high-priced marketing and psychology experts who planned today's event had said the color scheme of the fireworks' crescendo would appeal to Americans' patriotism and subliminally associate the team with the country. God bless America.

Blur, carrying Shay in her midnight black Ninja outfit, zoomed out of the distant horizon and into view. With his legs pumping like pistons, Blur zig-zagged through the crowd in seconds, accelerating as he approached the ramp.

Ninja's and Blur's bodies blurred, making it obvious why the speedster had taken his Heroic code name.

Blur hit the ramp and, thanks to his insane momentum, ran straight up its vertical side like adhesive was on the soles of his silver costume. In the blink of an eye, his legs cleared the top of the tall ramp. He shot straight up in the air like a rocket carrying Ninja as its payload. Powerful spotlights tracked the two Heroes as they rose toward where I was cocooned in the hovering Omega balloon.

Blur and Ninja reached the apogee of their rise. Ninja's katana, glowing pink thanks to her Metahuman ability, slashed the air. The glowing sword ripped through the poly-ester skin of the balloon I was in.

The balloon popped like a pimple and its specially treated fabric ignited with a fiery whoosh. Bubble gum sprayed out everywhere. Its shiny packaging glowed, making the packs of gum look like sparks shooting off a sparkler.

Free of the balloon's confines, I plummeted toward the ground with the wind screaming in my ears. Blur and Ninja tumbled below me. The snow-white cape of my Omega costume snapped and fluttered behind me like the tail of a kite.

Blur's arms windmilled, faster and faster, until his arms blurred like spinning airplane propellers. They spun so fast that he generated whirlwinds of air currents under him that slowed his descent. He went from plummeting like a rock to gently descending like a feather.

Ninja was no longer in danger of crashing, either. Isaac, who had transformed into a pegasus, swooped out of the darkening sky and caught her. Ninja sat astride Isaac's flying horse form like she had been born there. Still brandishing her glowing sword, she looked like a Valkyrie riding into battle. Her riding Isaac in his pegasus form reminded me of when he, Neha, and I, freshly graduated from the Hero Academy in Oregon, had set out on a cross-country trip to begin Apprenticeships under Amazing Man. Neha had ridden Isaac in his pegasus form the first leg of the trip. Though those times hadn't seemed simpler when I was living them, they had been. I missed them.

Unlike Ninja and Blur, I dropped like a stone until the last possible moment. Then I activated my telekinesis, using it to slow my body so I wouldn't go *splat!* like a dropped tomato.

I touched down with a loud thump on the stage in front of the crowd of spectators. The stage cratered and splintered around me from the force of the impact. My voluminous cape fell like a descending curtain as *Holding Out for a Hero* blared over the loudspeakers. My touchdown was dramatic, with my face turned down and a knee and a gloved fist touching the stage, as if I had caught myself after a hard landing. A classic superhero pose.

I felt like a complete idiot.

"But it'll look so daring!" the marketing consultants had assured me about the landing during rehearsals. "So Heroic!" Despite my misgivings, I had gone along with their plans for my landing, just as I had gone along with all the other embarrassing and undignified nonsense they had talked me into today. Lately, I had gone along with a metric ton of things I didn't want to. Living in the mansion where villains had plotted against me was number one on that list.

With *Holding Out for a Hero* still playing, Blur, Ninja and Myth landed simultaneously on the stage just a few seconds after I. With a shimmering glow, Myth turned from a pegasus back into his costumed human form. Slab and Flare stepped on stage as well, the platform groaning under the weight of the former. All five of my teammates formed a line behind my still-crouched body. On either side of the Heroes were seated VIPs: Astor City's mayor, the police chief, the fire chief, Maryland's lieutenant governor, the Deputy Secretary of the U.S. Department of Metahuman Affairs, other government officials, and a few private citizens whose lives I and the others had saved in the months we had been together as a team.

The Old Man—how Isaac and I referred to Amazing Man—had been asked to attend as a VIP as well, not only because he had been my and Isaac's Hero sponsor, but also because he was on the Executive Committee of the Heroes' Guild. He had declined. "I'm a Hero, not a prop," he had said.

Good for him. I didn't want to be a prop either. And yet, here I was, frozen in a carefully rehearsed pose, as much of a prop as a comedian's dummy.

I held my supposedly daring pose and didn't rise. We didn't have the crowd's full attention yet. Too many people were busy tearing into the glowing packs of gum that had fallen from the sky like hail. Well, more like a gentle rain, really, as I had used my powers to slow the packs' fall so people wouldn't get whacked upside the head. There was a time when controlling a thousand individual items would have been well beyond the capacity of my powers. A lot had changed since then. Including me.

Inside the packs were pink rectangular slabs of Omega Bubble Gum®, the official chewing gum of our new team. Omega Bubble's slogan was *Don't blow it: Chews me!*

Oy vey. The things I did for money. There was far more to forming a Hero team, it turned out, than simply clasping hands, declaring yourselves the super-friends, and calling it a day. Running one was expensive as heck. Ninja, who had inherited a third of Mechano's vast fortune and owned the mansion and the large parcel of land it was on, underwrote many of our expenses. Various licensing agreements and endorsement deals covered the rest. Most of those licensing agreements and endorsement deals—like the Omega Bubble one—were mine. After all, I was a household name, the most famous of the six of us. The marketing charts that tracked the UWant, Google, and social media searches for the names *Omega* and *Kinetic* over the past few years looked like an ad for an erectile dysfunction drug—limp, then rapidly shooting straight up like a steep mountain. I was, after all, the world's only Omega-level Hero, the white knight who had exposed the dark corruption at the heart of the Sentinels, the daring champion who had defeated the notorious Doctor Alchemy, and the avenging angel who had brought the Revengers to justice. It says so right here in my press packet, so it must all be true.

Ha! I had lots of help accomplishing those things, of course. But the public didn't want to hear that, and marketers weren't interested in selling it. People loved the trope of the lone, steely-eyed cowboy bravely facing down the overwhelming forces of evil. A lot of people thought of me as some sort of latter-day John Wayne: resolute, squinty-eyed, armed with only a six-shooter and pluck. Maybe I should title my upcoming autobiography *Alone in Astor City*. My second autobiography, that is. My first one was *Zero to Omega Hero*. It had been out for a while now, and the book was still a bestseller, even with the inane title. As far as I was concerned, the fact a thoroughly average guy like me had not one but two autobiographies was proof there was a god and he had a twisted sense of humor.

My recent legal troubles had only augmented my fame, though my approval ratings had taken a hit. My sagging approval ratings were the main reason the team was putting on this dog and pony show. Like it or not, I was the face of the new team. (I was in the *I don't like it* camp.) When my approval ratings took a hit, the team's ratings took a hit. And that meant less money in our coffers. Though I wasn't money-hungry, I was anxious to ensure the team was ready to handle any and every threat the world might face. That took cash, and lots of it. This spectacle was designed to get out in front of the burgeoning public relations crisis my legal troubles were causing.

My powers sensed some pushing and shoving in the crowd over the packs of gum. Still holding my face-down pose, I reached out telekinetically and gently separated people before the shoving degenerated into brawls. People were squabbling because there was not enough gum for everyone. There were only enough packs here for maybe a third of the crowd, though I knew for a fact there was a warehouse a few miles away full of the stuff, enough to rot the teeth of every man, woman, and child in the city. "Creating an artificial sense of scarcity is Marketing 101," the experts had assured me. I was learning a lot about branding and marketing. By the time this whole thing was over, I'd be qualified to get a job on Madison Avenue. Less momentous than being a licensed Hero, maybe. But safer. I'd never heard of an ad man getting his skin peeled like an orange by a Rogue.

The other reason people argued over the packs of gum was the packaging promised *Exclusive Collectors' Items Inside!!!* The gum packs contained collectible cards depicting each of us six Heroes, much like how gum used to come with baseball cards. More branding.

"Though gum isn't included in baseball card packs anymore," the experts had said, "people still associate the two. Baseball and baseball cards are as American as apple pie. By including cards featuring you six with the gum, we're tethering your brand to America." I had suggested we pelt the crowd with apple pie instead. After a few minutes of solemn debate while I listened in bemused disbelief that my tongue-in-cheek suggestion was being taken seriously, the consultants counseled against the idea.

"Too messy," one pencil pusher had concluded.

"And if the pie is hot, you risk burning people," another said.

"Remember that McDonald's hot coffee lawsuit?" The consultant shuddered.

"You'd have to increase your liability insurance coverage."

"Too much litigation exposure," a fifth person agreed.

"Good job with the out-of-the-box thinking though, Omega. We like where your head's at. Keep the ideas coming." It was then I'd realized that even the team's image consultants had drunk the Omega Kool-Aid. The problem with people thinking of you as some sort of can-do-no-wrong icon was that they treated your every statement, even a frivolous one, like it was uttered by the voice of God.

After waiting almost a full minute as the crowd scrambled and squabbled over the gum packs, Flare used her powers to set off another explosion of fireworks directly behind the stage. Those of us on the stage were bathed in red, white and blue light. We six Heroes in particular stood out as Flare used her powers to make us glow like fluorescent lights. Startled, the crowd gasped, ignored the gum, and focused its attention on us again.

That was my cue. I finally stood, grateful to no longer crouch as one leg had gone asleep. I ached to shake the pins and needles out of it, but didn't. Too many eyes were on me.

Gina would jump down my throat if I distracted from the calculated drama of the moment. She scared me more than some Rogues did.

Gina Hardshaw, the team's public relations chief and the mastermind of this three-ring circus, stepped to the podium at the front of the stage as the words to *Holding Out for a Hero* faded. Gina was plump, gray-haired, and rosy-cheeked; she wore a rose suit, sensible shoes, and compression stockings. She looked like someone's cuddly babushka whose favorite activity was baking cookies for her brood of grandkids. Appearances, as usual, were deceiving. Behind closed doors, Gina was as cuddly as a cobra and even sharper-tongued. Even so, I rather liked her. She was one of the few people left in the world who did not treat me deferentially, like I was a marble statue of a god come to life.

"Ladies and gentlemen . . . boys and girls . . . children of all ages . . ." Gina intoned, her voice pausing dramatically between phrases for effect. Her words echoed over the public announcement system and were beamed all around the world. "I'm proud to present the world's latest and greatest team of Heroes: The New Sentinels!"

The crowd roared. Its approval washed over us like a wave. Though the six of us had operated as a team for several months, this was the public unveiling of the team name and our official coming out party.

I'd almost winced when Gina said the team name, but had resisted the urge as my face was projected on one of the jumbotrons. The image of the rest of the New Sentinels was projected on the other screen. Thanks to Flare, we all still glowed like angels descended from heaven.

The New Sentinels. Branding again. The name had been poll-tested and focus-grouped to death. It tested best by far of all the names we had contemplated. Watchmen, Champions, Justice League, Defenders, Avengers, Legion of Super-heroes . . . unfortunately, so many alternative names were already trademarked or copyrighted by other superhero teams, real and fictional. Another legal issue on top of the ones I already had was the last thing we needed. *The New Sentinels* had the virtue of not infringing on someone else's intellectual property. And it capitalized on the world-famous Sentinels name while sufficiently distancing itself from the old name's tarnish. Like New Coke, the name was new, but the same. Bold, yet comfortable. Unique, yet famil-iar. Why reinvent the wheel when you can spray some Armor All on the old one and make it nice and shiny?

At least that's how Gina and the other marketing experts had sold me on the name. Unfortunately, it had built into it the name of the villains who had murdered Neha and my father and killed other innocents while trying to neutralize me. Before I was captured and tortured by Doctor Alchemy, Ninja had approached me with the proposal that I become a member of the new Sentinels team she was forming. I had literally laughed in her face. But, after tangling with Doctor Alchemy, I had realized I could not do everything on my own. Not if it was my responsibility to save the world as the old Sentinels had suggested it was. Too much was at stake. I realized I needed to surround myself with other Heroes. Living in the old Sentinels' mansion and repurposing the Sentinels' name was most definitely *not* what I had in mind back then, though. But as accountants, security consultants, and even Ninja had pointed out, the Sentinels already had in place all the infrastructure for a Heroic team. "Don't rein-vent the wheel, just realign it," they had said.

It all made so much sense. So, despite my squeamish-ness about all things Sentinels-related, here I was, standing on a stage at the same place where Seer, Millennium, and

Mechano had plotted against me and booby-trapped Neha. My new home. Our new home. The New Sentinels mansion.

The New Sentinels.

Ugh.

God, how I hated the name.

———

5

Lieutenant Governor Gowdy was the last of the VIPs to speak. I was irritated but trying to not show it as he droned on and on.

I was not irritated because Gowdy's speech was long and boring, though it was both. Gina had reviewed all the VIPs' speeches beforehand to make sure they were brief and sufficiently worshipful of the New Sentinels, but midway through his prepared remarks Gowdy had ignored the words on the teleprompter and started ad-libbing, making his speech more about him than about us. Like most politicians, Gowdy had never met a microphone he didn't want to deep-throat.

Gina stood off to the side of Gowdy as he spoke. She appeared to be listening respectfully. I knew from the hardening of her eyes, however, that she was not pleased by Gowdy going off script. She had planned this event down to the second. Everything had proceeded like clockwork until now.

Gowdy was saying, "The New Sentinels' recent capture of the last of the Revengers reminds me of the firefight I was in in the Kandahar province in Afghanistan while serving in this great nation's army. We were pinned down, and I knew I had to . . ."

Oh boy. Trying to not roll my eyes, I tuned the rest of what Gowdy said out. I had nothing but respect for people in the military—most were greater heroes than some licensed Heroes I could name—but I knew for a fact Gowdy had been a file clerk in the army. He had never even been to Afghanistan or a similar hot spot. The way he talked, though, you'd think he had shot five terrorists in the head before breakfast and built schools for their orphaned kids during lunch. In reality, the only things he had fought in the army were the venereal diseases he contracted in brothels. That's not what his official Pentagon record said, though. Gowdy's father being the Secretary of Defense during his army stint had everything to do with the embellishment of Gowdy's military record. Gowdy had ridden his supposed war record to being elected Lieutenant Governor, and would ride it higher still if the public didn't come to its senses. When I was a kid who'd barely stepped foot off his family's farm, I had thought the world was a meritocracy. Experience had taught me otherwise.

Though Gowdy's hot air was annoying, even more annoying was the fact he was here at all. We had expected the governor himself to attend. At the last minute, Governor Willard Flushing had backed out and sent the Lieutenant Governor in his stead. The governor's office said it was a scheduling snafu and could not have been more apologetic. Both Gina and I knew it was because Governor Flushing was distancing himself from the New Sentinels in general and me in particular because of my legal troubles. Flushing was positioning himself so he could disavow me if even more bad news came out about me or if I wound up in prison.

I really should not have been surprised by Flushing's behavior. After all, before he was elected governor, he had been the State's Attorney who charged me with murder for the destruction of Mechano, and then dropped those charges like a hot potato when people became aware of Mechano's crimes and public opinion swung my way.

One would think Flushing had been the Tonto to my Lone Ranger the way he cozied up to me once I was the toast of the town. Though I didn't like the guy, I had donated money to his gubernatorial campaign and didn't rebuff him when he made a point to be seen with me publicly. I had even let Flushing use footage of me in a campaign ad. Flushing was an ambitious fellow with his eye on the White House. It never hurt to have friends in high places. As Gowdy and his daddy amply demonstrated, often it was not what you did that mattered, but whom you knew.

I watched Gowdy drone on at the podium, careful to keep the disgust off my face. It ought to be Flushing up here giving us his stamp of approval instead of this second-stringer. And it had not gone unnoticed by me that Flushing had not lifted a finger these past few weeks to use his influence as governor to get me out of my legal woes. The trouble with buying a politician is they never stay bought.

I looked out over the sea of spectators that stretched out into the gathering darkness. They had been standing for a while and many stirred restlessly. They were getting bored and starting to tune out. I tried to catch Gina's eye to get her to do something before we completely lost the crowd's attention.

There was no need. No doubt also sensing the shift in the crowd's mood, Gina sidled up next to Gowdy, covered the podium's microphone while he was in mid-sentence, and whispered something in his ear.

Gowdy blanched, like he suddenly realized one of the terrorists he allegedly fought was behind him with a rocket-propelled grenade pointed at his head. Gina stepped back, smiling sweetly, looking as innocent as Mrs. Claus. I wondered what she said to him. Maybe that her husband would leave a lump of coal in Gowdy's stocking.

Gowdy did not finish the death-defying fairy tale Gina had interrupted. I hated cliff-hangers. I wondered if he made it out of the war all right. "And so, without further ado," Gowdy said into the microphone, the words tumbling out in his haste to get them out, his hands shaking as he fumbled with papers on the podium, "as a duly elected representative of the great state of Maryland, I am proud to proclaim today New Sentinels Day!"

The crowd, roused from the narcoleptic state Gowdy had nearly put it in, roared its approval. The reaction was goosed by Gina's flacks in the audience. Gina had planted them there to ensure the crowd reacted appropriately at the right times, much like television studios planted profes-sional laughers in sitcom audiences to get them to laugh in the right places. Gina believed people were nothing more than moist robots: "Punch this button, and people will react a certain way. Twist that knob, and they'll react in another. People, especially in large groups, respond predictably. Free will is an illusion. How do you think marketing got to be a trillion-dollar industry? 'Marketing.' Ha! We ought to call it programming instead. More accurate." I hoped her cynicism was wrong, but feared it was not. Watching Gina had taught me a lot about how we all were manipulated morning, noon, and night, usually without our knowledge.

The declaration of New Sentinels Day was my cue again.

I stepped toward the lectern, my cape swishing behind me. Gina's photographers scurried out of the wings and knelt in front of the lectern, their cameras at the ready. "Omega," Gowdy said into the microphone, brandishing a framed document, "I present you, the chairman of the New Sentinels, with this official proclamation of New Sentinels Day. You and your new team have the thanks of a grateful state, nation, and world. I speak for countless millions when I say we'll all sleep safer knowing you and the rest of the New Sentinels are on the job."

Gowdy and I shook hands, freezing for a moment to mug for the cameras. Flashes blinded me. I felt like an elementary school kid on picture day. I wanted to cross my eyes, but Gina would gouge them out later if I did.

The cameramen scurried away, Gowdy headed back to his seat, and Gina stepped up to take the proclamation so my hands were free. Gina took a spot just a few feet to the side of the lectern, almost side by side with me. According to what we had previously rehearsed, she was supposed to stand several feet behind me. If asked, she would probably say her changed location was an accident. Ha! When it came to Gina, nothing was an accident. She was sending viewers the subliminal message that, when they thought of Omega, they should also think of Gina Hardshaw, Chief Information Officer for the New Sentinels. *Freelance work accepted. Discretion assured. Ask about our special Heroes' rates!* Gina was all-in on hitching her wagon to my star, which was more than I could say about fair-weather friends like Governor Flushing.

All eyes were on me. I glanced at the flanking teleprompters to make sure my speech was loaded. Glossophobia—the fear of public speaking—was the most common of all the phobias. Years ago, I would have pissed my cape at the mere thought of addressing this many people. Now there was not so much as a flutter in my stomach as I adjusted the lectern's microphone. When you've been tortured by the likes of Doctor Alchemy, it puts all other fears into perspective. Though effective, I didn't recommend it as a glossophobia cure.

I began. "I'm sorry you all had to wait so long to hear from me. I just flew in from Indonesia, and boy are my arms tired."

That got a bigger laugh than it should have. I had objected to the cornball joke when Gina gave me the first draft of the speech days before. She responded, "You grew up on a dirt farm, and now you're one of the most powerful men in the world. Your brand is, 'The everyman becomes a superhero.' We need to lean into that, not run away from it. This dad joke aligns perfectly with your brand. It's just the right level of corny. Trust Auntie Gina. I've been rehabilitating public images since before you were born."

Based on the laugh the clichéd joke got, maybe Gina had been right. She usually was.

"But seriously folks, I appreciate you coming out this evening," I continued. "Even though it's dark out, it's the dawn of a new day. A new day where, uh—" I stumbled over the words, distracted by two attractive women at the front of the crowd. They had pulled off their shirts. Four words were written in red lipstick on their ample bare chests, one word on each breast: *WE LOVE YOU OMEGA*. The people around the two moved their smartphones off me and instead recorded the women as the two bounced and shimmied, staring up at me like hungry cats at a bird in a tree.

Younger me would have been stunned, unable to speak and barely able to think until the women covered up.

Younger me would also have taken a careful mental picture of the women for later . . . um, reflection.

But I was no longer that guy. Since becoming famous, I had been hounded by cape chasers. They no longer fazed me because now I understood their nature. Cape chasers didn't like me for me. Heck, they didn't know the real me. They only knew the costume and were only attracted to the fame, money, and power attached to it. Not to the man wearing it. They were energy and time vampires who would suck you dry if you got close enough to let them sink their teeth into you.

I had learned that the hard way months ago by dating one after my girlfriend Viola Simpson broke up with me. Worried about Viola's safety, I couldn't bring myself to reveal to her my secret life as Omega even after months of dating. As I was unable to explain my frequent absences and mysterious injuries, Viola said, more in sorrow than anger, that I was "emotionally unavailable and afraid of commitment." Then she broke things off. I could hardly blame her, because she was right.

The cape chaser's name was Amber Jasper, a Russian national and struggling actress who hit on me aggressively at a Beverly Hills charity event. Omega was the event's headliner and main draw. I'd been lonely post-breakup and—to be completely honest—horny. Otherwise, maybe I would've seen Amber for what she was. The fact a woman named Yekaterina Preobrazhensky adopted *Amber Jasper* as a stage name should've been my first clue of how fake she was. But I didn't pick up on the clue, and instead fell head over heels for the leggy beauty. It hadn't been love exactly, but it was more than lust. The tabloids couldn't get enough of our whirlwind affair. Ninja had taken one look at Amber and tried to warn me, but I wouldn't listen.

One night I woke up to find Amber taking nude pictures of herself next to my masked face. I broke things off so fast that I never found out if she intended to sell the pictures or if she was just going to use them to jumpstart her flailing career. Thank God I never revealed my secret identity to her and my Omega mask could not be removed unless I willed it. Last I heard Amber had parlayed her brief association with me into twenty-five million UWant Friends followers and a development deal for a TV reality show called *Stuck In Amber*. It sounded like a porno title to me. There's no business like show business.

Ignoring the jiggling cape chasers in the crowd, I picked right back up where I had left off. "A new day where we no longer worry if our Heroes are really Rogues. A new day where the strong protect the weak instead of preying on them. A new day where . . ."

I continued my speech as I watched Gina out of the corner of my eye. She had turned her back to the audience and was whispering into the transmitter clipped to her jacket's cuff: "We've got a couple of Hero hags causing a disturbance in grid A2. I need someone over there stat to collect the trash."

"To usher in that new day," I said, "we need a new team of Heroes. And that team is the New Sentinels." As I spoke members of our security staff reached the two flashers. They wrapped jackets around the women's torsos—the surrounding crowd booed—and hustled the disrupters away. "I'm proud to be the team's first chairman."

That last line, seemingly innocuous, had been the subject of an argument between me and Gina when I had reviewed the first draft of the speech with her. The line had originally read, *I'm proud the team has honored me by unanimously electing me chairman and team leader.*

"That's a lie, and you know it," I had protested to Gina about the original language. We had been in her office in the New Sentinels mansion. "Sure, I'm the chairman, but it's mostly a figurehead position. And the other five didn't unanimously elect me. Ninja, Myth and I agreed I should have the title as the public face of the team long before we even recruited the other three. And this 'team leader' stuff is a lie too. Ninja is in charge when the team is in the field since she has way more experience than I do. Not to mention she has three times the tactical mind I do. The only reason we don't call her the team leader publicly is because her name is still so closely associated in the public's mind with the disgraced Sentinels.

"It's not a lie," Gina had responded breezily with a dismissive wave. "It's puffery."

"Calling dog doo a chocolate puff doesn't change what it is. A lie is a lie. And what about what the speech says here? 'I'm completely innocent of the criminal charges against me. The New Sentinels know it, the millions who admire me know it, and soon the whole world will know it. I'm the victim of a witch hunt. An overzealous elected prosecutor named Draymond Miller is wrongfully targeting me to raise his own profile, troll for votes, and fill his campaign coffers. His goal is to take your favorite Hero down. Like Iceburn, Amok, Doctor Alchemy, and so many other villains I've faced who were only out for themselves, he will fail. My lawyers are drafting a multimillion-dollar lawsuit against him for malicious prosecution. You should call and email his office and demand his immediate resignation.'"

Gina had pursed her lips thoughtfully. "Okay, some of that is a lie," she conceded.

"Some of it? More like all of it." I shook the sheaf of papers containing the speech. "The entire speech is riddled with more of the same. I'm not going to stand up in front of all those people and tell a bunch of lies. I get that you're trying to rehabilitate my public image, but I'm not going to let you do it at the expense of the truth and people like Miller who are only doing their job."

Gina's blue eyes had flashed with irritation behind the thick glasses she was too vain to wear in public. "You're being naive. This is how the world works."

"After all I've been through the past few years, I'm the opposite of naive. I'm so jaded they'll break me apart and sell me as jewelry when I die. As jaded as I am, I'm not going to sink so low as to slander a public servant who's just doing his job." I shook my head in disgust. "Haven't you even heard of the Ninth Commandment?"

"Sure. It's my favorite one. It's the one that says, "Thou shalt not get caught.'"

"You're not funny. The Ninth Commandment is, 'Thou shalt not bear false witness against thy neighbor.' You ought to know, you were probably there when God handed Moses the tablets."

"Is that a crack about my age?"

"You know it was. Just like you ought to know I'm not going to stand on that stage and tell this pack of lies. And that's final."

And so, Gina and I had re-written the speech together. I had taken out all the lies and ad hominem attacks; she made sure it contained all the buzzwords and moist robot code designed to make the audience feel good about me and the New Sentinels. By the time we finished, the speech was cotton candy in word form—all taste, no substance. The speech positioned me as being foursquare in favor of things that were good, and opposed to things that were bad. Don't you love good things and hate bad things too, John Q. Public? See? I'm just like you. Pick up your Omega t-shirt on your way out, on sale for a limited time only!

I finished the bulk of the speech and swung into its peroration. The end of the speech was inspired by President Kennedy's 1961 inaugural address. I had worried about being accused of plagiarism, but Gina had poo-pooed me. "You *want* to be associated in people's minds with someone like Kennedy," she had said. "Besides, if you're going to steal, steal from the best."

"And so," I thundered to the crowd, "let the word go forth from this time and place, to non-Metahumans and Metahumans, Heroes and Rogues, good citizens and criminals, friend and foe alike, that the torch has been passed to a new generation of Heroes. A generation forged in hardship, tempered by tragedy, tested by toil and strife, yet still hopeful for the future. A future where every man, woman and child shall look to the sky and no one, Hero or Rogue, shall make them afraid.

"May God bless us all."

The crowd burst into applause and cheers. The people spread out before me blurred a little; I was getting misty-eyed. As cynical as this public relations offensive was and as hokey as my speech had been, I believed the fundamentals of what I had said. It was my responsibility to keep people safe, one I took very seriously. I had failed to keep people like Dad, Neha, and Hannah safe, and I was determined to not fail again. The crisis Mechano, Seer and Millennium had warned about still awaited me, and I had to be ready for it.

No, *we* had to be ready for it. I turned toward the New Sentinels still lined up behind me and joined the clapping by applauding the Heroes. The cameras moved away from me to project the five Heroes' images on the jumbotrons. I was lucky to be among such a fine group of Heroes:

Myth's secret identity was Isaac Geere. He had the Metahuman power to turn into various mythological creatures. Though I had more raw power than him thanks to my Omega-level status, Isaac's powers were probably the most versatile of all the New Sentinels. Isaac was a couple of years older than I and African American. "More like Mocha American," he often said, since his skin was more light brown than black. Or at least he used to say that—he didn't joke around with me much lately as he was too angry with me. Seamless, form-fitting, full-body black body armor protected Isaac's tall muscular form. The armor had light blue bands around its wrists and ankles and a red dragon on its chest. Its black cowl covered his brown face from the nose up. Though the body armor was reminiscent of the suit the Old Man had given Isaac when we Apprentices entered the Trials, it was a higher-tech upgrade from Isaac's old suit. Its light weight and flexibility belied how durable it was. Made of unstable molecules, the suit transformed when Isaac did so it was not destroyed every time he assumed a new mythological form.

Ninja's secret identity was Chie Sato, though Isaac and I called her by her nickname Shay. The rest of the New Sentinels only knew her by her code name, just as they only knew Isaac and me by ours. Though Shay, Isaac and I had vetted the other three New Sentinels as thoroughly as humanly possible, we weren't taking any chances considering the treachery that occurred in the ranks of the old Sentinels team. The level of trust it took to reveal our real identities to them would no doubt come with time. Keeping our identities secret made early mornings and late nights around the mansion awkward since all six of us lived together. Isaac, Shay and I wearing our masks at the dining room table felt weird, like wearing tuxes in a hot tub.

Shay's Ninja outfit was the same as that of the ancient class of Japanese assassins and spies she got her code name from. Her loose-fitting black robes were called shinobi shōzoku. The outfit covered her from head to toe, exposing only her eyes. Her sheathed katana was slung across her chest by a black leather strap that blended into her robes. The katana was her only obvious weapon; many others were concealed in the pockets and folds of her outfit. She once told me she even kept a small folding knife in her vagina. For emergencies, she said. I was pretty sure she had been kidding, but I wouldn't put it past her. In the unlikely event Shay and I ever hooked up, I'd run her through a metal detector first.

Despite looking like a mild-mannered librarian when she wasn't in costume, Shay could rag-doll just about anyone on the planet. She was the world's foremost martial artist and an Olympic-level gymnast. That last part was literal: Shay had won three gold medals, two silver, and one bronze in back-to-back summer Olympics when I was still a kid reading about superheroes in comic books. On top of all that, Shay had two Metahuman powers: a sixth sense for her opponents' weaknesses, and the ability to surround the weapons she carried with an energy field which allowed them to pierce anything.

Slab was otherwise known as Abdul Haddad. Slab was the team's strong man. What his super strength allowed him to lift had to be seen to be believed. Heck, I had seen it, and I still barely believed it. The Muslim man, originally from Algeria, wore a tight, concrete-colored costume that hugged his absurdly well-muscled body. He wasn't quite as wide as he was tall, but it sure seemed like it at first glance. In addition to his super strength, Slab's skin was nearly impenetrable.

Flare, otherwise known as Tiara Templeton. She could fly as well as emit and control heat and radiation. According to Isaac, she could also "turn a gay man straight and a saint into a sinner." In addition to being stunningly beautiful with a head full of cascading, flaming red hair, she wore an iridescent costume that left little to the imagination. Her posters were the only pieces of New Sentinels merch that outsold my Omega branded stuff. I couldn't blame the buying public. I too had eyes. The fact I could talk to Tiara without tripping all over my tongue was further evidence of how much I had changed over the years.

Blur was otherwise known as Eldridge Hollister. The short, lean speedster used to tout himself as *The Fastest Man Alive* until he got a cease and desist letter from DC Comics. The shiny silver costume he wore on stage now was relatively new. Months ago, shortly after Isaac, Shay and I had selected Blur from a mountain of applicants to join Slab and Flare on our new team, I had told Blur the canary yellow costume he then sported made him look like the world's fastest banana. I had just been kidding around, busting his balls, trying to get Blur to treat me like a comrade and friend instead of the marble statue he, Slab, and Flare treated me like.

Trying to bond with the Hero did not have the intended effect. Blur had stayed up that whole night, running around the world consulting with top fashion designers, to come up with a sleek silver costume he presented me with the next morning. Blur said he would start over from scratch if I didn't approve of his new threads. Mortified that Blur had taken my offhand joking comment so thoroughly to heart, I told him the new costume was the most awesome costume I had ever seen. I took greater care what I said to him, Slab and Flare after that.

That was the main problem I had with Blur, Flare and Slab: they treated me like an icon and a living legend instead of as a comrade. From the moment I met them, they had been standoffish toward me despite my best efforts to loosen them up. They acted normally with Isaac and Shay, so I knew the issue was me. I guess I could not really blame them for keeping me at a worshipful arm's-length despite how self-conscious it made me. I was, after all, one of the only four Omega-level Metahumans in the world, and the only one who was a Hero. My exploits were already the stuff of legend. Heck, Slab sometimes called me sir despite my continued protests, and the blockhead was over a decade older than I and married with three kids. Slab, Flare, and Blur treated me with worshipful awe, like the only reason why there was still hunger and disease in the world was because I hadn't gotten around to eradicating them yet.

I eyed my three newest comrades as I continued to applaud them. The other problem I had with them was something I could not put my finger on. They had been carefully screened and vetted by me, Shay, and Isaac. We had even hired Truman Lord, a Hero and private eye we had dealings with before, to do thorough background investigations. I knew more about the three Heroes than their parents did. They were tough as nails, as honorable as Boy Scouts, and as eager as puppies. They were some of the best Heroes in the business. They had acquitted themselves spectacularly in the field since we recruited them. If the crisis the Sentinels warned about was coming, I should have been comfortable facing it alongside these three.

I should have been. But I wasn't. Something did not feel right about the three Heroes. Not about them as individuals, but them as members of our team. It was like following a family recipe to the letter to recreate grandma's prize-winning blueberry pie. And yet, when you tasted it, something was not quite right. Too much sugar? Not enough sugar? Did I forget the nutmeg?

I hadn't shared my concerns with Isaac and Shay because I knew they were foolish. Those concerns likely only existed because, since I had screwed some things up so royally in the past, I was so worried about screwing something new up that I jumped at my own shadow.

Shoving my reservations aside, I stopped clapping and turned to face the assembled crowd again. The projectors focused on me once more and my image, larger than life, lit up the giant screens again. The carefully screened crowd roared its approval once more. They loved me. I had become the personification of the safety and security people everywhere craved.

A Bible verse popped into my head, the one that had inspired the last words of my speech. It was Ezekiel 34:28: *They will no longer be plundered by the nations, nor will wild animals devour them. They will live in safety, and no one will make them afraid.*

I looked out over the throng of applauding people. In my mind's eye, I imagined the millions more who watched remotely. If a crisis really was coming, so many were depending on me. I had let people I cared about down in the past, but there was no way I would let these people down now. Too much was at stake.

If things did not go my way, my legal troubles could land me in prison. What if the dream I'd been having was a precursor to the crisis the Sentinels had warned about? I could not deal with that crisis if I were cooling my heels in a power-dampening cell alongside the likes of Millennium and Chaos in MetaHold.

This public relations campaign to keep me out of prison was all well and good, but maybe I needed to do something a little more . . . proactive.

I felt my jaw tighten. I finally made a decision I had been wrestling with for weeks. If I didn't screw up the nerve to do what needed to be done, Dad, Neha, and the others the Sentinels killed while trying to kill me would have died in vain.

I stood at the podium and let the waves of cheers crash over me, washing away my remaining doubt.

I would do what I had to do to make sure the world was protected.

Even if I didn't like it.

6

I sat in the home's second-floor library wearing the full Omega suit and mask. Its cape felt especially heavy tonight. I was surrounded by dark wood, plush carpet, leather furniture, and law books. I wasn't reading. Reading the thick legal tomes would probably put me to sleep. I needed to keep my wits about me. I didn't know how lawyers waded through the stuff without developing narcolepsy. Amphetamines, maybe.

The night was overcast, so little light trickled in through the library's windows. I sat in the dark, brooding and waiting. In another room, a grandfather clock ticked loudly toward two a.m. Otherwise, the large house was still and quiet. Though the rest of the Queen Anne style showplace was spotless, apparently the live-in housekeeper had been forbidden to enter the library as a thin layer of dust was on everything. The inside of my nose itched. I fought off a sneeze. Even the dust smelled like money. The house was in Silver Sable, an upscale neighborhood in Astor City's northeastern quadrant. Shay owned a house not too far from here, though she now rented it out since she lived in New Sentinels mansion.

After that argument I'd had with Gina over the morality of my New Sentinels Day speech, I felt like the world's biggest hypocrite lurking here. But if I had to choose between being a hypocrite and ensuring the protection of the world . . . well, the choice was easy.

That didn't mean I had to like it.

My powers sensed someone approach the other side of the library's closed door. I shooed away my second thoughts and put my game face on.

The door opened and the lights flicked on. Astor City State's Attorney Draymond Miller jumped when he saw me.

"Jesus!" Wild-eyed, the prosecuting attorney blinked furiously, taking a startled step back. Recognition and confusion washed over his face, erasing the initial surprise and fear. "Omega! How did you get in here? How did you not set off the alarms?"

"Oh, you know . . ." I waved my hand vaguely and made a *whoosh* sound.

"The better question is, what are you doing here?"

"I was thinking about you, so I thought I'd swing by and have a chat."

"In the middle of the damned night?"

"I don't need much sleep, so I'm something of a night owl. As are you, it turns out. Close the door. Your wife's upstairs asleep. We don't want to disturb her."

Miller hesitated, his uncertainty obvious.

"Come on in," I urged. "You know who I am. I'm a Hero. I'm not going to hurt you. Close the door and have a seat. I want to talk."

Miller frowned, but finally closed the door. He sat down

behind his mahogany desk; I was already on the other side of it. Miller was in his early forties and mostly slim, but with the hint of a spare tire beginning to swell his light sweater. His curly golden-brown hair was cut close to his skull. He was a black man with a reddish tint to his light skin. Isaac would call Miller a redbone; if I called him that, the NAACP would probably picket me. Miller's complexion reminded me of the black comedian John Elroy Sanford, who had taken the stage name Redd Foxx because of his skin's reddish hue. I learned that bit of trivia from the Old Man. Not everything I learned under the Old Man's Apprenticeship related to crimefighting.

Mounted on the wall opposite me were degrees and honors including Miller's Harvard University *summa cum laude* undergraduate degree, Yale Law School degree, an editor-in-chief of *The Yale Law Journal* certificate, a Phi Beta Kappa honor society certificate, and a framed U.S. Supreme Court opinion signed by the chief justice Miller had clerked under. God, how I hated an underachiever. Underneath the degrees and honors were framed pictures of Miller shaking hands with the last two U.S. Presidents and of Miller with various CEOs and celebrities. Including Willow Wilde, the reality TV star known for the shows *Born to be Wilde* and *Buck Wilde*. Neha had been her head of security when Neha was kidnapped by the Sentinels in an attempt to bend me to their will. Willow was probably the most famous woman in the world. She had given herself the nickname The Queen, but those weren't crowns I was looking at.

"Okay, I'm dying to know." I pointed at Willow's ample chest. "Are those things real?"

Miller looked over his shoulder at where I pointed, then snorted dismissively. He impaled me with light eyes. "Surely you aren't lurking here in the dead of night to discuss Ms. Wilde's endowments. What do you really want to talk about?" Miller had already recovered from his startle over finding me here. As a trial attorney, he was used to rolling with the punches.

"Let's talk about my case," I said.

"Then this conversation is over before it's begun. You're a defendant I'm prosecuting who's represented by counsel. Ex parte communications between us about your case are strictly prohibited. Does Ms. Leonard know you're here?"

"No. Laura would be aghast if she knew." *Aghast*. I tried to step my verbal game up when speaking to Ivy League graduates.

"Rightly so. Ms. Leonard is a good lawyer. We attended the same law school, though she graduated a few years before I. If you want to discuss your case, have Ms. Leonard call my secretary in the morning and make an appointment for you both to come in."

"You don't want Laura to hear what I have to say to you."

"I also don't want to hear what you have to say to me. If your case is the only thing you want to discuss, I'll have to ask you to leave."

I leaned back and crossed my legs. "I don't think I will."

Miller stared me down. Or at least he tried to. Despite our age disparity, I was not some public defender fresh out of law school or a gangbanger with two strikes already on his record begging for a favorable plea agreement. I've matched stares with Doctor Alchemy. A lawyer in the burbs couldn't make me flinch.

Miller was the first to look away. He reached for the telephone on his desk. "Since you won't leave voluntarily, I'm calling the police."

He could not lift the receiver from the cradle. Frowning, he tugged harder.

"Before you dislocate something," I said, "you should

69

know that I'm exerting my powers on the phone. My colleague Slab couldn't pick up that phone right now, and he has Class 5 Metahuman strength. I doubt even Avatar in his prime could pick it up, God rest his soul. There was a time when that wasn't the case, but I've been taking Flintstones vitamins and eating lots of spinach since then."

Miller stopped trying to lift the phone. One hand casually slipped under the lip of the desk.

"And good luck pushing the panic button you've got under the desk that sends an SOS to the cops," I added. "Buttons aren't my Kryptonite. My powers work on them just as well as they do on phones. Doors too, so you won't be leaving this room. Not until we talk. And don't insult me and embarrass yourself by pulling that gun out of the drawer. You and I both know even a howitzer can't stop me. Let's reason together. Once we talk, if you want to call the police, Laura, the Heroes' Guild, or Miss Manners to complain about my boorish behavior, be my guest."

Miller gave me his dead-eyed stare again, the one cops and prosecutors must practice in the mirror until they've got it down pat. "There's a legal term for what you're doing to me," he said, calmly and somberly, like a father lecturing his wayward son. "It's called false imprisonment. Not to mention the crimes of trespassing and breaking and entering you committed by coming in here. You're wading in treacherous waters."

"Oh my goodness. Treacherous waters? Yikes! How terrifying. You're already prosecuting me for the false imprisonment and kidnapping of the Rogue Mad Dog. Add the other charges to my tab."

"I think I'll do that. Judge Shepard released you on your own recognizance pending trial. Pillar of the community, and all that. Considering your behavior and flippancy tonight, she'll undoubtedly revisit her decision. By this time tomorrow, I suspect you'll be rethinking your actions in the federal Metahuman Holding Facility."

"Just call it MetaHold like everyone else does. Do you lawyers get paid by the syllable?"

Ignoring me, cool as a cucumber, Miller folded his hands on the desk. "Since I seem to have no choice in the matter, talk. But know that I'm engaging with you under protest and against my will."

"If it comes to that, I'll be sure to tell the judge you made that clear and that you didn't violate your ethical obligations as a lawyer and officer of the court. But it won't come to that. I want to talk to you about dropping all the charges against me."

Miller barked out a laugh. He seemed comfortable and in his element despite the fact I could squish him like a bug. In his eyes, I had transformed into just another dirtbag defendant like the ones he had easily handled thousands of times before. "I can't do that."

"Sure you can. Rule 4-247 of the Maryland Rules of Procedure says, and I quote, 'The State's Attorney may terminate a prosecution on a charge and dismiss the charge by entering a nolle prosequi on the record in open court.' Not bad for someone who went to a state school, huh? A friend helped me with the big words."

"I know all about Rule 4-247. It's called a nol pros."

"I prefer the full Latin phrase. Nolle prosequi. 'I refuse to prosecute.' Saying it makes me feel smart."

"Clearly you aren't smart. You did break into the home of the city's top prosecutor, after all." Miller shook his head. "But you misunderstand my meaning. I have the prosecutorial discretion to dismiss the charges against you. I *can* do it. I *won't* do it."

"Why not?"

"You're charged with kidnapping and confining a man—the aforementioned Mad Dog, aka Antonio Ricci—in a cell for over two years without a trial, a lawful arrest, or any due process whatsoever. Not to mention depriving Mr. Ricci of adequate food, recreation, medical care, and sanitation facilities."

I was glad I had Amnesia wipe Mad Dog's and the rest of the Revengers' knowledge of The Mountain and of my and Isaac's secret identities before I turned those Rogues over to the authorities, or else it would be Theodore Conley and not just Omega in legal trouble. At least with that I had not broken the law; under the federal regulations implementing the Hero Act of 1945, such a memory wipe was as legal as driving through a green light. Keeping Heroes' identities a secret was why the Guild kept Amnesia on retainer. "Mad Dog is a murderer," I said. "If what you say I did is true, he got what he deserved."

"Perhaps. But that's not relevant here. You are not the arbiter of what people deserve. As I said earlier, false imprisonment is a crime. So is kidnapping. Heroes aren't the police. They aren't prosecutors. They aren't judges. They aren't above the law. In this country, no citizen is, super-powered or not. If the allegations against you are true—and I have no reason to doubt they aren't, especially considering your behavior tonight—you will go to prison for quite some time. Deservedly so, I might add."

"I think I can persuade you to drop the charges."

Miller barked out another laugh.

"And I think I have the body of an Adonis. Alas, merely thinking something doesn't make it so." Miller shook his head at me. "Besides, this is not the first time someone's asked me to drop your case. Various federal, state, and local officials have contacted me about you. Mayor Stone calls to plead your case at least once a week. His Honor himself, not one of his flunkeys. I wonder why he's so insistent that I end your prosecution. Was he, perhaps, the subject of an earlier nocturnal visit from you?"

Truth be told, I was holding something over Mayor Stone's head. He was the mayor I had seen with a needle in his arm on the Sentinels' surveillance system known as Sentry when I burst in on Mechano, Seer and Millennium to confront them for trying to assassinate me. A few weeks ago, I made a point of letting Stone know I knew he was a drug addict and that I had access to recordings of him getting high. As with Governor Flushing, I had also given a bunch of money to the mayor's election campaign. The money was the carrot; the threat of exposing his drug habit was the stick.

But I couldn't tell Miller all that, of course. Instead I said, "Nah. The mayor's a big fan, is all. Word on the street is he doesn't leave the house without Omega brand underwear on. Would you like a pair?"

Miller stared at me in disbelief. "You're awfully flip for someone who's put himself in such a precarious situation." He gave me a grim smile. "And I've seen your underwear in stores. Tighty-whities, as I recall. Thanks, but no thanks. I'm a boxers man."

"Wow. TMI."

"You brought it up. As far as the mayor and other officials lobbying on your behalf is concerned, unfortunately for you, the State's Attorney is an elected position. I answer to the voters, not other politicians."

"The voters don't want you to prosecute me either. I've seen the polling."

"I said I answer to the voters. I'm not ruled by them. If I were, who went to jail would become a popularity contest."

"You mean it's not already? I know some well-heeled, well-connected white-collar criminals whose continued freedom says otherwise."

"I'm not going to debate the fairness or unfairness of the criminal justice system with you."

"You're quite right. I'm not here to debate. I'm here to persuade." Using my powers, I floated a large yellow envelope from where it had been tucked next to me in the chair to above Miller's desk. The thick envelope fell to the desk with a loud plop when I released my hold on it.

Miller stared at the envelope. "What's this?" he demanded.

"It's persuasion. Open it. Don't be shy. It doesn't contain anthrax or anything that will hurt you. Not hurt you physically, at any rate." Miller eyed the envelope like it was a rotten fish and didn't move. "No? Fine, be that way. Allow me."

Still using my powers, I unsealed the envelope and pulled out a sheaf of enlarged color photos. I spread them over Miller's desk so he could get a good look at them. His eyes widened.

"How'd you get these?" Gone was the calm, in control voice. Now Miller sounded like he was being strangled.

"Why do you keep asking questions the answer to which you already know? You know who I am, you know what I can do." Miller's eyes were big and disbelieving as he stared down at the photos. "You weren't kidding when you said you were a boxers man. I don't see a single brief in all those pictures. Or much clothing of any kind. Do you know what these pictures are? No, don't answer. I can see that you do. They're of you in flagrante delicto. Saying that Latin phrase makes me feel smart too. Roughly translated, it means these are pictures of you dipping your pen in ink that's not your wife's. Multiple inkwells, as a matter of fact. At the risk of mixing my metaphors, you're quite the busy bee. You've been dipping your proboscis in an awful lot of flowers. How do you find the time to practice law?"

Miller didn't look up or respond. He sat frozen. I could practically hear the wheels of Miller's mind turn as he gaped at the pictures.

"I know what you're thinking," I said. "You're thinking, 'This is not such a big deal. I can survive this. Lots of people have affairs. Infidelity is not a crime. This is not the 1920s. If my indiscretions become public, they don't have to be fatal to my career as a public servant. Heck, if I spin this right, they'll be *good* for my career. They're evidence of my virility. People will start to see me as a lady's man instead of the Ivy League nerd they now think of me as.'"

I shook my head.

"And maybe your thinking's right," I conceded. "I'm reminded of something I read Louisiana Governor Edwin Edwards say to reporters when he ran for reelection in 1983. He said, 'The only way I can lose this election is if I'm caught in bed with either a dead girl or a live boy.' He won that election, as it turns out. You might not be so fortunate though, Dray. Can I call you Dray? I think I will. You might not be so fortunate as Edwards because, in your case, there *is* a live boy involved. Two, as a matter of fact. Look at those pictures in the upper right-hand corner."

Miller's bronze face drained of blood.

"As it turns out, you're an equal opportunity adulterer. Don't get me wrong—I couldn't care less who you sleep with. I personally am exclusively heterosexual but, hey— live and let live. But I don't need to tell you that a lot of black people do have a problem with homosexuality. Mostly because the church is such an integral part of the black community, especially the voting portion of the black community. Maryland's not in the Bible Belt, but we're right above it. Call it the belt buckle of the Bible Belt.

"Black people make up almost a third of the electorate in both Astor City and the rest of Maryland. They turned out in droves to vote for you in the last election, and yet you still squeaked into office by the skin of your teeth. You've done a good job as State's Attorney, so you're more popular now than when you got elected. Even so, if you lose as little as three percent of the black vote, you'll lose your job next year. If these pictures become public, especially the ones in the right-hand corner, you'll lose a heck of a lot more than three percent of the black vote. And that's not even counting the non-black vote you'll lose. Your political career would be over. And you have such a bright future, too. You're a kid from the projects who kept his nose clean, studied hard, earned a bunch of scholarships, and made good. There's talk of you one day being the first black governor of Maryland. They say you've been eyeing the governor's chair since high school. If you pull off getting there, after that, who knows how high your star would rise?"

Miller wasn't looking at me. I didn't think he was even looking at the pictures anymore. His head was hung. I felt like I was kicking a puppy. But I knew I couldn't let up. By all accounts, Miller was an honest and straight-shooting prosecutor. I didn't know if the threat of losing his job alone was enough to bend him to my will.

"And then there's the not so small matter of your wife," I added. "A lovely woman from a conservative family. Of the two of you, she's the wealthy one. An oil heiress. Canola, not petroleum. Who would've guessed there was so much loot in vegetable oil? Not me. Anyway, without her you couldn't afford this ritzy house in this swell neighborhood. Or to send your two kids to private school. Or your vacation homes in Miami and Aspen. Or your sailboat and luxury cars. Or countless other aspects of your comfortable life-style. Not on a government salary while you're busy climbing the greasy political pole to greatness. How would Mrs. Miller feel about you greasing your own pole with your extracurricular activities? Hmmm, I wonder." I snapped my fingers. "You know what we should do? Let's pop upstairs and ask her."

I stood. Miller's head snapped up. "Wait! Wait, goddamn you, wait!"

Miller didn't speak again for several long beats. Then he let out a long exhale. He seemed smaller than when he had first walked in, like he was a deflating tire.

"What do you want?" For the first time tonight, Miller sounded tired.

I looked down at him. "Again with the questions you already know the answer to. I want you to dismiss the charges against me. Before close of business tomorrow. If you don't, those pictures and the names of the men and women depicted in them will anonymously make their way to every news organization and tabloid in Maryland. Not to mention posted to social media. Not only will you never be elected to office again, there's a good chance the public outrage will be such that you'll have to resign before you finish your current term. I'd hate to see that happen. Truly I would. You're a good prosecutor. You've crusaded against public corruption and you've done a lot to clean up the cesspool that the municipal government used to be. You have a high conviction rate and yet you treat people fairly.

Can't seem to keep your dick in your pants, but no one's perfect."

Miller let that sink in. "And if I do dismiss the charges?"

"Then you'll go on with your life, and I'll go on with mine. It will be as if this conversation never happened."

The room fell quiet. The only sound was that of the grandfather clock, faintly ticking down the moments.

"If I do this," Miller finally said, "I want your word that the pictures will be destroyed. Assuming your word's any good."

"C'mon Dray. Do you take me for a fool? If I destroy the pictures after you dismiss the charges, you'll simply refile them. The statute of limitations hasn't run yet." I shook my head. "No. I'll keep the pictures to ensure our deal stays our deal and that you keep your mouth shut about it. I will give you my word, though, that no one other than I will ever see them. Assuming you hold up your end of the bargain and keep your nose out of my business."

The room was quiet once more. Miller looked around the room with unfocused eyes. Maybe he was picturing what he would do if it were all gone.

"Fine. I'll do it." Miller's voice was small. "How will I explain my office's change of heart?"

"How should I know? You're the silver-tongued politician. Come up with something that sounds good. Or don't. It doesn't matter. Your prosecutorial discretion in matters like this is absolute. You don't have to explain yourself to anyone. Except, eventually, to the voters. Don't look so glum. If you're smart—and I know you are—you'll use the dismissal as a campaign selling point. I'm a pretty popular guy, even under indictment. My public approval ratings are way higher than yours. If you play your cards right, you can ride an association with me right into the governor's office.

Why should you be any different? That's what Flushing did."

"What about the civil suit? You must know Mad Dog's lawyers are champing at the bit to file one. They're probably just waiting for the criminal case to resolve first. I don't have any authority in civil matters."

"You let me worry about any civil case. I'll be sure to demand a jury trial. A Hero versus a guy like Mad Dog with a record and Mafia connections who is on tape attacking that Hero alongside the likes of Doctor Alchemy and the rest of the Revengers?" I shrugged. "I like my chances with a jury. Besides, even if I were to lose a civil suit, it's only money. I've got plenty of that. Not going to prison is what I'm really concerned about. I've got too many responsibilities to risk getting locked up."

I stepped toward a window. Now that we had an agreement, I had to get out of here. I felt three inches tall and sick to my tiny stomach. It seemed everyone had skeletons in their closets if you rummaged in them long enough. It was disheartening, especially for someone like me who naively once believed good people were all good and bad people were all bad.

I slid the window open with my powers, then paused. I turned to face Miller.

"I almost forgot. That digital recorder under the lip of your desk that you activated when you sat down? When you listen to it after I leave, you'll discover it recorded absolutely nothing at all. Nothing's wrong with the device; I enclosed it inside a soundproof force field the instant you turned it on. Don't look so glum. I'm saving you from yourself. After all, recording a conversation without the consent of the other party is a violation of Maryland's Wiretapping and Electronic Surveillance Act. A very serious crime. I would think the city's top prosecutor would know better." I shook my head in mock sadness.

Then my voice hardened. "Nice try, Dray. But you're punching above your weight with me. There's no way out of this for you other than doing exactly what you've agreed to do. Don't screw with me on this.

"Oh, and the pictures?" I jerked a thumb at the desk. "Keep them. I've got lots of copies."

I turned back to the window. Miller called out behind me: "You're not much of a Hero, are you?" It came out in a husky whisper. The guy sounded like he might cry.

I didn't respond. The only answer I had was one I didn't like.

I flew out the window, shutting it gently behind me with my powers despite feeling disgusted enough to slam it closed. I rose into the chilly night air, orienting myself, preparing to fly back to the mansion. Maybe on the way there I'd find a nun to mug, or some butterflies to pull the wings off of. I felt like showering, but knew water wasn't enough to wash the filth off me.

That's when I realized it. My telekinetic touch sensed a nearby presence.

Someone was following me.

7

I touched down on the sloped roof of a nearby three-story Greek Revival mansion. The other person up here and I were shrouded in shadows.

I did a quick scan with my powers. Though people were in the house below us, they were asleep. No one else was nearby.

"You're following me," I called out in a low voice to the other person.

At first, there was no response.

"No shit, Sherlock," finally returned Isaac's voice. A memory of how Isaac and I had first met hit me. He had said the identical words when we had been assigned to clean the Hero Academy latrine together. I missed how well we had gotten along back then.

Isaac was well-camouflaged in the shadows thanks to his dark Myth costume. If it hadn't been for my powers, I never would have been aware of his presence. I stepped closer to him, my powers keeping me clinging to the angled roof like a spider.

"How long have you been tailing me?" I asked.

"Ever since you snuck out of the mansion."

Despite the situation, I was impressed; I had been on the lookout and would have sworn no one had followed me. The fact I detected Isaac now when I hadn't before told me he wanted me to spot him. "I didn't sneak out."

"That's not how it looked to me. Guilt was written all over your face. You looked like a teen creeping out of the house to steal a car and go joyriding. Papa Myth wondered what you were up to. Especially since you have a history of hiding things and being sneaky." Isaac had been angry with me ever since discovering I had imprisoned Mad Dog in The Mountain, the secret retreat I inherited from Avatar. I told Isaac what I had done shortly after the New Sentinels captured Mad Dog a few months ago so that he'd hear it from me instead of the press. I knew Mad Dog would sing like a canary as soon as he was in the hands of the civilian authorities, and he had not disappointed. I didn't know which Isaac was madder about: the fact I had illegally imprisoned Mad Dog, or the fact I had not told him about it sooner.

"How'd you follow me without me detecting you?" I asked.

"I'm a Hero too, you know. Why do you keep asking questions the answer to which you already know?"

My stomach sank. Isaac was throwing in my face words I had said to Miller. It confirmed what I suspected.

"You eavesdropped," I said.

"Obviously."

"How? Miller's place is several houses away."

"The short answer? Again, I'm a Hero. The long answer? I turned into a Coraniaid. It's a type of dwarf from Celtic mythology. A Coraniaid has absurdly acute hearing. In that form, I can hear grass grow from a mile away."

"Impressive."

"Far more so than your behavior. Jesus, Mary, and Joseph! It's one disappointment after another with you lately. What's gotten into you? How did you even get those pictures of Miller? Please tell me you didn't hire Truman and get him mixed up in this foolishness."

I was reluctant to answer, but did anyway; they say confession is good for the soul. "I'd heard rumors about Draymond's dalliances from some of my sources in local government. I tried to hire Truman to chase down the rumors and verify them. He turned me down. He said the things he wouldn't do for money outnumbered the things he would. Certain things trump money, he said. Told me I should already know that. I told him I'd do the job myself. I think he's disappointed in me."

"He's not the only one. Blackmailing a public official? What the hell are you thinking?"

"The world needs me. I'm no use to the world if I'm stuck in a MetaHold prison cell with my powers removed. That's what would happen if I let the case against me proceed."

"The world needs you? Of all the narcissistic, self-serving BS. Do you even hear the words coming out of your mouth? First you lock Mad Dog up in your own personal black site and throw away the key. Now this. I often wonder what other shady things you're doing or have done that I don't know about." A wave of guilt washed over me. Despite promising myself I would, I still had not told Isaac I had cheated during the Trials so that he and I could both pass. I was waiting for the right time. The right time never seemed to arrive.

Isaac shook his head. "The New Sentinels are supposed to be a team. A team can't truly be a team without trust among its members. I used to trust you, but can't anymore. I feel as though I don't even know you anymore. Maybe I never did."

My frustration at this whole situation and my soured relationship with Isaac came to a boil. It all came out of me in a torrent. "You know, I'm getting pretty sick of your lectures. And of you snapping and snarling at me these past few months. You of all people know the responsibility on my shoulders. I'm the Omega. The Omega spirit that's supposed to keep the world safe resides in me. Do you think I'm happy about it? About any of this? Dad died because of the Omega spirit. So did Neha. So did a lot of other people. If I could give the blasted thing to someone else, I would. But I can't. I'm stuck with it. I'm doing the best I can. I'm doing what needs to be done. Mad Dog deserved what I did to him and more. How many lives did I save, I wonder, by locking him up where he couldn't hurt anyone? And if you can't see all of that, maybe I don't know *you* like I thought I did."

"This 'I'm doing what needs to be done for the greater good because the end justifies the means' nonsense you're spouting reminds me of someone. Mechano said the exact same thing when he explained why the Sentinels sent Iceburn after you and right before they murdered Neha. You're acting just like him."

I recoiled, feeling like I'd been slapped. "I'm nothing like that murderer," I hissed.

"Aren't you? I'm reminded of what we were taught in our Heroic Feats, Ethics, and Theory class in the Academy. The Old Man taught us that a Hero is an instrument of the law, not a subverter of it. He said that 'A Hero must follow the law. If he doesn't, he's no better than the criminals and Rogues he fights.' Or maybe you missed all those lessons. Too busy mooning over Neha and making goo-goo eyes at her, probably. Maybe she'd still be alive if you thought more with your big head than your little one."

My fists clenched and I took a step toward Isaac. He was bigger than I, but if he thought that would stop me from pummeling him, he was mistaken.

I stopped. With an effort, I unclenched my fists. It was several seconds before I trusted myself to speak.

"That was a low blow, what you said about Neha." My voice was hoarse.

Isaac was quiet for a long while. He breathed heavily, his breath coming out as a mist in the chill of the night.

"You're right," he finally said. "I was out of line. I'm sorry. I apologize." His voice hardened. "But not for the rest. I'm dead right about the rest of what I said."

"It must be nice, living in your pristine ivory tower where everything is black and white, looking down at those of us wrestling with reality that's full of shades of gray."

"You don't even sound like the guy I used to know. What in the world has happened to you?"

"The real world and responsibility. They're what happened to me."

We were both quiet for a while. A cat yowled in the distance, then fell silent again.

"I want you to report what you've done tonight to the Heroes' Guild," Isaac said quietly. His voice sounded almost pleading.

"You know I can't do that."

"You can. But you won't."

"Same difference." I hesitated. "You could report me yourself."

"I could. I should. In fact, I'm supposed to."

"Will you?"

The tension in the air was so thick, I could taste it.

"To quote the world's most powerful jackass, 'You know I can't do that.' Isaac's grin flashed in the dark, cutting the tension like a knife for an instant.

"Why not?" I asked.

"For one thing, I'm no narc. For another . . . well, you know why. We've been through a lot together. We've grown up together, fought together, seen wonders together, lost friends and family together." Isaac paused, then recited: "'We few, we happy few, we band of brothers. For he to-day that sheds his blood with me shall be my brother. Be he ne'er so vile, this day shall gentle his condition.'"

"Henry the Fifth's Saint Crispin's Day speech. You're chock-full of quotes tonight."

"I'm very smart. It's a curse."

"Especially for those of us forced to listen to your erudition."

"Don't try to compete with my smartness by using words like erudition."

This banter was like old times. Better times. The old Isaac was back, though I knew he wouldn't stay long. He was so idealistic. And I . . . wasn't. Not anymore. Not when there was so much at stake.

We fell quiet again for a long while, lost in our own thoughts.

Finally, I said, "Let's head back to the mansion and get some shut-eye. The Diabolical Dozen are still at large, and we need to resume our search for them."

"One more thing before we go."

"Yeah?" I said, turning back toward him.

Isaac's fist collided with my jaw. I saw stars. My legs shut off, I fell and slid down the sloped roof. Only a last-second exertion of my powers kept me from falling off and plunging down.

There was a faint glow and suddenly Isaac hovered over me in his bare-chested and haloed angel form. Isaac was normally taller and more muscular than I, and he was even more so now that he had transformed. His snow-white wings beat the air.

"Regardless of what we've been through together, regardless of what we are to each other," he declared, his eyes flashing with angelic fire as he looked down at me, "my patience and indulgence only go so far. Like I said, I'm a Hero too. If I catch you doing something else even close to what you've done tonight, I'll put you in chains and drag you in front of the Guild myself. And if you think I won't or can't do it, Mister Omega-Level Savior Man, then you were right before—you don't know me as well as you think you do. Capisce?"

"Understood," I said. I touched my jaw gingerly. Despite the fact the Omega suit covered it and had absorbed much of the blow, it had not absorbed all of it. It hurt like hell. There would undoubtedly be a bruise.

Isaac's eyes softened. He dipped in the air and extended a hand. I took it, and he helped me up. "Whatever your faults might be," he said, "you're not one to get caught flat-footed. Your powers must've sensed the punch was coming. You could have blocked it. Why didn't you?"

Wincing, I worked my jaw from side to side. It popped. Maybe I'd have soup for dinner instead of the steak I had planned on. Solid food was overrated anyway. If mush was good enough for a Gerber baby, it was good enough for me. "I thought you hitting me would make both of us feel better. Did it work?"

Isaac considered it.

"Nope," he concluded. "How about you?"

"Me neither."

"On that, at least, we agree. C'mon, let's head back to the mansion."

We went airborne. I didn't go as fast as I normally did so Isaac could keep up.

After a little while had passed, I said, "You hit like a girl."

"I was holding back. I was trying to make a point, not bust your head open," Isaac said as the wind whipped around us. Astor City looked like a giant Lite-Brite below us. "And even if I do hit like a girl, this girl still managed to knock you on your ass."

"Good point."

"You up for racing back? I feel like stretching my wings. Last one back pulls double monitor duty." At least one of us New Sentinels was on duty in the Watch Room around the clock, keeping an eye open for any threats the team might need to deal with. The old Sentinels had done something similar in their Situation Room, but both Isaac and I had insisted on shuttering the Situation Room since that was where Mechano, Millennium and Seer had confined Neha after they kidnapped her.

"A race wouldn't be fair to you," I said.

"Don't go polishing your gold medal before you've won it yet, Junior." Isaac was two years older than I, but he acted like it was 2,000 years when it suited him. "This old dog has learned some new tricks."

"Uh-huh. I'll give you a ten second head start."

"Deal," Isaac said immediately.

"You were awfully quick to take me up on that. What happened to your new tricks?"

"I'm still ironing out their kinks. This is no time for foolish pride. Double monitor duty sucks."

I slowed to a stop in mid-air. Isaac kept going, glowing and transforming out of his angel form as he flew. He became a reddish-brown bird with a white head. The bird was almost the size Isaac's angel form had been.

With a whoosh and a whiz, the bird abruptly accelerated out of view, though not out of the range of my telekinetic touch. Isaac had changed into a Garuda, a bird from Hindu mythology that could fly faster than the wind. I had seen Isaac turn into a Garuda before. So much for new tricks.

I doubled the time and waited a full twenty seconds. Then I rocketed after Isaac's bird form. I soon zoomed past him. The wake of my air turbulence sent him tumbling with a squawk and spray of feathers.

I didn't have to fly so close that I sent him spinning. But my jaw still hurt. He had hit me pretty hard.

But mostly, I was still sore about what he had said about Neha.

8

The ridiculously blue ocean lapped at the milky-white beach far below where I stood on the promontory. As always, the strange sun with its dancing fiery tentacles was directly overhead. The storm clouds were still on the horizon, but further away and looking less threatening than they had before.

The dream was back. Assuming it really was just a dream. The last thing I remembered was falling asleep in bed as usual.

I spun around, examining the area. I did not see the little Asian girl I had spoken to before. I really wanted to talk to her again to determine if this was merely a recurring dream or something more.

As usual, I could not move to the right, deeper into the grassland. Going too far to the left would take me off the edge of the promontory. A steep cliff was below the edge, with jagged rocks at the bottom. The narrow beach and then the ocean water extended beyond that. Without my powers in this supposed dreamworld, I didn't want to risk falling off the cliff. Maybe I'd wake up when I hit the rocks far below. Or maybe I would never wake up at all. I didn't know.

Careful to not get too close to the promontory's edge, I began walking. As before in these dreams, it seemed like time passed both slowly and quickly, all at the same time. I walked for what simultaneously seemed like hours and mere moments.

I eventually spotted something: a dot in the distance, hovering above the promontory.

As I got closer, the dot enlarged into a person. It was the Asian girl again. She wore the same bunny shirt and other clothes I had previously seen her in. She hovered several feet in the air in the lotus position, legs crossed, each foot on the opposite thigh. She faced the ocean, with her eyes closed. Her arms were lifted at her sides, bent slightly. She was saying something.

As I got closer, I heard her.

"Ooooooooommmmmmmmmmm," she intoned, over and over.

I stopped walking once I was abreast of her. "I have questions for you."

"Ooooooooommmmmmmmmmm."

"Who are you?"

"Ooooooooommmmmmmmmmm."

"What is this place?"

"Ooooooooommmmmmmmmmm."

"Who is this Progenitor person you spoke of before?"

"Ooooooooommmmmmmmmmm."

I asked more questions, but it was like talking to a wall. With her eyes closed, not acknowledging me at all, the girl continued to float and say the same mantra, over and over.

I gave up. I supposed the girl would speak again when she was good and ready.

Like the girl, I turned to face the ocean. I looked out over it, careful to not look directly at the storm clouds on the horizon. They still made me uneasy.

After a while—maybe a few minutes, though it could have just as easily been a few hours—one of the girl's eyes peeked open. Out of my peripheral vision, I saw the girl examine me from her cracked eye. I pretended like I didn't notice. If peppering the girl with questions didn't work, maybe ignoring her would.

The girl abruptly stopped mid-*ooommm*. "Aren't you going to ask what I'm doing?" she asked petulantly. Both her eyes were open now.

"No." I continued to look at the ocean.

My disinterest took the girl aback. "You're not the least bit curious?"

"No."

"Oh." She sounded disappointed.

After a few seconds, the girl closed her eyes again. She resumed *ooommm*ing, but her heart didn't seem to be in it anymore. I continued to look straight ahead. I felt like I was on the right track.

After a short while, the mantra broke off again. The girl's eyes flew open and she said, "Well if you *must* know, you nosy parker, I'm contemplating the answer to the universe."

I was interested despite myself. "There's an answer? Just one?"

"Of course. Even idiots know that."

I ignored the slight. "Well, what's the answer?"

"Twelve," she said definitively.

"Twelve? Just twelve? What's that supposed to mean?"

"Isn't it obvious?"

"Not at all."

The girl rolled her eyes heavenward. "Morons," she muttered. "Why must I work through morons?"

"That's the second time you've called me a moron. I don't like being called one. Or an idiot, for that matter." I felt like an elementary school teacher telling a precocious yet socially delayed student it wasn't nice to call people names.

"You heard that? Oh. Sorry. I don't talk to people much. Or at all, really. Not for decades. My social skills are rusty. It's just that, from my perspective, you *are* a moron. No offense intended. Almost everyone is, compared to me. I am a nth level genius, you know." She didn't say it in a bragging way, but as a simple statement of fact. Like she was saying *Fire is hot, ice is cold, and I'm scads smarter than you.*

"No, I don't know," I said. "I don't know anything about you." *Assuming you're real and not an obnoxious figment of my imagination*, I added silently.

"We'll rectify that tout de suite. It's why you're here, after all." The girl's legs untangled from their lotus pose. Still floating in the air, she stuck her hand out. "My name's Mastermind. Pleased to meet ya. Not that I don't already know you. But you don't know me. Hence the introduction."

I looked at the girl's extended hand warily and didn't touch it. The girl frowned, then her expression cleared as she realized why I was reluctant to shake. "Don't worry. I won't zap you again. Pinky swear. Before I was just proving this is not a dream, is all."

Still dubious but feeling like a heel for not taking the proffered hand, I reached out and swallowed her small hand in my own. I wasn't hit by the excruciating pain I had felt when the girl touched me before. The girl's hand was warm and entirely normal feeling.

"See, I don't bite." The girl beamed at me like I was a

child who had successfully gone potty in the toilet for the first time instead of in his diaper.

"What kind of name is Mastermind?"

"It's my code name, of course." She slowly and deliberately pointed at herself, then at me. "Me Mastermind, you Omega."

I felt a flash of irritation. "You're treating me like I'm a moron again."

"Yeah, but I didn't come right out and call you one this time. That's progress."

"Not much. It's like shooting somebody three times, yanking out one of the bullets, and calling it progress."

"What an over-the-top analogy. You should change your code name to Drama Queen."

I refused to be diverted. "What's your real name?"

"I just told you. M-a-s-t-e-r-m-i-n-d." She pronounced the name slowly, like I had been too stupid to understand it the first time.

I wasn't about to call someone young enough to be my daughter Mastermind regardless of how smart she allegedly was. "No, I mean your birth name. The one your parents gave you."

"Despite looking like I was born yesterday, I'm old enough to be your grandma. And therefore old enough to know the first rule of the superhero club is you don't talk about your secret identity."

I eyed the little girl dubiously. I had shoes older than she was. "You're telling me you're a Hero?"

"Am I a licensed Hero? No. I've been too busy all these years to jump through those hoops. All that running and leaping and sparring and test-taking? Blech! Looks exhausting. Grandma's too old for that tomfoolery. But I'm a superhero, all right. After all, for over eighty years I've been the only person standing between the world and *him*." She jerked her chin at the distant storm clouds. Then she balled her fists and pressed them to her waist, thrusting her flat chest out. "Mastermind's my name, protecting the world's my game."

If I was going to determine whether this was just a dream, I needed something more tangible than grand assertions from someone who could easily be my sleeping mind talking to me. "What's your name?" I insisted. "Your real name."

"Yeesh! You're like a dog with a bone. Fine Fido, I'll tell you my real name. Hopefully it'll move things along. We have much to discuss and not a ton of time.

"My name is Lim Qiaolian. Some of the books you Westerners have written insist on calling me Liam, but it's Lim. Liam's not even a Chinese name. So much for fact-checking." The girl sniffed disdainfully.

"Anyhoo, like you, I'm an Omega-level Meta. One of the only four in the whole world. And we're the only two not in the pokey. It's a mighty exclusive club."

The girl's face suddenly lit up.

"You know what we should do?" Her hands fluttered with excitement. "We should have a secret handshake!"

9

Lim Qiaolian. I knew the name instantly. Not knowing it would be like the President of the United States not knowing his predecessor—there were so few alive and they were all so prominent that of course they knew of one another. The same was true of Omega-level Metahumans, only more so as there were fewer of us than there were living Presidents.

As the girl had indicated, other than me, there were only three Omega-level Metas in the world: Lim Qiaolian, the Rogue Chaos, and the ex-Sentinel and ex-Hero Millennium. The latter two were both imprisoned in MetaHold. As for Lim, when the Chinese telepath and super genius was five-years-old, she put herself in a coma for reasons only she knew. Since then, she had sat unmoving in her Beijing childhood home for over eighty years, her child's body perfectly preserved and not aging a day. Over the years, her home had been converted into a shrine. A sizeable and still growing Chinese sect known as Qiaolianism worshipped her as a god. Because of that sect, I did not know what Lim looked like. "Only believers in the truth may know the face of god," Qiaolianists often said when refusing to allow Lim's body to be photographed or otherwise recorded.

I didn't need to know what Lim looked like to know this dream girl's claim was ridiculous.

I said, "If you're Lim Qiaolian, I must be Thor. It's nice to meet another god face to face." I glanced around. "Where are Zeus and Shiva? You'd think gods would show up on time for the universe's first divine meetup. I hope Zeus brings those little cheese balls I like so much."

"Hysterical, Mr. Smarty Pants. I'm dying of laughter. Not! Fortunately for you, my followers are misguided and I'm not actually divine. If I were, I'd smite you for blasphemy."

"Lim is in a coma on the other side of the world. If you're her, how are we speaking?"

"Uh, telepathy. Duh!"

"Prove that you're Lim. If you're a telepath, what am I thinking right now?"

The girl put a hand on her forehead, stretched the other toward me, and got a distant look in her eyes. "Lim to Theodore, Lim to Theodore. I've almost found the right frequency. Wait . . . wait . . . got it. It's coming in clearly to me now: you're thinking you don't believe me."

Giggling, the girl dropped her hands. She was obviously pulling my leg. "I don't need my powers to discern you don't believe me, silly boy. It's written all over your face. In reality, I *can't* read your mind right now. Haven't been able to for years. Not since you absorbed the Omega weapon and turned it into your costume. It makes you resistant to psychic energy. I'll bet you didn't even know that."

"If I'm resistant to psychic energy, how are we speaking now?"

"I said you're resistant, not immune. It's why I contact you when you're asleep. Your natural psychic defenses are lower then. It's why succubi and incubi only try to seduce people when they're asleep."

"Succubi? Incubi?" I shook my head in disbelief. This girl, whoever or whatever she was, was nuts. Or thought I was. "Myths. Legends. Supernatural nonsense. None of that stuff's real."

"So says the guy who can lift a tank with the wave of a hand and whose best friend turns into the Minotaur. What did I tell you before about the universe being queerer than you imagine? But we're getting away from the subject at hand, namely how I'm able to communicate with you when you're asleep. I've essentially set up a mental conference call between you, me, and—unfortunately—him." Her eyes darted to the storm clouds. The girl spread her arms wide, encompassing the colorful surroundings. "Think of this place as your mind trying to make sense of all the unusual data it's getting from two strangers' minds. The reason why this is only the second time we've spoken but you've visited here more times than that is because it took me a while to cut through the Omega weapon's interference so we can talk. That thing is no joke, even in the face of someone as powerful as I."

The girl studied my face. "I can tell you still don't believe I am who I say I am. I don't have to be a mind reader to interpret your body language. Though I can't read your mind now, I did delve into your mind before you absorbed the Omega weapon once I became aware the Omega spirit had chosen you as its latest vessel. Hmmm, what can I tell you to prove I've read your mind? Something you've never told anyone else . . ." The girl trailed off as she thought.

She snapped her fingers. "I know. Remember the first time you slept with Neha Thakore? She told you to stand up, bend over, and she . . ." The girl proceeded to tell me something that had happened between me and Neha the night I lost my virginity that I most definitely had never told anyone else, not even Isaac.

"Enough!" I exclaimed, interrupting the girl's enthusiastic blow-by-blow recount of the incident. It made me squeamish to have someone who appeared to be a child speak of such things. I shook my head. "This proves nothing. If you are a figment of my imagination, of course you would know everything that happened between me and Neha."

"Are you still tooting that old 'this is all just a dream' horn? I thought I had already disabused you of that silly notion by marking you with that psychic stigmata." She tapped her chin thoughtfully. "But you have a point about how I'd know everything about you if I were just a manifestation of your subconscious. I've got it. I'll tell you some secret stuff about Isaac and Shay. Stuff they've never told anyone else. I've read their minds too, of course. Had to, to figure out if they were suitable. Because, though you're the key to this whole thing as the carrier of the Omega spirit, you're still going to need help. Lots of it."

My head was spinning. "I still don't know what you're talking about."

"I'm trying to explain it to you. Hasn't anyone ever told you patience is a virtue? All in due time. First to prove I'm a telepath and who I say I am.

"I'll start with Isaac. After his sister Lilly deliberately overdosed on sleeping pills after their stepbrother Trey raped her, Isaac unsuccessfully tried to beat Trey up. The attempt led to Isaac's stepfather convincing his mother to throw Isaac out of the house. He had to go live with his paternal grandparents."

"I already know that," I said impatiently. "If I know it, my subconscious knows it too. You telling me this doesn't disprove this isn't just some bizarro dream."

"Slow your roll. What did I just say about patience? I'm getting to the part you don't know, the part Isaac has never shared with a living soul.

"When Isaac's mom threw him out of the house, she told him he was to blame for Lilly's death and that he had driven a wedge between her and Isaac's stepfather. 'I hate you,' she told him. 'I wish you had never been born.' Imagine, saying that to your kid *ever*, much less after his sister died. That lady is messed up in the head.

"Anyway, the first week Isaac was with his grandparents, he was so despondent over both his sister and his mother that he hung himself. He would have died if the rafter he tied the other end of the rope to had not snapped. The rafter's wood was thick and solid. It should have easily supported Isaac's dangling weight. And yet it didn't. An act of god, maybe." The girl shrugged. "I don't know. As smart as I am, whether something is an act of god is above even my pay grade.

"Regardless, that's how Isaac interpreted it—as a sign that his god didn't want him to die. From that moment on, Isaac dedicated himself to helping people, just as his police officer father had before he was killed in the line of duty. His biological father, I mean, not his crappy racist stepfather. Isaac fights to ensure what happened to his sister never happens to anyone else. Impossible of course, but all one can do is try. It's why he accompanied you when you broke into Mad Dog's apartment to try to scare him into not abusing Hannah Kim anymore. Isaac knew it was a bad idea, but went along with it anyway."

"Jesus!" I couldn't think of anything else to say. What if

what the girl said was true about Isaac's suicide attempt? I had no idea.

"Talk to Isaac. He'll confirm what I told you. As for Shay, there's an evil stepfather in her past, too. 'You're a woman, now,' Hideo said the first time that louse crawled into bed with her after he discovered she had started menstruating. 'It's my job to teach you what that means.' She was ten.

"The nightly rapes occurred, off and on, for months. Hideo told Shay he would kill her mother if Shay ever told her or anyone else.

"Finally, one day Shay had enough. She waited until her mother was out of town on business, then snuck into Hideo's bedroom late one night with a kitchen knife. She was going to kill him before he carried out his threat to hurt her mother. The knife began to glow as Shay raised the knife over Hideo's heart. Her powers were manifesting for the first time. Meta powers are often triggered in times of extreme stress, as you know.

"The glow awakened Hideo before Shay could work up the nerve to plunge the knife into his chest. He easily disarmed Shay. She was just a kid, after all. Then and there, he raped her again, in the same bed he shared with Shay's mother. He laughed at Shay while he did it. He *laughed* at her."

The girl's eyes welled up with tears. Mine did too. Maybe this girl was my imagination. Maybe she was something else entirely and was trying to trick me for reasons I didn't comprehend. But whatever else she was, she was convincing. I began to believe what she was telling me. Only the cynical calluses hard experience had made me grow over the years kept me from completely swallowing her story.

"But the universe had the last laugh," the girl continued. "The very next day, Hideo was crossing the street. A moving truck's tires blew, the vehicle spun out of control, and it slammed into Hideo. Kablammo! Japanese spaghetti. Killed him instantly. Too quick of an ending for the likes of him, if you ask me. Another act of god? Again, I dunno. God moves in mysterious ways, his wonders to perform. Sometimes he takes his own sweet time about it, though. Seems to me he should have moved in his mysterious ways months earlier and saved Shay a lot of pain and trauma. But who am I to criticize the divine? Despite what my deluded worshippers think, I'm no god myself. Running the multiverse is probably harder than it looks."

She sniffled and wiped her eyes with the back of a hand. "Shay started training in martial arts shortly thereafter. She never again wanted to feel so powerless as she did when Hideo was on top of her."

My jaw was clenching and unclenching. When I realized it, I forced myself to stop. I couldn't imagine someone as strong and tough as Shay ever being weak and vulnerable. If what the girl said was true, maybe that was why Shay presented a granite facade to the world.

"I wish you hadn't told me this stuff," I said. "If these stories are true, I understand why Isaac and Shay keep them to themselves. Hearing them without their permission is an obscenity. A massive violation of privacy."

The girl sniffled some more and wiped her nose on a sleeve. She seemed embarrassed to cry in front of me. "How do you think I feel, buster? You're just hearing about the memories. I had to *see* them. Relive them. Both Isaac and Shay feel them acutely, as if the memories were formed seconds instead of years ago."

"Me, Isaac, Shay. All of us have tragedies in our background." Amazing Man too, I thought, whose sister was murdered by her own husband. Even Truman, the guy who never thought of a joke he couldn't resist saying aloud, came from tragedy. He had told me that, when he was fourteen, his parents and sister were killed after his father, driving drunk, rammed them all into a tree. "Why do so many Heroes have darkness in their backgrounds?"

"When the world's lucky, intense pressure forms a diamond," Lim said. Though I was by no means convinced the girl really was that Omega-level Meta, I would mentally call her that until I proved her identity one way or another. "A diamond who takes the darkness within herself and tries to transmute it into light. When the world's not lucky, intense pressure forms someone like him." She pointed at the storm clouds.

"I'll find out whether or not what you told me about Isaac and Shay is true when I wake up. Let's assume for the sake of discussion you really did read their minds and you really are Lim Qiaolian. Why have you contacted me? Why have you brought me here?"

"I'd think that would be obvious by now. Because of him." Lim pointed at the dark clouds in the distance again. "Because of Progenitor."

"And who is he?"

"He is the greatest threat the world's faced since . . . well, since the last time Progenitor walked the earth well over a thousand years ago. At the time, Britain's King Arthur carried the Omega spirit and wielded the Omega weapon in the form of his sword Excalibur. The good king and his allies barely defeated Progenitor and his dark forces back then. Unable to kill him, Arthur instead imprisoned Progenitor."

"Imprisoned him where?" I glanced at the weirdly colored scenery surrounding us. "Here?"

"Not exactly. As I said, think of this place as the site of a three-way conference call. A little of your mind is sharing space with a little of my mind and a little of Progenitor's. Though I've hit the mute button, so to speak, so Progenitor can't hear us. If he heard us, it would hasten his escape. He'll be out soon enough as it is."

That sounded ominous. "So where is he imprisoned, then?" I pressed.

"How do I describe something so complicated to a mor —uh, someone like you?" Lim chewed her bottom lip thoughtfully. "Are you aware there are multiple dimensions?"

"Yes. My Hero Trials took place in another dimension. Earth Sigma."

"Oh yeah. Earth Sigma. Home of the tiger-bat." Lim shuddered. "Gruesome things. On that version of the Earth, they're the reason why the dinosaurs went extinct and why hominids never climbed down from the refuge of trees. Anyway, King Arthur and his amazing friends imprisoned Progenitor in another dimension. An otherwise empty, non-corporeal one where Progenitor exists only as mental energy."

Mechano and the other corrupt Sentinels had told me King Arthur was a previous carrier of the Omega spirit, so I wasn't surprised by the revelation. "Three cheers for King Arthur. I'd say, 'Long live the king!' but I guess it's almost two thousand years too late for that." I often said silly things when my mind was awhirl, and it most definitely was now. "All of that still doesn't tell me why you brought me here. And how you're related to this whole thing."

"Progenitor grew more powerful in confinement. Over the centuries, he grew almost powerful enough to free himself from the chains that bound him. When I was five, I telepathically sensed him stirring. Progenitor was about to awaken, to free himself from the prison Arthur and the rest bound him in. I knew I had to do something to stop it from happening. So I put my body into suspended animation and uploaded my consciousness to the same dimension Progenitor is trapped in. Actually, suspended animation overstates the case as my body is still functioning, but just barely. Enough to keep my physical shell alive until I returned to it. Call it a form of hibernation, one where the aging process was slowed to an almost imperceptible crawl. It's why my physical body looks the same as it did when I took a powder over eighty years ago.

"Once in the dimension Progenitor was in, I devoted my formidable mental resources to keeping him confined. I assumed I could keep him bound indefinitely. I am, after all, an Omega-level telepath and genius. I thought I could do anything."

Lim stared at the storm clouds. Perhaps it was my imagination, but they seemed closer than before. Lim's face darkened.

"I was a fool," she said bitterly. "Arrogant. Too confident in my power and will. I fear arrogance is the Achilles heel of all true genius. I only delayed the inevitable. I'll continue to hold him at bay for as long as I can. But Progenitor *will* free himself. And soon. He'll be even more powerful post-imprisonment than he was before. It's why I reached out to you. To the Omega, to the vessel of the spirit that's protected the world since time immemorial. I've been studying Progenitor for over eighty years. I know things about him you don't. I must teach them to you, to do what I can to prepare you for what's to come."

I let all that sink in.

"And what is to come?" I demanded. "What happens when Progenitor is free?"

"It's not like he has a definite plan. He's been locked up for many centuries, after all, unaware of how the world has transformed in his absence. But I know this: Progenitor is a predator. It's his nature. You grew up on a farm. You had a front seat to nature, red in tooth and claw. You've seen predators in action. You tell me—what happens when a fox or a coyote gets into a henhouse?"

"Dad only grew fruits and vegetables. But my Uncle Charles had farm animals. Including chickens. I saw his coop after a coyote got in by chewing through the chicken wire." I winced at the gruesome memory. "There were bodies and blood everywhere. The coyote had killed everything. And the funny thing is, only one of the chickens was partially eaten. The rest hadn't been fed on at all. The coyote killed all those other chickens not because he was hungry. He did it for fun. For sport."

"Bingo. Progenitor is a coyote who's about to run wild in the henhouse that is the world. Once he's free, Progenitor won't stop wreaking havoc. He must be stopped. That's where you come in. Lucky you." Lim still looked at the dark clouds on the horizon. I looked too, was overwhelmed by a feeling of dread, shuddered, and averted my gaze.

I thought about what Lim had said. Then, I forced myself to look at the storm clouds again despite the fact everything inside me screamed at me to look away. Pink lightning played around the edges of the storm. Thunder rumbled ominously. It wasn't my imagination—the clouds were darker and closer than they had been earlier.

I would of course try to independently verify what Lim had told me, but in my heart, I already knew:

She was telling the truth. I didn't know how I knew, but I knew. Maybe it was the Omega spirit whispering to my soul.

"This is the cataclysmic, world-threatening crisis the Sentinels warned me about, isn't it?" I asked Lim.

Lim's head jerked back. She twisted in the air away from the clouds and stared at me. My question seemed to stun her.

"Hi! My name's Lim, alias Mastermind. Welcome to the conversation, slowpoke!"

10

—————

"Y ou don't have to get smart," I told Lim.

Lim rolled her eyes. "I wouldn't have to get smart if you got smarter, sloth for brains. Of course this is the crisis the Sentinels warned you about. What'd you think they were talking about? The perils of social media?"

I bit back a retort. If everything the girl had said was true, despite the fact she was an eighty-plus year-old genius, her socialization had ended when she went into suspended animation at the age of five. In ways, she was still the undeveloped little girl she appeared to be. Politeness and courtesy were social lubricants Lim had clearly never mastered.

Besides, Lim had apparently sacrificed over eighty years of her life trying to keep the world safe. I respected that.

So instead of putting Lim over my knee and giving her the spanking she probably needed, I said, "Teach me what I need to know."

Thunder rumbled in the distance. Frown lines sprouted between Lim's eyebrows. "We'll have to pick this up later," she said. "It takes my full concentration to keep Progenitor imprisoned. When my energy and attention are diverted, like now to talk to you, the Ancient One gets all kinds of restless. Momma needs to go and rock him back to sleep before he wakes up prematurely. You're not ready for that to happen yet. Speaking of which, before I reach out to you for the next lesson, there's a homework assignment you need to work on."

Lim waved her hand. Like magic, glowing green symbols popped out of nowhere and floated in front of us. The lines of symbols took up more space than an eighteen-wheeler would.

Lim eyed the floating symbols with pride. Their light gave her face a greenish tint. "Do you know what this is?"

I studied the symbols. Trying to make heads or tails of the stuff made my head hurt, like when I'd been introduced to linear algebra in Hero Academy or when I tried to wrap my head around the quantum mechanics described in the book I'd misplaced. "It's math. Equations. But beyond that, I couldn't begin to tell you."

"Ding! Ding! Ding! You get a gold star for the day. Perhaps there's hope for you yet. Yes, these are equations. More specifically, these are probability equations. Well, that's not entirely accurate—it's like saying a laser rifle is the same thing as a flintlock. I had to invent a whole new field of math to come up with this stuff, much like how Newton invented calculus to further his studies of gravity and motion. He was a genius too, you know. Not as smart as I, but competent enough in a thumb-fingered sort of way."

Lim looked at the equations with affection and smug satisfaction, like a mother gazing at her newborn. "I took regression analysis, married it to game theory, and gave birth to a whole new mathematical discipline. I call it Limathematics. The portmanteau has a nice ring to it, don't you think?" She hugged herself gleefully. "When the world learns of my achievement, getting the Fields Medal will be a cinch. Not to mention the Chern Prize and the Morningside Medal, but those math awards are Chinese-specific. The Fields Medal is where the real prestige is at. It's the Nobel Prize of math. Doctor Higginbotham will turn positively chartreuse with envy. That know-nothing abacus flicker. He practically has to take his shoes off to count higher than twenty."

I eyed the rumbling clouds nervously. "The equations," I urged, trying to get Lim back on topic. "What about them?"

"Eh? Oh yes! The equations. The point I'm trying to make is I've looked at every variable, examined every eventuality, and run the numbers. Do you know what the chances are of you prevailing against Progenitor if you face him alone?"

The way she asked meant I wouldn't like the answer. "Fifty-fifty?" I suggested hopefully.

Lim snorted. "Ha! You wish! Against someone like Progenitor, I'd take coin flip odds every day and twice on Sunday. No, you adorable rose-colored glasses optimist. The odds are zero. A big fat goose egg. If you try to tackle Progenitor alone, you will lose. No ifs, ands, or buts about it. Which means that the world loses."

I didn't like the sound of that, but didn't despair. "But I'm not alone," I protested. "I'm a part of the New Sentinels."

"That's the point I'm trying to make. With the New Sentinels by your side, the odds are worse against Progenitor than they are if you face him all by your lonesome. Don't get me wrong—Isaac and Shay are all right. In fact, they're critical. The math says you need them. As I said earlier, you'll need help facing Progenitor. Isaac and Shay must be a part of that help. Numbers don't lie."

Lim's face was as serious as a heart attack.

"But Blur, Slab and Flare?" She shook her head. "While fine Heroes, they are all wrong for this job. Get rid of them. We need to recruit a different team. The odds of you prevailing are still terrifyingly small, but it's the only way you and the world have a fighting chance."

11

—————

"Let me see if I've got this straight," Isaac said. "A girl claiming to be a superpowered Nostradamus appears to you in a dream, informs you some ancient monster is about to run amok, tells you the Book of Revelation is an overly sunny depiction of the future, demands you disband one of the world's premier Hero teams, insists you replace it with a motley crew of unknowns, and your response is, 'Sure thing hoss, no need to tell me twice. I'll get right on that.'"

"When you put it that way," I conceded, "it sounds ridiculous."

"You think?"

Unmasked and wearing civilian clothes, Shay, Isaac and I sat at a small circular conference table in The Mountain. This was the first time I had seen Isaac unmasked in months as he had refused to hang out with me outside of team duties. It looked like he had been out in the sun; his shaved head was browner than the last time I'd seen him unmasked. His darker than usual skin color made the jagged pale scar on his forehead stand out more than usual.

He had gotten that scar when, back in our Academy days, he, Neha and I fought Iceburn, the Rogue assassin Mechano, Seer and Millennium had hired to kill me.

The Mountain was a massive cavern carved within a mountain in Asia's vast Himalayan mountain range. The rocks of its floor and walls were grey with flecks of white and gold; the flecks reflected light from glowing globes hovering high overhead like the flecks were glittering gemstones. I never figured out how the globes were powered or what kept them aloft. Maybe Avatar had simply told them to stay lit and airborne, so they did. If he were alive and told me to do something, I sure as heck would. He had been one of the greatest Heroes in history.

Despite having come to The Mountain more times than I remembered, the cavern's size always made me feel like an ant. Far off to the right of us was a huge hole in the cavern, protected by an almost transparent force field. Through that hole, one looked down on snow-capped mountains of varying heights. When I came up here, I felt like a god, looking down at the mundane world from Mount Olympus, Asgard, or Mount Kailash. If what Lim had told me the night before was true, I would need to channel my inner god if I had any hope of defeating Progenitor. Unfortunately, I seemed to have misplaced my thunderbolts.

Truman had discovered this secret mountain retreat of Avatar's years ago when he investigated Avatar's murder, and he told me about it later when I searched for where Avatar had hidden the Omega weapon. The jagged fissure in the cavern floor was a result of me tipping over Avatar's absurdly heavy neutronium spear to uncover the Omega weapon. Now the spear was upright again, once more concealing Avatar's hidey-hole. The hidden area now contained the Philosopher's Stone, Doctor Alchemy's book of alchemy formulas. With it, Doctor Alchemy had caused a lot of trouble over the years, and he had the handicap of being a lunatic. If the book ever fell into the hands of someone smart, unscrupulous and sane, watch out. Which was why I had hidden it under the neutronium spear. As far as I knew, I was the only person on the planet with the raw power to move the spear.

The Mountain was littered with memorabilia from other adventures as well. Mostly Avatar's, like the giant robot exoskeleton in which Doctor Diabolical had partially destroyed the White House and Capitol building, the V'Loth mothership from the aliens' 1960s invasion, and the torch from the now-destroyed Statue of Liberty. The torch was encased in leaded glass; Black Plague had irradiated the statue before throwing it at Avatar like a giant javelin. But The Mountain also housed a few artifacts from my own experiences, like the Philosopher's Stone and the Little Green Men's ray guns. The Mountain also contained the power-nullification cell I had imprisoned Mad Dog in. It was like a Hero and Rogue museum in here. In fact, I had once considered donating the artifacts here to actual museums, but later decided against it—like the Philosopher's Stone, there were too many things here that could do a lot of damage and cause a lot of trouble in the wrong hands. That, and I saw myself as the custodian of all these artifacts rather than their owner. Just as Avatar had inherited some of them from prior Heroes, added to the collection, and then left them for the next generation of Heroes, I would do the same. Assuming there would even be another generation of Heroes after mine. I had my doubts thanks to how dire Lim's warnings were about the threat Progenitor posed.

Due to how dangerous many of the items here were, I limited who knew about The Mountain and its contents.

The only people who knew were me, Shay, Isaac, Truman, and Truman's friend Shadow. I'd never met Shadow, and I didn't like the fact someone I didn't know was aware of the lair's existence. Truman said she was trustworthy despite being a high-priced mercenary and thief. I had my doubts. To be on the safe side, I had considered getting Amnesia to wipe Shadow's memories of The Mountain just as she had done to the Revengers. I didn't go through with it because Truman would have a fit if he found out I messed with his friend's mind. Despite Truman's clownish demeanor, he was not to be trifled with. He was scary sometimes, even to someone like me.

Not even the other three New Sentinels knew about The Mountain, which was why the lair was the perfect place for this secret meeting with Shay and Isaac. A matter transmitter—or matmitter for short—had whisked us here nearly instantaneously from the New Sentinels mansion on the other side of the world; it was hidden in the bowels of the New Sentinels' underground compound, password and retinal scan protected. Not to mention monitored 24/7 by the tireless Minerva. Shay, Isaac and I had agreed when we formed the New Sentinels that all major team decisions would be made by the three of us exclusively. I had insisted on it. Knowing there was some sort of world-threatening crisis on the horizon, I'd been unwilling to create a team where the big decisions were made democratically by the entire team. The more power that was in my hands and the hands of people I trusted, the better I liked it.

As I sat with Isaac and Shay, it occurred to me we made decisions behind the backs of the rest of the New Sentinels just as Mechano, Seer, and Millennium had behind the backs of the original Sentinels. I squirmed at the sudden realization. Maybe Isaac had been partially right outside of

Draymond Miller's house—maybe I was more like the corrupt Sentinels than I cared to admit.

"Isaac's right about Lim," Shay was saying. The table we sat at was positioned in front of a curved computer panel with a massive monitor above it. "Assuming that's really who the girl in your dreams is. There's little evidence to support her claims."

"More like no evidence," Isaac insisted. "A dream acorn fell on Theo's head, and now he's Chicken Little, running around screaming, 'The sky is falling!'" A notepad was in front of him with a half-complete drawing of a sphinx on it. During our meeting, Isaac had alternated between doodling and mocking what Lim had told me. If I could choose between the two, I'd prefer the doodling. An artist by trade before becoming a full-time Hero, Isaac used art to help him conceptualize the creatures he turned into. The sphinx he'd been sketching was ram-headed. Ram-headed sphinxes were called criosphinxes; the ones with male heads, like the one depicted by Egypt's Great Sphinx of Giza, were androsphinxes. *Black don't crack*, criosphinxes, and don't sit still for a right cross—Isaac had taught me very eclectic lessons over the years.

"It's not true there's no evidence," I said. I was trying to remain calm and dispassionate on the outside despite being freaked out on the inside. I had prepared for years for the crisis the Sentinels had foretold of. And now it was imminent. If I wore my heart on my sleeve and got worked up and emotional, however, Isaac and Shay would never go along with what needed to be done. "I just got back from Beijing. Fame, like rank, has its privileges. Otherwise I never could've gotten the Chinese government to pull strings with the Qiaolianism sect to allow me inside their central temple to view Lim's body. The girl I saw in my dream is definitely Lim Qiaolian."

"The girl in your dreams *looks* like Lim Qiaolian," Isaac said. "The fact she looks like that comatose Chinese girl doesn't mean she's the real McCoy. Hell, describe her for me and I'll turn into a creature that can replicate her down to her pigtail and breathtaking nerve. I'll use a doppelganger. Or an etiäinen from Finnish mythology. Or any one of a dozen other creatures." Isaac shook his head in disbelief. "My point is that appearances can be deceiving. How do we know this Lim look-alike is not a Rogue pursuing some fiendish agenda? Or that she isn't really just a dream?"

"How did a dream cause that mark on my forehead?"

"Doctor Agrawal explained that."

"Agrawal didn't explain anything. He gave a song and dance about the power of the human mind without committing to anything. Besides, can Agrawal explain what I told you about your past, Isaac? Or yours, Shay?"

Isaac opened his mouth to argue some more, then abruptly shut it. He couldn't explain what Lim had told me. Lim had been right about my teammates' pasts. I had already confirmed the stories with them. I had pulled them aside separately, of course, so no one else would learn their secrets. It was bad enough that I knew them. I felt like a voyeur.

Shay said, "The fact this girl knows incidents from our backgrounds doesn't mean she is who she says she is. Or that the rest of what she says is the gospel truth." I had the feeling that, unlike Isaac, Shay had not yet made up her mind one way or the other about Lim. Rather, it felt like she was playing devil's advocate and looking at the argument from all possible sides so she could make an informed decision. "Perhaps this girl knows what she knows because she read our minds, but that does not mean she is Lim Qiaolian. After all, Lim is not the only telepath in the world."

"Come on," I scoffed. "Telepaths are rare as hen's teeth."

"Rare," Shay agreed. "But not unheard of. And not all of them are on the side of the angels. Mind Reaper, for example."

"Who's cooling her heels in a MetaHold power nullification cell."

"True enough. But you see my point."

"I do. But that doesn't change the fact there's evidence Lim is Lim and that she's telling the truth."

"The evidence—such as it is—is at best inconclusive," Isaac said. "It's not enough to make me change what I have for breakfast, much less make me agree to fire three insanely accomplished Heroes and instead bring in new people we don't know and don't trust."

"But Lim made clear that, if we don't get rid of Blur, Slab and Flare and bring in the new people, we will lose and Progenitor will win."

"She's making that prediction based on what?" Isaac demanded. "A fortune cookie? Poking around in chicken entrails? Reading tea leaves? Staring into a crystal ball?"

"I already told you. It's math. Probability analysis. She showed me the formulas."

Isaac flung his notepad toward me. Papers fluttering, the pad hit the table in front of me like a shot bird. "Finally, some evidence we can sink our teeth into," he said. "Math doesn't lie. Jot the formulas down, and we'll have Minerva run an analysis. If she concludes the four horsemen of the Apocalypse are galloping toward us, I'll personally give Flare, Slab and Blur their pink slips."

I stared down at the blank pages. "I can't do it," I

admitted reluctantly. "There was too much to take in to memorize it. And what I saw, I didn't understand."

"Don't feel bad," Isaac sneered. "It was probably all just nonsense anyway. Bait to snare a gullible fish. And you fell for it, hook, line and sinker."

Despite my best efforts at restraint, I began to lose my temper. "You're being unreasonably pigheaded."

"Are you kidding me, Theo? I oughta change my name to Spock. I'm the personification of logic and reason right now. You're the one who's pigheaded. Don't call me names when it's your own mouth that's full of bacon. I'm starting to think you're so eager to get rid of the other New Sentinels because they're not buddy-buddy with you the way they are with me and Shay."

"That has nothing to do with it," I protested. Despite my words, I couldn't help but wonder if there was some truth to what he said. Being treated like a marble statue by the other New Sentinels when I just wanted to be one of the guys was irksome.

Isaac gave me a knowing look. "Doesn't it? Work out your longing for a surrogate family issues with a therapist, not at the team's expense." He shook his head. "Imagine, being so trusting as to fire three experienced Heroes on the say-so of an imaginary friend who might not be at all friendly. A few nights ago, you were behaving as cynically as a hooker with thirty years of tricks under her garter belt. Yet now you're as gullible as a virgin whose boyfriend is talking her into putting just the tip in. A little consistency would be nice."

"You know what I think?" I asked, my voice almost rising to a shout. "I think you're just salty about what happened the other night. You're so pissed at me that everything I say and do must be wrong."

"What happened the other night, gentlemen?" Shay interjected quietly.

Isaac and I both froze. I don't know when it happened, but we both had stood and were pointing our fingers in the other's face. Isaac lowered his hand, looking as sheepish as I felt. We both sat back down.

"Nothing," we intoned simultaneously to Shay. That got a wry smile out of Isaac. We sounded like kids who had been asked by their mother what they had done to get them suspended from school. Shay did not know about the pressure I had brought to bear on State's Attorney Miller. As Isaac had said that night, he was no narc, and God knows I hadn't been stupid enough to tell Shay myself. She only knew that Miller had dropped the charges against me. When she had asked me about the nol pros days ago, I had avoided and then changed the subject. What I had done was bad enough; I didn't want to add bald-faced lying to Shay to my growing list of sins. But Shay was a smart woman—she must have known something was up. She certainly didn't now look like she believed our denial about the other night.

"Look," I said, more calmly than before, "I realize I have nothing definitive to prove the truth of what Lim said. Or even to prove that she is Lim. All I can say is that I know she is Lim and that she's right. I feel it in my bones. This is the crisis foretold of. We have to do as Lim suggests to prepare for it. Even then there's no guarantee we will prevail against Progenitor. But following her recommendations at least gives us a chance, however slight."

Isaac barked out a laugh. "Oh, you feel it in your bones? Why didn't you say that before? I'm convinced. If I've said it once, I've said it a thousand times—never doubt Theo's bones. Dem bones, dem bones, dem infallible bones. Shakira's hips don't lie, and Theo's bones don't either." Isaac shook his head in disbelief. "This whole thing is nuts. Theo, you're so anxious to finally face the crisis you were warned about that you're grasping at straws to find it. And even if, for the sake of argument, everything this girl says is as true as a mother's love and this Progenitor character is the crisis, we already have a team in place to face it and him. We'd be fools to throw away the other three's training and experience."

Isaac faced Shay. "Theo's position is clear. As is mine. You're the tiebreaker. What do you say?"

Shay considered it.

"I'm sorry, Theo, but Isaac's right," she finally said. "There's too little to go on to make such a momentous change in direction for the team. If a Rogue is behind the dreams you're having, by doing as the girl says, we would be playing right into some villain's hands. If new evidence appears, we can reevaluate and revisit this discussion. Until then, I say we stay the course with the team we have."

I sighed. I was sorry it had come to this.

"Let's take a vote," I said.

"We just did," Isaac said. "I voted no, Shay voted no, you voted yes. The noes have it. Election day's over. Where's my 'I Voted' sticker?" Isaac rubbed his hands together. "I'm starved. Electioneering is hungry work. Who's up for some pizza? Does Mario's deliver way up here?"

"Let's take a formal vote," I insisted.

"Why waste the time?" Isaac asked.

I ignored him. "You there, Minerva?" I called out, activating a secure satellite link back to the mansion. Minerva's servers resided deep underground there.

"Yes, Mister Chairman," returned the AI's saucy, half-amused contralto from a speaker on the nearby computer panel. "Thanks for finally inviting me to your super-duper secret clubhouse. So secret that I'm programmed to forget I know about it after this tête-à-tête is over."

Unlike usually, I didn't correct Minerva in her use of my title. "Confirm my voiceprint."

"Omega voiceprint confirmed. And what a sexy voiceprint it is. If you were a computer like me, I'd slip a Trojan onto your throbbing hard drive."

Isaac groaned. "Now you know how the rest of us feel," Shay told him. "No one made you give her your sense of humor."

I again ignored them and said to Minerva, "This is a formal New Sentinels' executive council vote pursuant to the official bylaws."

Isaac rolled his eyes at the formality. Shay's mouth puckered slightly, like she had unexpectedly tasted something sour, before her face smoothed over and became expressionless.

"Noted and logged." Minerva's voice was different now, brusque and all business.

"I move that Slab, Flare and Blur be immediately removed as New Sentinels. I further move that they be replaced by new individuals, said individuals to be determined by me, Theodore Conley, team chairman."

"Motion noted and logged."

"I vote in favor of the motion."

"Vote noted and logged."

"Shay?" I said, gesturing at the computer equipment.

Shay's dark eyes glittered knowingly at me. "I vote against."

"Ninja voiceprint confirmed. Vote noted and logged."

"Isaac?"

"This is so stupid, Theo. You already know you've lost. I vote against too."

"Myth voiceprint confirmed. Vote noted and logged."

"Everything's nice and formal now, Theo. Happy?" Isaac demanded.

"Almost. Minerva, tally the votes."

"Two votes nay, one vote aye," Minerva said in her unusually clipped voice. "The sole aye has it. Motion carried. Slab, Flare and Blur are hereby terminated as New Sentinels. This executive council session is adjourned."

Isaac jumped out of his chair so quickly it overturned and smacked loudly against the rock floor. "What?!" he sputtered.

"Who are the new members going to be?" Minerva purred, her voice now back to normal. "I do so love making new friends."

12

The plane flight seemed longer than it actually was because of the ear beating Isaac gave me during it.

We were over Arkansas, though the conversation had stretched out over several states. Isaac was saying, "Of all the underhanded, dirty, low-down, contemptible, slimy, deceitful, shady, despicable, underhanded—"

"You said underhanded already," I interjected from the pilot's chair, my eyes and hands steady on the controls before me. "Repetition is an early sign of dementia. You should have Doc Agrawal give you the once-over."

My comment brought Isaac up short. He glared at me from the co-pilot's chair. We were both in costume, though with our cowls off as we were alone in the New Sentinels jet.

"Do you think this is funny?" he demanded. "Do you think this is a joke?"

"No."

"Because you sound like you think this is a joke."

"I was just trying to lighten the mood, is all."

We zoomed through clouds that reminded me of fluffs of

cotton candy. It was nighttime, and I flew by instruments. I adjusted our course slightly by tugging on the joystick that poked up between my legs from the jet's floorboard. I had gone from being a boy afraid to drive on the interstate highway near my family's farm to a man who piloted a cutting-edge jet halfway across the country in the middle of the night like it was no big deal. What a difference a few years made. This was but one of the several airships and other vehicles in the New Sentinels' fleet. Having vehicles like this at our disposal was one of the perks of repurposing the former Sentinels' property instead of starting a super-hero team from complete scratch.

"I'm not looking for my mood to be lightened," Isaac grumbled. "I'm looking for an explanation as to why my supposed friend pulled a fast one on me."

"I didn't pull a fast one. When we created the New Sentinels, you were given a copy of the team's proposed bylaws just like Shay and I were. It's not my fault you signed them without reading them."

"Bylaws that your personal lawyer Laura drafted. I didn't read them because I knew you had. 'If it's good enough for my trustworthy old pal Theo, it's good enough for me,' I thought as I put my John Hancock down." Isaac snorted in disgust. "Little did I know I should've hired a gang of lawyers to review every comma with magnifying glasses and minds full of mistrust. Never in my wildest dreams did I think my best friend would sneak language into the bylaws that made him the de facto dictator of the team." Isaac recited from memory, "'In a vote on a motion made during a formal New Sentinels executive council session, the team chairman's vote negates the votes of the other council members when said votes are in conflict.'"

"Oh, so you *have* read the bylaws. Good for you. No need to go see Doctor Agrawal after all. Your memory seems to be working just fine."

Isaac gave me a glare that would make a car's paint job bubble. "I thought you said you didn't think this was a joke."

"I'm still trying to lighten the mood."

"Well knock it off already. I'm really pissed. I trusted you."

Trusted. Past tense. "I know you're angry," I said. "But try to look at it from my perspective. The Sentinels said I was the key to victory or defeat regarding the looming crisis. When we recovered the Omega weapon from The Mountain, the Omega spirit came to me in a vision and told me essentially the same thing the Sentinels had. Making sure the world stays safe is ultimately my responsibility. When we formed the New Sentinels, I needed to make sure I had the authority to do what I thought best to carry out that responsibility. Which is why that provision is in the bylaws. Responsibility without the power to satisfy that responsibility is doomed to fail. How is it that British Prime Minister put it? 'Responsibility without power—the prerogative of the eunuch throughout the ages.'"

"For the love of Mike! Not only are you unscrupulous, but you can't even source your unscrupulousness appropriately. That quote's not from a real British Prime Minister. It's from a character on a British TV comedy called *Yes Minister*. Humphrey Appleby. And the character wasn't even the Prime Minister in the show."

I really liked that quote and was proud I had pulled it out of my butt. "Are you sure?"

"Sure I'm sure. Unlike someone else I know, I wouldn't lie to you."

I opened my mouth to argue I hadn't lied, but shut it before saying anything. I could argue until I was blue in the face, but Isaac would not understand why I did what I did and why I'd continue to do it. Because he did not have the weight of the world on his shoulders like I literally did, he *couldn't* understand. Despite being only a few feet apart, in reality a massive gulf separated us. That gulf had existed ever since I assumed the mantle of the Omega, but it had taken time's passage to fully expose it. It was the difference between a caddie who gave advice and the golfer who had to actually sink the putt when the tournament was on the line. At the end of the day, the golfer had to put his own judgment ahead of the caddie's because the ultimate responsibility for winning or losing rested on the golfer's shoulders.

Was what I had done with the bylaws entirely aboveboard? Maybe not, especially since I'd assumed Isaac would sign them without reading them. But this was the real world, not a theoretical discussion in the Academy's Heroic Feats, Ethics and Theory class. What would people say if I doomed the world because I was afraid to cut a few corners here and there? *Yeah, maybe Omega stood idly by and let disaster strike, but at least he conducted himself honestly while watching the world burn. He's useless, but virtuous. That's my kind of Hero! Too bad he let us all die, otherwise we could name a monastery after him.*

Screw that. I would continue to do what I thought best. And if people like Isaac didn't like it, that was just too bad. The time for coloring strictly inside the lines was when the whole world wasn't at stake. The appropriate time for *Please* and *May I?* and *Beg your pardon* was during a tea party, not when you're stopping your house from burning to the ground.

Isaac was the first to break the sullen silence that had descended over the cockpit. "Any other nasty little surprises you're waiting to spring on me?" he asked.

I thought of how I had cheated during our Trials duel. I feared if I told Isaac about it, it would destroy what remained of our friendship. "As a matter of fact, there is something that's been weighing on me. Something I've wanted to tell you for some time, but haven't found the right words for until now: Sylvia and I have been having a torrid love affair. She wants to marry me instead of you. Says your breath smells like a sewer, you have a micropenis, and you're lousy in bed. Plus, you snore."

Isaac snorted. "That tall tale's definitely a lie. I don't snore."

"Have you guys set a date for the wedding yet?"

"No. Since the world's supposedly coming to an abrupt end soon," Isaac added sarcastically, "I guess there's no need."

Isaac hadn't asked me to be his best man or to join his wedding party at all. With anyone else, I'd be grateful to not have to don a monkey suit and wrack my brain for a wedding toast. With Isaac, though, him not asking me to be his best man hurt my feelings. It was further evidence of our growing estrangement.

The jet's computer beeped, seeking my attention. I pushed the thought of Isaac's wedding aside and focused. Still shrouded by clouds, I slowed the jet to a halt.

"We're above the location Lim gave me." I studied my sensors and frowned.

Isaac, looking at his own instruments, saw it too. "Pastureland for as far as the eye can see. The sensors read no sign of human life below for miles. Was your fantasy girl wrong? How could it be? Who would have guessed? Oh wait, that's right—I did." He shook his head in disgust. "This is nothing but a wild goose chase. We fired the other New Sentinels for nothing. They probably wouldn't come back now if we got on our hands and knees and begged them."

My heart was sinking. Could Isaac be right and my instincts about Lim were totally wrong? I said, "Thank goodness you're too gracious to even dream of saying 'I told you so.'"

"My graciousness is exceeded only by how right I always am."

I began our descent. My body pressed into the top of my seat's straps as the jet dropped straight down. It was designed for vertical takeoffs and landings. "We've come too far to turn around before checking things out in person. I'll put us down in the empty pasture near the location Lim gave me."

Isaac didn't respond, but his body language said he thought we were wasting more time. For the first time since my discussion with Lim, I feared he was right.

I could have come out here alone in search of the first person Lim said we needed to recruit to face the crisis. However, Isaac had insisted on coming with me. Though he hadn't come right out and said it, I knew it was because his growing distrust made him want to keep an eye on me. Shay was back at the mansion, on monitor duty in the Watch Room with Minerva's assistance. I hoped there wasn't a major Rogue attack or natural disaster until we had a new team in place. Right now, we were woefully short-handed.

Soon, the jet touched down softly in an open field surrounded by trees. I grabbed a small computer tablet from the supply chest mounted on the wall. As it was after midnight and we were in a rural area with no streetlights, I also took three hands-free flashlights. They were more sophisticated versions of the ones bicyclists strapped to their heads so they could ride in the dark. I used my powers to make the lights hover overhead.

After donning our masks, we exited the jet via the ramp that telescoped from its side. With the push of a button on the tablet, the ramp retracted and the exit silently closed. I pushed another button. The ivory jet shimmered, and seemingly disappeared. I had activated the jet's light-bending stealth mode. Light now went around the jet instead of bouncing off it, making the jet invisible. We'd never know it was here if we hadn't just exited from it. We had an invisible jet, but didn't have to don skirts and bustiers to get one. Eat your heart out, Wonder Woman.

"Everybody remember where we parked," Isaac muttered, eyeing the seemingly empty space the jet occupied.

The line sounded familiar. "*Star Trek IV: The Voyage Home?*" I asked.

Isaac shrugged. "Like Gina says, if you're going to steal, steal from the best."

"*The Wrath of Khan* was the best."

"First Lim, now this. You must get sick of being wrong all the time."

The closest town Beaufort—assuming that one-horse hamlet should be called something as lofty as a *town*—was miles away. We were in the middle of nowhere; it was as if the civilization we were used to had ceased to exist. It was completely still and quiet in the middle of the empty pasture. Not even insects chirped. The moon was full and yellow, giving everything an otherworldly glow. The trees ringing the pasture's perimeter looked like giant skeletons. The air was humid and heavy with the smell of the outdoors. It carried a faint whiff of something rotten, like an animal had died nearby.

"Well, this isn't at all creepy," Isaac said in a hushed voice as his eyes danced around.

"You're a big, strapping Hero. What are you worried about? Afraid Jason Voorhees is going to get you?"

"Well, it *is* Friday. And the black guy is always the first one killed."

"It's not Friday the thirteenth, though."

"You and I know that, but Jason doesn't strike me as a stickler about dates." Isaac glanced at the surrounding gloom nervously. "Unlike you Old MacDonald, I didn't grow up on a farm. The mean streets of Los Angeles are more my speed. Muggers and rioters and out of work actors I can deal with. But this place gives me the heebie-jeebies."

"I'll hold your hand if you want." Despite my flippancy, I was uneasy too. Just as a big city had never-ceasing nightlife sounds, so did the country—insects chirping, owls hooting, frogs croaking, and the like. None of that was present here. It was as if everything around us was holding its breath, waiting for something dreadful to happen. My hackles were rising.

I tried to shake the feeling off. As I had told Isaac, we were Heroes. There was nothing to worry about.

I consulted the computer tablet. The location Lim had given me was north of here, beyond the ring of trees around us. I turned on the orbiting flashlights so we wouldn't run into something in the gloom. I could practically hear the breathless nightly news report if I stumbled in the dark: *Breaking news good citizens of Astor City: Omega is dead! No, he wasn't killed by a Rogue. He broke his neck after tripping on a tree root. In related news, Mad Dog has died from laughter.*

"C'mon, this way," I said to Isaac, pointing. I led the way

toward the copse of trees, still unable to shake the feeling the other shoe was about to drop.

On the way there, Isaac froze. "Crap!" he exclaimed.

I nearly jumped out of my skin. My head swiveled, alert to danger. "What? What?"

"Literally crap." Isaac looked down at his boots with dismay. "I stepped in a cow patty."

My heart pounding, I exhaled with relief. "What did you expect? Cows don't use toilets. Their leavings litter the ground like landmines. Watch your step."

"Now you tell me." Isaac twisted his boot into the ground, trying to wipe away the excrement. "I hope Elsie the cow is getting a good laugh at my expense. You know what they call cows with a sense of humor? Laughing stock."

"If you make a pun like that again, I swear I'll bury you in dung and leave you here."

We entered the thicket of trees. Leaves crunched and dry twigs snapped underfoot, sounding like firecrackers in the quiet. We could have flown toward the woman Lim wanted us to recruit, but I didn't want to spook her. Two Metahumans zooming toward a stranger would seem more like an attack than an invitation.

We cleared the trees, entering another open pasture, this one larger than the one we had landed the jet in. The tablet said the location Lim had provided was in the dead center of this pasture.

The smell of death was stronger here, and it got stronger to the point of cloying as we cautiously advanced toward the center of the pasture. The Hero Lim had promised was not here. There was only a group of large dark forms lying on the ground, seeming to glisten under the yellow moon.

I covered my nose to reduce the rotten stench that threatened to gag me. Fear tickled my backbone. Isaac and I looked at each other and wordlessly agreed to split up. We walked cautiously among the bodies.

For that was what they were—bodies. Lying on their sides, they were arranged in a circular pattern covering an area larger than a professional basketball court. The stench of death lay over everything like a heavy blanket.

"Psst!"

I ignored Isaac trying to get my attention. I was too busy running my telekinetic touch over the bodies. A shudder of revulsion ran through me.

"Psst!"

"All cows," I called out to Isaac in a low voice, my voice carrying in the still of the night despite the distance separating us. "Dozens of them. All dead. Some fresh; their bodies are still warm."

"How did they die?"

"Psst!"

"How should I know?" I asked. "What am I, a veterinarian?"

"You're more of one than I am, farm boy. Why would that dream girl of yours direct us to a cow graveyard?"

"Psst!"

"Would you stop making that stupid noise?" I snapped, irritated. "You already have my attention."

"Psst!"

"I'm not doing it," Isaac insisted. "I thought *you* were doing it."

"Psst!!!"

The sound was even more urgent than before. I realized it came from the center of the swirl of bovine bodies.

Isaac and I exchanged a mystified look. Then we cautiously advanced toward the sound.

We met over the body of a black and white Holstein

Friesian dairy cow. The large cow must've weighed nearly a ton. My telekinetic touch indicated the cow did not have a pulse. It was as dead as the rest of the animals.

One side of the cow's face was on the ground. The other side was exposed. The cow's dark eye glittered under the lights of the hovering flashlights.

"What are you guys doing out here?" the dead cow whispered in a female's voice through thick mottled lips. "Beat it! You're going to ruin everything! You're putting all our lives at risk."

Isaac and I stared at the cow, then at each other. Isaac's eyes were saucers; he was as stunned as I. "It's official," he said in a hushed voice. "I haven't even hit thirty, and yet I've seen everything. Maybe my body absorbed a magic mushroom when I stepped in that cow pie."

"Get out of here!" the cow whispered urgently. Its big black eye rolled from Isaac to me. "Scram! Before they come."

"Before who comes?" I asked her. I was talking to a cow. Isaac had seen everything; I had now done everything.

"The chupacabras!"

"Chupacabras? The monsters from urban legend? That's ridiculous." I was telling a talking dead cow something was ridiculous. It was shocking I didn't choke on the irony.

The words were barely off my tongue when there was a barrage of wet pops all around us, like a series of underwater explosions. The smell of death was overwhelmed by an even more offensive odor, as if someone had opened a mass grave. Dense oily clouds about four feet tall appeared outside the circular perimeter formed by the cows' bodies.

The clouds rapidly coalesced into solid creatures. The creatures were coated with an oily sheen, like they had been dipped in dirty motor oil.

Rows of sharp fangs glittered in the flashlights' illumination. Claws like daggers clicked together like the chirping of a swarm of locusts. Dozens of hot coal eyes burned in fierce monster faces as dark as sin.

The monsters charged us.

13

The monsters—chupacabras, I guess—bounded toward us on crooked legs that reminded me of kangaroos' legs. The chupacabras had exoskeletons like crustaceans did, but theirs were black, shiny and greasy, almost metallic, like the creatures wore armor they had gone drilling for oil in. Their bodies glinted in the illumination of the flashlights still hovering over us. Instead of hair on their heads, the creatures had tentacles that writhed like snakes. Sharp black quills ran down their backs. Their snarling, hissing faces were otherworldly. Demonic. Evil. Even if the monsters hadn't been charging us from all sides, I would've instinctively known from just looking at their malicious faces they meant us harm.

"Get out of here!" a woman in an all-black costume shouted at me and Isaac as she scrambled up from the ground. In the blink of an eye, the talking cow had disappeared, replaced by this masked woman. "I'll take care of this."

No, I'll take care of this, I thought, pushing aside another thought about how nutty the night had become. I reached out with my powers, intending to grab the chupacabras and hoist them into the air, where they couldn't do us harm.

It was like trying to grab a handful of polluted air. My telekinesis didn't work on the approaching creatures. I felt their bodies with my powers, but couldn't seem to affect them.

I changed tactics, and hastily erected a large domed force field around us three humans. It was invisible to others, but through my eyes I saw it shimmer with energy around us. My force fields were powerful enough to stop missiles. I wasn't worried about stopping a gaggle of monsters, no matter how fearsome they looked.

The chupacabras hopped through the force field as if it didn't exist, not slowed by it in the slightest. I was stunned, and I didn't stun easily. The monsters advanced on us like a demon army from hell.

"Don't let them bite you!" Grimoire yelled above the monsters' nerve-grating chittering and hissing. For that's who the cow-turned-woman was: Grimoire, the Hero Lim had sent me here to recruit. I recognized her from pictures online and in the news. "They're in the vampire family. They'll turn you into one of them if they penetrate your skin." Grimoire fumbled with a black pouch hanging from her costume's belt. She tugged out a thick wooden stake, over five feet long. It looked like a magic trick—the stake's length was many times the depth of the shallow pouch she had pulled it from.

In the vampire family? There wasn't time to contemplate the absurdity of what Grimoire had said and done. Or how absurd this entire night was.

The first wave of chupacabras reached us. Thanks to Grimoire's warning, with a thought I made the Omega suit cover the unprotected parts of my skin, leaving only my eyes and nostrils exposed.

Just in time. Two chupacabras leaped on me, almost bowling me over, fangs snapping at my arms. They reeked, smelling like rotten meat and onions dumped on a tire fire; inhaling their stench burned my nose and lungs. Fortunately, their bites did not penetrate the Omega suit. Not even Doctor Alchemy had figured out a way to penetrate the tough suit when he captured me.

But I dared not let the beasts continue to gnaw on me; maybe they'd eventually succeed where the deranged Rogue had failed. I punched the monster clinging to my left arm, hitting the beast square in its forehead. Despite its carapace looking metallic, it wasn't. The chupacabra's head dented and there was a satisfying crunch, like stepping on a roach, though much louder. The chupacabra shrieked and fell off me. Its continuing screams set my teeth on edge.

Its companion was on my back, trying to bite my neck and claw my eyes. I grabbed at it, my fist closing around one of its long black quills. I bent at the waist and yanked, flinging the thing off my back and slamming it into the twitching body of the one I had punched. Both screamed in pain, getting tangled up in each other's writhing bodies. Neither seemed incapacitated, though. Tough little buggers.

A roundhouse kick sent two more chupacabras flying. I glanced at Isaac to see how he fared. He had transformed into a male lion that glowed faintly red. I questioned his choice of mythical forms until I saw three monsters snapping at him. The bites did not penetrate his hide. He must've transformed into the Nemean Lion, the creature from Greek mythology with impenetrable skin.

With a roar, Isaac's lion form chomped down on a charging chupacabra. Oily black blood spurted, and the monster's body ripped in two. With a shake of his maned head, Isaac flung mangled monster pieces away. When the monster's upper torso hit the ground, it began crawling back toward Isaac despite the fact it lacked the other half of its body. Tough buggers indeed.

Grimoire was using the wooden stake like a spear, stabbing at the attacking chupacabras with the stake's sharpened end. The beasts seemed strangely averse to the wood, shying away from it, hissing in fear when the wood jabbed too close. However, Grimoire appeared to only accomplish keeping them at bay.

No, she was doing more than that. When the stake hit the dead center of one of the monsters' chests, the chupacabra exploded with a spray of oily smoke and disappeared.

"Can we destroy these things by driving wood through their chests?" I yelled at her over the pandemonium. If so, I'd rip a tree out of the ground and go jousting like Sir Galahad. A chupacabra dove at me. I sidestepped it, grabbed it as it sailed by, spun and tossed, using the creature's own momentum against it. It crashed into a cluster of other chupacabras, knocking them all over.

"Only cedar wood," Grimoire yelled back. She tugged a chupacabra off her back and sent it hurtling through the air. Based on how far the thing went flying, Grimoire was superstrong. Also, the black leather of her outfit must've been super-tough; it was still intact despite being clawed and bitten repeatedly. "Driving cedar through their hearts destroys them. Like staking a vampire."

Of course. Just like staking a vampire, I thought sarcastically. I swept a monster's legs, then kicked it, sending it tumbling end over end. *I should've known. After all, I staked three vamps before breakfast.* The problem was, though we were surrounded by trees, I was no arborist—I couldn't tell a cedar from a seder even in the best of times. Being attacked by monsters that were all but indestructible wasn't the best of times.

Fortunately, a proven piece of cedar was handy. "Give me your stake!" I ordered Grimoire.

She stabbed another chupacabra in the chest. With a *plop*, it exploded and disappeared. "Nothing doing, greedy!" Grimoire yelled, dodging the snapping jaws of another chupacabra. "Get your own!" For the first time, I missed Flare, Slab and Blur. When I gave them an order, they obeyed instantly, assuming I knew what I was doing, even when the order didn't seem to make sense.

There wasn't time for explaining or arguing. I had to end this fight before someone got hurt.

I ripped the stake out of Grimoire's hands with my powers. I sent it spinning high overhead like a helicopter rotor.

"Hey!" Grimoire exclaimed. "What's the big id—"

"Get down!" I yelled.

She punched a chupacabra's head clean off its shoulders, blood and viscera flying in the wake of the head. The headless body still raked at Grimoire with its claws. "I'm not getting down. *You* get down! Of all the—"

Grimoire didn't finish the thought. Isaac, still in his lion form, leaped and tackled her, knocking her down. He, at least, listened. He knew what it meant to function as a team.

I locked onto each of the chupacabras' chests with my powers. Like breaking a frozen candy bar into pieces with a hammer, I broke the spinning cedar stake into long, thick splinters. One for each chupacabra targeted in my mind's eye.

Like the days of yore when an array of longbowmen let

loose a volley of arrows to decimate an opposing army, the cedar shrapnel rocketed down at my mental command.

Each piece of cedar found its target—the dead center of the chupacabras' chests. Like dozens of balloons poked with needles, the chupacabras all exploded into oily smoke in a barrage of wet bangs. They disappeared.

The pasture fell silent. The abrupt quiet was in stunning contrast to the hellish scene the pasture had been an instant before. Even the echoes of the chupacabras' cries were gone.

14

"Get off! Get off me!" Grimoire's voice cut through the silence like a buzz saw. She shoved Isaac's mythic form away like he was a lap dog instead of a full-grown lion. "Do I look like Dorothy from *The Wizard of Oz*? I like lions as much as the next gal, but not enough to hook up with one."

Huffing indignantly, Grimoire clambered to her feet. I got my first good, chupacabra-free look at her.

Grimoire was tall for a woman and solidly built, like she got a lot of exercise but didn't count calories. Like Ninja, Grimoire obviously had an affinity for the color black. She wore tall black boots covered by leather greaves carved in an ornate pattern. Matching gauntlets covered her hands and forearms. From the neck down her body was covered by black leather that hugged every curve. It gave the impression of being functional armor more than the bondage outfit it might have passed for in a different context. A black belt was around her waist, from which hung the shallow pouch she had miraculously pulled the long wooden stake from. A silver pentagram buckle was in the center of the belt.

A black mask like that of a bandit in an old Western covered Grimoire's face from the nose down, leaving her upper face bare. She had glossy, shoulder-length black hair. For some reason, despite the fact I saw the top half of her face, I felt like I would have a hard time describing her face later other than the fact it was white. I was looking right at her and I couldn't testify as to the color of her eyes. I couldn't begin to guess how old she was.

Grimoire brushed dirt and chupacabra blood off her outfit indignantly.

"Amateurs! Dummies! Fools! Imbeciles!" she exclaimed. "You could've gotten yourselves killed. Or worse, me. Or even worst, what if the chupacabras had escaped? They would've gone on a rampage that would make the Snallygaster's look like a Sunday picnic."

"What's a Snallygaster?" Isaac asked. He had transformed back into his human form.

Grimoire blinked at him, then recovered. "Who said anything about the Snallygaster? I didn't say anything about it. I don't know nuthin' 'bout no Snallygaster." She jabbed a finger into the dragon on his chest, making him step back. "If you ever tell anyone I even so much as whispered that word, I'll swear on a stack of Bibles that you're a low-down dirty liar. And sue you for slander. And attempted bestiality too, you horny lion man!"

Isaac and I looked at each other, both of us taken aback. Despite the fact we were still relatively young Heroes, we were both famous. The world knew us as the Davids who had vanquished Goliaths like Doctor Alchemy and the Sentinels. We usually got a certain amount of respect and deference from other Heroes. Not that we expected it, but we were used to it. We certainly weren't used to this kind of reaction. This woman treated us like we were her annoying kid brothers who had ruined her weekend plans.

"How about you calm down?" I suggested. "You would have been overrun by those monsters had we not been here. We probably saved your life. You're welcome."

Grimoire looked like she would explode. The best way to get someone to not calm down was to tell them to calm down. "You arrogant, airheaded as—" Grimoire stopped herself, swallowing the rest of the word. "God bless America! You almost made me curse. Saved my life? Saved my life?! You're the know-nothing who put it in danger. Everything was going according to plan until you buttinskies showed up. The chupacabras would have appeared and gorged themselves on the blood of all these cows I left for them. And then, when they were fat as ticks and docile as lambs, I'd get up and stab them in the chest with the stake. It would've been as easy as clubbing baby seals. Instead you butted in, looking all hale and hearty, triggering the chupacabras' prey drive. What should've been a walk in the park turned into a fight for our lives."

"This was a trap?" I asked incredulously. "A ruse?"

"Didn't I just say that? Use your lips less and your ears more."

"You killed all these cows to set a trap?" Isaac was aghast.

"Of course not," Grimoire huffed. "What do I look like, a moo mass murderer? I got them from the local slaughterhouse. They were dead when I got them. If I hadn't bought them, someone else would've just turned them into hamburger. Just as the chupacabras would've turned a bunch of innocent people into hamburger had I not set this trap for them. A trap which you loused up."

"What the hell are chupacabras anyway?" Isaac asked. "I

thought they were just fake legends. Or dogs and coyotes infected with mange people mistake for supernatural creatures. Those things we fought certainly weren't mangy dogs. And what was it you said about vampires?"

"Chupacabras are—" Grimoire began, then abruptly stopped. "Never mind what they are. And vampires aren't real. Everybody knows that. If you ever say I said otherwise, I'll sue you for that too. We prevented the chupacabra outbreak from spreading. That's all you need to know. In fact, it's more than you need to know. What in blue blazes are you knuckleheads doing out here in the middle of nowhere, anyway?"

"We could ask you the same question," Isaac said. "I thought Washington, D.C. was your stomping ground."

"I go where I'm needed," Grimoire said breezily. "Just like you two go where you're not needed. Why aren't you off stopping an asteroid from hitting the earth or chasing Rogues with ridiculous names or chilling in that tricked out mansion of yours instead of meddling with matters you don't belong in?" Despite the disrespect with which she treated us, she obviously knew who we were after all. Our fame had struck again.

Isaac and I looked at each other. Because of our history, his brown eyes were as easy to read as a street sign. I saw what he was thinking: Grimoire had been exactly where Lim had said she would be. It wasn't enough to convince Isaac everything Lim had told me was true, but it was a point in her favor.

"We're here to see you," Isaac told Grimoire.

"What for?" Grimoire's inscrutable eyes narrowed. "Is this about the fire at the White House? Did Mirage tattle? Whatever it is she said I did, I didn't do it. I was out of state at the time. Come to think of it, I was out of the country. It's not my fault gremlins got loose in the Oval Office. That video of me torching the *Resolute* desk is fake news."

Mirage was a Hero who worked under Ghost in the Heroes' Guild's investigation division. I didn't understand what was going on in this conversation at all, like I had come into the middle of it. "We're not here because of a fire," I told Grimoire. "At least not a literal one. We're here because we need your help to save the world."

Grimoire just stared at me for several beats.

Then she burst out laughing.

Her guffaws finally trailed off. She rolled her eyes heavenward, speaking as if to herself: "First Ghost, then the Wandering Jew, then Agatha, then Mirage, and now these do-gooders. Too many people want to drag me into their soap operas. I've half a mind to change my name, move into Goatman's hut, and become a hermit."

Her eyes came back down to ours and she shook her head ruefully. "The last time someone roped me into saving the world, it got me into so much trouble that I'm still neck-deep in it. There's an old saying: Fool me once, shame on you; fool me twice, and I'm a dummy."

"That's not the saying," Isaac said.

"No?" Grimoire blinked at him, flustered. "Well . . . it ought to be. It's also not the point. The point is, I've learned my lesson. If the world needs saving, I'm sure you Johnnies-on-the-spot are more than capable of dealing with it. I'll be in my apartment with my robe on and feet up, cheering you on as I watch your death-defying feats on TV with a tub of popcorn to keep me company. Saving the world is what you sort of people live for. Laying traps for chupacabras is more my speed. That one time I saved the world was more than enough. I've had my fill."

"But you haven't even heard the details," I protested.

Most Heroes would at least want to know how the world was at risk. What kind of Hero was this?

"Don't need to." Grimoire shook her head firmly. "The answer is no. How many ways can I say it? No, negative, nah, nyet, nerp, nope, nuh-uh." Her hands and arms began weaving an elaborate pattern in the air. "I'm out. Good luck with that whole saving the world thing. Let me know how it all works out. Better yet, don't. I'm too busy tending to my own weed-infested garden."

Grimoire ended her hand-waving with a flourish. A blue and black hole, shimmering with some strange form of energy, opened under Grimoire's feet like a trapdoor. She dropped into the hole and disappeared, as if the hole had eaten her. The shimmering hole vanished after Grimoire did.

With my powers, I cautiously probed the ground where the hole had been an instant before. There was nothing unusual there, just grass and dirt. It was as if Grimoire and the hole she'd fallen into had never existed.

Isaac and I looked at each other with astonishment.

"Sure, she's weird," Isaac finally said. "And a little on the abrasive side. But you know what? I kinda like her."

15

I wasn't about to let Grimoire go that easily. Lim had said each person she wanted me to recruit was critical if we had any hope of abating the threat posed by Progenitor.

"Grimoire must have used some kind of teleportation," I told Isaac. "Can you track her?"

Isaac's form glowed and morphed, shifting into one of his go-to forms, that of a black-furred, yellow-toothed, red-eyed werewolf. He raised his hairy snout, his big nostrils expanding and contracting as he sniffed the air.

"No," he concluded in a half-snarl. "I only smell her spoor right here. She didn't teleport to anywhere nearby."

"I'll do a long-range scan for her. Wait here."

Leaving the flashlights behind for Isaac, I shot straight up into the air, with my personal shield around me to protect me from rushing winds, random stuff like insects and birds, and the g-force caused by such a rapid ascent.

When I was about half a mile up, I slowed to a halt. The wind whistled around me. I extended my arms out straight so they were at ninety-degree angles from my sides, closed my eyes, and concentrated. It was easier to do a long-range scan with my telekinetic touch when I was high in the sky. It was why, when I needed to do a city-wide scan of Astor City, I often went to the top of the UWant Building, the tallest in the country. Despite what Isaac told people, I didn't ascend the UWant Building because it made me look taller.

If Grimoire was still in the general area, I was confident I could locate her. If Grimoire had teleported far away, however, I would not find her with my telekinetic touch. Despite all my power, it had range limits. I was a Hero, not a god. Unlike Lim, no one worshipped me. And if someone did, they needed to develop better taste in divinities.

Gotcha, I thought after less than a minute's search. There Grimoire was, in a building several miles away in the nearby town of Beaufort. Unless someone else was dressed in a Grimoire costume, it had to be her. It wasn't close to Halloween, so I assumed the latter.

With my shield still around me, I zoomed toward Beaufort, keeping my rate below the speed of sound to avoid damaging property and injuring people with sonic booms.

Despite not flying as quickly as I was capable, it did not take long before I entered the tiny town of Beaufort and rocketed toward the building Grimoire was in.

The Beaufort Inn read the dilapidated sign outside the building. The Beaufort Inn wasn't the Four Seasons of Arkansas—it needed painting, fumigating, and an army of competent maintenance men. Every small town in the country seemed to have a motel like this, one that rarely got guests but managed to stay open year after year. I never understood how such places survived. Sheer stubbornness, maybe. Or by laundering meth, opioid, and weed money, as was the case with too many motels in Nowheresville, USA. My time as a Hero had given me an education I certainly hadn't gotten at the straitlaced Catholic high school I graduated from. If I weren't so focused on Grimoire, I'd keep my eyes peeled for Walter White.

Grimoire was in a tiny room on the second story. The room was above an empty parking lot. No Grimoire-mobile or any other vehicles were in sight. If Grimoire was staying here, I wondered how she had gotten all the way here from Washington, D.C. without transportation. Maybe she was capable of long-range teleportation in addition to short hops like the one she'd taken from the dead cows to here. If so, I needed to convince her to help us before she hopped aboard the teleportation train again.

I landed on the concrete breezeway in front of Grimoire's room. No one else was nearby. I scanned Grimoire's door with my powers. It was locked and the security chain was engaged. Fortunately, I was a superpowered master key.

I unlocked the door with my powers, removed the security chain, and pushed the door open. Bright light from inside spilled out. Standing in the open doorway, I peered inside.

Grimoire's head shot up. Unlike in the pasture, her entire face was uncovered. Her bandit mask hung limply around her neck. Her face looked completely different unmasked than masked. It was oval, whereas when masked it had been more . . . square-shaped, maybe? She also looked younger than she had before; now she looked just a few years older than I. And I would have sworn her eyes were . . . some other color before. Green, black, brown? I couldn't remember. Certainly she hadn't had the arctic blue eyes that now flashed with surprise and outrage at my abrupt appearance. It was strange I couldn't remember the details of her prior appearance; I was no

Ninja, but I wasn't a total amateur when it came to absorbing details.

And, unlike in the pasture, Grimoire wore a cape now. Crimson red, the heavy cape was fastened around Grimoire's neck by a gold clasp shaped like an eagle with its wings spread wide.

"What the heck!" Grimoire exclaimed at my sudden appearance. Her voice sounded different than it had before, but maybe that was just her startle over my unexpected appearance. Like it had a mind of its own, Grimoire's mask flew up, covering the bottom half of her face again. Strangely, her blue eyes were no longer blue. Her face looked completely different too, though I could not explain how other than she looked older with her mask on. Maybe her mask contained the same face-scrambling technology some other Heroes used.

A small designer suitcase containing clothes and sundry items was open on the bed. The bed, like the rest of the room, was stained and raggedy. Resting on it, Grimoire's high-end bag looked like a diamond atop the cow patty Isaac had stepped in. I wondered why Grimoire, if she could afford a bag as pricey as this one, was staying in a dump like this cramped room, the smallest in the motel.

I said, "We're going to talk about why I've come to see you whether you want to or not."

Grimoire slammed her suitcase shut and tucked it under an arm. "Whether I want to or not? Ear rapist. We've already talked." Her voice was back to how it had sounded before she was unmasked; maybe her mask contained voice-scrambling as well as visual-scrambling tech. "I told you the answer is no. You need it notarized to understand it? Go somewhere else to find a patsy. They're out of stock here."

Grimoire's hands and arms began weaving in the air, just

as they had before she teleported from the pasture. *Oh no you don't*, I thought. My own hands twitched.

Grimoire's arms and hands immediately froze, like I had hit their pause button. The rest of her body shuddered as she resisted my telekinetic hold. She definitely had some measure of super strength—restraining a normal woman would not be this hard. Not that restraining Grimoire was hard, just harder than it would be with a typical person.

Grimoire, realizing what was happening, stared daggers at me. "Let go! I've done nothing wrong. You've got no right to detain me. And you a Hero and everything. Just wait until my lawyer hears about this."

"I'll let you go once you hear me out."

Grimoire just stared at me with her strangely indistinguishable eyes. "You've got more nerve than an exposed tooth. When I get loose, I'm going to slap the taste out of your mouth."

"C'mon, Grimoire. Don't make threats you know you can't carry out. You obviously know who I am. It's more likely that your lawyer will slap me with a lawsuit than you ever getting close enough to slap me. Now, are you ready to stop being silly and start listening?"

Grimoire's strange eyes glittered. Then I felt her body relax.

"Fine," she said, admitting defeat. "But do you have to stand all the way over there shouting at me? Unless you want to share this save the world business with all of Mayberry."

I didn't walk into the room immediately, not liking the crafty look in Grimoire's mysterious eyes. *"Will you walk into my parlour?" said a spider to a fly.* Grimoire had somehow defeated Millennium, an Omega-level Meta. I'd be a fool to underestimate her.

I did a quick but thorough security sweep of the room with my powers. Other than the inside of the walls containing enough mice and roaches to jump-start a plague, there was nothing threatening inside.

Assured I wasn't walking into a trap, I stepped over the door's threshold.

Intense pain arced through me like I had stepped on a downed power line.

A strangled cry ripped from my throat. I collapsed onto the room's threadbare carpet. I was not the only one crying out in pain. Inside my head, countless voices screamed in anguish. The ever-present burning of my hands ceased, and my telekinesis shut off. My powers felt like a subway car I had just been shoved off of; they were receding from me down a dark tunnel, click-clacking far out of reach.

I couldn't get up or otherwise move on my own volition. Nothing on my body worked correctly. I could barely even think.

All I could do was lay writhing on the floor.

"Serves you right," Grimoire said smugly as she looked down at me from across the room, able to move again without my powers restraining her. "That's what you get for busting in here without an invite. I bet you'll think twice before messing with me again. So long, sucker."

Her arms and hands danced again. Another shimmering teleportation hole like the one Grimoire had created in the cow pasture opened next to her.

Her suitcase in tow, Grimoire stepped through the hole.

16

My muscles seized up and relaxed, over and over, like I was being electrocuted. I began to convulse. My teeth chattered. I was simultaneously insanely cold and absurdly hot, like I was an ice cube plunged into boiling oil. The Omega suit began withdrawing into my body, leaving naked skin behind. The anguished screaming from countless voices in my head grew fainter, like the screaming entities rode the receding subway car containing my powers. Somehow I knew—without knowing how I knew—the screams came from the residue of the countless people down throughout the ages who had carried the Omega spirit before me.

Grimoire paused. Half her body was in the shimmering hole; that half was gone, as if the Hero were a piece of paper cut in half. Half of her masked face frowned as she looked down at me. "Dude, are you alright?"

I didn't respond. I *couldn't* respond. The Omega suit completely withdrew into my body. I was naked now, writhing on the floor in the most intense pain I had ever been in. My heart pounded like a jackhammer, feeling like it would burst out of my chest. My vision dimmed and got hazy.

Grimoire withdrew from the hole, her body becoming whole once more. The shimmering hole disappeared as if it had never been. Dropping her suitcase, Grimoire rushed to me and crouched down. Her cape partially draped over me; it felt like it groped me, but that had to be a figment of my fevered imagination. One of her gauntlets disappeared, and Grimoire touched her bare hand to my neck.

"Puck, he's burning like a stove and his pulse is racing," Grimoire said rapidly, her eyes shining with concern. I had no idea who she was talking to; no one else was in the room. I was probably hallucinating. Frankly, I was past caring. I looked forward to death's sweet release, which I knew was right around the corner when my heart gave out. "That ward is just supposed to knock a human out. But it's like Omega's having an allergic reaction to it. What do I do? I think he's dying."

Head cocked, Grimoire seemed to listen to a voice only she could hear.

"Are you sure? In its raw form, the dust is lethal to humans." She paused, listening again. "Okay, you're right, we have to risk it."

She opened the pouch on her belt and hastily pulled out what looked like a rubber squeeze coin purse. Grimoire's gauntlet mysteriously reappeared on her bare hand, then she squeezed the rubber container open. Inside was dust glittering all the colors of the rainbow.

Grimoire scooped a bit of the stuff onto her gloved finger, dropped the rubber container back into her belt pouch, then gingerly held the small pile of glowing dust on her finger near my shaking head. "Omega, I need you to swallow this stuff. Omega. Omega!"

I heard her but couldn't respond. I certainly couldn't do as she asked. I had lost all control of my faculties. My vision was tunneling. I felt the Omega spirit slipping further away from me like water draining from a sink. Its screams grew fainter.

Seeing I wasn't cooperating, Grimoire grabbed my nose with her free hand and roughly pinched it closed. I gasped for breath. Grimoire shoved into my open mouth the finger carrying the shimmering dust.

Whatever the dust was, it dissolved like powdered sugar on my tongue. It tasted the way a sunrise looks. The substance made my lips pucker and my mouth go numb.

Then my mouth began to tingle, like a leg gone to sleep when feeling was returning to it. The tingling rapidly spread from my mouth and through the rest of my body like an ever-strengthening wave.

The screaming in my head, which had become faint, abruptly got as loud again as it had been when it first started. Then the screaming stopped altogether. I stopped convulsing. The horrific pain ended.

I sat up abruptly, like I was an android whose on switch had been flipped. I no longer felt terrible anymore. Quite the opposite. I felt amazing, like I had gotten a full night's rest, eaten a nutrient-dense breakfast, downed a shot of espresso, and gotten a vitamin B-12 shot. The burning of my hands was back. As a test, I lifted the bed, then set it back down. My powers had returned.

"What was that you gave me?" I asked Grimoire. Whatever it was, I wanted more.

She sat back on her haunches, breathing hard, looking at me with obvious relief. "Raw pixie dust."

"Pixie dust? The street drug?"

"No. Well, yes. Kind of. It's a long story." Grimoire's brow was furrowed with concern. She said, "How do you feel? Any pain, heart palpitations, light-headedness, racing thoughts?"

"No. I feel great. Better than great. This is the best I've felt in my whole life." I had never done illegal drugs before, but if this was what they felt like, I understood how people got hooked. The only other time I ever felt this good was right after I had absorbed the Omega weapon into my body in The Mountain. I had been losing sleep over Progenitor, but now knew the anxiety had been wasted energy. Dealing with him would be a snap. I was so giddy at the thought, I started giggling and couldn't stop.

Grimoire watched my reaction dubiously. "You feel great, huh? Doctor Grimoire will be the judge of that."

She grabbed my chin, pulled me close, and stared into my eyes as giggles bubbled out of me like gas from a soda. She waved her hand, and her index finger burst into flame like it was a lighter. She moved the flame back and forth in front of one of my eyes, then the other.

She shook her finger, extinguishing the flame. "You're high as Snoop Dogg riding a comet," she concluded, "but it appears you're otherwise fine. Which begs the question . . ."

She trailed off, her eyes moving to the still-open door. She stood, her cape swishing around her. I got to my feet too, turning to watch as she went to the door, stuck her head out, looked both ways, then closed the door and locked it behind her. She made a wide circular gesture in front of the door while murmuring words I couldn't catch. I felt a weird vibration, like someone had tapped a tuning fork and pressed it against my skin.

Grimoire spun to face me. "Now no one can overhear. It's cards on the table time. What *are* you?"

I still had the giggles. "I'm a licensed Hero. Omega, at your and the world's service. You already know that."

"C'mon bro, ain't nobody here but us chickens. My protective ward wouldn't have affected you like that and the pixie dust wouldn't have healed you if you were just a man." Grimoire looked down. "Speaking of chickens, you mind doing something about that worm? Not that I'm against a little eye candy, but it's distracting."

I looked down too. I felt myself flush with embarrassment and my giggles died off. Because the Omega suit had withdrawn into my body during my seizure, I was as naked as the day I was born. Maskless, too.

Mortified, I made the Omega suit re-manifest with a mental command, covering me and my so-called worm again. "You called it little on purpose," I accused Grimoire. "It's not little."

Her mask's fabric twitched. "I call 'em like I see 'em. Don't change the subject. What are you? Human, Otherkin, Halfling, or something else entirely?"

Little of what this woman said made any sense. "I'm human."

Grimoire looked at me with faraway eyes, more like she was looking through me than at me. "Uh-huh. Your mouth says you're human, but your aura says otherwise. Don't fib to a fibber."

"I'm telling you, I'm human. I don't know what those other words you used mean. Though I do have something called the Omega spirit inside of me." I surprised myself by admitting that. Only Isaac, Shay, Truman and Lim knew about the Omega spirit. I could only assume the pixie dust had turned me into a chatty Cathy.

Grimoire didn't respond at first, eyeing me the way a cop eyes someone she's pulled over for suspected drunk driving.

Then she said, "Maybe he's telling the truth."

"What's this 'he' stuff? I'm right here."

"I wasn't talking to you," Grimoire replied. "Tell me about this Omega spirit."

My tongue apparently still loosened by the pixie dust, I told her about how the Omega spirit has been around as long as humanity has been, moving from host to host, helping those hosts be humanity's champion against the forces of evil and darkness. I told her the Omega spirit had passed from Avatar to me upon his death.

Grimoire said, "I remember the Wandering Jew saying you had possession of the Relic that is the Omega weapon, but he lied so much, I didn't know what to believe or disbelieve."

"What in the world is a Relic? And who's the Wandering Jew? The guy from Christian mythology? You mentioned him before."

She frowned. "I did? I shouldn't have. Forget I mentioned him. The Omega spirit explains why the ward affected you the way it did, though. It's obviously a super-natural entity, and the ward is designed to keep things in the spirit world out. The same thing with the pixie dust—if you were just a human without a supernatural entity riding shotgun inside you, the dust would have killed you for sure. Instead, it healed you."

"The Omega spirit isn't supernatural."

"Oh? What exactly is this Omega spirit, then? A type of liqueur?"

I opened my mouth to respond, but just as quickly closed it. I didn't have an answer. "How do you know so much about the supernatural, anyway?" I demanded instead.

Grimoire made a dismissive motion with her hand. "No

reason. Don't worry about it. Let's get back to you. Let me guess—the Omega spirit is why you're on a world-saving spree and why you've come to me."

"Not exactly." Before I came to Arkansas, I had a big speech prepared where I would recruit Grimoire by appealing to her Heroic idealism. That would work on a traditional Hero. It certainly would work on me if I weren't already hip-deep in this thing. But Grimoire was clearly a non-traditional Hero.

No, a *once more unto the breach, dear friends* rah-rah type speech would not work on someone like Grimoire.

Instead, probably still under the influence of the pixie dust, I told Grimoire the unvarnished truth. I told her about Lim, Progenitor, and the coming crisis.

And, the strange thing was, it felt good to be completely honest with someone for a change. I withheld information from, shaded the truth with, and outright lied to so many people that it was refreshing to "tell the truth and shame the devil" as my Dad would say. It was a Jamesism, what I called the phrases he often used. A lot of wisdom was in the clichés he had spouted. Sometimes, though, I wondered if that wisdom was better suited to a more innocent world that died long before I was born. Or maybe that world never even existed outside of wishful thinking.

"Let's see if I understand correctly," Grimoire said once I finished spilling my guts. "Recurring psychedelic dreams are warning you about some Big Bad named Progenitor slash The Ancient One slash The Adversary slash Hellscape. Mr. Tall, Dark and Scary will do gods know what to the world when he breaks out of the interdimensional prison he's spent the last dozen centuries cooling his heels in. The only reason why he hasn't busted out already is because a five-year-old girl is beating him in a mental game of Red Rover. But he will bust out soon. And when he does, if you don't have certain superpowered Merry Men in place, the world's in trouble. Though you don't know exactly what that trouble is. And the odds are terrible for the Merry Men even if you do assemble them."

"I know it sounds crazy."

Grimoire barked out a mirthless laugh. "I hate to say it, but as far as crazy stories people have tried to sell me on go, yours is on the more believable side. You wouldn't believe the whoppers I've heard before." She shook her head, then said, "Puck, have you heard of this Ancient One joker?"

"Who's Puck?" I demanded. "Who are you talking to?"

"An old friend. A *very* old friend. He's something else you shouldn't worry about."

Grimoire cocked her head, appearing to listen to something I most definitely couldn't hear. The longer she listened, the paler she got.

"Oh, this is bad," she said. "This is very, very bad."

"What? What can you hear that I can't?"

"Don't worry about it." I was getting really sick of her saying that. It was like people were gossiping behind my back right in front of me.

"You know all the irons I have in the fire," Grimoire said, obviously not speaking to me. "This stuff with Agatha's heating up. How can I take the time to help? On the other hand, how can I *not* take the time to help?" Whatever Grimoire heard that I couldn't had visibly shaken her.

Grimoire obviously was wavering. I had already appealed to her better nature, so it was time to appeal to a different part of her nature. I was no math whiz like Lim, but Grimoire's luxury suitcase plus her staying in this shabby room seemed to equal expensive tastes on a poor woman's budget.

"The job pays," I said. "A lot."

Grimoire's eyes lit up. "How much is a lot?"

I smiled triumphantly on the inside, though I kept the expression off my face. It was like that old story where a man walked up to a stranger in a bar and asked her if she would sleep with him for a million dollars. The woman looked him up and down, and said yes. Then the man instead offered her five dollars to sleep with him. She rejected the offer.

What do you think I am, some kind of whore? the woman demanded angrily.

We've already established what you are, the man replied. *Now we're just haggling over the price.*

When Grimoire asked how much "a lot" was, I knew she was on board.

Now we were just haggling over the price.

17

I had anxiously awaited having the dream again, and it took far too many days to finally happen.

I marched along the vividly green grassy promontory, looking for Lim. I thought about Grimoire as I walked. The strange Hero was an enigma.

Assuming she actually was a licensed Hero. I had my doubts, especially once I looked into her background. That had been a snap once I discovered her secret identity. Grimoire hadn't told me, of course. Neither had Lim. "That's none of your beeswax," the pint-sized Meta had said when I asked about Grimoire's secret identity when Lim had tasked me to find and recruit her. "It's safer for you and her both if you don't know her true identity. All you need to know is that you need her to help you deal with Progenitor. So stop asking so many fool questions and make sure you get her on our side. Chop, chop!"

The only reason why I knew Grimoire's real name was, after we parted company at the Beaufort Inn, I doubled back and grabbed a half-drunk glass of water Grimoire had left on the nightstand. When I returned to New Sentinels mansion, I had Minerva scan the glass for prints and run them through all the state, federal, and international databases she had access to. Minerva could have run the prints remotely by scanning them from the jet, but I didn't want Isaac to know I was seeking Grimoire's real name. He wouldn't approve, and I was sick of butting heads with him. It was a felony under the Hero Act to attempt to uncover a Hero's real name, and an even more serious felony to actually unearth it. But there was too much at stake for me to simply close my eyes to the type of person I was dealing with and hope for the best.

Minerva had reported back with Grimoire's real name almost immediately: Sage Hawthorne. Sage was in her late twenties, her last employment was as a security specialist with Capstone Security Consultants in Washington, D.C., and she rented a basement apartment in the D.C. neighborhood known as Columbia Heights. To remove all doubt that Sage was Grimoire, Minerva showed me a picture of Sage. Sage definitely was the same person I had seen in the motel room before her mask had flown up, seemingly of its own accord, somehow changing her facial features and making her masked face impossible to remember. I had no issue remembering what her unmasked face looked like, though.

The picture Minerva had shown me of Sage was not merely a picture—it was a mug shot. Sage was an ex-con. It was why her prints were on file.

Years ago, Sage had spent three years as a guest of the D.C. Department of Corrections for threatening a public official, criminal contempt, and assault and battery. She also had tons of debt and lousy credit, which explained why she was so eager to take my money.

The only other publicly available information regarding Sage was really more about her father than about her. An old *Washington Post* article reported that Anwell Hawthorne, a D.C. public school history teacher, was murdered when he returned home and surprised a home invader who was about to molest his sixteen-year-old daughter. The *Post* didn't name the sixteen-year-old as she was a minor, but the teenager described had to be Sage as birth records indicated she was Anwell's only daughter.

The *Post* stated the home invader escaped, and the police had no suspects. Minerva had found no indication that Anwell's murderer was ever caught. The only other mention of Anwell's death was in the trash tabloid the *National Inquiry*, known for its tongue-in-cheek reporting and ludicrous headlines like *I Was Bigfoot's Love Slave* and *Noah's Ark Found Floating In Bermuda Triangle—Unicorns Still Aboard*. The tabloid had a voracious readership despite how ridiculous it was. Or maybe because of how ridiculous it was. The *Inquiry's* piece about Anwell suggested with a wink and a nudge he was killed by a demon; the article ran under the headline *D.C. Man Can't Outrun Demon Due To Failure To Exorcise*. I believed in the First Amendment, but the *Inquiry* took freedom of speech too far.

Sage and I had at least two things in common: we both had fathers murdered in front of us, and we both had been guests of the D.C. Department of Corrections. Though Sage far longer than I. I'd gone to jail for only a few days for unauthorized use of Metahuman powers after capturing Iceburn during my Apprenticeship. The charges against me were later dropped. Unlike Sage, I had never been convicted of anything. It didn't stop Isaac from gleefully calling me a jailbird.

While it was not unheard of for a convicted felon like Sage to have a Hero's license, it was highly unusual. A felon who aspired to be a Hero usually wasn't accepted into the

Trials, and an already established Hero being convicted of a crime was an express train to having your cape snatched off you. Heck, I'd been afraid I would be defrocked after I destroyed Mechano, and I had merely been accused of a crime, not convicted of one.

Grimoire's less than Heroic behavior and discovering her criminal record had made me wonder if she really was a Hero at all. It was, of course, illegal to use powers and wear a superhero costume without a Hero's license.

I had checked the Heroes' Guild's computerized membership records. To my surprise, Grimoire's code name was on the official roster.

Even so, I still harbored doubts. Ghost had been mighty evasive when I reached out to him to get more information about Grimoire. And, other than Grimoire being listed as a licensed Hero, the Guild's records about her were as sparse as snow in South Carolina. The ones Ghost hadn't classified, that is. It was hard to believe Ghost and the Guild were allowing someone to hold herself out as a Hero when she really wasn't one, but I had been through enough over the years to know the world didn't work the way the civics books said it was supposed to.

There was no doubt about it: there was something weird about Grimoire, over and above her strange behavior and powers. I thought I knew why. I'd confirm it if I ever managed to find Lim again.

After walking what seemed like forever, I spotted Lim. Finally! I strode up to her.

"Where have you been?" I demanded impatiently.

"Hello! How are you?" Lim replied. "I'm fine, thanks for asking."

"Don't be smart. I asked a question: Where have you

been? Do you know how long it's been since you've pulled me into another of these dreams?"

"I've been vacationing in Monaco, of course. How do you like my tan?" Lim rolled her eyes, then jerked her head at the distant storm clouds. "I've been busy with *him*, of course. He's getting more and more restless. It takes energy and attention away from him to come to you for these talks, you know. I don't want him to wake up prematurely. Before I can get you ready."

"How are you supposed to get me ready if I never see you?"

"You're seeing me now. You're like a child crying about getting a toy today instead of four days ago. Grow up."

"That's mighty ironic, being told to grow up by someone who looks like a kid dressed up for Halloween."

Lim looked down at herself with pride. "You noticed my new ensemble. I didn't think you would."

"How could I not notice it?" Gone were her bunny shirt, black pants and pink ballet shoes. Now she wore an above-the-knee red skirt, matching red galoshes, and a long-sleeved white top with red accents. Her clothes looked like shiny latex; the outfit dully reflected a fun house mirror version of my body. On the front of the shirt was a stylized image of a gray brain. Superimposed on top of the brain was a large red *M*. Wrapped around Lim's head was what looked like a man's red power tie. Holes had been cut out of the tie to expose Lim's eyes.

Lim looked giddy as I stared at her. "The M is for Mastermind, of course. This is my new superhero costume. I figured since I'm mentoring you, it's only appropriate. When in Rome, do as the Romans and slap on a toga. How do you like my ensemble? I designed it myself."

She looked ridiculous. "You look great," I said.

Lim's face fell. "You don't like it."

"I just said it looks great."

"You didn't mean it. You're just being nice." Lim's face shifted from disappointed to sullen. "Who cares what you think, anyway? You're just a mor—uh, someone who doesn't have an eye for fashion. I think I look smashing. Intrepid. Heroic. You're just jealous. After all, you're the guy who dresses like a discount Captain America who can't afford to add red to the white and blue of his costume."

"I'm definitely jealous. It's been a long time since I looked like a trick-or-treater. I miss those happy childhood days."

"Now who's being smart?"

I changed the subject. We had important matters to discuss, Grimoire being one of them. "Did you know that magic is real?"

"Duh. Of course magic is real. I'm the one who told you."

"No, you didn't."

Lim looked like she was about to argue, then her mouth twisted to the side as she thought. "Okay, maybe I didn't come right out and say so," she concluded. "But I alluded to it. It's not my fault you didn't pick up on what I was putting down. I'm surprised you didn't connect the dots based on your interactions with Doctor Alchemy. His alchemical concoctions had a magical component, you know. If you didn't learn magic is real from me, whom did you learn it from?"

"Grimoire."

"I take it you successfully recruited her."

"Yes. Don't you already know?"

"I told you—I've been busy. Too busy to expend the energy reading minds. Progenitor has got my hands full, especially since he's so close to awakening and breaking free. Yours is the only mind I'm reaching out to these days, and I'm only doing it because I need to teach you some stuff about Progenitor. I'm surprised Grimoire told you about magic. She'll get into a lot of trouble if the people who run the magical world catch her blabbing."

"Grimoire didn't tell me. Not in so many words. But creatures like chupacabras my telekinesis won't work on? Vampires? Healing pixie dust? An undetectable protective field that hurt the Omega spirit and nearly killed me?" I shook my head. I could still hardly believe what I'd witnessed and experienced. Now that I was wrapping my head around magic being real, I wondered if there was a nugget of truth to that *National Inquiry* story about Sage's father being killed by a demon. Reality was turning out to be far stranger than fiction. "On top of all that, Millennium described himself as a magician. I thought that was merely an affectation on his part, something he let people believe to hide the true nature of his power. But he made the same sort of hand and arm gestures Grimoire makes when she triggers her powers. It's not hard to put two and two together."

"Well, buy a hat and keep your discovery under it," Lim advised. "The Conclave takes the First Rule super seriously."

"Conclave? First Rule? What are you talking about?"

"I'm talking about magic. Do try to keep up. The Conclave is the loose federation of magicians and magical creatures running most of the supernatural world. You're a *Star Trek* fan, right? Think of the Conclave as the United Federation of the Paranormal, with the First Rule as its Prime Directive. The First Rule states, 'There is no magic.' Meaning, everyone in the magical world is supposed to deny and hide the existence of magic. The magical world went into hiding centuries ago, and it does what it needs to do to stay hidden. Even you wouldn't be safe if you started running your mouth about what you know."

"What would they do to me?"

Lim looked me dead in the eye and slowly ran a finger across her throat. I blinked at how somber she was. Not too many people scared me these days. This supposed magical world being so dangerous was perhaps why Lim had said earlier it was safer if I didn't know Grimoire's real name. I decided to keep to myself the fact I had figured it out on my own.

I asked, "Could they really do that? Kill me?" I thought about how the chupacabras had hopped right through my force field like it didn't exist.

"They'd kill you and not lose a wink of sleep over it. They've done it before and will do it again. The unscrupulous members of the magical world, I mean. There are good and bad people in every society, but it seems like the bad ones are running the magical one right now. They're committed to remaining hidden, at least until they think they're strong enough to come out into the open, throw their weight around, and start running things in both the magical and mundane worlds. As they once did eons ago after Progenitor took his first powder and exited the world stage. It's no accident that every human culture has legends about elves and witches, ghosts and goblins. They're not really legends—they're racial memories. The only thing that stops magical folk from taking over again is fear of people like us. Metahumans, I mean, not the sartorially gifted like me and the sartorially challenged like you. Maybe you'll be a part of the inevitable reckoning between the mundane and magical worlds. In the extremely unlikely event you survive your looming encounter with Progenitor, I mean."

The weight of the responsibility on my shoulders, never

light to begin with, got even heavier. The way Lim always talked, it was clear she wasn't optimistic about our chances against Progenitor. "When this thing with Progenitor is over, you should get a job as a motivational speaker."

"Nah. I'd rather not cast my pearls before swine." Lim clapped her hands and rubbed them together. "Speaking of which Wilbur, granny Charlotte has much to teach you. Or else you'll be heading to the slaughterhouse for sure. Let's begin this evening's lesson. What do you know about the Neanderthals?"

"The Japanese rock band?"

"That's The Cro-Magnons!" Lim snapped. Her face clouded over like she was about to explode. She caught herself, peered up at me suspiciously and said, "Are you kidding around again, or is this additional evidence of imbecility?"

"I'm kidding. A bit of retribution. Wilbur from *Charlotte's Web*? Don't think I don't know you just called me a pig. The Neanderthals are a species of humans who went extinct tens of thousands of years ago. *Homo neanderthalensis*. They were—"

"Hey! Are you running this mentoring session, Mister Funny Man, or am I? Zip it. The Neanderthals went extinct around 40,000 years ago to be more precise about it. Living in Eurasia, they were bigger, stronger, and smarter than another human sub-species they shared the planet with. Namely the ancestors of modern humans, *Homo sapiens*."

"Neanderthals weren't smarter than *Homo sapiens*," I protested.

"Do you have doctorates in anthropology and archeology I don't know about? I told you to zip it, especially since you don't know what the hell you're talking about and I do." Lim shook her head. "Despite Neanderthals being bigger, stronger, and *smarter*," she said, emphasizing the word irritably, "*Homo neanderthalensis* suddenly went extinct and *Homo sapiens* survived. And it happened after the two human species co-existed for over 170,000 years. Any guess why, Professor Know-It-All?"

"There's speculation they died because of climate change, war with *Homo sapiens*, disease, some sort of massive natural disaster, or a combination of those factors. History doesn't know for certain."

"History may not know." Lim poked a thumb into the M on her chest. "But *I* know. A shame I can't publish an anthropological paper on the subject once this whole thing with Progenitor is over. Clear up the historical ambiguity. Oh well."

"Why can't you?" I asked.

"For one, if I know Progenitor, there's not likely to be anybody left standing to read the darned thing. For another . . ." Lim trailed off, her face becoming unreadable. "Never mind, it's not important. What's important is what happened to the Neanderthals. It all relates to Progenitor and what you'll be up against. Take my hand."

I looked at Lim's proffered hand warily. I had not forgotten what her touching my forehead had felt like. "Why?"

"Because we're going steady. All couples going steady hold hands." Lim rolled her eyes so hard, I thought they might get stuck. She muttered oaths under her breath before saying, "I want you to hold my hand because I'm taking you on a field trip. Think of you taking my hand as your consciousness giving me a permission slip to take little Theo out of school and on the trip."

I still didn't take her hand. "Where are you taking me?"

Lim jerked her head toward the distant dark storm

clouds. "There. Into Progenitor's mind. More specifically, into his memories." She waggled her outstretched hand. "Are you going to take my hand or not? Come on, homey. Don't leave a sista hangin'."

I swallowed my lingering apprehension and grabbed Lim's hand. Fortunately, it was like when I shook her hand the last time I saw her and not like grasping a cattle prod; holding her hand was like holding any small child's hand. Not that I could remember the last time I held a child's hand. Despite being as famous as him, I wasn't Michael Jackson.

"Whatever you do, don't stop making physical contact," Lim warned.

"What will happen if I do? Will the bogeyman jump out and get me?" I often got flip when I was nervous, and I was certainly nervous now. Dealing with garden-variety Rogues I was used to. Traveling into the mind of an ancient evil trapped in another dimension alongside a preschooler was an entirely different kettle of fish.

"You're more right than you know, smart aleck," Lim said. "If you let go of me, your consciousness will be trapped in Progenitor's mind. I won't be able to extricate you, and your sleeping corporeal body will waste away until it dies due to your mind no longer being able to regulate its functions. Assuming an acute case of embarrassment over being so stupid doesn't kill it first."

I felt a lot less flip now. I squeezed Lim's hand tighter. "Don't let go. Got it."

Staring at the distant storm clouds, Lim took several deep breaths, like she was psyching herself up for a race.

"Okay, let's get this horror show on the road," she said.

Like we had been launched from a superpowered cannon, Lim and I rocketed off the promontory. We sailed over the ocean, higher and higher into the indigo sky, toward the dark storm clouds. Unlike when I flew with my powers, there was no stress of acceleration, no blowing of the wind, no tug of gravity. It was as if we traveled through an empty void rather than the clear sky we appeared to be in.

We entered the dark storm clouds. It felt like jumping into a pool of water that simultaneously scorched us and chilled us to the bone.

The clouds swallowed us into their murky depths.

18

A kaleidoscope of images flashed around us, like we had been tossed into a television set whose owner tapped the channel button feverishly. I saw castles being stormed, the clash of armies, men mowed down like blades of grass, women being ravished, children being enslaved, a large man in strange silver armor being bound with heavy chains to a boulder in the center of Stonehenge, and countless other images. Most of them of conquerors and the conquered.

The flashing images eventually stopped. The icy-hot sensation that began when we entered the storm clouds faded. A single scene formed around us.

Still holding hands, Lim and I stood deep in a large cave made of reddish-brown rock. Sunlight trickled in through an entrance over to our right. The cave obviously served as a dwelling. Furs and plant matter lay in clumps on the rock floor, forming rough bedding. Ashes and partially burned wood were in the corner, under a small hole in the ceiling that evidently served as a natural chimney. Near the dead fire were stones that looked like rough-hewn tools. The cave reeked of food, smoke, burnt matter, and body odor.

"Where are we?" I asked Lim in a low whisper since we were not alone in the cave.

"Over 40,000 years ago in a cavern in a part of the world you know as Turkey," Lim said in a normal tone of voice, not keeping her voice down at all. No one else in the cave seemed to hear her. "The people in here are all *Homo sapiens*. Or at least *Homo sapiens* as they looked back then. Now hush! This next part is the hardest. You're the kinda guy who barges into an operating room and tugs on the surgeon's elbow. Let me focus."

Lim touched her free hand to her head and stared intently at a dark-skinned boy who was in the cave with us. He was seven or eight at the most. Lim frowned as she concentrated on him, like he was a difficult math problem she was trying to solve in her head. Her dark eyes turned clear as crystal and shone.

In addition to the boy, there were several other dark-skinned people in the cave, all female. Everyone ignored Lim and I as if we weren't here. The females ranged in age from middle-aged to younger than the boy. It was hard to tell anyone's exact age, though, because these people were unlike any I had seen before. They were very hairy, they had prominent brow ridges over their eyes, and the older females wore animal skins around their waists. The girls and the boy were completely naked. Height-wise, the adults were smaller than modern females; the tallest was under five feet tall. Otherwise, everyone was stockier and more robust than modern people, with little fat on their bodies other than the pendulous breasts dangling from the torsos of the eldest women.

All but one of the females, even the little girls, clutched

stones and sharp sticks. They were clustered around the cave's entrance. Shouts, yelps, and grunts came from outside the cave. Sounds of combat.

The sole unarmed female was shoving the boy into a narrow crevice in a wall at the far end of the cave. Before I could ask Lim further questions about what was going on, she announced triumphantly, "Got it!"

Lim and I became translucent; looking down, I saw the cave floor through our bodies. Our linked bodies shrank like we were being miniaturized, and we were pulled forward. We were sucked into the boy's skull as if his head was an impossibly powerful vacuum cleaner.

In the blink of an eye, Lim and I were inside the boy's mind, seeing what was going on in the cave from his perspective. I had complete access to his memories and could understand his people's long dead language.

AROUCH'S MOTHER CHEKA HASTILY SHOVED SOME OF THE plant matter their tribe used as bedding into the crevice, concealing her son from view. If Arouch weren't small for his age, he never would've fit into the narrow crack.

"Promise me you'll stay hidden and quiet, Arouch," Cheka told him. "The barbarians may spare us females and take us for bed wenches. As a male, they will definitely kill you if they find you. No matter what you see, no matter what you hear, stay here. Don't make a sound. Promise me."

Arouch nodded solemnly. He was trying to be brave. In truth, he was terrified. Fear had snatched his voice away.

Cheka finished tucking the plant matter into the crevice, completely hiding Arouch's small body. With a last glance at her hidden son, she turned away, moving to retrieve a spear she had left on the cave floor. The instant her back was turned, Arouch stuck a couple of fingers in the plant matter, making a hole big enough that he could see out clearly by pressing an eye right up against it.

Cheka moved to join the other armed women and girls clustered around the cave's entrance. These females were all Arouch's relatives—mother, aunts, and cousins—just as all the males fighting outside the cave were his relatives. They all lived together as a small, nomadic tribe, just like countless other groups of humans did.

Men suddenly appeared at the mouth of the cave. Arouch's insides quivered with terror. They were not Arouch's tribemates or humans from another tribe. These were barbarians. Neanderthals.

The Neanderthal men were far stockier than Arouch's male relatives, with heavily muscled builds and barrel chests. They had short forearms and lower legs, but were still taller by several inches than the tallest of the females in the cave. Instead of being garbed in roughly tailored animal skins as Arouch's people traditionally wore, the Neanderthals wore animal hides as loose ponchos. Their skin was lighter than Arouch's and his people's. Their heads were big with prominent bumps on the backs of them, their foreheads were sloped, their chins recessed, and their eyes and eye sockets were bigger than those of Arouch's adult relatives.

The Neanderthals' appearance at the cave mouth was a horrible sign. It meant Arouch's male relatives had been defeated defending their home. They were likely all dead. Arouch almost whimpered with fear and grief but swallowed the sound, remembering his promise to his mother.

The females inside the cave, the tribe's last line of defense, were ready. As soon as the Neanderthals appeared, the females let loose with a volley of rocks that pelted the interlopers. Their aim was true, even that of the little girls. Their marksmanship was a finely honed skill because their lives often depended on it. Arouch was proud of them, but ashamed of himself. While girls younger than him fought, he cowered in the crevice like a trembling rabbit. Only his promise to his mother stopped him from springing out of the crevice and trying to help. Arouch knew his mother had made him hide because, if Arouch survived to adulthood, he could father a multitude of children with his seed, ensuring the continuance of the family line.

Two of the Neanderthals were clocked in their large heads by the females' rock volley. They collapsed and fell from view. The rest of the barbarians rushed into the cave, armed with rocks and sticks like the females.

A wild melee ensued. It was clear to Arouch, though, what would happen as soon as the battle was joined: the Neanderthals would win. They outnumbered the females two to one and were stronger and faster.

The battle in the confined space was soon over. The females who had not been killed were disarmed.

Then what Arouch feared would happen happened. The Neanderthals held the females down and took turns raping them. Not even the little girls or the dead were spared.

Sick to his stomach, Arouch wanted to turn away, but forced himself to watch. He used what he saw to feed the fire of hate burning within him. He had seen sex before—the older members of his tribe did not conceal their coupling from the younger ones. But he had never seen sexual violence before. The temptation to break his promise to his mother and try to help his relatives was almost too much to resist, but he knew he alone was no match for the barbarians. Arouch would be killed instantly. His sacrifice would not do his mother or the others any good.

Instead of needlessly throwing his life away, Arouch silently stared at the man thrusting away atop his screaming mother. The man's long, shaggy hair was red, like it had been scorched by the sun. Arouch carefully memorized the man's features.

Arouch was too small and weak to kill all of the Neanderthals here. The red-haired man who was violating his mother, though, he would find a way to kill. Arouch swore it to himself and to all the gods.

After what seemed like an eternity, the Neanderthals had slaked their filthy thirsts. They began grunting loudly and gesturing at each other, seeming to argue. The sobs and anguished moans of the few still-living females served as a heartbreaking counterpoint to the argument. Though Arouch could not understand the Neanderthals' language, he assumed the Neanderthals were debating whether to kill the females, keep them as slaves, or keep them as human currency to be sold to other tribes. It was the way of the world—the conquerors showed no mercy to the conquered.

The Neanderthals must have come to a decision. They killed all the females, either by bashing their skulls in with rocks, stabbing them with spears, or slitting their throats with sharp rock chips. The redhead killed Arouch's mother by stabbing her repeatedly in the chest. He laughed as he did it, like it was a game.

Arouch surprised himself by not crying as he watched his mother die. Though he grieved for her and his other relatives, the grief was eclipsed by cold, implacable fury. How he loathed the Neanderthals in general and the redheaded one in particular.

Once the Neanderthals slayed everyone, they ransacked

the cave for anything of value, including stripping the women of their clothing. Arouch silently resolved to spring out of the crevice and claw the eyes out of any Neanderthal who uncovered his hiding place. The Neanderthals overlooked Arouch's thatch-covered hole, however, and he remained hidden.

The Neanderthals collected their spoils and shambled out of the cave. They took a few of the youngest of the dead females with them. Arouch knew why—as they were not fully grown and not yet corded with muscle, the flesh of the youngest was the tenderest. Cannibalism between warring tribes of humans was not unheard of, but it was downright common between Neanderthals and humans. Had the battle gone differently, Arouch would almost certainly be eating roasted Neanderthal meat tonight.

Arouch waited a while to make sure the Neanderthals were not returning. Then, he shoved the plant matter out of the way and squeezed out of the crevice. Stepping over dead bodies, he crept to the cave entrance. He got on his belly and, wiggling like a worm, cautiously stuck his head out of the cave and looked down.

The invading Neanderthals were below, threading their way down the rock formation containing the cave Arouch was in. Scattered on the gently sloping rock were the bloody bodies of the males of Arouch's small tribe as well as a few dead Neanderthals. Arouch could see his father and two of his uncles from here. His father's head had been smashed open; bits of his brain littered the rock he lay on. Arouch certainly was not happy to see his father dead, but it did not affect him the way his mother's death did. Men died in battle and on hunts all the time. Arouch had known his father would not live forever. Arouch's mother had seemed timeless, though, like she would hold him in her lap and love him forever. Perhaps she would have had it not been for these filthy Neanderthals.

The Neanderthals paused to collect weapons from the fallen. They also gathered the bodies of Arouch's youngest male relatives. More fresh meat for the Neanderthals' fires. A group of additional Neanderthals waited for the marauders near the tree line far below. Though Arouch could not clearly see the individuals in the group from this distance, he surmised they were women, small children, and men too injured or too old to fight.

The Neanderthal raiders joined the group awaiting them. All told, there were several dozen of the barbarians. The entire group disappeared into the trees.

Arouch was sorely tempted to follow the Neanderthals now, try to catch the redhead unawares, and kill him. He knew, however, that would be foolish. In the daylight, the Neanderthals would spot, capture, and kill him. The only way to exact vengeance on the redhead would be to wait until dark, creep into the Neanderthals' camp, and catch the redhead while he was asleep. The redhead was a grown man and Arouch was but a child—in a fair fight, Arouch had no chance of killing the man. Subterfuge was Arouch's only way to settle the score, albeit in a small way.

Arouch looked at the sun's position in the sky. Darkness would not fall for hours. He had a while to wait before leaving.

Arouch withdrew back into the cave. He knelt over his mother's bloody and defiled body.

For the first time that day, he cried. His sobs echoed off the rock walls, distorting them into something akin to laughter that mocked Arouch's impotence and anguish.

Before he knew it, the cave darkened. Not as much sunlight spilled into the cave as before. Darkness would soon arrive. Hours had passed like minutes. Arouch had spent them in a cloudy haze of grief.

There was no more time for wallowing. Now was the time for action.

Arouch rose from his mother's body. He regretted not being big and strong enough to carry her and the others down to the soft soil near the tree line to bury them. By leaving his dead relatives here and outside the cave, their remains would be devoured by cave hyenas, cave lions, cave bears, wolves, and other predators. He was lucky the scavengers had not already arrived.

Ah well, there was no help for it. If he took the time to drag everyone down the slope for burial, the nomadic Neanderthals would no doubt travel too far away for Arouch to track them.

Arouch went outside, startling squawking birds who already pecked at the dead. Feeling like a ghoul, he took an animal hide from one of his relatives and wrapped it around his own naked waist. Wearing it was a mark of adulthood. A man's garb for a man's task. After picking through the other corpses for a bit, Arouch found a stone secured to a thick stick by a knotted vine. It was a stone cudgel, almost as long as Arouch was tall, but still small enough for Arouch's immature body to carry and wield. He also found a short, sharpened stick, and tucked it into his waistband. Neither weapon would do much good if he were attacked by a large predator while pursuing the Neanderthals, but inadequate weapons were better than none at all.

Arouch's stomach rumbled as he straightened. The red deer he and his tribe had feasted on seemed like forever ago. There had been some food stored in the cave—nuts, root vegetables, dried berries, and the like—but the Neanderthals had taken it all. Arouch could get nourishment by hacking off some flesh from the bodies around him, but the thought turned his empty stomach.

Arouch tried to ignore his hunger. The hollowness of his stomach would be gone soon enough. There was, after all, no hunger in the afterlife. For Arouch knew he would not survive his looming encounter with the Neanderthals.

However, as long as the redhead did not survive the encounter either, Arouch would die content.

With his stone cudgel in his arms, Arouch picked his way in the twilight down the rocky slope leading to the tree line, his thickly calloused feet barely feeling the sharp edges of the rocks. A half-moon was bright in the sky. Bright enough to see by in the dark. Good. The only thing that did not bode well was distant storm clouds. If the clouds obscured the light of the moon and the stars, it would be impossible to track the Neanderthals in the dark.

With the night rapidly approaching, Arouch slipped into the forest, on the trail of the vile redhead and his wretched Neanderthal kin.

19

Arouch's father and uncles had taught Arouch well. Tracking the Neanderthal tribe through the forest was as easy as tracking a herd of straight-tusked elephants. The Neanderthals had done nothing to conceal their trail, thinking they had nothing to fear. They believed they had completely wiped out Arouch's tribe.

After trekking through the woods for hours, Arouch caught up with the Neanderthals. They had made camp for the night in the Silver Rock Clearing. The area was called that by Arouch's tribe and neighboring ones because it was a large clearing in the middle of the woods littered with shiny, silver-colored rocks. In the dark, the rocks glowed faintly, as if each contained their own moon. The rocks ran the gamut from as big as boulders to as small as pebbles.

According to tribe legend, generations ago Silver Rock Clearing had once been lush forest just like the surrounding greenery it was amid. But then, during a pitched battle between the god of the sky and the god of night, the head of the sky god's mighty stone ax came loose from its haft. The stone head fell, breaking up and burning in the night sky like a torch due to a curse from the devious night god, who had long envied the sky god's powerful weapon. Cheka had told Arouch that one of their distant ancestors had personally witnessed the fall of the ax head from the night sky. The same ancestor had also supposedly witnessed the night god put his finger over the sun, turning midday briefly into nighttime, so Arouch was not sure how much that distant ancestor's stories could be trusted. It had been a big moment in Arouch's young life when he realized not all the tribe's legends were real, especially the ones the men recounted from sacred visions they had after eating mushrooms that sprang up from cattle manure.

When the remnants of the sky god's ax head hit the forest floor, they slammed with such force they flattened trees and killed animals all around the point of impact. And so, Silver Rock Clearing was formed. The shimmering, silver-colored rocks in the clearing were all that remained of the sky god's once mighty stone ax.

Cheka had told Arouch their tribe's forebearers had experimented with using the divine rocks as weapons and tools, but the rocks were too soft and brittle. Also, long exposure to the always warm rocks made people sick; prolonged exposure killed them. It was a sign, the tribe believed, that man was not meant to meddle with the tools and weapons of the gods. As a result, Arouch's tribe and all the neighboring human tribes avoided Silver Rock Clearing. Even animals, it was said, steered clear of the area. Other than patches of sickly-looking grass, no vegetation grew in the clearing either.

The fact the Neanderthals settled down for the night in the clearing told Arouch they must be new to the area. The center of the large clearing must have looked like an ideal campsite to the barbarians: it offered a clear, unobstructed view on all sides, it was surrounded by woods one could readily retreat into, and the silver rocks provided light and warmth.

Creeping forward stealthily, Arouch easily avoided the sentries the Neanderthals had posted among the trees surrounding Silver Rock Clearing. The Neanderthals reeked like musk ox during rutting season, so it was easy to smell and avoid the shadowy sentries, even in the gloom of night.

Soon, Arouch crouched at the edge of the clearing, his heart beating like a hammer.

Other than the sentries in the surrounding woods, it appeared the entire tribe of Neanderthals was asleep in the clearing. Under the illumination of the moon, starry sky, and faintly glowing rocks, the Neanderthals' husky forms were shadowy lumps on the ground, like shallow graves.

I wish they all really were in graves, Arouch thought fiercely. Reluctantly, he pushed the savage thought aside. He could not kill all these Neanderthals by himself. He had to focus on his primary target.

Arouch put his short spear and stone cudgel down; carrying the weapons into the clearing would only hamper his movements. Getting so low to the ground he was almost crawling, Arouch inched forward into the clearing. Arouch silently prayed to the snake god, hoping the stealthy deity would guide his movements. Arouch crept cautiously, stopping every few feet, like he was stalking a skittish ibex or reindeer. If one of the sentries on the perimeter looked his way, he hoped to look like just another sleeping member of the tribe. He was less worried about the sentries, though, than he was about waking the people in the clearing. The sentries, after all, would concern themselves more with threats approaching the clearing than they would with people already in it.

Fortunately, there were no fallen tree branches in the clearing to accidentally snap, nor any leaves to crunch underfoot. There was only anemic grass and, here and there, faintly glowing rocks of varied sizes.

Moving like a shadow, Arouch searched the faces of the sleeping Neanderthals for the redheaded man whose features he had so carefully memorized.

After what seemed like an eternity, Arouch found the man. He lay alone. Arouch wasn't surprised filth like this hadn't been able to attract a mate. His long red hair looked like shimmering quicksilver under the pale night lights, forming a ghostly halo around the barbarian's head.

Arouch did not have to look for a suitable weapon. One was just feet away from the redhead—a silver rock the size of a deer skull. Arouch felt himself grin fiercely. The rock was light enough for a boy like Arouch to pick up, yet heavy enough to cave a man's head in. A sign from the gods of their approval.

His hands trembling with excitement, Arouch picked the rock up with both hands. He lifted it overhead, preparing to dash it into the skull of the sleeping savage.

A shudder of pleasure ran through Arouch.

He was about to avenge his mother.

But that was only a part of the joy singing in Arouch's heart and quickening his blood. The other part was because Arouch was about to take someone's life. During animal hunts, his father had sometimes let Arouch land the death blow. But Arouch had never killed a humanoid. He liked this feeling, holding someone's life in his hands.

For the first time, he felt equal to the animal hide signal of manhood around his loins. He felt like an adult.

No, not like an adult, Arouch realized as he held the warm, glowing rock overhead.

He felt like a god.

Savoring the feeling, drunk on it, Arouch made his first mistake:

"This is for Cheka, daughter of Ghull," Arouch said aloud.

The redhead's eyes snapped open at the words as the rock plunged toward his skull.

Moving faster than Arouch thought possible, the redhead rolled to the side. Arouch's falling rock struck only a glancing blow against the man's thick skull.

Before Arouch could raise the rock to try again, the man's muscular arm swept out like a striking snake. Arouch was bowled over. He fell.

Arouch's head hit something hard. He yelped. His vision went dark, darker even than the gloom surrounding him.

Cries of alarm from roused Neanderthals sang Arouch into a deep sleep.

20

Whenen Arouch awoke, it was bright, hot daytime. The bright sun stabbed at Arouch's throbbing head, making him blink.

No, he *tried* to blink. But he couldn't. It was like reaching for something with your right hand, only to realize the appendage was missing, with only a bloody stump remaining.

Arouch was physically incapable of blinking. He realized what must have happened: the Neanderthals had cut his eyelids off. He had heard tales of them doing that to their prisoners. The inability to blink led to sharp pains in the eyes and, eventually, blindness. Especially when exposed to bright sunlight, as Arouch now was.

Arouch had sharp pains in his eyes, all right—his eyes felt like hot coals shoved into his face. But he could still see, though his vision was limited and blurry.

Arouch ached all over, like he had been beaten. He looked down to assess his injuries. All he saw through his bleary, burning eyes was soil and silver rocks of various sizes.

He was buried in the ground from the neck down. The soil had been tightly packed around him. He could barely move at all, much less move enough to free himself.

But still he tried, straining and squirming as much as he could. He felt silver rocks, buried under the soil, cutting into his legs, arms and torso with their unnaturally warm sharp corners and edges.

It was no use. He was trapped. And even if he weren't, freeing himself wouldn't do any good. He was surrounded by Neanderthals. He could not see them through the worsening vision of his lidless eyes, but he could hear them.

Soon enough, he felt them. Once the Neanderthals realized he was awake, they kicked him and threw rocks at his exposed head. One particularly long rock-throwing session was punctuated by children's giggles. Neanderthal children, Arouch surmised, using his head for target practice.

Arouch accepted the abuse as stoically and steadfastly as he could. He counted as a victory each time he managed to keep himself from crying out in pain. Arouch wanted to deny these animals the pleasure of knowing the agony he was in.

HOURS AND THEN DAYS PASSED. AROUCH SOON LOST TRACK OF time as well as most of his vision. The Neanderthals continued to toy with him, abusing him for sport. He could not see at all through one eye thanks to a well-thrown rock; it had smashed into his eye socket like it was designed to fit there. All he could tell through his remaining working eye was whether it was day or night. He was feverish, one moment burning hot, the next freezing cold. The Neanderthals did not give him food or water. His tongue swelled up, making it impossible to speak and hard to close his mouth. Many of his teeth had been broken; bitter pus from jaw infections dripped down his throat.

Arouch knew that if the abuse or the sickness or the constant exposure to the elements didn't kill him, the lack of water surely would.

Death beckoned invitingly, promising a warm embrace. And yet Arouch resisted its siren call. If he succumbed to death, if he gave in to the wishes of his too weak flesh, he would never kill the redheaded monster. Back in the cave, he had sworn to the gods he would kill him. Arouch feared the wrath of the gods over a broken promise more than he did pain and anguish.

But not only that. When Arouch had the silver rock over that man's head, when he had held the man's very life in his hands, the taste had been sweeter than any fruit. More succulent than any roasted meat. Arouch had felt more alive than at any other time in his short life.

He wanted to feel that feeling again.

And so, instead of letting go and slipping into the beguiling darkness whispering to him, Arouch stubbornly held on, fighting to stay alive despite the lack of food, the lack of water, the pain of his failing body, and the unrelenting abuse by the Neanderthals. His hate sustained him. Hate for the redhead, yes, but also hate for the entire raiding party that had killed and raped Arouch's tribe. That life-sustaining hate grew like wildfire, fueled by the Neanderthals' continuous abuse. The inferno of Arouch's hate grew to encompass the entire Neanderthal tribe and then all of Neanderthal kind wherever they might be.

Though they resembled men, they were in fact monsters, Arouch concluded. Evil shadows of man that resembled him in form, but that were merely dark doppelgangers of true men. They were abominations who should not be suffered to live.

Wetness suddenly splashed Arouch's face. Completely blind now, the moisture startled him. Could it be there was some kindness in the Neanderthal heart after all? Could it be one of these brutes was giving him life-sustaining water?

No. Though Arouch was deaf in one ear thanks to repeated cuffs and he could barely hear out of the other due to the infection running through his body, he faintly heard a crack and then thunder. His head was drenched now, giving much needed relief to Arouch's fevered brow. High winds whipped his matted hair. There was another crack, with thunder rumbling on its heels.

A thunderstorm was raging around him, Arouch realized. The sky god was on the rampage. Arouch's tribe believed thunderstorms indicated the sky god's displeasure. Was the sky god angry with the Neanderthals' treatment of Arouch? Was this a sign?

Arouch tilted his aching head back. Rainwater trickled into his mouth through bloody, swollen lips. The water felt like ice against his burning flesh. Maybe it was Arouch's fevered imagination, but he thought he felt his hair begin to stand on end.

"If it is your will, mighty sky god," Arouch croaked, able to speak for the first time in days thanks to the refreshing water, "grant me the strength to destroy the Neanderthals, take their women, and erase their footsteps from the soil of the earth."

As if in response, lightning cracked and thunder boomed.

Arouch's body felt as though it was being ripped into pieces, like when a falcon dive-bombs a pigeon, resulting in a spray of flesh and feathers.

Suddenly, unexpectedly, impossibly, Arouch could see again. Completely naked, clean, and whole, he floated above where his body had been buried in the ground.

Where I'm still buried, he realized with a shock as he looked down at his dark head poking out of the ground. He was somehow in two places at once. Only his floating body could see, though; the body still stuck in the ground looked at the world with lifeless eyes. Torrential rain passed right through his floating body, as if he were not there.

The version of him still buried in the ground was being struck by lightning. Through the floating Arouch's miraculously healed eyes, the lightning strike seemed to be happening in slow motion. Arouch's floating form could somehow see underground and witness what was happening to the part of his body that was buried.

The lightning arced through Arouch's injured body, its incredible power drenching the silver rocks touching him. The lightning melted the rocks. The hot liquid metal began to flow into Arouch's body through his pores, like his body was a piece of meat plunged into boiling oil.

The liquid metal reacted with something deep in the core of Arouch's body. The reaction began to heal, strengthen, and change him.

The slow-motion lightning strike ended. Arouch's exposed head was completely healed. All the injuries inflicted on him by the Neanderthals were gone.

But something was wrong. Arouch's floating body looked down at still lifeless eyes.

With a flash of insight, Arouch realized *he* was what was wrong. The part of him that floated above his body was his soul. His spirit. He and his buried body were two parts of a whole. Without his soul, Arouch realized, his body was as dead as his tribe was.

He could join his family, Arouch thought. He could let go of what remained of him in this life and join his tribe in the next. There the shelters were always warm, the food was plentiful, health was assured, and no man or animal could make you afraid. Or so the tribe's stories foretold, and Arouch now knew for a certainty they were true. He felt it, deep in his core. Just as he felt the calls of his mother, other tribe members, and ancestors he had never even met. He could join them all in paradise and be happy forever.

He also somehow knew that if his soul rejoined his body, he would be bound to earth forever, never able to die, never able to see his mother again.

Arouch was sorely tempted to abandon his mortal coil and float to where his mother awaited him.

Then his resolved hardened.

No! He had made a promise to the gods. And to himself.

Arouch dropped back into his body. His earthbound body absorbed his floating form like a dry sponge sucking up water. Arouch's halves became one whole again.

Arouch blinked away the water pouring into his eyes. He could blink again because his eyelids had somehow regrown. Just as all of Arouch's wounds had been healed. An answer to his prayer. A gift from the sky god.

A gift Arouch would not squander.

With a thought, Arouch rose from the packed ground he was entombed in. It was laughably easy, as easy as rising from a cave floor after a night's slumber. Only instead of standing, Arouch hovered in midair above the hole the Neanderthals had intended to be his grave.

Floating in the air just as his soul had a moment before, Arouch looked down at his new body. For that was what it was: a new body. The liquified silver rocks had coated him from the neck down and hardened, like the scales of an armored reptile.

The rain pounded his new armor, washing it of the dirt and grime he had previously been trapped in. The metal encasing him gleamed in the glare of lightning. Arouch still had a child's body, but he was far more muscular than before. Corded muscles rippled under his silver armor like writhing snakes when he moved.

Acting on some unknowing impulse, he willed the metal encasing his body to disappear. The metal sank into his flesh like a stone dropped into a pond. Rain pelted Arouch's naked, uninjured flesh. With a thought, the metal bubbled back out of his skin and hardened, encasing him in silver armor once more, this time from head to toe.

Arouch had not merely been healed. He felt better than he ever had before. Better than he ever could've imagined.

Again acting on some deep instinct, Arouch extended an arm palm up.

In answer to Arouch's silent command, a thin bolt of lightning erupted from the dark clouds above and struck his hand. Arouch laughed with delight as the bolt danced on his palm. The lightning strike did not hurt at all. Quite the opposite. The lightning's power running through Arouch's body felt like bathing in the warm waters of a summer river.

The lightning felt like it was a part of him. No, not merely the lightning. The entire thunderstorm felt like an extension of Arouch's new body. As readily as opening or closing his fists, Arouch could command the powers of the storm at will.

Days ago, Arouch had felt like a god when he had been about to snuff out the redhead's life. Now, thanks to the sky god's kiss, he had the powers of a god to match.

It was time to put those powers to good use.

21

The Neanderthals were no longer in Silver Rock Clearing. They had taken shelter from the violent storm in the cover of the surrounding forest. Arouch felt their bodies huddled under the shelter of various trees. Rainwater dripped off the monsters. The rain was like Arouch's fingers, allowing him to sense everything it touched.

But, even without the rain, Arouch would have known exactly where all the Neanderthals were. Their spoors wafted to him like dozens of well-marked trails; their ragged breathing was as distinct as drums. All of Arouch's senses had been heightened. He now had the nose of a wolf, the eyes of an eagle, and the ears of a bat. Not to mention the strength of a bear. His mind worked more swiftly and efficiently, too, making connections between facts and drawing conclusions about information at a heightened pace. Arouch realized that, all his life, his mind had been as blind as his eyes had recently been. His supercharged mind was already sorting through all the things he had seen and heard in his short life, separating rumor from evidence, superstition from fact, and what he had been taught from what was actually true. For the first time, he could truly see.

Arouch floated approximately in the center of the clearing. He could direct the wind to carry him to his enemies, but Arouch wanted to expend some of the restless energy that bounced around in his body like a ball.

Arouch dropped out of the air onto the sodden ground. He began to run, toward the tree line, splashing mud and water in his wake. Faster and faster, faster and faster he ran, until his legs were but a silver blur. Exulting in the power that coursed through his enhanced body, Arouch knew he was running faster than the fastest cheetah.

The closest Neanderthals did not even know Arouch was approaching until he was right on top of the evil brutes. A barrel-chested male huddled with a female under the relative dryness of a tree with big leaves and low-hanging branches. Despite the darkness of the stormy night, Arouch saw the monsters with his enhanced vision as clearly as if they were next to a campfire.

Lightning turned night to day, letting the crouched monsters see Arouch's approach. Startled by Arouch's abrupt appearance, the Neanderthal male tried to stand as Arouch zoomed toward him. Arouch raised a clawed hand as he approached the monster, like Arouch was about to pluck an apple out of a tree.

Arouch's hand and arm slammed into the Neanderthal's stout chest like they were the tip and shaft of a well-thrown spear. His hand plunged into the Neanderthal's chest, boring through inches of muscle and snapping through thick bone. Wriggling like a speared fish, the Neanderthal was propelled backward.

Arouch stopped running. His feet and legs plowed a furrow in the wet ground as he skidded to a stop with his metal-encased hand and arm deep inside the Neanderthal's chest.

Though Arouch came to a halt, the Neanderthal did not. Propelled by the force of Arouch's impact with his chest, the Neanderthal kept flying backward. Thanks to Arouch's clenched fist, the Neanderthal's large heart was ripped right out of his chest.

With the gaping hole in his chest trailing blood, the Neanderthal sailed through the air. He smacked into the trunk of a nearby tree, crunching bones and cracking wood. The monster bounced off the thick trunk and hit the ground, dead before his flesh touched the wet earth.

The Neanderthal woman was shrieking loudly enough to wake the dead. Arouch spun and threw the still-beating heart at her as hard as he could.

The heart smashed into her ugly face, exploding like a dropped melon. She toppled over with a spray of blood, both her own and the heart's.

Arouch approached the prone female. Her legs were splayed open, exposing her hairy womanhood. Arouch thought about what the Neanderthal men had done to the women of his tribe. He would not do to the Neanderthal female what the Neanderthals had done to his relatives. The opening between the female's legs that so enthralled grown men held no allure to Arouch.

To ensure the female was dead, Arouch reached down and twisted her head all the way around. Her neck snapped like it was a dry twig instead of a heavily muscled body part.

Even with the noise of the storm, the commotion Arouch had raised in killing the two Neanderthals had not gone unnoticed. Neanderthals approached from all around, most armed. The redhead who killed Cheka was not among them.

Encircling Arouch, the monsters approached warily. Though they had not witnessed what happened to the dead Neanderthal male and female, with his shiny silver body, Arouch did not look like anything they had ever seen before.

Arouch laughed out loud. *I am the last thing they'll ever see*, he thought, raising his hands. He silently summoned a bolt of lightning from the sky.

A jagged white bolt ripped from the heavens. Darkness became the brightest of days. The accompanying thunderclap drowned out the panicked yelps of the surrounding Neanderthals.

Despite the lightning strike, the Neanderthals surrounding Arouch still stood. For Arouch had made the lightning hit him instead of the monsters. His now-glowing silver body blazed and crackled with energy absorbed from the lightning.

Frozen with fear and wonder, the Neanderthals gaped at Arouch. He literally smelled their fear. Arouch grinned, savoring their fear even more than the power coursing through his body.

The Neanderthals came to their senses, realizing the danger they were all in despite them outnumbering Arouch. To a man, they turned to run.

They barely took a step before Arouch discharged the energy he had absorbed from the lightning. It crackled out of him like jagged white spears, striking each of the Neanderthals square in their backs. The Neanderthals stopped dead in their tracks, trembling like leaves in a storm.

When Arouch finally ended his energy blast, the Neanderthals slumped to the ground. They were all dead. Their charred bodies sizzled and smoked under the falling rain like meat pulled from an open fire.

Arouch regarded the steaming bodies with deep satisfaction. *A good start*, he thought.

Using his enhanced senses, Arouch went hunting for the remaining Neanderthals. Including, most importantly, the redhead.

Arouch found the redhead almost immediately. Arouch knocked him out and tied him high up in a tree so Arouch could deal with the beast at his leisure.

Then Arouch stalked and slaughtered the rest of the Neanderthal tribe, from the oldest woman to the smallest child. It was laughably easy. Each time he killed a Neanderthal, Arouch did it in a different way to learn more about Neanderthal bodies and their threshold for pain. Using flint knapping, he made stone knives and dissected the last few Neanderthals he slaughtered to better familiarize himself with their anatomy.

It took less than two days to eradicate the redhead's tribemates and give himself a crash course on Neanderthal anatomy. Armed with his newfound knowledge, Arouch turned his attention back to the bound redhead who had raped and killed his mother.

First, Arouch started a fire using sparks his hands generated. He had discovered while killing the other Neanderthals that, not only could he control storms and their lightning, but the energy that composed lightning somehow had become a part of him. And the fire he created was under Arouch's command as well; he could enlarge it into a raging wildfire or extinguish it entirely, and anything in between. Arouch had not merely been touched by one of the gods, he realized—they had made him one of their number.

Then Arouch rendered the fat of a particularly plump Neanderthal woman's corpse by slowly heating her fatty flesh in a large bowl he fashioned from metal rocks from Silver Rock Clearing. With her fat, he greased a pole he'd made from an immature tree. The green pole was strong enough to support a Neanderthal's weight and long enough that someone atop it couldn't touch the ground. Arouch had sharpened one end of the pole, careful to not make the point too sharp. He dug a hole deep enough to cover the bottom quarter of the pole, but did not secure the pole upright in the hole just yet.

His preparations in place, Arouch flew like a bird to the top of the tree where the redhead was bound. The Neanderthal had been up here for days, exposed to the elements, without food or water. Even so, there was much life left in the monster. He pleaded with Arouch for his life as Arouch hovered before him. Arouch's hyperactive brain had by then deciphered the monster's primitive language.

Ignoring the beast's pleas, Arouch swiftly choked him unconscious with a tight metallic arm around his neck. With the burly beast slung around Arouch's shoulders like a dead deer, Arouch floated back down to the ground.

Arouch stripped the monster naked. His flesh crawled as he touched the poncho; it was the same one the monster had worn when he defiled Cheka. Arouch tossed the poncho into the fire. If only it were as easy to burn the memory of what this Neanderthal filth had done to his mother.

Arouch tied the unconscious Neanderthal's arms and legs with thick vines. Then, angling the sharpened end of the greased stake carefully, Arouch eased the stake's end into the naked Neanderthal's anus. The Neanderthal moaned softly as the stake entered his body, but did not awaken.

Arouch then lifted the stake and secured it in the hole in

the ground, with the Neanderthal impaled atop it. The man's dangling weight and the grease on the stake made the wood slide further into the man's insides.

The Neanderthal awoke screaming, his eyes bulging and rolling.

Arouch laughed.

The more the Neanderthal struggled, the faster the stake slid deeper into his body. The Neanderthal quickly realized this and stopped thrashing, slowing the greasy stake's inexorable slide, prolonging his life and agony. Thanks to Arouch's study of Neanderthal anatomy, the stake was angled in such a fashion as to not pierce any vital organs. Arouch had made the end of the stake not too sharp for the same reason.

At first, the redheaded Neanderthal begged for his life. Arouch only laughed more in response. He was having the time of his life.

After a day passed of the Neanderthal creeping further down the stake, the monster stopped begging for his life and started begging for death. Again, Arouch only laughed in response. Fortunately for Arouch and the joy he took in watching the redhead suffer, the Neanderthal was too weak to struggle now; a struggle would hasten the end of both the redhead's pain and of Arouch's pleasure. Eschewing eating and sleeping, Arouch didn't take his eyes off the Neanderthal for a second. Arouch didn't want to miss an instant of his suffering.

After a few days, the sharpened end of the stake burst through the back of the Neanderthal's head. Happiness wrestled with sadness in Arouch's heart as the redhead took his last shuddering breath. His death was bittersweet: sweet because Arouch had satisfied his oath to exact vengeance; bitter because Arouch's plaything was dead. Arouch never had enjoyed himself so much as while watching the Neanderthal suffer. It even eclipsed the joy of slaughtering the redhead's tribemates.

Arouch brightened. The thought of the redhead's tribemates chased away some of the sadness brought by the redhead's death.

After all, Arouch thought, the Neanderthals he had killed were not the only tribemates the redhead had. Weren't all Neanderthals everywhere the redhead's tribemates? A red deer was a red deer whether the deer stood here or a hundred miles away. Where it was located did not change its nature. It was always prey.

Similarly, the fact the Neanderthals in the rest of the world had not participated in the murder of Arouch's tribe and in Arouch's torture did not change their inherent nature: they were subhuman filth who should not be allowed to live.

The more Arouch thought about it, the more he realized his quest to kill the redhead and all his tribemates was at its beginning rather than its end. The world was full of the redhead's tribemates. How many Neanderthals remained? A few dozen tribes? Arouch had seen so little of the world, he didn't know. It was Arouch's sacred duty to rid the world of the subhuman filth. All of them, not merely the ones who'd camped at Silver Rock Clearing. Why else had the gods elevated Arouch to their level? The Neanderthals were stronger, more cunning, and more ruthless than humans like Arouch. Given time, they surely would eradicate humans and be the dominant hominid.

Arouch could not let that happen. The Neanderthals were a blight. A disease plaguing the earth.

The gods had made Arouch the cure.

22

A rouch's body grew abnormally quickly after he killed the redheaded Neanderthal. Within two months, he developed the body of a full-grown man despite being less than ten summers old.

Arouch's god-given powers strengthened and grew as the months passed as well. It quickly became clear that, in addition to Arouch's ability to control and harness the weather, he could control all natural forces, from earthquakes to plants, from water to animals. With each passing day it seemed like Arouch discovered a new ability, or a new use for an old one. That was all in addition to his ability to fly, his apparent invulnerability when the miraculous silver metal coated his skin, and his heightened strength, speed, senses, and intelligence. Also, injuries he suffered when not encased in metal quickly healed, as if they had never been.

Arouch put his evolving abilities to good use. In the months after the redheaded Neanderthal's death, Arouch hunted and killed more Neanderthals than he ever dreamed existed. Other than eat and sleep, all Arouch did was hunt and kill the monsters. His quest to rid the world of them consumed him.

However, regardless of how quickly and efficiently Arouch found and kill Neanderthals, there always seemed to be more. It was like trying to exterminate a nest of ants— the more you stomped them, the more there seemed to be. Contrary to Arouch's initial ignorant speculation, there were more Neanderthals in the world than he had thought. Incredibly more.

Arouch's travels quickly made him realize why there were far more Neanderthals than he had dreamed: the world was much larger than he had been taught as a child. The elders of his tribe had said the world was a big plate— large enough to contain all the resources men needed, but small enough that a man could walk across its surface and fall off its edge in a few weeks if he were foolish enough to walk continuously in a straight line.

The span of territory Arouch covered on foot and in the sky and the sheer number of Neanderthals he killed made him realize that, like so much else he had been taught as a child, the world being a flat plate was nonsense. Not only was the world round, but it was larger than the elders had said. Much larger.

Arouch took a break from hunting Neanderthals to ponder just how large the world must be. To calculate its size, Arouch needed a system of numbers and measurement. Unfortunately, Arouch's fellow men could only count as high as the number of their fingers and toes; any number beyond that was simply *many*. Distance was measured in how far a man could walk; anything further than a few days away was simply *far*.

Fortunately, Arouch was no longer like his fellow men.

After several days of pondering and many more days of intense scratching, erasing, and rescratching in the dirt, Arouch's super-charged mind created a system of numbers and measurement. He then invented geometry, algebra and trigonometry.

Afterward, he stuck two straight sticks in the ground many miles apart from one another and took careful measurement of the distance separating them and the length and angle of the shadows cast by those sticks at solar noon, when the sun was directly overhead. Armed with the data gleaned from the sticks and using the mathematical disciplines Arouch had invented, he made a rough estimate of the world's circumference.

That can't be right. Arouch took the measurements once more and did the math again.

The answer was the same shocking number as before. Arouch was stunned. The elders had not only been wrong about the size of the world, they had been wrong by several orders of magnitude. It was no wonder the Neanderthal blight persisted regardless of how many of the subhuman scum Arouch killed. There were far more than dozens of them. More, even, than hundreds. Perhaps many tens of thousands, Arouch theorized, considering the world's vast size. There were simply too many for one person to locate and kill, even someone like Arouch. What if he thought he completed his Neanderthal extermination quest but over-looked some of the monsters? The survivors would breed like roaches and continue to pollute the world.

Arouch considered the problem.

The answer was clear.

To ensure the Neanderthals' destruction, he needed more than one set of eyes, ears, and hands.

He needed help.

Arouch fell from the sky, landing in the middle of a forest encampment in a land far from where Arouch's tribe had lived. This was the semi-permanent home of a human tribe Arouch had secretly observed for a couple of days from far overhead, like a hawk surveying a band of ground-nesting birds. Numbering well over one hundred people, this was the largest tribe Arouch had found in his travels.

The smell of food and fire mixed with the stench of human waste in the tribe's camp. Arouch's sensitive nose twitched with distaste. Sorting through the things he had seen and heard, his agile mind made yet another miraculous connection: it was no wonder, he suddenly realized, that human life was so brief. By humans eliminating in the same place they ate, they were quite literally consuming disease and death. Not to mention humans having to constantly vie against the threats posed by hunger, harsh weather, man-eating animals, each other, and the vile Neanderthals. Soon, Arouch resolved, he would change all that.

The people of the tribe were smelly, dirty, and parasite-ridden; it was hard for Arouch to believe he was like them. They approached warily, gaping at him, clutching crude weapons but not yet attacking. Instead they muttered to each other with fear and wonder, not knowing what to make of Arouch, uncertain whether to flee or fight.

Arouch had to admit he did present a spectacle. Not only had he fallen from the heavens like a star, but his metallic body was bigger and taller than that of the largest men of the tribe. Also, for just this occasion, Arouch had slain a cave lion with his bare hands. Its golden-brown pelt dangled down his back like a cape, and its head surrounded Arouch's like a helmet. The lion's upper and lower fangs framed Arouch's face like sharp stalactites and stalagmites. Only a mighty warrior could kill a cave lion. Arouch wearing its pelt attested to his status more eloquently than words could ever express.

Arouch let the people's language wash over him as they murmured to each other about the stranger in their midst. Thanks to Arouch's acute hearing, their murmurs might as well have been shouts. Their tongue was different than that of Arouch's tribe, but it shared some linguistic commonalities. In less than a minute, Arouch's facile mind understood enough of their language to allow him to speak in it:

"Take me to your leader," he said.

Still muttering amongst themselves uncertainly, the tribe members surrounded Arouch and, alert to any aggression from him, escorted him deeper into the tribe's territory.

The tribe's leader was a squat, husky man named Ghekk. Arouch reckoned Ghekk had seen the passage of thirty-five summers. Old for a world where human life was brutal and short. Ghekk's scarred body and two missing fingers testified to all the scrapes the man had survived. He wore furs and a crude crown made of raptor feathers, indicating his high status. Ghekk eyed Arouch's lion regalia greedily as he brandished a stone ax. It was obvious what Ghekk was thinking: soon, Arouch's adornments would be his own. After all, regardless of Arouch's size and intimidating appearance, Ghekk was surrounded by dozens of his own people. By now the entire tribe had turned out to gawk at the unusual stranger in their midst.

"I am Arouch," he announced to Ghekk, the tribe's

language still tasting foreign to his tongue. Though Arouch did not speak the words particularly loudly, with a mental command Arouch made the wind carry his words to the entire tribe like they had been trumpeted by an elephant. "I am a god. You are but a man. Surrender leadership of this tribe to me willingly and I will let you live."

Ghekk looked surprised by Arouch's words. Then he laughed, followed a beat later by the rest of the tribe. People were as hierarchical as a wolf pack, Arouch thought, with the timid, weak and stupid following the lead of the bold, strong and cunning.

Ghekk's laughter neither angered nor surprised Arouch. A man who had risen to lead such a large tribe had undoubtedly been challenged many times before. Such a man did not frighten easily, especially when his followers' presence bolstered his courage and gave reason to conspicuously display it.

Power is never surrendered, Arouch realized. *It is always taken.*

Arouch stepped toward Ghekk. Several armed men moved to bar his path. Arouch could easily push through them or drop them where they stood, but he had no desire to hurt or kill unnecessarily. These were not Neanderthals.

Looking over the heads of the men stopping him from advancing, Arouch spread his empty arms wide and said to Ghekk, "Are you such a cowardly old woman you're afraid to face an unarmed man?"

The two men stared at each other, neither willing to look away and show submissiveness. Arouch read uncertainty behind Ghekk's surface bravado, but he knew Ghekk could not ignore his challenge. If Ghekk displayed cowardice today, ambitious young bucks in the tribe would be at his throat tomorrow. And they would not be so foolish as to challenge Ghekk unarmed.

Ghekk barked a command. The men barring Arouch's path fell back, as did the rest of the people surrounding Arouch, forming a large circle around Ghekk and Arouch.

Ghekk approached Arouch warily, with the stone ax in his whole hand and a rock knife in the other. Arouch merely stood placidly, with his arms folded, letting the tribal chief get close. Ghekk's wariness spoke well of him, Arouch thought. A lesser man would be confident he would prevail against an unarmed stranger.

Without warning, Ghekk attacked. The ax slashed. It slammed into Arouch's still torso. Stone clanged against metal, and the ax head shattered. Fragments flew everywhere.

Ghekk was left holding a headless wooden handle. He looked astonished, but that did not stop him from slashing at Arouch with the knife. Arouch knew if the knife hit him, it would suffer the same fate as the ax.

It did not hit Arouch, though.

Arouch spun out of the way, toward Ghekk, moving behind him. He moved as quickly as a striking snake and as gracefully as flowing water. In the blink of an eye, Ghekk was slashing at thin air and Arouch stood behind him.

Not wanting to embarrass Ghekk by prolonging the inevitable, Arouch cupped Ghekk's ears and twisted his head. With several meaty pops, a ripping of flesh and a crimson spray of blood, Ghekk's head twisted all the way around until Ghekk's face and his back pointed in the same direction.

"You fight well, my friend," Arouch murmured to Ghekk's face. But Ghekk could no longer hear Arouch. The glassiness of his eyes showed he was already gone to where all men were eventually fated to go. Arouch let go of Ghekk's almost completely decapitated head. The chief's body tottered for a moment, then collapsed into a heap.

Stunned, frozen in place, none of the onlookers said a word. The fight had ended more quickly than it had begun.

Arouch's display of power and dominance was not over, however.

Arouch whistled loudly. The whistle was not actually necessary; he had already mentally summoned the creatures who roosted silently in the surrounding trees. However, Arouch wanted to make it obvious to the tribe who controlled the creatures. To rule, one must not only possess power, but conspicuously display it.

The trees exploded with movement and feathers. A bevy of birds of various species descended on Ghekk's dead body. They covered him like a feathered blanket writhing with different colors. The birds screeched and cawed as they fought over the choicest morsels of flesh. It would not be long before picked-clean bones were all that remained of Ghekk's beefy body.

Arouch lifted himself into the air. He hovered several feet over Ghekk's body and the mass of feeding birds. The tribe looked up at him, equal parts awed and terrified.

Arouch surveyed the people. *His* people. Like him, except untouched by the gods. Though some looked as well-fed as Ghekk had been, many more were almost gaunt with malnourishment. Plump and thin alike were filthy and riddled with fleas, lice, and even worse parasites. Arouch sensed the tiny creatures feeding happily on and within the tribe.

Arouch had thought he needed people like these to help him eradicate the Neanderthals. Arouch now realized they and people like them needed *him*. Only with his wise guidance could humanity fulfill its potential, which currently lay dormant due to the demands and brutality of the state of nature men lived in. Man could not turn his attention to higher pursuits if his stomach was growling, a leopard was stalking him, or a Neanderthal was at his throat.

A realization hit Arouch like the lightning bolt that elevated him from man to god:

With great power came the great responsibility to rule.

"I am Arouch," he boomed once more, again letting the wind carry his words to all the tribe, including those out of sight, huddling fearfully behind trees. "I am a god. I am now the leader of this tribe. Anyone who wants to leave may do so now without being harmed. Anyone who stays will follow me without question. In return, I guarantee that you and your children will never go hungry again. Furthermore, I promise that many more will join us. At the end of a spear's point, if necessary. Soon the whole world will lie at our feet."

Arouch paused, letting his words sink in. Only the tumult of the feeding birds marred the quiet.

"Who is with me?" Arouch asked.

One of the young men who had barred Arouch's path stepped forward. "I am!" the wooly-haired young man cried as he hoisted his spear overhead.

The young man's enthusiasm spread like a fever. Soon almost the entire tribe was shouting Arouch's name and brandishing weapons.

Arouch did not let the display go to his head. He knew that, in a crowd, passion spread like wildfire. It was only after time doused the heat of passion that Arouch would be able to ascertain who truly was a friend and who was a hidden foe. Ghekk doubtless had friends and relatives in the tribe who would try to kill Arouch or sabotage his efforts the instant his back was turned.

Arouch let the shouts of the tribe wash over him. He closed his eyes and luxuriated in it. It was good to have a tribe again. He had been so obsessed with pursuing Neanderthals that he had not realized how much he missed belonging to a larger group.

He would separate the tribe wheat from the chaff later.

For now, the tribe was his.

23

"It's done, my lord," Bheb said, looking up at Arouch as he sat on his high obsidian throne. The two men were alone in Arouch's throne room. It was the largest chamber in a series of caves that served as Arouch's headquarters. Torches mounted on the walls provided light. This form of torch was one of Arouch's many inventions. Dipped in sulfur mixed with lime, the torches stayed lit for so long that Arouch's people considered them nothing short of miraculous. Holes Arouch had strategically bored in the cavern walls with his powers provided both fresh air and egress for the torches' fumes.

Bheb was the wooly-haired man who had been the first to support Arouch's takeover of the tribe a few years ago. In that time, Bheb had become Arouch's most trusted lieutenant. *Completely trustworthy*, Arouch thought, *though not too bright*. Arouch valued slavish loyalty over intelligence, anyway. People who thought too much were dangerous. Arouch knew that better than anyone—he considered himself the smartest and therefore the most dangerous person in the world. He planned to keep it that way. Hence the mission he had sent Bheb on.

"Are you sure all the rocks have been removed from Silver Rock Clearing?" Arouch pressed his lieutenant.

"Yes. I supervised their removal myself," Bheb said proudly. Though Bheb had just returned from a months-long journey to and from Silver Rock Clearing, no evidence of the arduous trip was visible on his person. The dampness of his dark hair and the absence of pungent body odor indicated Bheb had bathed before reporting to Arouch. Arouch was a stickler for cleanliness and demanded it of all his followers. Arouch's calculations projected that the soap he had invented and the sanitation measures he had instituted since assuming a leadership position would lengthen his followers' average lifespan by at least a decade.

"And you hid the rocks as I ordered? Somewhere where no one will accidentally stumble upon them?"

"Yes, my lord. Are you certain you don't want to know where we hid them?"

"Quite certain," Arouch said firmly. "What I don't know, I can't tell." Arouch considered it unlikely he would ever not guard his tongue, but better safe than sorry. Especially because he had grown quite fond of the fermented beverages he had experimented making. They sometimes made him quite foolish until their influence wore off.

Arouch's powers had made him a god. If someone else was struck by lightning while surrounded by the rocks, perhaps that person would be elevated to godhood as well. As things stood, Arouch reckoned his unique abilities made the achievement of his long-term goals inevitable. Someone else sharing Arouch's abilities might derail or outright deny that inevitability. In addition to that, some primal instinct warned Arouch the silver rocks could somehow be used to negate his powers.

"And what of the men who helped you excavate and hide the rocks?" Arouch asked Bheb.

"All dead. Executed as soon as we reentered the village. They spoke of the magic rocks to no one." The twenty-five men had been hand-picked by Arouch for this task. Composed of malcontents, criminals, and men with no strong family ties, few in the tribe would mourn the dead men. Though Arouch had little to fear from tribal unrest. A few people had tried to assassinate Arouch in the early days of his reign, but mass executions of the would-be assassins, their families, and all their friends had set an example and forestalled further attempts.

"Good. No one can know where the rocks now rest." Arouch stood, stepped off the stone dais the black throne rested on, and clasped Bheb on the shoulder with his metal-plated hand. Bheb's eyes widened in awe at the unexpected gesture. Arouch made a point to not touch his followers casually. For him to rest his hands on someone was a great honor. It was rumored Arouch's touch was so potent, it could raise men from the dead. Arouch could do no such thing, of course, but he didn't stifle the rumor. When ruling a superstitious people, myth was often more important than reality.

"You have served loyally at my side," Arouch said to Bheb, looking down at the much shorter man. "In many ways, you're the brother I never had. The only real friend I have. I will sorely miss you."

Confusion crept into Bheb's awestruck eyes. "Miss me?"

Completely trustworthy, Arouch thought again sadly, *though not too bright.*

Arouch let some of his body's energy surge through his

arm, into his hand, and through Bheb's body. Bheb's body stiffened and shuddered. The smell of charred meat filled the air.

It only took a couple of seconds before Arouch heard Bheb's heart stop. To ensure it did not resume, Arouch continued letting his energy flow into Bheb.

Finally, Arouch removed his hand. Bheb's smoking dead body toppled and hit the ground with a thump. Arouch looked down at him. Unlike when Arouch killed a Neanderthal or an enemy who opposed him, joy did not fill Arouch's heart. Instead, sadness lay there like a leaden lump. Arouch had spoken truly earlier—Bheb *had* been like a brother to him. An older brother in fact; despite his adult appearance, Arouch had not even reached his teen years yet. Regardless of his affection for Bheb, however, his trusted lieutenant could not be permitted to live. Bheb had been the sole remaining person to know where the silver rocks were hidden. As trustworthy as Bheb had been, the only sure way to keep a secret was if all the people who knew it were dead.

Arouch suddenly got the strangest feeling he was not alone, like someone was looking over his shoulder. He looked up and caught a quick glimpse of a small brown-skinned girl and a pale-skinned man, holding hands as they stared at Arouch.

Like a shadow chased away by exposure to the sun, the two disappeared the moment Arouch tried to focus on them. Arouch strained his every sense, but the two were gone.

The apparitions troubled Arouch. Even an animal as stealthy as a wolf left behind the smell of fur, the sound of paws clawing the ground, or a disturbance of the air as the animal retreated. Not these two—the girl and the man left behind no trace Arouch's acute senses could detect. It was as if they had not been real, mere hallucinations triggered by Arouch's grief over Bheb.

Arouch might have accepted that explanation if this were the only time he had seen the apparitions. It was not. Arouch had caught quick glimpses of the two together over the past few years, and of the girl alone for what felt like Arouch's entire life. When Arouch had discussed the visions with Bheb, Bheb had suggested the strange people were heralds sent by the gods. Since Arouch had risen so far so fast, the heralds were no doubt assisting Arouch in his rise, the gullible Bheb had assured him. They were a sign of good fortune. Arouch was not so sanguine about the apparitions. They often seemed to look at Arouch with judging, disapproving eyes, as they had just now as they watched Arouch stand over Bheb's body. Moreover, something about the girl in particular made Arouch wary, as if she were an ancient foe despite her immature appearance. Perhaps it was like a child being instinctively wary of a snake—the child did not have to be bitten by one to know it was not his friend.

Having matters of state to attend to, Arouch tried to dismiss thoughts of the apparitions from his mind. Even so, he could not shake the feeling the two were somehow still here, watching his every move.

Leaving Bheb where he lay, Arouch donned the same lion regalia he had worn when he'd confronted Ghekk. Arouch wore it whenever he dealt with official business.

Arouch warned the guards outside the animal hide flaps enclosing the throne room that no one was permitted to enter in Arouch's absence. He strode to meet with his satraps, thinking of Bheb on the way.

The tribe had previously been told Bheb and the twenty-five men he led had been scouting new territory for the ever-expanding tribe. Now Arouch would announce the twenty-five men plotted against Arouch, hence their executions. As for Bheb, no one would believe it if Arouch told them the ever-loyal Bheb had been a part of the treasonous plot. Instead Arouch would tell the tribe the plotters had tried to recruit Bheb, and Bheb pretended to go along with them until the group returned from their journey and Bheb could report their treachery to Arouch. Smitten by Bheb's loyalty, the sky god had swept the loyal man into the heavens and rewarded Bheb with a seat at his renowned Table of Eternal Feasting.

Not everyone in the tribe would swallow that tall tale, of course. But most would. There seemed to be something inherent to human nature that, the bigger the lie, the more believable it was.

Arouch made a mental note to take Bheb's body out of the caverns in the dead of night, fly him far from here, burn his body, and scatter the ashes. Arouch would even take the time to bury the bones so predators wouldn't gnaw on them. It was the least he could do for his loyal brother.

Pushing thoughts of Bheb aside for now, Arouch entered the cavern in which five of his satraps were assembled. They hastily got to their feet, competing with one another to show Arouch the most respect the fastest. These five were the local leaders of the closest segments of Arouch's ever-expanding tribe. There were six other satraps, but they were not present as they were too far away to make the trip to Arouch's headquarters. Arouch would fly to those far-flung satraps in the coming days and tell them what he was about to tell these five.

Arouch set general tribe policy; his satraps executed the details of that policy depending on the specific circumstances of the part of the tribe they led. As Arouch's tribe now consisted of many thousands spanning an ever-widening territory, a system of central command but local execution made the most sense to Arouch. Gone were the days when Arouch could intelligently micromanage the affairs of the entire tribe.

Constantly acquiring new lands and new resources, Arouch's tribe was spreading like water poured on a flat rock. Each group of humans Arouch's tribe encountered during its expansion was met with a simple directive: *Join, or die.* When given a glimpse of how much better life was as a member of Arouch's tribe, most people joined voluntarily. After all, under Arouch's leadership, life was no longer a touch-and-go daily struggle for survival. Tribe members led longer and better lives than humans previously had thanks to Arouch's many innovations and reforms, including sanitation, advanced weaponry, crop cultivation, and animal husbandry.

If a group did not join Arouch's tribe voluntarily, the second half of the directive was executed: the men and children were killed, and the women were taken as bed wenches.

Despite Arouch having an adult male's body, he had no interest in those bed wenches. Or any other woman, for that matter. At least not in a sexual way. The mere thought of sexual relations turned his stomach. It brought to mind the image of that redheaded monster grunting over his mother's struggling body. Perhaps Arouch's revulsion regarding sex would change when his chronological age caught up with the apparent age of his body, but Arouch doubted it.

It was just as well. Women seemed to dominate the thoughts of most men, especially the young ones. Arouch not being a slave to bodily urges gave him ample time to concentrate on more important matters. Like the foundational reason for why he had forged this powerful tribe.

Arouch motioned for his satraps to resume their seats. Once they had settled down again, he said, "As you know, our people and Neanderthals are ancient enemies and competitors for food and other resources. The evil Neanderthals have been content with crimes of opportunity, raiding human settlements when those settlements were not large enough to defend themselves.

"Until now. Intelligence from spies scattered around the world indicates the Neanderthals are organizing. No longer content with opportunistic raiding, they now intend to attack us humans systematically. To kill us and take our women and resources."

Arouch paused to let his satraps' angry muttering die down. There was no grand Neanderthal conspiracy, of course; the monsters were too individualistic to cooperate on such a grand scale. But, as with Bheb ascending into heaven, when you were selling a lie, lie big. "We must strike before they are ready," Arouch thundered. "Kill them before they kill us."

"Which ones do you mean?" one of his satraps interjected. "Which tribes?"

"All of them!" Arouch snarled. His fist smacked his palm angrily; the Neanderthal conspiracy might not have been genuine, but his rage was. "We'll keep some of the women as bed wenches if we must. But every Neanderthal man and child must die. If humanity is to live, Neanderthals must die!"

Arouch paused again, blinking. The two apparitions were back. The man and the girl stood facing Arouch, behind his chattering satraps, holding hands as they always did. Their bodies threatened to fade away just as they had many times before, like fish squirming off a hook.

Acting on some unthinking instinct, Arouch latched

onto the couple's bodies with his mind, forcing them to solidify and stay visible. The two came into vivid focus; everything else in the cavern froze. Arouch's mind suddenly felt clearer, like something weighing on it had gone away.

Arouch got his first good look at the two who had dogged Arouch's every step over the past few years. They were whispering together, not even looking at Arouch. The brown-skinned girl looked like she had seen no more than four or five summers. She wore a shiny ceremonial dress unlike any Arouch had ever seen before. The man was taller than the men Arouch was used to and, based on the fact he was not lean and sinewy like most men, he was far better nourished. The man had pale skin, paler than even Neanderthals, who tended to be lighter-complected than humans. Though he was not dressed as the girl was, he too was not dressed in any way Arouch recognized. Arouch wondered what sort of strange animals had been used to fashion the garments they wore.

Arouch's satraps were unmoving, like they were encased in invisible ice. Other than the couple holding hands and Arouch himself, everything else was deathly still and quiet. Even the torches on the walls had stopped flickering and hissing.

Arouch raised a closed metal fist. Energy sparked around it as he pointed it at the girl and the man.

"Who are you?" Arouch hissed at the two.

24

_____

L im and I were stunned when Arouch seemed to speak to us. No longer were we riding piggyback in his mind. Instead, we stood across the cavern from him, looking at his glowing fist. Tendrils of electrical energy danced on it like it was a Tesla coil.

Looking at that glowing fist felt like looking down the barrel of a loaded gun. I wasn't an expert on caveman diplomacy, but this hardly seemed like an *Ugh! Me come in peace* moment.

"He can see us," I whispered to Lim urgently, not taking my eyes off Arouch and that ominous fist.

"Of course he can't. That's impossible." For the first time since I had known her, though, Lim sounded less than certain of herself.

"Who are you?" Arouch, aka Progenitor, repeated. His harsh, guttural language sounded like a drowning dog. I somehow understood his words even though they weren't English, just as I had understood everything he said when Lim and I were inside his head. "Answer, or I'll strike you down where you stand." The electricity around his fist crackled menacingly. Other than he, Lim and I, everyone and everything else in the cavern were frozen, like a paused movie.

"Okay, maybe he can see us," Lim reluctantly conceded. "Though I don't understand how. But none of this is real, not in a physical sense. These are his memories. He can't hurt us here. That I'm certain of."

I wasn't so sure. Fate hadn't blessed me with a Spidey-sense, but hard experience had taught me to not ignore alarm bells going off in my head.

And now they were clanging like a five-alarm fire was about to incinerate us.

Which was why I was on the move before the electrical blast left Progenitor's fist. Snatching Lim off the ground, I flung myself between Lim and Progenitor's fist, trying to spin us out of the way.

I reacted in just the nick of time. The blast missed Lim but grazed me, scorching my side before Lim and I hit the rock floor. The graze felt like being stabbed by a red-hot knife.

The sparkling blast hit the cavern wall right behind where Lim and I had stood an instant before.

Boom! Rocks went flying. A hole was blasted in the previously solid rock face.

I've never been one to stay where I clearly wasn't wanted. I scrambled to my feet. With Lim tucked under my arm like a wriggling sack of potatoes, I jackrabbited through the hole, and took off running into pitch darkness. My burning side throbbed with every step. I didn't know where I was going, and didn't much care. Anyplace where Progenitor wasn't doing his best Thor impersonation would do.

Another electrical blast zoomed past me, just feet overhead, lighting up the dark area I ran in. I was no longer in

Progenitor's warren of caves as I had assumed I was. Instead, I ran on and amid roiling dark storm clouds. It was as if running on water vapor had miraculously become a part of my power set.

I didn't stop to puzzle over what was happening; I was too busy putting distance between us and Progenitor. I didn't know how I felt him pursuing us, but I did. It felt like, any second now, his metal fist would wrap around my throat. I felt naked and completely vulnerable without my powers.

Lim was squirming so much I almost dropped her. "Put me down!" she squealed. "The mighty Mastermind is the rescuer, not the rescued!"

"Oh shut up!" I spat. "This isn't a game." The world's youngest octogenarian was showing her immaturity again. Lim had never been in a life or death situation before, but I had. Too many times. This definitely was one of them. I felt it in my gut. I knew it just as sure as I knew Progenitor was chasing us. Lightning strikes sizzled near us, each one closer than the last.

"Let me go, you lummox!" Lim cried, pounding my sides with her tiny fists. "You're taking us the wrong way, deeper into Progenitor's mind. You're going to get us lost! I know the way out."

Though it felt as counterintuitive as a deer skidding to a halt in the face of a pursuing grizzly bear, I slowed to a stop. Panting, I put Lim down on the cloud I'd been running on; it seemed as solid as concrete despite its appearance. I was careful to not let go of her. I hadn't forgotten what she said about being lost forever in Progenitor's mind if I released her. After what I'd seen, this dude's mind was the last place I wanted to take up permanent residence. "Why didn't you say you knew the way out?" I wheezed.

"I just did," Lim sniffed. "Now shut your trap. I gotta focus."

Closing her eyes and still clutching my hand, Lim extended her free hand with her index finger pointed. With her face screwed up in concentration, she spun in a slow circle like a dowser searching for water. Meanwhile, I fretted with impatience mixed with a heavy dollop of fear. The lightning strikes were so close now, they would be dancing atop our heads soon. On the plus side, they were the only things letting me see. On the negative side, death. Given a choice, darkness please.

Lim's outstretched arm finally dipped. Her index finger pointed down at a steep angle. Her eyes flew open. "Got it!" she said triumphantly. "The road to freedom. Let's go."

As if rocket-propelled, Lim shot down through the clouds in the direction her finger pointed. I was pulled behind her, the tail to her kite. The clouds we zoomed through felt like countless taloned fingers clawing our bodies, trying to hold us back.

Soon we exited the dark storm clouds. The beach and promontory we had left seemingly so long ago became visible again. But it was not the sunny beach and promontory we had left behind. The storm clouds that previously had been far off in the distance were now directly overhead, completely blocking the sun, darkening everything. A thunderstorm raged, whipping up the waters of the ocean. Rain poured in heavy sheets. It burned my eyes and skin like it was mixed with sulfuric acid.

We landed on the promontory. The light was so dim and the rain was so heavy, the grass seemed black instead of the vivid green it had once been.

Lim looked around like someone who had come home to find the dog she was fostering had ripped the house apart and might leap out of the gloom to rip her apart too. Between her Mastermind costume and being sopping wet, she looked like Krypto the Superdog half-drowned in a pool. "This is bad," Lim shouted over the storm's tumult. "This is really, really bad. He's nearly free from his confines. I'll have to try to soothe him back to sleep."

I'll have to try. I didn't like the uncertainty in her voice. "Don't you think you can do it?" I yelled back, blinking stinging water out of my eyes and shivering. Though the rain burned like acid, temperature-wise it was ice cold. I was chilled to the bone. This storm might be taking place in my head, but it sure as heck felt real.

"I think I can." Lim hesitated. "I hope I can." Cocky Lim was sometimes annoying; unsure Lim was terrifying. "Shake a leg and recruit the rest of the people we discussed. Do whatever it takes. We may not have much time left. You need to have your team in place before Progenitor busts loose."

Our jaunt into Progenitor's mind had answered some questions, but raised plenty others in their place. Lim was the only person I knew with the answers. "Will we talk again?"

"I'll reach out once I get Mr. Black Hat to bed again. For now, get out of here. You're a distraction; I need my full concentration."

Lim shoved my leg, trying to push me away. She looked stunned when nothing happened. She pushed again, harder this time. Once more, nothing happened.

"What's wrong?" I shouted, the storm nearly drowning out my words.

"I don't know. That should've awakened you. If you're still here when Progenitor wakes—" Lim trailed off. "Let's just say the ballgame will be over before we even get a chance at bat. Lemme see what's wrong."

Lim popped off the ground, getting eye level with me. Gazing into my eyes, her own usually dark ones turned clear and shone, just as they had when she had transported us into Progenitor's mind. I felt the strangest pressure in my head, like I was being mentally frisked. I had the sudden urge to cover myself, as if Lim were staring at me naked.

"I see the problem," she yelled after a few moments. "Progenitor has wrapped his mind around yours like it's an octopus' tentacles. I'll have to jar you loose."

Lim's arm reared back. I had seen this movie before and hadn't enjoyed it the first time. "Hold on to your hat," she said grimly. "This is gonna hurt."

Lim's palm slammed into my forehead. Pain lanced through my head like a flaming sword was stabbing me. I got a mental image of Progenitor and I somehow simultaneously occupying the same space and then abruptly being ripped apart.

I did not merely see the ripping, however. I felt it.

I screamed. I was not the only one screaming. The raging storm screamed too. It sounded like the whine of countless buzz saws slicing through metal. The force of the noise made my insides shudder, like I stood in front of a high-powered subwoofer during a rock concert.

Everything went dark. Lim and the stormy promontory disappeared. I hurtled through the dark void of space, toward a pinprick of light that got bigger and brighter as I fell toward it.

The light consumed me, searing my flesh like a laser, blasting me into nothingness.

———

SCREAMING, HEAD POUNDING, SIDE HURTING, I SAT UP.

I panted like a locomotive. My hands danced over my wet body, ensuring everything was where it was supposed to be despite feeling like I had been blasted into nonexistence an instant before.

It took a few confused moments for me to realize I was back in bed in New Sentinels mansion. I was wet because I was sweating, not because an acid rainstorm had drenched me.

Staggering into the bathroom, I flipped on the light and saw in the mirror what I expected to see: a small handprint in the center of my forehead like a brand.

But not only that. I lifted my shirt to examine my throbbing side.

I found a black and blue raised bruise right where Progenitor's blast of lightning had grazed me. It undulated slowly, like a small black squid had crawled under my skin and was lazily writhing its tentacles.

25

"You're saying this Progenitor lunatic is responsible for the extinction of the Neanderthals?" Isaac asked.

Both in costume, he and I were on our way to recruit the next team member Lim had identified. We flew in the same New Sentinels jet we had traveled to Arkansas in. This time, Isaac was piloting. The jet rocked as we hit turbulence over New Jersey. Isaac changed altitude to get us out of it. I was a better pilot than Isaac—it was one of the few things I was better at than he was—but I resisted the temptation to needle him about it. Our chilled relationship had warmed somewhat lately, and I didn't want to derail the rapprochement.

"Apparently. I didn't actually see Arouch and his men wipe out the Neanderthals. But the events I witnessed took place right around the time the Neanderthals died off as a subspecies."

"The events you *think* you witnessed," Isaac said. "I'm still not convinced Lim is who she says she is. And even if she is the same Lim who's doing her Chinese knockoff version of Sleeping Beauty, that doesn't mean what she's showing you is real. Lim is an Omega-level telepath, not an Omega-level Heroic telepath. Meaning she could be a comatose bad guy. Uh, bad gal. She could be leading us down the primrose path for some unsavory reason we don't understand."

"How do you explain the black pus Doctor Agrawal drained from where Progenitor blasted me, then? It contains electrical and psionic energy plus trace DNA from someone other than me. It's unlike anything he's ever seen before." Though Agrawal did not think the writhing stuff posed a threat to anyone, to be on the safe side he had sealed it inside a shatterproof container and enclosed it in a force field in the mansion infirmary. I told Minerva to monitor the substance around the clock and instructed her to blast it back into the Stone Age with the mansion's interior defenses if it did anything more threatening than wiggle.

Despite those precautions, I would've felt better about the stuff if I chucked it into space. I felt like a masochist, living under the same roof as the tapeworm that had been teased out of him. Watching the black goo stretch and contort like a giant amoeba made my skin crawl. Looking at it gave me the same feeling of dread I got when looking at the storm clouds in Lim's dreamworld. As much as I didn't like it, I would have to learn to live with the unease of sleeping under the same roof as whatever the writhing substance was. It was, after all, our only tangible connection to Progenitor.

Or at least I knew it was. Isaac wasn't convinced. He said, "The fact I can't explain the black goo doesn't mean that our little tar baby is the residue of an attack from some prehistoric superpowered serial killer."

"Tar baby?" I repeated. "How come you get to use a term

like that but, if I said it, you'd organize a Black Lives Matter march outside the mansion?"

"It's a reference to Uncle Remus' Br'er Rabbit story, not the pejorative for my people."

"Los Angelenos?"

"Black people, smart-ass. Thinking of black people when I say tar baby goes to show where your head's at, Mr. South Carolina. You can take the man out of the Confederate state, but not the Confederate state out of the man." Isaac took his eyes off the jet's viewscreen long enough to shoot me a look. "Don't think I don't know what you're doing. You're trying to get me off the subject of your pint-sized girlfriend."

"She's not my girlfriend."

"You're right. My bad. She's your sleeping psychic sensei who's taking you on strolls through the mind of a guy who's equal parts Captain Caveman, Vandal Savage, and a Neanderthal-hunting Dexter. If that sounds preposterous, it's only because it is."

I felt my jaw tighten. I itched to respond, but didn't. There was nothing I could say to make Isaac believe the way I believed. If I tried to convince him, it would devolve into a fight and I'd wind up biting Isaac's head off.

I didn't like the way Isaac mocked Lim. She and I were in an exclusive club as Omega-level Metas. Just as all Metahumans shared a bond—the blessing and the curse of superpowers—Lim and I shared an even more special bond. She was like a long-lost sister I'd always heard about but was just now getting to know.

Maybe I should have taken Lim up on inventing a secret handshake.

I admired Lim. She had spent most of her life trying to prevent Progenitor from escaping and wreaking havoc again. She had seen a need and filled it without any expectation of reward. She did what she had to do for the greater good. Just like I tried to. Unlike Isaac, Shay, Truman, Draymond Miller and everyone else, Lim understood the pressure I was under. She operated under the same pressure: to keep the world safe at all costs, regardless of the sacrifices one had to make and the corners one had to cut. Though she was not a licensed Hero, her eighty-plus year sacrifice made her a hero in all the ways that mattered.

On top of admiring Lim, I liked her. Yes, she was arrogant and emotionally stunted. But she was also quirky, interesting, and fun in a *since we're stuck here on this bloody battleground, we might as well play soccer with this skull* sort of way. I was growing fond of her despite how irritatingly smug she often was. I hated leaving her alone to deal with a rampaging Progenitor. I didn't know what I could do to help her had I stayed in the dream, but I didn't like running from a fight. Not that Lim had given me any choice in the matter.

I hoped she was all right. Not only because she still had much to tell and show me about Progenitor, but also because I didn't want anything bad to happen to her.

"We're crossing the state line into New York," Isaac announced, tearing my worried thoughts away from Lim.

I reached for my controls. "Activating stealth mode." Recruiting this particular new team member required stealth; it was hard to be stealthy if you were spotted zooming overhead in a state-of-the-art superhero jet. Isaac frowned as I rendered the jet invisible, but he didn't say anything. He didn't like being sneaky, especially when it involved keeping another Hero team in the dark.

We were flouting protocol by not informing the Empire State Champions we were entering their jurisdiction. The Champions were a regional Hero team, much like the

Heartland Heroes, the Gulf Coast Guardians, and the Sunshine State Warriors. The New Sentinels and the Sentinels before us were pretty much the only US-based team with a national and international profile. Though there was no law or regulation saying one Heroic team couldn't operate in the stomping grounds of another without a heads-up, it was considered bad form, like a sheriff entering a neighboring county to investigate a lead without giving the native sheriff notice. Additionally, telling another team you were in their jurisdiction was just hard-nosed good sense—they would know to come running if you ran into trouble you couldn't handle on your own. However, if we told the Champions we were on our way to New York City, word might leak out and tip off the person I needed to recruit. As Benjamin Franklin said, three people could keep a secret, but only if two of them were dead. The Founding Father was chock-full of wisdom. He'd also told a young friend about the many merits of having an old woman as a mistress, which some later wit distilled down to *Older women don't tell, don't smell, don't swell, and are grateful as hell.* For some reason, when the government slapped Ben's wrinkled face on the one hundred-dollar bill, it left off that bit of Franklin wisdom. Not enough room, maybe.

"Let's assume Lim is who she says she is and she really did show you the memories of this Arouch character," Isaac said. "How did he get his powers? Is he a Metahuman, or are his powers solely due to the meteorite?"

"Lim doesn't know for sure, but thinks it's a bit of both. That's what we were discussing when Progenitor attacked us. She believes Arouch had a latent Metahuman gene, and that gene was activated by his body's interaction with the meteorite fragments being struck by lightning."

"And why does she call him Progenitor?" Isaac asked.

"She mentioned something when you first encountered her about him being the father of us all. Is he supposed to be the first Meta all the rest of us are descended from? My long-lost Pop-Pop is coming for a visit and I'm empty-handed, without even a casserole to greet him with. I wonder if Hallmark sells a great-great-great-great-great granddaddy's day card."

I shrugged. "I don't know why she's dubbed Arouch Progenitor. Maybe I would've seen for myself if my walk down his memory lane hadn't been interrupted. Hopefully I'll find out the next time I see Lim." *If I see her again*, I thought, then pushed the bleak thought away. Despite her appearance and sometimes childish demeanor, she was an Omega-level Meta. And older than I to boot. She could take care of herself.

"We're jumping through an awful lot of hoops based on the say-so of someone who's told you a whole lot of nothing." Isaac held up a hand, seeing I was about to argue. "I'll move on before you launch into another riveting episode of *Omega Knows Best*. Let's say Lim's right and Progenitor will go buck wild if he's let loose in the world. How are we supposed to prevent that from happening? Please tell me the plan is not just hoping my greeting card will mollify him."

"We'll capture him before he goes on a rampage, of course," I said.

"Based on the doom and gloom predictions of both the old Sentinels and Lim, what you've told me about his abilities, and how he's supposed to be even more powerful when he gets free, capturing him sounds easier said than done. But let's say we and this team of misfits we're assembling pull off the improbable and capture Progenitor. Fantastic. Yay us. We should get medals. Then what do we do with him? Turn him into the authorities? For what, exactly? Killing a bunch of Neanderthals and cavemen millennia ago?"

"There's no statute of limitations on murder."

Isaac snorted. "Now you're talking even crazier than you're acting. No prosecutor is going to embarrass himself by prosecuting someone for crimes committed in a state of nature before laws even existed. A judge would laugh the prosecutor right out of court. I've got the giggles myself. Not to mention there's a total lack of evidence of Progenitor's supposed crimes. Admissible evidence, I mean. Under the original Hero Act and its later amendments, evidence gleaned by telepathic means is not admissible in court. I could recite the applicable parts of the Act to you, but I know I don't need to—I sat next to you in our Hero Law class at the Academy. You were even awake for parts of it."

Isaac shook his head. "You're no dummy. Surely you've already realized everything I'm saying about the legal system and how it's not equipped to deal with someone like Progenitor." Isaac shot me a sharp look. "Tell me you're not planning to put Progenitor into the same sort of black site prison you kept Mad Dog in."

"Of course not. I've learned my lesson. Once we capture Progenitor, we'll turn him over to the Guild and let it figure out what to do with him. Unlike the civilian authorities, the Guild will understand the threat Progenitor poses."

"Uh-huh." Isaac's grunt was fraught with more meaning than the Bible.

"What's that supposed to mean?" I demanded.

"It means I get the feeling the lesson you learned from Mad Dog is to not get caught again. But maybe I'm just getting too cynical in my old age."

"What can I tell you, gramps? Some of us age like wine. Others like you age like milk, more sour each passing day."

Isaac grunted again, focusing his full attention on flying. We had entered the always busy New York City airspace. I was glad to let the subject drop. For Isaac's suspicions were correct—I was contemplating doing more to Progenitor than merely turning him over to the Guild. Isaac hadn't felt Arouch's exuberant joy when he killed all those Neanderthals. But I had. It made him feel the ecstasy I'd felt when Grimoire dosed me with pixie dust. Someone addicted to a drug's high would not give it up easily. As demonstrated when he killed Ghekk and Bheb. Arouch fooled himself into thinking he regretted killing them, but I had access to all his emotions. Deep down, he had relished killing those two men as much as he did killing Neanderthals. He had been a junkie jonesing for a fix. And Lim had implied I'd just scratched the surface of witnessing his depravity. What would he do if set loose in this modern world containing billions of people?

Isaac altered course to avoid Liberty Island in New York Harbor. Liberty Island was restricted airspace because it housed MetaHold, the crown jewel of the country's Metahuman prison system. Isaac and I didn't know for sure if the federal government had technology or a Hero on patrol that could detect us while cloaked, but better safe than sorry about being blown out of the sky by a surface-to-air missile. MetaHold would become my new home address should the authorities discover the things I'd been up to lately. I could swap stories with Iceburn about the bad old days. The Rogue assassin was back in custody there, recaptured by the New Sentinels after Doctor Alchemy broke him out of MetaHold to help him attack me with the rest of the Revengers.

Considering MetaHold, Liberty Island really ought to be renamed Not At Liberty Island. It probably retained the name Liberty Island out of nostalgia. The island had been the site of the Statue of Liberty before Black Plague's 1980s fight with Avatar destroyed most of it.

The Hudson River was to our left, the East River to the right. The skyscrapers of Manhattan loomed up ahead, gleaming in the late afternoon sun as they stretched to touch the sky. I got a small thrill at the sight, just as I always did when I came here. Astor City was one of the largest cities in the country population-wise, but the Big Apple was the biggest. And it felt the biggest. Even from a distance, New York City seemed to crackle with pent-up energy, like anything was possible here, good and bad. A certain bracing energy came from millions of people stacked on top of each other like ants in an anthill. New York always struck me with awe, like I was fresh off the farm, visiting the concrete jungle for the first time.

Soon Isaac slowed to a stop at the coordinates Lim had given me. Hovering below the city's cloud cover, we were directly above Fifth Avenue, which ran through the middle of Manhattan, connecting the northern and southern parts of the borough. More specifically, we were above Georgette and Company's flagship store on the corner of Fifth Avenue and 57th Street. It was an unseasonably cold Sunday. The traffic below, while hardly light, was as light as it ever got in the city that didn't sleep.

From this high up, the luxury jewelry company's multi-story building was just a dark speck in a sea of specks, even with the jet's viewscreen set to maximum magnification. "You'll have to descend," I told Isaac. "From up here we can't see what's what."

Isaac nodded, pushing his joystick forward. The jet

descended. The top of the Georgette building grew and came into sharper focus on the viewscreen. Fifth Avenue got bigger as well, looking like a dark ribbon of water on which floated cars and trucks. The sidewalk on both sides of the avenue became visible.

Isaac stopped our descent and we again hovered. "If we go down any lower," he said, "someone's bound to hear the engines despite the noise-muffling system. I can hear the pedestrians now: 'Listen! Up in the sky! It's a flatulent bird! It's a plane! It's super-men!' Unless you've abandoned the idea of stealth."

I still couldn't see what was happening on the ground as clearly as I would like. But Isaac was right—any lower and we would surely be detected despite our cloak. Especially with security so tight at the Georgette building today. "This'll have to do," I said. "Besides, based on what Lim said, we shouldn't get too close. I've an idea how we can get an even better view. Minerva, can you hear me?"

Minerva was programmed to not listen to our conversations, but the use of her name activated her. "Loud and clear, Chairman Mao," she said, beaming to us from the mansion through the cockpit's speakers. "The jet's transponders tell me you're in my favorite city. New York, New York— the city so nice they named it twice. A shame you didn't invite me along. We could've gone to see *Hamilton*. I'm dying to find out what happens to the ten-dollar Founding Father at the end."

Isaac raised an eyebrow. "Chairman Mao?"

"It's a long story," I said.

"Unless it's too cold and they cancel tonight's performance," Minerva continued. "Be a real shame if *brrr* kills *Hamilton*."

Isaac and I groaned simultaneously. "It's your fault she's like this," I told him.

"Don't blame me. Maybe her personality matrix is degrading. My jokes are better than that."

"That's what you think."

"You two know I can hear you, right?" Minerva sniffed. "I'm not deaf. Speaking of which, did you hear about how Ninja's gynecologist has lost his hearing? It's okay, though—he can still read lips."

"Minerva," I said hastily before she assaulted us with another statement like that, "we're above the Georgette building. Can you access the store's security cameras, the ones for the old Victoria building around the corner on 57th Street, and the camera feeds for the street and sidewalk in between?"

"I'll answer your question with a question." Minerva sounded insulted. "Are you aware that I'm the most advanced known artificial intelligence on the planet, capable of well over a quintillion operations per second?"

"I take it you can do it."

"Not only can I do it, but I've already done it. If you talk to the off-site Georgette folks who are monitoring the camera footage from New Jersey, you might want to mention the risk they took in hooking their computer network to the Internet while having laughably bad security protocols. Stealing candy from a baby kind of bad. Tell them they oughta sell that 175-carat monstrosity they call the Georgette Diamond and use the proceeds to upgrade their network security."

"So much for a diamond being a girl's best friend," Isaac muttered. "Maybe the cliché only applies to human girls."

"Thanks, Minerva," I said. "Put the footage onscreen."

"Since 'it' is footage from almost 700 separate camera

feeds, I think it's safe to say the jet's monitor is not big enough," Minerva responded.

Isaac whistled. "Maybe the computer security is lousy because they spent all their money on cameras."

I said, "How about just the view right inside the main entrance to the Georgette building, and the views right outside both that building and the Victoria one?"

"Now you're talking," Minerva said. "That's doable."

"Project it onto the jet's cockpit windows," Isaac suggested. "There's more real estate there."

Minerva complied. The three normally clear cockpit windows became dark and opaque, as if black ink had been injected into the glass. Soundless color images formed on each, showing the three areas I had asked Minerva to focus on. And, of course, we still had the straight down view of the building, street and sidewalk on the cockpit monitor. I said, "That should work, Minerva, but keep monitoring the other feeds. Give a yell if you spot something unusual."

"A Confederate rebel yell, a Tarzan yell, or something else?"

I was about to tell Minerva to surprise me, but that would be a mistake. She might burst our eardrums with something like *Show me the money!!!!* bellowed at top volume. I said, "'Hey guys, look at this,' in a calm tone of voice will be sufficient."

"Your definition of yelling and mine are completely different," Minerva said, "but you're the boss." She played the first few seconds of *Hail to the Chief* before the jet's speaker clicked twice and shut off, indicating Minerva was no longer actively listening.

"When this is all over," Isaac said, "we should reprogram her. I'm not too big to admit using my personality as a model was a mistake. One of me is bad enough; two are more than the world can stand."

"Hate to break it to you, but just one of you is more than we can stand. Maybe we should give you a personality transplant too while we're at it."

"And destroy perfection? How dare you."

Isaac and I settled in to watch the activity in and outside the polished granite Georgette building. Customers browsed, women tried on jewelry, and the men with them looked uncomfortable. Knowing how expensive the jewelry could be, I couldn't blame the guys.

"What are we looking for exactly?" Isaac asked. "Audrey Hepburn carrying her breakfast?"

"We'll know it when we see it. In the meantime, keep your eyes peeled for more modern references. You sound like an old man."

"You young whippersnappers have no appreciation for the classics."

Soon the remaining customers were gently shooed out of the Georgette building, despite it being two hours from the store's standard Sunday closing time. The women looked indignant at being hustled out; the men looked relieved. The front door was locked, and a *Closed* sign went up.

Like a well-oiled army ordered to attack, Georgette employees sprang into action. They and armed security guards erected barriers on the sidewalks, blocking off access to the sidewalk stretching between the Georgette building and the old Victoria building around the corner. The barriers were tall, well over nine feet high. Similar barriers were erected on the edge of the sidewalk as well, blocking what was happening on the sidewalk from the view of passing vehicles and pedestrians. The barriers were topless, however, so we could still see from our overhead perch what was happening behind them. Not to mention we had the feed coming in from Georgette's security cameras. A contingent of New York City police looked on as the barriers were erected; they ordered pedestrians curious about the unusual activity to move along.

The barriers were the color of the jewelry company's signature Georgette Green, the distinctive light olive color the company had trademarked. Inspired by Georgette's example, Gina had once tried to talk me into trademarking the uniquely blue color of the Omega suit. "We'll brand it as Omega Blue, of course," Gina had said with excitement, dollar signs dancing in her eyes. I had refused. I'd done a lot of things to keep money flowing into the New Sentinels' coffers, but I drew the line at monopolizing a color. Where would the madness end? Babies trademarking baby blue?

Georgette employees within the building were equally as industrious as those outside. Under the watchful eye of more security guards, they bustled about packing up all the jewelry in the store. A total of 112,599 rings, necklaces, brooches, and every other conceivable gewgaw. Not that I counted. I only knew because Lim had told me. She, of course, had informed me about this entire operation.

It was moving day for Georgette and Company. After all the jewelry was transferred to the temporary location in the old Victoria building, Georgette's ten-story flagship building would be closed for renovation. Georgette planned to have the temporary store open by Monday morning, less than eighteen hours from now, with no downtime other than the original location closing two hours earlier than usual. It warmed my heart to see the efficiency of American capitalism in action. Or maybe that was just heartburn from the burrito I had for lunch. The fact this move was happening was a tightly guarded secret to reduce the risk of robbery while the jewelry was in transit. But there were no secrets from an Omega-level telepath like Lim.

The jewelry was packed into cushioned boxes which were itemized, sealed, and barcoded. The boxes were in turn packed into rectangular cases which, when stood on end, were as tall as a man. They had Georgette Green tambour doors which were padlocked once the cases were packed full. Then the cases were sealed in plastic shrink-wrap. No cops were inside the store during all this, only security guards in Georgette's employ. A wise precaution if New York City cops were anything like the sometimes sticky-fingered Astor City police. Surprisingly, the security guards' uniforms were not Georgette Green. No doubt an oversight on the part of Georgette's vice president of brand marketing.

"Do you suppose Georgette has a vice president of brand marketing?" I asked Isaac.

He snorted. "Does a bird sing? Heck, I'm surprised we don't have one."

"We do. Gina. She just doesn't have the title."

"Don't give her any ideas. She'll expect a pay bump along with it. Pretty soon, she'll be making more than we do. And we're the ones out here risking our necks."

Once the packing and sealing process was complete for a case, burly men picked it up and gently placed it upright on a dolly. A gloved workman carefully wheeled the case outside, escorted by a security guard and a well-dressed, sharp-eyed Georgette employee. The guard's eyes darted from side to side like he suspected Butch Cassidy and the Sundance Kid lurked nearby.

The case was pushed down the cordoned-off sidewalk, around the corner, and to the old Victoria building. A Georgette Green tent had been set up around the building's front door. Once concealed in that tent, a different Georgette employee carefully inspected the case to ensure none of the shrink wrap had been removed or otherwise tampered with during the short trek. Everything was handled with military precision. The journey—less than a couple hundred feet—was hardly Sherman's March to the Sea, but the Georgette employees treated it like it was. I kept my eyes open for Johnny Reb.

Once the case was approved, it was wheeled into the Victoria store, where another contingent of Georgette employees unsealed, unlocked, and unpacked the case, placing the unpacked jewelry in display cases in the new location.

There was soon a steady one-way stream of shrink-wrapped cases between the Georgette and Victoria buildings. The cases seemed to be packed and moved in a specific order, but I couldn't make heads or tails of what that order was or why it existed. I was no gemologist.

"It's almost as if they're worried someone might be tempted to steal hundreds of millions of dollars of jewelry," Isaac said about the precautions. "I count thirty security officers, not to mention the five-o."

"You Yankees sure are paranoid," I agreed.

"I'm an Angeleno, remember? That makes me a Westerner, not a Yankee."

"I was taught that anybody who didn't fight on the side of the angels during the War of Northern Aggression is by definition a damned Yankee."

"Where'd you learn that? In school or at a Klan rally?"

The jet's cabin fell quiet again as Isaac and I continued to watch the move, waiting for the people Lim had told me about to make an appearance.

Darkness swallowed the waning daylight. The city below

us lit up like a Christmas tree, illuminating eight million stories in the naked city. A concrete jungle where dreams were made. A helluva town where people rode in a hole in the ground. A great place to visit, but my heart told me it was a better place to live. If I could make it here, I could make it anywhere. I wondered how many more TV and song references to New York City I knew. We continued to wait. My stomach rumbled. I wished I had gotten a second burrito to go. A shame I couldn't get some food delivered. I doubted Katz's Delicatessen delivered to invisible jets hovering high in the air. If you were a New York landmark, you could be persnickety about your delivery areas.

We waited and watched for what seemed like forever. I was starting to think Lim had gotten a wire crossed when, on the jet's direct monitor, a case moving from the Georgette flagship store to the temporary location stopped rolling. The leg of the man pushing the case froze in midair, as if it rested on an invisible step. The well-dressed woman and the security guard who accompanied the mover were frozen in mid-stride as well, as still as if they were trapped in ice. The other security guards and the police who lined the perimeter of the route were still as statues as well. In fact, everything within the area marked off by the Georgette Green barriers was frozen. Everything outside that area moved normally, however, with cars still zooming by and annoyed pedestrians walking in the street along the edge of the high Georgette barriers. Due to those high barriers, no one outside them could see the frozen people inside them.

Stranger still, despite the frozen scene shown on the jet's direct monitor, the bigger image of the exact same location that Minerva projected onto the cockpit windows from Georgette's security cameras moved normally.

Isaac and I looked at each other. "Minerva," I said, "is there something wrong with the jet's monitor?"

"Running diagnostics," she said. A moment's hesitation, then, "It's working like a top. Why? Did your in-flight movie shut off? Is *Saving Ryan's Privates* not coming in clearly for you guys? I'll summarize the plot, if you want. What there is of it."

"Anything unusual going on in or around Georgette's?" Isaac asked her. "Any unexpected third parties on the footage you're monitoring?"

"Have I yelled 'Yahtzee!' yet as Chairman of the Board Frank Sinatra instructed? Then no."

"Then explain the discrepancy between what's shown on the jet's direct monitor versus what we're seeing through Georgette's security cameras," Isaac said.

"Working." A long pause. "I see what you mean," Minerva said thoughtfully. "I can't explain it. Maybe they're playing freeze tag down there."

Isaac and I looked at each other again, then back at the monitor with the motionless people on it. One of the Georgette Green barriers sealing off the sidewalk shifted. Four costumed men darted through the barrier's narrow breach and toward the front door of the Georgette flagship store, with everything and everyone else around the four as motionless as statues.

The four men all wore solid-colored jumpsuits—black, blue, red, and yellow. Except their faces, the jumpsuits covered them from head to toe. Their faces were concealed by white face paint, on which in turn was painted black minute and hour hands, making the men's faces look like clocks. Satchels were slung across their chests.

On the jet's direct monitor, we watched the costumed men disappear into the Georgette store. Despite the fact one of the security feeds we monitored covered the front door, the men did not also appear on the security feed. It was as if two radically different things were happening in the exact same time and place.

Isaac whistled. "If I didn't see it with my own eyes, I wouldn't have believed it. I guess Tempus Fugit is real."

26

Tempus Fugit: *time flies* in Latin. It was the name of an apocryphal gang of Metahuman thieves with time manipulation powers.

The group was an urban legend in the Heroic community, something Heroes speculated and joked about but nobody with any sense thought was real. Like Bigfoot or the Loch Ness Monster. According to legend, Tempus Fugit was responsible for crimes as varied as the theft of Rembrandt's masterpiece *The Storm on the Sea of Galilee* from the Isabella Stewart Gardner Museum in Boston, the stealing of 26.5 million pounds sterling from the Northern Bank in North Ireland, and the theft of Gold Man's 24-karat heart from the Heroes' Guild's national headquarters in Washington, D.C. "Tempus Fugit has struck again!" we Heroes often joked anytime something valuable went missing. I said it myself not long ago when I misplaced the book I had been reading.

Unlike Bigfoot, however, Tempus Fugit apparently was as real as I was. The frozen scene we watched was an indication of them in operation. First they froze time in a localized area, then they went in and stole everything they could.

They were smash and grabbers with superpowers. According to Lim, thanks to those powers, the Rogue gang had stolen untold millions over the years, never getting caught, leaving only barely believed rumors and legends in their wake.

Also according to Lim, Tempus Fugit had been tipped off about Georgette's move by someone high up in the company's management; for her trouble, Tempus Fugit would cut her in on a percentage of everything the gang stole. The Meta gang was composed of four Rogues: Stopwatch, the one in black, who could freeze time in a localized area in short spurts and who must've been responsible for the frozen tableau below us; Chronon, in yellow, who could shoot blasts of chronons, the particles time was composed of; Rewind, in red, who could rewind time to replay what just happened; and Timeline, in blue, who could electronically project events that were transpiring elsewhere in the temporal multiverse.

Temporal multiverse. Sheesh. The term sounded like something out of a comic book. According to Lim, just as there were many other dimensions, there were a vast number of timelines all simultaneously sharing the same plane of existence. The way she had explained it to me, reality was like a never-ending library housing a multitude of never-ending books. Each book was a separate dimension; each page was a different timeline. Different events happened on each page, but the pages were a part of a greater whole. On this page I was in pursuit of Tempus Fugit, but on another page I'd never developed superpowers. Ad infinitum.

First magic, now the temporal multiverse. Lim and John Burdon Haldane had been right: the universe was much queerer than I had supposed.

Timeline's powers were why Georgette's security cameras indicated the move proceeded as scheduled—the off-site Georgette employees who monitored the hundreds of security feeds were seeing another reality, one where Tempus Fugit wasn't robbing Georgette blind. The only reason why Isaac and I hadn't been fooled was because we watched what was happening below us directly through the jet's monitor instead of relying solely on what Georgette's security feeds showed. Timeline would have been able to trick the jet's monitor too, which was why it had been so important for Isaac and me to remain hidden—Timeline couldn't try to fool us if he didn't know we were here.

Tempus Fugit's plan was this: Freeze time within the confines of the barriers, then go in and rob Georgette, where the store's most expensive items had thoughtfully been packed up in a few cases in one area. Since the barriers blocked outsiders' views, those outsiders wouldn't know anything was amiss. The people who monitored Georgette's security feeds also wouldn't know anything was amiss since they watched a projection from another timeline, one where nothing untoward was happening.

"What was it you were saying about Lim earlier, doubting Thomas?" I asked Isaac. "If I sound smug right now, it's only because I am."

"Thanks for not rubbing it in." Isaac stood. "But the fact I was wrong about Lim's prediction about Tempus Fugit doesn't mean I'm wrong about everything. Let's get down there before Tempus Fugit cleans Georgette out. Minerva, while we're gone, you have the jet's conn."

"Aye, aye, captain," she said. "Lieutenant Minerva reporting for duty. I refuse to put on a red uniform, though. I know what happens to redshirts."

Masking our faces, Isaac and I hustled to the center of

the jet. With a click and a whir, a circular part of the floor lowered us through the bowels of the jet.

"I'll neutralize Stopwatch first," I told Isaac as we descended. "He's the biggest threat. If he spots us, he'll time-freeze us and the entire gang will get away. Can you handle Chronon and Timeline while I go after Rewind?"

Isaac just stared at me.

"I withdraw the question," I said. "You can handle Chronon and Timeline."

"Damn straight. What am I, an amateur?"

The circle we rode fell open like a trapdoor, dropping us in the air underneath the jet. I held us aloft near the jet with my telekinesis, not wanting to reveal our presence by exiting the jet's stealth field or to descend farther and get caught in the time freeze field Stopwatch had erected below us. Lim had told me how high we'd need to hover to stay above Stopwatch's field.

Under us, the cops and Georgette employees inside the barriers were still frozen. It was not only they who were frozen, though—stray bits of windswept trash and even a few pigeons were frozen in front of the Georgette building. Literally everything was still in Stopwatch's time stasis field.

No, not everything. As Isaac and I watched, Tempus Fugit burst out of the Georgette building. The men struggled with their satchels; they were no doubt full of loot the men had just stolen. Good. It was important to catch these guys red-handed.

Their thievery was not yet complete, however. The Tempus Fugit gang hustled toward a frozen case on the sidewalk that had been on its way to the Victoria building. According to Lim, the gang's plan was to save the best for last. The case on the sidewalk contained, among other items, Georgette's crown jewel: the Georgette Diamond.

Maybe Minerva wasn't a fan of the iconic jewel, but Tempus Fugit was. More to the point, they were a fan of the jewel's worth. Valued at more than thirty million dollars, the Georgette Diamond was likely worth more than everything else the gang had taken inside the store.

Once they grabbed the Georgette Diamond, the plan was for the gang to dash back to their nearby getaway car, and have blended in with the rest of the city's traffic by the time Stopwatch's fifteen-minute time freeze wore off. The Georgette employees would be robbed in what would seem to them the blink of an eye, with no footage of a robbery left behind nor any clues as to the robbers. It would be just the latest mysterious and unsolved heist for cops and crime historians to scratch their heads over.

I was able to closely monitor what was happening below with my telekinetic touch. Apparently, Stopwatch's time stasis field only affected people present in the area when he initially triggered it. The field was like a grenade—it affected you if you were next to it when it exploded, but it wouldn't affect you at all if you wandered along five seconds after detonation. It didn't make sense, but a lot of things in this line of work didn't make sense. Time, like so many other things in the Meta world, was weird as hell.

Stopwatch carefully shifted the frozen workman whose hands were still on the upright case, moving the workman like he was a mannequin. Then Stopwatch placed his own hands on the case, squeezing his eyes shut in concentration, like he was a faith healer praying cancer away.

The case emitted a dull white flash as it reentered the conventional time stream. With a box cutter, Timeline sliced away the case's plastic shrink-wrap. Chronon grabbed the case's padlock. It crumbled in his hand and fell away. Chronon wasn't super strong, so he must have blasted the lock with chronons, making the lock age like a fraction of a second was centuries.

Timeline and Chronon tilted the case over until it lay lengthwise on the sidewalk. The two opened the case and rifled through it, tossing boxes full of jewelry aside. They must've not been interested in anything other than the Georgette Diamond.

While the robbers were busy, I carefully probed Stopwatch's body with my telekinetic touch. I was really good at big splashy stuff, like picking up eighteen-wheelers and throwing them at an opponent. Subtle stuff like what I was trying to do now was much harder despite requiring a lot less raw power. It was akin to destroying a computer: smashing it with a sledgehammer was easy; reaching into its messy innards to snip the tiny connection of a key component without touching anything else was hard.

Finally, I was ready.

I stopped Stopwatch's heart.

The effect was immediate. Making a strangled sound, Stopwatch clutched his chest. He stepped forward, staggered, then slumped to the ground. Rewind leaped to catch Stopwatch, partially breaking his fall. Timeline and Chronon spun to stare at Stopwatch, unsure what was happening.

Once I was certain the black-garbed Rogue was unconscious, I restarted Stopwatch's heart. Blood resumed its flow to his brain and other organs. I wanted to render him a nonfactor, not kill him. Even with Stopwatch out cold, though, the cops and Georgette employees around him were still frozen and would remain so until the fifteen-minute time freeze lapsed.

I released my hold on Isaac's body. Exiting the jet's stealth field, he plummeted headfirst toward the sidewalk, glowing and transforming as he fell. His descent caught the attention of the Rogues below.

Cursing, Chronon raised his fists, bringing them together, pointing them at Isaac. A barely perceptible wave of energy blasted out of them. The energy blast was colorless and translucent, but it made the air shimmer.

Isaac, in his angel form, twisted in midair, dodging to the side, avoiding the shimmering wave. The blast of temporal energy shot past Isaac and kept going. Isaac had angled himself so the Rogue's blast would go harmlessly into the sky instead of hitting the tall buildings that formed an urban canyon around us. It was easy to forget how good Isaac was until you saw him in action. According to Lim, Chronon's temporal blasts could disintegrate the hardest of substances and age a person centuries in an instant, reducing him to dust. She thought maybe even my force fields couldn't withstand Chronon's blasts.

Isaac reoriented and dove again, with his snow-white wings tucked tightly into a V shape. He shot toward Chronon like a hawk after a dove. Chronon shot at him again. Isaac turned ever so slightly mid-dive, making the energy blast miss once more.

Isaac slammed into Chronon, knocking the Rogue off his feet, driving him back-first into the sidewalk. Using his dive's momentum in his favor, Isaac tumbled off of Chronon, pushed off the sidewalk with his hands, and landed on his feet like a gymnast positioning himself for the next part of his routine. Maybe Ninja with her Olympic medals could've pulled off the move as gracefully, but I doubted it.

Chronon didn't stir, knocked out cold. Wings flapping, Isaac took flight again, soaring over the barriers to go after Timeline. That blue-garbed Rogue had already squeezed through the narrow gap Tempus Fugit had opened in the barriers and was hightailing it up 57th Street.

That left Rewind. Seeing that Isaac pursued Timeline and ignored him, Rewind ran toward the opening in the barrier. Neither he nor Timeline had made any effort to help their unconscious comrades. Truly there was no honor among thieves.

I dropped out of the sky like a stone, landing on the sidewalk directly in front of Rewind. He slammed full tilt into my personal force field, then bounced off it like a cue ball. He would have gone sprawling had I not grabbed his red costume right under his throat. The loose-fitting fabric balled up in my fists as I yanked the man's pasty-white clock face close. He was shorter than I and about my weight. Pudgy and thin-limbed, the Rogue looked like a bowling pin with arms. Like all of Tempus Fugit, he wore a watch that counted down the minutes until Stopwatch's time stasis field dissipated.

"Leaving so soon, Xander?" I asked. "And I was so looking forward to us having a little chat."

Rewind's eyes widened at my use of his real name. His gray eyes darted from my face to the Omega emblem on my chest, and back again. The dismayed recognition in his eyes said it all. He knew who I was. Ah fame, that fickle food. "Fuck my life," Rewind groaned.

"Yeah, that pretty much sums it up," I agreed. "But guess what? Today's your lucky day. I need your help with something. If you help me, maybe you won't spend the rest of your life in prison."

Rewind said something about my mother. I gasped. Despite knowing he was trying to get my goat, his words were so breathtakingly vulgar that he succeeded. Rewind must've read *Zero to Omega Hero*; I had feared discussing

Mom's brain cancer was a mistake, but the book's ghost-writer had talked me into it. Even though I'd been a kid when she died, Mom was still a touchy subject.

My hands shifted as if they had a mind of their own, moving to Rewind's neck. His eyes darted toward the crack in the barriers where Isaac could be seen flapping after Timeline. My throat tight, I said, "Listen here, you piece of sh—"

I stopped mid-sentence. My hands were around Isaac's throat.

27

Isaac and I blinked at each other, both confused.

Isaac recovered before I did. He grabbed my wrists, dipped his head between my arms, rolled out of my front choke hold, and stepped away from me.

"What's the big idea?" he sputtered, rubbing his throat. "Reenacting the good old days, Captain Confederacy?"

"I'm sorry . . . I didn't mean to . . . it's just that—"

"It's just that Rewind got the jump on you, is what happened." Isaac shook his head. "And just when I'd gotten close enough to Timeline to French kiss him. You asked before if I could handle Timeline and Chronon. The better question is if you can handle Rewind."

Annoyed at myself, I felt my jaw tighten. "I've got him."

"Good. I'll get back after Timeline before he gets away clean." Isaac morphed into a werewolf as he spoke, his last words coming out as a snarl from a slavering mouth. With his snout's nostrils flaring as he picked up Timeline's scent, he dropped to all fours and bounded away. He leaped over a ten feet tall green barrier like it was merely a step stool and disappeared. Seconds later, screams rose from unseen pedestrians. If was as if they had never seen a werewolf loping up a city street before.

I went airborne, shooting clear of the Georgette Green barriers so I could look for Rewind. My face was hot with embarrassment. I was annoyed with myself for letting Rewind escape my clutches. It was one thing for Lim to tell me Rewind had the ability to reverse time for several seconds while simultaneously swapping positions with someone else; it was quite another to see his ability in action. Still, letting him get away was the sort of rookie move I thought I had left behind with my Apprenticeship. I'd be careful to not get caught off guard by him again.

I twisted in the air, looking for Rewind on the streets below. He couldn't have gotten far. I remembered Minerva's remark about redshirts. Rewind was a redshirt from head to toe due to his red Tempus Fugit costume. Even at night, he shouldn't be hard to spot in the city's lights. Assuming he hadn't darted into a building, but I'd cross that bridge if I came to it.

There! Rewind was running west on 57th Street. Fellow pedestrians paid him no mind. They didn't seem to bat an eye at a costumed man running like hell, yet Isaac's were-wolf form had gotten a reaction. New Yorkers had seen everything, but apparently even their jadedness drew the line at werewolves.

I swooped toward Rewind like a bird of prey with a pigeon in its sights. I lifted the running Rogue off the side-walk with my telekinesis, twisting him so he faced me as he rose. My fist tightened in anticipation. A punch in the gut ought to take the starch out of him, making him more amenable to conversation.

Plus, I was still irritated at the Rogue. You didn't talk smack about my mother.

Rewind's legs and arms windmilled the air, like a cartoon character who hadn't realized he had run off a cliff and was defying the laws of gravity. His eyes widened when he saw me dropping toward him like an anvil. His head twisted frantically, down toward the traffic on 57th Street as my punch was about to land.

My fist slammed into the belly of an old lady.

Her scream was cut short by the force of the punch, turned into gagging and wheezing.

"Omigod, I'm so sorry," I apologized in a rush. At the last instant I had seen whom I was about to hit and checked the punch. But not much—the woman had still taken the brunt of it. "Are you all right?"

The old woman was too busy choking and trying to breathe to answer. Her watery eyes looked like they would bulge out of their sockets. Stout and gray-haired, she had to be at least seventy.

Feeling an inch tall, I landed, setting the woman down gently on the sidewalk, propping her back against a building. She gasped for breath, shaking her arms and fluttering her hands like she was conducting a frantic symphony. Pedestrians clustered around us. Some muttered angrily. They didn't know I had been in hot pursuit of a Rogue; all they had seen was me slugging someone's meemaw.

I gently ran my telekinetic touch over the gasping woman's body. I felt a little better: I hadn't broken bones or done other serious damage. I had simply knocked the wind out of her. Based on her flailing, I'd also scared the crap out of her. She probably had gone her entire life without being punched. Must be nice.

Kneeling, I grabbed her liver-spotted hands and held them, both to comfort her and because I feared she was going to pull a muscle the way she flailed. "I'm so sorry. It was an accident. My name's Omega, I'm a Hero, and I'm not going to hurt you." I kept my voice calm and soothing despite my insides dancing with impatience; the longer I lingered, the farther away Rewind got. The woman's arms began to relax; her face indicated she now recognized me. "You're going to be all right. You've just had the wind knocked out of you. Keep trying to breathe and the feeling will pass. In through the nose, and out through the mouth. Like this." I demonstrated until the woman calmed further and began breathing somewhat normally.

"There. That's better." I smiled at the woman reassuringly. *Welcome to Dr. Bedside Manner's world-renowned postpunch clinic. Yeah, maybe he'll gut punch grandma, but he'll comfort her afterward.* "Now, what's the last thing you remember before I hit you?"

"I was driving my car," she answered shakily.

As I suspected. The last thing I remembered of Rewind was him looking at the cars on the street as he rushed up toward me. First Rewind had stared over my shoulder at Isaac before pulling his switcheroo routine, now this. I didn't need Ninja-level tactical awareness to deduce Rewind needed to look at the person he was going to exchange places with in order to trigger his power. "Which direction were you going?" I asked. "And what do you drive?"

The woman told me. I apologized to her again and told her I'd make sure she got her car back. I stood, glancing at the people gathered around us. "You," I said, pointing at a middle-aged woman with kind eyes and an air of competence. "Call an ambulance and see that this lady gets checked out. Tell them to send the bill to the New Sentinels in Astor City." The woman pulled out a cell phone and dialed. Hero Academy taught and experience had confirmed that people usually did what you told them when you said it with authority and were in uniform, which was one of the reasons why Rogues and Heroes alike tended to wear costumes. "In the meantime, I've got a Rogue to catch."

A man piped up as I went airborne: "Next time, pick on somebody your own size!"

"Working on it," I muttered. The guy hadn't said boo to me on the ground. Everyone's a tough guy when the other guy's walking away.

Following 57th Street, I quickly flew west, traveling low enough to distinguish the make and model of the various vehicles. The old woman said she had been driving west on 57th in a red Ford Escape. The irony of an Escape being Rewind's getaway vehicle wasn't lost on me. The old woman had even known her license plate number, which was more than most people could say.

Finding the Escape was easy enough. It was double-parked a few blocks away with its hazard lights on and a line of cars and irate drivers behind it. I was not at all surprised to find that the guy behind the wheel was not Rewind. Suspecting I would chase after him, Rewind had ditched the vehicle. Smart.

"I don't know what happened," the coveralled man in the Escape said, his eyes wild with confusion. "I was driving my truck, minding my own business, and all of a sudden ... bam! I'm behind the wheel of a strange car. I must be going crazy."

"You're not," I assured him. "It's the work of a supervillain. I'm hot on his trail. What kind of truck were you driving and which way were you headed?"

He told me, and I took off after Rewind after asking the man to return the Escape to where I had left its owner.

I found the man's truck in short order, also pulled over, also with a confused driver behind the wheel. After hastily interrogating that driver, I took flight again. If Rewind thought he could shake me with a game of vehicular whack-a-mole, he had another thing coming.

Several more cars and confused drivers later, I found Rewind driving south, heading out of the city. I thought it was him based on the car's description—a late model gray Dodge Durango with racing stripes—and a probe of the SUV's interior with my telekinetic touch from where I flew overhead confirmed it. Not too many people drove while wearing a unitard.

Rewind drove the speed limit, blending in with the other traffic. He undoubtedly thought he had gotten away clean and was taking pains to not draw attention to himself. Little did he know I had him in my sights from high overhead. I had positioned myself so he'd only be able to see me if he stuck his head out the window and looked straight up. I didn't want him to spot me, nor did I want to brace him directly as I had before. If I did, he would reverse time and switch positions with someone else once more. Maybe I wouldn't be able to find him again.

I reached out with my powers and gently squeezed Rewind's eyes shut. Startled, unable to see, Rewind jerked the Durango's steering wheel. He would've crashed had I not picked the Durango up, lifting it off the street and out of traffic. I brought the car abreast of me. Rewind clawed at his face, unsuccessfully trying to force his eyes open. The SUV's wheels spun uselessly in the air. When the creators of *The Jetsons* envisioned flying cars, this was probably not what they had in mind.

Carrying the Durango with me, I moved higher in the night sky. The people below shrank into dots and then disappeared into a latticework of city lights. Isaac in one of his forms with enhanced vision could've still seen the people, but I sure as heck couldn't. Which meant Rewind couldn't either. I had deduced that if he couldn't see someone, he couldn't swap places with them. If he could, he would have swapped places with someone on the other side of the planet to get away from me instead of leapfrogging from person to person on the street.

Floating next to the driver's side door, I rolled down the window with my powers and turned on the vehicle's interior lights so I could see Rewind better. I shut the engine off. Saving the world one car emission at a time. I should change my name to Captain Planet.

Only then did I release my hold on Rewind's eyes. The Rogue blinked furiously, able to see again. Him clawing at his face had smeared his face paint, revealing ruddy flesh underneath. His face now looked like one of those melting clocks in Salvador Dalí's *Persistence of Memory*. More like *Persistence of Supervillainy*.

It took a few seconds for Rewind to focus his watering gray eyes on me. I wagged my fingers at him. His lips tightened into a grim slash. He cautiously stuck his head out of the window and looked down. Cold wind whistled in our ears. A murder of cawing crows was barely visible as it flew far beneath us.

Rewind hastily pulled his head back in. He gulped and looked at me again.

"Is there a reason you pulled me over, officer?" he said gamely. "Did I do something wrong? I could've sworn I renewed my registration on time."

"I am not amused. You can switch places with me if you'd like, Xander, but that would just mean you'd fall out of the sky. There's nowhere to run this time."

Rewind glanced out the window again. He grimaced and leaned back in the driver's seat. He did it carefully and gingerly. As if, if he moved too quickly, he might jostle the vehicle out of the sky and he'd plummet to his death. "Appears so," he conceded. "Your name's Omega, right? I caught part of your New Sentinels Day speech on the news a while back. Very inspiring. Made me wanna go out and beat a mugger to death. Your fame is how I know your name. How do you know mine?"

"I know lots of things about you. You're Xander Waylett, age forty-eight, raised in foster homes, divorced, one kid in the custody of your ex Holly, resident of Las Vegas, amateur high-stakes baccarat player, unregistered Metahuman, member of the Tempus Fugit gang—"

"'Gang' is such a nasty word," he interrupted. "Makes me sound like a criminal."

"Because that's what you are: a professional criminal."

"My clean record says otherwise."

"The fact you haven't been caught before now doesn't change what you are."

"I haven't been caught now. Me and my friends are dressed like this because we were on our way to a costume party. And this car? I don't know how in the world I got into someone else's vehicle. The work of a supervillain, no doubt. There oughta be a law. I was just driving down the road, minding my own business, when you picked me up and brought me up here. I'm fairly sure that's kidnapping. I should have you arrested." He waved his hand, stopping me from pointing out the many and obvious flaws in his story. "But I'll save all that for court. You said something before about asking for my help."

"Not asking. Demanding. You help me and maybe I'll keep you out of prison."

Isaac flew up from below in his angel form before Rewind responded. I wasn't glad to see him; I would much rather deal with Rewind alone. Isaac's bare brown torso was heavily muscled and there was a faint halo around his head. His snow-white wings flapped slowly as he hovered next to me and the car.

Rewind looked at Isaac, then tilted his head back on the car's headrest. "Oh goody, a dark angel," he muttered. "I've died and gone to hell."

"Have you taken care of Timeline?" I asked Isaac.

"Of course. He and the other two are unconscious and tied up in a neat little bow in front of the Georgette building within the time freeze zone. All the cops have to do is wander along and open their late Christmas presents." Isaac jerked his chin at Rewind. "This dirtbag on board?"

"Who you callin' a dirtbag, dirtbag?" Rewind shot back. He eyed Isaac's bare chest. Isaac was jacked in his human form, and his angelic form took his musculature to the next level. "Though I will admit you're in good shape. How do you do it? Jazzercise? Jane Fonda workouts? Oh, I know—a tall drink of chocolate milk like you must stay fit by eating an all watermelon diet, playing lots of basketball, and chasing PAWGs. Am I right, my brotha?"

Isaac didn't react to Rewind's words, but the look in his glowing eyes told me he bristled on the inside. He normally kept his cool, but racial stuff was a sore subject for him, probably because of his racist white stepfather and stepbrother Trey, aka the Revenger Elemental Man. Yeah, this was not going well. To say that Isaac was less than pleased about the prospect of collaborating with a Rogue was an understatement. Still, I wish he kept his annoyance to himself. Antagonizing Rewind, whom we needed, wasn't helpful. "Take it easy guys," I said. "I was just explaining to Xander that helping us is his get out of jail free card."

"Help you with what? Increasing your mean IQ?"

Rewind jerked his thumb at Isaac. "It's not my fault homeboy is dragging the average down."

Isaac's eyes tightened. "An ancient supervillain is about to escape the prison he's been confined in," I rushed to say before Isaac lost his temper. "We want your help bringing him down. In exchange, we'll talk to the authorities about shaving some time off for your role in your attempted heist. Maybe keep you out of prison altogether."

"I see." Rewind glanced at his watch. Its countdown indicated there wasn't much time remaining before Stopwatch's time freeze wore off. Rewind stared out of the windshield for a few seconds, thinking. Then he said, "Alright, you want my help? Here are my demands."

Isaac laughed derisively. "You just tried to rob a jewelry store. Plus, look where you are. We could drop you out of the sky like bird poop. You're in no position to make demands."

"That's not how it looks from where I'm sitting, Othello. From here I see two Heroes willing to let a thief escape with a slap on the wrist. Something you wouldn't do if you didn't need his help bad. Help you probably can't get elsewhere." Rewind might be a crook, but he clearly wasn't stupid. "So like I said, here are my demands: One, not only do you not turn me over to the cops, but you don't turn over the rest of Tempus Fugit either. If you act in the next few minutes before Stopwatch's powers wear off, the cops don't even have to know we were ever here."

Isaac snorted. Rewind made a shooing gesture at him and said, "Quiet crack baby, I'm talking. Two, we get to keep all the merchandise we, ah, liberated."

"Screw you and screw this," Isaac said. "No deal."

"You walk," I countered, "but the jewels and your accomplices stay right where they are."

Isaac looked thunderstruck. He turned to face me. "I can't believe you're negotiating with this trash."

"You can't get something for nothing," Rewind told Isaac. "But it's no surprise someone raised on welfare doesn't know that."

"Shut up," I told Rewind. I remembered what he had said about my mother; his default move seemed to be to get under people's skin. Plus, Isaac and Rewind had taken an instant dislike to one another, which was making this harder than it already was. "Myth, why don't you go wait in the jet? I can handle this."

"I've no doubt you can handle it," Isaac responded. "But based on your recent behavior, it's *how* you'll handle it that's got me worried."

Rewind watched us intently. I didn't like airing our dirty laundry in front of him. It was like a family fighting in front of a stranger. "I said I'll handle this," I repeated. "Go wait in the jet."

"Yeah, go wait in the jet, Kayne," Rewind chimed in.

"Shut up," Isaac told him. His eyes flashing, he said to me, "Go wait in the jet? What am I, your lapdog? Who do you think you are? The Old Man? You can't give me orders."

I grew increasingly impatient. The clock was ticking. If the Georgette employees unfroze with Tempus Fugit and their loot in their midst, the police would get involved, meaning I would no longer have a free hand to deal with this situation. Plus, with the rest of the gang in police custody, some of my leverage over Rewind would be gone. There was no time to tiptoe around Isaac's feelings. "I think I'm the team chairman. Which means we'll recruit the people I say the way I say. We had a vote on it. I won, you lost. So, for the last time, go wait in the jet. Don't make me tell you again."

"Yeah, don't make us tell you again," Rewind added.

"Shut up!" both Isaac and I snapped simultaneously. Rewind opened his mouth again, saw the looks on our faces, abruptly shut it, and turned away to grab the Durango's steering wheel. He *vroomed, vroomed,* pretending to drive away.

Isaac and I glared at each other for several beats, neither of us wanting to give in.

Finally, Isaac said, "Fine. Have it your way. For now, I'll follow your lead. Just remember there's a limit to how far I'll follow. There's going to come a time when you go too far."

Without a further word, Isaac tucked his wings in and plummeted out of sight. Rewind leaned out the window and blew him a kiss. "Don't know about you, but I for one am glad he's gone."

"He's worth a thousand of you, and don't you forget it," I snapped. Rewind's watch said there were only a few minutes left. I spoke quickly. "You help us, you walk, your colleagues don't, and the jewels go back to where they belong. We have a deal?"

"No. I already told you what I want. Take it or leave it."

"I'll leave it. Let's hand you over to the police." I began descending, towing the Durango with me. I tried to keep my anxiety off my face. I would free every criminal in MetaHold and clean out every jewelry store on the planet if that was what it took to stop Progenitor, but I didn't dare admit that to Rewind. It was hard to negotiate from a position of weakness, and it was bad enough that Rewind already had an inkling of how badly I needed him.

"Wait, wait, wait," Rewind said hastily.

I brought us to a stop. We were still up high enough that Rewind couldn't swap places with someone else. "Jew me down, why don't you?" the Rogue said. "Maybe there's room for negotiating after all. How's this: all of Tempus Fugit walks, and we only keep half of the jewelry we took."

I considered it. Tempus Fugit would still get millions. But I didn't care about the jewelry; surely Georgette had it all insured, anyway. However, I had to sell whatever deal we arrived at to Isaac. I needed him to stay on the team just as much as I needed to recruit Rewind onto it. I'd seen the look in Isaac's eyes—he hadn't been bluffing about walking away. I couldn't imagine Isaac going along with Tempus Fugit getting away with half of their loot. He'd say we were accessories after the fact. He'd be right.

"Here's my final offer," I said. "You and the rest of Tempus Fugit get away scot-free. But the jewelry stays where it belongs. It will be as if the crime never happened. No harm, no foul."

Rewind probed my face for a moment, then leaned back in his seat. He stared straight ahead, looking deflated and trying to hide it. "Then you might as well give me to the cops. I can't take that offer." It was interesting he hadn't tried to throw his fellow gang members under the bus and keep the spoils to himself. Maybe there was some honor among thieves after all.

I floated closer to the SUV, putting my head almost in the window. "You won't take the offer because, unlike with your previous heists, you don't merely want the money. This time, you *need* the money. For your eight-year-old daughter Michaela."

Rewind almost jumped. "How do you know about her?"

"The same way I know your name, where you live, and the fact you gambled away almost all the spoils of your previous robberies. Little did you know as you were pissing away millions at the baccarat tables that your little girl would develop cardiomyopathy, a disease causing the enlarging and weakening of heart muscles. If Michaela doesn't get a heart transplant soon, she'll die. The problem is, there are lots of kids ahead of her on the organ donor list. The legal one, at least. It'll be months if not years before a compatible heart becomes available for Michaela. She doesn't have that long to live. It's why you and the rest of Tempus Fugit came out of semi-retirement—to pull off one last big score so you'd have the funds to buy a heart on the black market, pay an unscrupulous surgeon to perform the transplant, and subsidize Michaela's post-procedure care."

Rewind looked at me with wide eyes. "How do you know this stuff?"

"The how is not important. What's important is this: if you help me, I'll see that Michaela jumps to the head of the donor list. I'll even do you one better: I'll make sure the finest doctors in the world perform the surgery in a state-of-the-art facility and that she gets the best aftercare humanly possible. You won't have to rely on a shady doctor with a medical degree from a Third World country who barely understands germ theory."

Rewind stared at me, transfixed, hope flickering in his eyes like a flame fighting for oxygen. "You really can do all that?"

I shrugged modestly. I was just an earnest, humble Hero leveraging the life of a sick child to bend a desperate father to his will. Funny how they leave this kind of stuff out of the biographies of people who tried to get big things done. I didn't like the taste of this, nor did I like the prospect of bumping kids who'd been on the donor list longer than Michaela further down the list. But didn't the needs of the many outweigh the needs of the few? The concept had been my guiding light, lately. They should put the words on my tombstone. Right under *He did what he thought he had to do.*

That rat bastard. I said, "I've already leaned on the right people, twisted some arms, and called favors in. I can make it happen. I *will* make it happen. But only if you agree to help me."

Rewind's eyes were wary. "Say I help you and you in turn help Michaela. I still insist the rest of Tempus Fugit goes free. I won't have them sent to the joint because of me."

"Deal," I said immediately. If we acted quickly, I could get the gang away from the Georgette building and no one would be the wiser. The loot Tempus Fugit had bagged wouldn't be in the cases they were supposed to be in, but no one would be able to trace that to Tempus Fugit and two Heroes making deals with crooks.

And, to be completely honest, Rewind wanting to save his friends made me feel better about the guy. Despite him being a criminal and a degenerate, his loyalty to his gang confirmed what I had learned over the years: no one was all bad or all good. I myself had turned into Exhibit A for that credo.

Rewind was looking at me like a guy who had been thrown a lifeline but was afraid it would be jerked away like it had been too many times in the past. "How do I know you'll do as you say if I throw in with you?"

I held his gaze. "Because I give you my word I will."

He searched my eyes. He must have liked what he saw because he extended a red hand.

"Shake on it," he said.

And we did.

28

I strode purposely through the top floor of the high-rise UWant Technology building in downtown Seattle, Washington. My white cape gently swished behind me. UWant employees stared as I passed; excited whispers swirled in my wake. It was as if these people had never seen a costumed superhero stalking through an office building before.

Considering the circumstances, I was in a good mood. While I certainly wasn't confident about defeating Progenitor—hard experience had taught me the dangers of over-confidence—I was becoming cautiously optimistic. With only one more person left to recruit on Lim's Metahuman wish list, I felt rather good about how things were progressing.

I was at UWant to recruit that last person. I had come alone. Everyone else was otherwise occupied. Grimoire was in Washington, D.C., checking on her mother. When I asked if her mother was sick or something, she had brightened and said, "Gods, I hope so." An interesting one, that Grimoire.

Ninja was en route to Wyoming to deal with a group of Jacobites who had barricaded themselves in a National Guard armory. They threatened to kill a bunch of hostages if their nutty demands weren't met, including the repeal of the Hero Act, the execution of us Metas who used our powers, and the imprisonment of the rest. Jacobites were a fringe Christian sect who believed Metahumans weren't human at all, but rather a plague sent by god to punish man for his sins. How they knew what was in god's mind was beyond me. Maybe they had his personal cell phone number. I had lots of questions for him, so I wished they'd share it. Stingy.

Ninja would be facing those twenty-six well-armed misers all by herself. Terrible odds. I was tempted to call the Jacobites and warn them Ninja was on her way so the nutjobs could ship in reinforcements and make it a fair fight. I almost felt sorry for them.

Almost.

Isaac had stayed behind at the mansion with Rewind to —as Isaac had put it—"Make sure this crook doesn't walk off with the china." *Quis custodiet ipsos custodes?* In answer to that age-old question of who watches the watchman, I had asked Minerva to keep an eye on Isaac while he in turn kept an eye on Rewind. The way Rewind relished baiting Isaac, I was afraid one of them would kill the other if they were left alone long enough. When I was a kid, I'd kept two crickets in a terrarium, only to come home one day to find one cricket had eaten most of the other. My money was on Isaac if a terrarium race war death-match went down at the mansion.

I knew Isaac babysitting Rewind was only partially the reason he had stayed behind. Left unspoken was the fact Isaac couldn't stand to be around me right now. Unspoken by Isaac's mouth, at least. His eyes had said it loud and clear.

It was just as well. I was heartily sick of Isaac second-guessing me and jogging my elbow. Without him underfoot, I could do what needed to be done without pandering to his delicate sensibilities.

I smiled and winked at a particularly cute engineer as I strode by her cubicle. She recognized me. Her return smile hinted at infinite possibilities. Though I was tempted to linger and explore those possibilities, I kept moving. Saving the world was a jealous mistress.

Well-dressed and attractive, the cute engineer reflected the company she worked for. The exterior of the UWant Technology building gleamed with shiny metal and glass. The interior was plush and luxurious, decorated with high-end furniture, expensive tapestries, rare paintings and objets d'art. It was also cluttered with prototypes for technology that maybe Buck Rogers would recognize, but I did not. I was careful to not touch anything. If the Pottery Barn rule of *You break it, you bought it* applied here, I would probably have to liquidate some assets to pay off the debt.

UWant Technology was a subsidiary of UWant Corporation, the company behind the world's leading Internet search engine. UWant's world headquarters was the giant emerald green building in Astor City that I often perched on top of like a blue gargoyle. Last night I had examined the organizational chart for the UWant umbrella of companies. It looked like a giant octopus with UWant Corporation as the head, and countless other companies forming its tentacles. Though technology was UWant's main revenue source, it also had interests in products as diverse as oil, natural gas, sugar, cotton, and pharmaceuticals. Economists said that for every American dollar spent, an average of ten cents went to a UWant company. If I woke up one morning to find a *Property of UWant* tattoo on my chest, I wouldn't be surprised.

There had been talk for years about the government going after UWant for antitrust violations and breaking the company up, talk that intensified after Truman uncovered its founder's involvement in Avatar's murder. Nothing ever came of all that talk, though. UWant lobbyists had probably twisted regulators' and politicians' arms, and money had likely quietly changed hands. Me leaving Dad's farm hadn't made me a better person, but it certainly had opened my eyes as to how the world worked.

I stopped walking in front of a gleaming desk. It probably cost more than the entire mobile home I lived in on the farm. The desk's nameplate read *Bernice Hennigan, Executive Secretary for Sonya Copeland, Chief Technical Officer and Vice President of Information Technology*. It took me a moment to digest the title. I was surprised the nameplate wasn't the size of a billboard. Maybe one of the prototypes I passed on the way here was revolutionary tech that had squeezed in all the words.

"Hi Bernice," I said, surmising the woman furiously typing behind the desk was Hennigan. With awesome deductive abilities like these, what chance did Progenitor have? "I'm here to see Sonya."

The woman didn't even look up as her manicured nails continued typing with a frenzied speed she somehow made elegant. When I pictured someone named Bernice, I didn't picture this beauty. Whoever coined the acronym MILF probably had this stunner in mind. Her face had high cheekbones and was impeccably made up. Her long blonde hair was in a chignon, with not a strand out of place; potentially errant strands were probably too scared they would ruin the woman's sleek look. Her ivory pantsuit was perfectly tailored. Her crimson nails matched the color of her high heels. A clutch of pearls was around her throat. I couldn't decide if her desk or her outfit cost more. This lady was obviously extremely well paid, yet she didn't risk getting punched in the nose daily the way I did. If Progenitor didn't bring the world to an end, after the crisis was over, maybe I'd find a job as an executive secretary. Or even an under-executive secretary if it was Bernice I was under. Maybe wise old Ben Franklin had been right about older women.

"Do you have an appointment with Ms. Copeland?" Bernice asked, still not looking up as her computer's keyboard clattered like machine gun fire. She had empha-sized the *Ms.*, a subtle rebuke of a lowly peon like me daring to use Sonya's first name.

"No," I replied, though Bernice had asked the question in a tone which implied she already knew the answer. An elite assistant like Bernice probably knew everything about Sonya's schedule, including what she planned to have for breakfast two weeks from now.

"Then meeting with Ms. Copeland is quite out of the question," Bernice said, still focusing on her computer screen and not looking at me. "She's very busy. If you tell me the nature of your business, perhaps I can help you." Her tone hinted she very much doubted it.

Years ago, I would have slunk away at the woman's tone with my tail between my legs. Assuming I worked up the courage to speak to this mature, stunningly beautiful woman at all. Those days were long gone. "Bernice, stop typing," I said, putting a touch of the whip into my voice. "Look at me. Get Sonya on the phone and tell her I'm here to see her."

Bernice's fingers faltered at my tone. She frowned, and then her blue eyes looked up and found the Omega emblem on my chest. She did a double take. Her wide eyes danced all over my costumed body, taking me in. Her ice queen demeanor slipped, and she suddenly seemed years younger. "Omigod, omigod, you're Omega!" she gushed.

That's what my mother named me almost slipped out, but that would've been a breathtakingly stupid thing to say. What sort of lunatic named her kid Omega? Maybe I wasn't as accustomed to talking to pretty women as I thought. Old habits died hard. Instead I said, "Indeed I am. Tell Sonya I'd like to see her."

Bernice's hands fluttered nervously, knocking over a pen holder on her immaculate desk. Pens went flying. I caught them with my powers, putting the holder upright again and the pens back into place. Between my miraculous pen-wrangling powers and Holmesian detecting abilities, Progenitor was surely shaking in his prehistoric boots.

Bernice stared at her pens and me like I had walked on water. Her mouth opened and closed wordlessly. She seemed to have lost her voice, completely flustered by the fact the world-famous Hero Omega stood before her. *In the flesh!* I could imagine her crowing on the phone to her girlfriends as soon as I was out of earshot. *Even with the mask, I could tell he's much better looking than that actor who played him in The Fall of the Sentinels.* My fame had struck again. Sometimes I wondered what Gina and the rest of the New Sentinels' marketing department did to justify their high salaries. This was not one of those times.

"Ms. Copeland explicitly said she did not want to be disturbed," Bernice finally managed to get out. I didn't respond. I just gave Bernice my best encouraging smile, the one immortalized on my New Sentinels Day commemorative poster, the same one Gina had made me practice in the mirror until my lips cracked. Gina had said my old smile made me look like I was introducing myself to someone while holding back a bean fart. A wordsmith, that Gina, always looking to spare your feelings.

Bernice blushed as I smiled at her. I guess all that grimacing in the mirror had done some good. She hastened to add, "But I'm sure she'll make an exception for you. You went through the Hero Trials together, didn't you?"

"We did. We're old pals. Sonya tried to teach me everything she knew. The fact I still can't turn a computer on without electrocuting myself says a lot about my learning capacity."

Bernice laughed harder than the remark justified. With shaking hands, she touched a button on her desk telephone, then the bud in her ear. "Ms. Copeland? Yes, I know what you told me, but Omega is here to see you. Yes, *that* Omega." Bernice paused, listening. Her smile faded, turning into a frown. Her eyes darted up at me, then away, her voice lowering to a whisper. "But Ms. Copeland, I don't think I can bring myself to say that to him. Are you quite sure?"

I knew it was rude, but I did it anyway: I hit the speakerphone button on Bernice's phone with my powers.

"—got some gall," boomed Sonya's voice through the speakerphone. "You tell Omega what I told him on the phone yesterday—I'm not going on some crazy snipe hunt with him. I don't care how much money he tries to bribe me with. I've got more money than I could ever spend already. Tell him to take his money, fold it up until it's all sharp corners, and shove it up his—"

Sonya's voice cut off when Bernice's fumbling fingers finally managed to silence the phone. Her face red, she looked like she would die of embarrassment.

"I wish you wouldn't have done that," I said mildly. "I'm just dying to hear where Sonya recommends I put my money for safekeeping. I'm always on the lookout for sound investing tips. Be a dear and get her back on the phone and ask what the rest of that sentence was. Better yet, I'll ask her myself."

I was already moving around Bernice's desk toward Sonya's closed office door. Protesting weakly, Bernice hopped out of her chair and click-clacked in her heels after me, bleating half-heartedly at me to stop.

I opened Sonya's door and went inside with Bernice in lukewarm pursuit. An office the size of an airplane hangar unfolded before me. The floor was metallic and so shiny, it was almost mirrored. Straight ahead, through the transparent floor to ceiling glass wall, I saw Mount Rainier far off in the distance; to my right lay sparkling blue Elliott Bay. The Space Needle was behind me. The image was so cunningly wrought that it looked like I viewed the Space Needle through yet another glass wall. However, unlike Mount Rainier and Elliott Bay, the image was just a hologram.

Sonya was yelling into a cordless phone's handset, not having yet realized Bernice was no longer on the other end. Sonya's language was colorful. She must've supplemented her technical reading with some pretty racy fiction since the last time I had seen her. She certainly had not picked up those words in the manuals and electronics journals she devoured like a greedy kid scarfing down cake.

As Sonya ranted into the phone, she walked briskly on a treadmill desk facing Mount Rainier. A black metal panel was mounted on the treadmill's side. Sonya had her phone-free hand pressed into it. While Sonya ranted and walked, lines of computer code rapidly appeared on multiple computer screens that were fanned like giant playing cards in front of her. Sonya was transmitting her thoughts through the metal panel and transmuting them into code. Walking, talking, and coding. If Sonya added gum chewing to the multitasking, I would've been truly impressed.

Sonya finally noticed my and Bernice's entrance. Looking confused, her ranting trailed off. She yanked the phone from her ear and glared at it like it had betrayed her. She flung it at me.

I slowed the phone down and altered its flight path, making it smack into my hand. Though Sonya did not have much need for her Heroic combat training anymore, clearly her muscle memory was still sharp—the phone would have smashed into my forehead had I not changed its trajectory. It had been a fantastic throw, especially considering the size of the office.

"You're missing your true calling as a Mariners' pitcher," I called out to her.

"Go away!" Sonya cried, glowering at me. Lines of code still rapidly appeared on the screens in front of Sonya as she continued to power walk.

"Not until you hear me out," I said, walking closer to her. I noticed a Ninja action figure on her desk. It was the only thing there not tech-related. The action figure looked vintage; it was not one of the new ones Gina had commissioned for each of us when we formed the New Sentinels.

Sonya's green eyes flashed with anger. "I did hear you out. On the phone yesterday. And I didn't like what I heard. I don't want you here. You're trespassing on private property."

The expansion of the code on the monitors faltered for an instant, warning me Sonya had diverted her attention for a moment. So I was ready when several copper-colored metal balls about the size of my fist shot out of Sonya's treadmill desk and the back wall. Like the phone had, the balls rocketed toward my head. Bernice screeched and ducked, covering her head.

I wasn't so foolish as to catch the balls like I had with the phone, especially considering Bernice's reaction to them. Instead, I grabbed them with my powers, gathered them together, and trapped them in a spherical force field overhead. The metal balls spewed a pink gas as they caromed inside my invisible field. It was a good thing I had the foresight to make the field airtight. The pink vapor was probably knockout gas. Sonya had antisocial tendencies, but not so much that she would try to gas me to death. Or so I hoped.

I leaned toward Bernice and stage-whispered, "Bernice, I'm not positive, but I'm starting to get the idea your boss wants me to leave."

Bernice grinned. Sonya turned her glare on her, and Bernice hastily wiped the grin off her face. "Shall I call security, Ms. Copeland?" Bernice sounded like she'd rather jab a nail into her eye than do it. My practiced smile was more effective than I thought. I'd have to slip Gina a little something extra this Christmas. Assuming any of us were still around to celebrate Christmas. After watching what Progenitor did to the Neanderthals, I had my doubts.

Sonya snorted at Bernice's suggestion. She looked with disgust first at her trapped balls, then me. "And have security do what, exactly? Shake their fingers disapprovingly at Omega? Wiggle their tails at him like you're doing?"

Bernice sputtered. "I'm doing no such thing."

"That's not the way it looks from where I'm walking. Get ahold of yourself, Bernice. For shame. What would your husband think? You've got kids older than Omega." Sonya shook her head. "Don't bother security. I know better than most Omega's not going anywhere unless and until he wants to. He's stubborn as a . . . as a . . ."

"A mule? A goat? A dog with a bone?" I suggested.

"I don't need your help," Sonya snarled.

"That's not the way it looks from where I'm standing."

"Just go back to your desk, Bernice. I'll get rid of this . . . this . . . animal-referencing interloper."

I raised an eyebrow. "Animal-referencing interloper?"

"You know I'm not good with insults," Sonya snapped.

With a final look and faint smile at me, Bernice click-clacked away. I wanted to examine her retreat to see if she really was wiggling her tail at me, but Sonya was riled up enough as it was. I didn't want to add *MILF Ogler* to her list of my deficiencies.

Bernice closed the door behind herself. The opening disappeared into the seemingly real image of the Space Needle as if the door had been a mirage. I wondered if I could find it again. I wished I had left a trail of breadcrumbs.

Still walking briskly like she was training for the Olympic race walking event, Sonya shook her head disgust-edly at where the door had been. "And to think, normally she's the very picture of maturity and gravity. It's why I hired her."

"It must be the Omega suit. Chicks dig the suit."

"It's certainly not the man in the suit."

I ignored the dig. Sonya was trying to bait me into an argument. "You're looking well, Hacker."

"No one calls me that anymore. My name isn't Hacker. It's Sonya."

"Miss Jackson if you're nasty."

Sonya's forehead wrinkled. "Huh?"

"Never mind." I wasn't surprised she didn't catch the reference. Back when we had gone through the Trials together on the planet Hephaestus, Sonya hadn't even known who Spider-Man was. Sonya was technologically highly literate, but culturally illiterate. If she did not know who one of the most iconic fictional superheroes was, she certainly wasn't going to know the lyrics to Janet Jackson's *Nasty*. Heck, the only reason I knew the lyrics was because Isaac was a huge fan. Janet Jackson was his future sugar momma and second ex-wife, he was fond of saying. Never in front of his possessive and fiery-tempered fiancée Sylvia, though. Isaac didn't have a death wish.

I glanced around Sonya's large office. Looking like a futuristic junkyard, it was the opposite of Bernice's immaculate workspace. Computers, computer equipment, and related tools were piled on the furniture, even the chairs, and strewn all over the floor. If I were to walk from one end of the office to the other—there was so much clutter, running was out of the question—I would have to do it in a zigzag.

I turned my attention away from Sonya's stainless steel rat's nest of an office and back to her. I had not been flattering her before—she *did* look well. When I met her during the Trials, she had been boyish and pale. Now she had the sleek, well-kept look that people with a lot of money often had, even when they were sloppily dressed as Sonya was now. Her hair was the same it had been during the Trials: short, dyed albino white with pink highlights, and in a pixie cut. Gone, however, was the green and tan form-fitting costume she had worn during the Trials, as were the thick black goggles that had hidden her face. Now she wore ratty sneakers, cut-off jean shorts, and a black midriff-baring t-shirt. Her toned, tanned arms and legs gleamed with a light sweat. On the shirt, written in pink lettering, was *I'm not antisocial. You can email me anytime.*

Based on her clothing, Sonya looked like she should be working for Bernice rather than vice versa. But rank had its privileges, apparently including the privilege of making every day super casual day. The only person Sonya reported to at UWant Technology was the CEO, and I heard that even he stayed out of her way. The CEO didn't want to muzzle the mouth of the ox that treads the grain, as the Bible puts it. For Sonya pretty much *was* UWant Technology, at least on the software side of things. She was, after all, a licensed Hero with the Metahuman ability to communicate with any computer, however crude or complex, by simply touching it. When she had jumped ship from her previous tech firm to here, the other firm's stock price had crashed and never fully recovered. Sonya had become quite wealthy post-Trials thanks to her one of a kind skill set. She wasn't the richest person I knew—that distinction belonged to Shay thanks to her inheritance from Mechano—but Sonya was certainly in the top ten once her UWant stock options were factored in. It was quite an accomplishment for someone only about a year older than I.

I looked at the sailboats on Elliott Bay and then at snow-capped Mount Rainier. Pretty as a picture postcard. "Nice view," I said.

"Thanks. It looks even better from *outside*." Sonya's emphasis on the word was not lost on me. But I wasn't going to leave until Sonya agreed to help us with Progenitor.

"Here's a fun fact," I said, procrastinating, dreading what I knew I'd be forced to do. "At a height of 14,410 feet, Mount Rainier is the highest volcanic peak in the contiguous United States."

Thump, thump, thump. Sonya still speed-walked on the treadmill while coding. "It might be a fact, but it's not fun. And what the hell is Mount Rainier?"

Had it been anyone else, I would have thought she was pulling my leg. Sonya's shocking ignorance about certain things and her sometimes odd behavior often made me wonder if she was somewhere on the autism spectrum. I pointed. "That humongous mountain that's been sitting out there ever since you moved to Seattle after the Trials? That's Mount Rainier."

"Oh." Sonya shrugged with indifference. "I knew a mountain was there, of course. I'm not blind. I just didn't know its name. I wish I still didn't. You know I don't like cluttering my mind with needless trivia. It supplants useful information and leads to faulty thinking. Like you thinking I'm going to help you with your wild goose chase. Isn't it enough that I helped you by designing Minerva and Augur?"

Augur was the computer system I had used when I operated alone as Omega before we formed the New Sentinels; it had alerted me about issues and threats I needed to deal with. "You got paid to do that. Handsomely, I might add."

"Exactly. Because that's my job. Just like it's your job to save the world. I don't ask you to design an artificial intelligence matrix from scratch. Don't ask me to save the world."

"If it's more money you're looking for, I already told you that we'll pay you for helping us. Think of it as just another job."

"If I offered you a million dollars to perform brain surgery, would you do it?" Sonya asked.

"Of course not."

"Exactly. You're not qualified to perform surgery, so you wouldn't attempt it regardless of how much money was dangled before you. It's the same thing here. My talents lie with computers, not with world saving."

"The problem with your analogy is that, as you point out, I'm not trained to perform surgery. You are trained to be a Hero, though. Heeding the call to help people goes with the title. Weren't you paying attention when you swore the

Hero's Oath when we got our license?" Feeling a little like a doofus, I recited it:

> "No cave so dark,
> No pit so deep,
> Will hide evil from my arm's sweep.
> Those who sow darkness soon shall reap,
> For in the pursuit of justice,
> I will never sleep."

I didn't feel like a doofus by the time I finished. In fact, I was a little misty-eyed. I took the Oath very seriously, which was why I was willing to do things I rather wouldn't in order to live up to it. It was hard to wrap my head around the idea a fellow Hero like Sonya didn't feel the same way.

But she didn't.

"The Hero's Oath is aspirational, not prescriptive," Sonya retorted primly. "I got my Hero's license because I needed it to use my powers without running afoul of the Hero Act. Not because I long to run around in a neon leotard getting shot at and helping ungrateful little old ladies cross the street. There are lots of Metas better suited for that sort of thing. Your teammate Ninja, for example. She's got the do-gooding and derring-do down pat. She's the best. But just because I admire her and respect what she does, it doesn't mean I want to be her. I'm doing exactly the kind of work I want to do right now, and I'm making a mint while doing it. For me, it's the perfect life. I'm not going to derail my career for god knows how long to chase after some phantasm you dreamed about. Not to mention risking my neck if that phantasm turns out to be real."

"Do you need reminding you wouldn't have a neck to risk if it weren't for me?"

Sonya shook her head. She was breathing hard now, likely more because she had gotten herself worked up arguing with me than because she was tired from walking on her treadmill. Her leg muscles' definition suggested she could walk to the moon without tiring. "I like you, Omega. Always have. You've thrown me a lot of business since the Trials, which I appreciate. And as you alluded to, during the Trials you risked your life by coming back for me during that worm swarm on Hephaestus when you could have just saved yourself. I was in your debt for that. Note how I said *was*. Past tense. I discharged that debt by reprogramming Overlord to give you and Myth a fair shot at both of you winning your Trials' duel. You did something for me, and I did something for you in return. We're even. Don't come in here now trying to guilt-trip me into a fool's errand."

Sonya shook her head again, more firmly this time. "If you want to talk about something other than do-gooding silliness and irrelevancies like mountain names, pull up a chair. Otherwise, get out. If you continue to refuse, you'll discover I have more potent defenses in place than knock-out drones. Stuff you can't even dream of, much less guard against. You've only been here this long because I've tolerated your presence for old time's sake. I'm not someone to trifle with. As you're so fond of reminding me, I'm a Hero too."

Aside from the whir of the treadmill and the pounding of Sonya's feet, the room fell quiet. Despite Sonya's refusal to help, I was undeterred. So far this visit had gone pretty much the way I expected it to. As much as I hated to do it, I'd have to play my trump card.

"I'm glad to hear you've built the perfect life for yourself," I said. "But should the Heroes' Guild discover you tampered with Overlord during the Trials, they'll yank your license. Without your license, you can't legally use your powers. And without your powers, you're of no use to UWant. I visited UWant's human resource office late last night and sneaked a peek at your employment contract to confirm my suspicions."

Sonya's mouth dropped open. "You broke into our personnel files? That's illegal!"

"So was hacking into Overlord. What's a little light felony between friends? Your contract says that maintaining your Hero's license in good standing is a prerequisite to your continued employment as an executive here. It's also a prerequisite to your stock options vesting, and most of your wealth is derived from those options. Good luck getting another baller job like this one without the use of your powers. And without such a job, this perfect life of yours all goes away. I can ruin your life with a simple phone call to the Guild."

Sonya still gaped at me. "Are you threatening me?"

I held her gaze. "It sure seems like it."

She thought about it, then barked out a laugh. "You can't expose what I did with Overlord without exposing yourself. If my license is revoked, yours will be too. Probably Myth's as well. On top of that, they'll throw all of us in prison for fraud and who knows what else. Turning me in would be like burning down your entire house to kill a single mouse. You're neither stupid nor suicidal. Don't make threats you won't carry out."

"Getting locked up doesn't scare me. I've been to jail before. It's not so bad. Peaceful, even. I could use the rest." I shrugged. "As I told you on the phone, if I can't recruit all the people we need, Progenitor will have already won before he steps foot out of the prison he's in. I've got nothing to lose."

I waved Sonya's phone. "Either help us defeat Progenitor, or I'll call Ghost right now and tell him what you and I did during the Trials." Threatening to sic the Guild's intimidating chief investigator on a Hero was like threatening to sic a pack of pit bulls on someone afraid of dogs.

Even so, Sonya laughed dismissively again, still walking and working. "You're bluffing."

I shrugged again and hit the speakerphone button on Sonya's phone so she could hear the call. I dialed a number. Despite my surface nonchalance, my pulse raced. I tried to keep my mounting apprehension off my face.

"It's ringing," I announced, though Sonya could hear the phone ring as well as I could.

"You're bluffing," Sonya repeated. For the first time, though, she stopped walking, placing her feet on the footrests on the sides of the treadmill's spinning belt. She took her hand off the metal pad she exerted her powers through and instead touched the phone's cradle on the desk. Her eyes narrowed in concentration. She was no doubt using her powers to confirm whether I really was calling the Guild.

"It's still ringing," I said. "You only have a few seconds left to change your mind."

Sonya's eyes were distant, then they widened. I surmised she had confirmed I really was calling Ghost. Before coming here, I had memorized the direct number to Ghost's office in the Guild's secret space station headquarters, knowing my conversation with Sonya might come to this. If Ghost didn't pick up, the call would roll over to his deputy Mirage. Either would do.

"You're bluffing," Sonya said again. She sounded a lot less sure of herself this time. She began tapping her cheek with a finger. It was her nervous tic.

"I'm all in," I said, my heart beating faster the longer the phone rang. "Call or fold."

"Hello?" came Ghost's deep voice from over the speakerphone.

Sonya didn't say anything. She just stared at me with a stricken look on her face. Maybe she was envisioning the life she had built for herself collapsing around her. Between her splayed legs, the treadmill whirled like a conveyor belt carrying the debris of her cozy life away.

I hesitated, swallowed the lump in my throat, then said, "Ghost, this is Omega. I'm calling to report—"

"Hang up. Hang up, damn you!" Sonya hissed. "I'll do it. I'll help."

I hit the phone's mute button so Ghost couldn't hear. "Do I have your word?" I asked Sonya. Her word, once given, was good. I wondered if mine still was should I find living up to it inconvenient.

"Yes, yes, you have my word," Sonya hissed, staring at the phone like it was a poisonous snake. "Just hang up."

I hit the mute button again. I noticed my hand was shaking. "Sorry Ghost, false alarm. I'm sorry to bother you." I hung up before Ghost could ask questions I didn't want to answer.

Silence descended. The only sound was the faint tapping of Sonya's finger against her cheek and the whirring of the treadmill belt. Sonya was staring at me like I was someone she thought she knew, but she had been mistaken and I was actually just a stranger.

Finally, she spoke again.

"You're a real asshole, you know that?"

29

I was relieved beyond words when I found myself standing on the grassy cliff above the absurdly blue ocean again. A storm was no longer raging unlike the last time I had been here. Never before had I been so glad to find myself in a dream.

It seemed like I walked forever before I finally discovered Lim again. I grinned as I approached her. Surprising myself, I scooped her up and hugged her.

"While I appreciate the interest," she said, her voice muffled by my chest, "you're too young for me. I'm no cradle-robber." Despite her words, she didn't push me away. Instead she patted my shoulder affectionately.

Embarrassed by my unexpected display of affection and Lim's surprising return of it, I put her back down. "After what went down the last time I was here, I'm glad to see you're okay." I hesitated, unsure what to say next, unsettled by how quickly I had grown attached to the pint-sized telepath and not knowing how to appropriately express the fondness. We were the Wonder Twins, the only two Omega-level Metas in the world on the side of the angels. Lim was the Jayna to my Zan, but I knew better than to call her a cartoon character to her face. "I kinda want to tousle your hair right now."

Lim recoiled as if I'd threatened to slap her. "Resist the impulse. Imagine the nerve!"

"Okay, jeez, I won't actually do it." I wiped the grin off my face. Now that my initial excitement over seeing Lim again was waning, I looked at her more critically. "You look terrible."

"Wow! You sure do know how to make a girl feel beautiful. It's no wonder you're such a big hit with the ladies."

"Sorry. Your appearance just caught me off guard, is all." Lim didn't have her Mastermind costume on again, thank goodness. It had been hard to take her seriously in that getup. Meeting her in this dreamworld was surreal enough as it was. Instead of the costume, Lim wore the black pants, pink ballet shoes, and beige shirt with the bunny on it she had worn when we first met. Only now her outfit was scuffed, stained, and had holes in it, like she was the child of a homeless person. Lim's body matched the raggedness of her clothes—her arms and face were smudged with dirt, her face was wan, and her usually shiny hair was dull and unkempt. Her ponytail was gone. Even her normally high-pitched voice was raspy, like she had spent all five years of her pre-suspended animation life smoking heavily.

Lim looked down at herself and frowned.

"I do look a mess," she conceded. "I've been wrestling with you-know-who ever since you left. It was a struggle, but I got him back under control." The weird sun shone brightly over the promontory, and the storm clouds that represented Arouch's consciousness were off in the distance instead of raging around us like they had when I was last here. The storm clouds were not as distant as they had once been, however. Their thunder rumbled threateningly, far louder than before. "You're seeing a manifestation of the current state of my mind. I could clean myself up some, but it would take needed bandwidth away from my focus on him. What do you care what I look like, anyway? I won't be a victim of the male gaze. This is a Progenitor 101 seminar, not a date. Despite how handsy you've suddenly become."

"You don't have to bite my head off. I was just making an observation."

Lim looked like she was going to snap at me again, then stopped herself with a visible effort. "Sorry. Getting Progenitor buttoned up again was quite a strain. Still is, as a matter of fact. But it's nothing I can't handle." Lim brushed some errant strands of hair out of her eye and tucked them behind her ear. Her Asian face was almost as pale as my Caucasian one. There was bruising under the dirt on her face, as if Lim had been in a wrestling match in the mud. She really did look terrible.

I said, "Maybe this will make you feel better: I finished recruiting everyone you said I need to help me against Progenitor. Everyone's on board."

"What do you want, a pat on the head and a treat? You don't get a cookie for doing what you're supposed to do."

I felt deflated. I thought she'd be pleased at my progress and was disappointed she wasn't. My initial gladness that Lim was all right was rapidly turning into irritation, both at her and myself. Why was I so eager for the approval of someone who looked younger than my breakfast eggs? I said, "Well, aren't you just a big bundle of sunshine and rainbows today."

Lim reddened and looked like she was about to give me a tongue-lashing. She caught herself and took a deep breath. "Sorry. I don't mean to snap at you. I'm tired and stressed and worried and I'm taking it out on you. I'm turning into a termagant in my old age." I didn't know what a termagant was, but didn't volunteer my ignorance at the risk of being called a moron again. "Good job assembling the new team. Really. I mean it. Like I said, getting Progenitor bottled back up and keeping him that way is a strain. More so than usual as he almost got loose. Keeping him under wraps has made me ill-tempered."

"You mean more ill-tempered than usual. At the best of times, you're not what I'd call cuddly."

"Yeah, well, I've got a lot on my plate. You try keeping a homicidal mindmate under house arrest for over eighty years and see if you still have a sunny disposition. Besides, never trust anyone who's cheerful all the time. They're either stupid, medicated, or distracting you so they can pick your pocket."

"You should put that on a fortune cookie."

"It's too many words. What sorta big ass Fukushima mutant fortune cookies have you been eating?"

"Fukushima is in Japan. Fortune cookies are a Chinese tradition."

"Thanks for whitesplaining that to me. You do know I'm Chinese, right? You want me to put on a qipao to make it more obvious?"

"Qipao? I don't know what that is."

"Color me surprised. As usual, I'm right and you're wrong—fortune cookies are derived from a Japanese tradition. In the U.S. during World War Two, Chinese-American manufacturers took over fortune cookie production from Japanese-Americans when the latter were rounded up and sent to internment camps. That's why, in your country to this day, the cookies are so strongly associated with Chinese food despite their Japanese origin. Got it straight in your head now, pink skin? Thanks for coming to my TED Talk." Lim made a dismissive motion. "But enough of the hello again banter. We've got a lot of work to do and not much time left to do it. I reached out to you again today because we're heading back into Arouch's mind. I want to show you as much as I can before he gets free and his thoughts are closed to you. I especially want to show you why I dubbed him Progenitor."

"We barely escaped the last time."

"I think I've made it so he won't detect our presence again."

"You only think?" Though my side had healed from its graze with Progenitor's electrical blast, I certainly hadn't forgotten what it had felt like. "That's hardly comforting. I'd like it better if you were certain."

Lim said somberly, "The only thing that's certain in life is death."

"Don't forget taxes. You wouldn't believe the size of the check I just wrote to the IRS. You'd think they'd cut me some slack after I stopped Gigantica from pocketing the Washington Monument." I was trying to lighten the mood. Lim was as grim as the Reaper today.

"Nope, just death. I've never paid a tax in my life, so that just goes to show what that randy old lech Benjamin Franklin knew. He should've spent more time raising his bastard kid and less time thinking up inaccurate aphorisms and chasing every woman in a petticoat. Besides, how bright could someone really be who thought it was a good idea to fly a kite in a lightning storm?" Lim held her hand out. "Come on, let's get rolling. I'm not getting any younger."

After a moment's hesitation, I took her hand. It felt as different as Lim looked. Her hand was much hotter than before, as if she ran a fever. "Are you sure this is wise?" I asked.

"Wise? Probably not. Necessary? Almost certainly. I want to make sure you're as prepared as humanly possible for your inevitable confrontation with him. I don't know what you might see that'll prove useful. Maybe none of it will be. Or maybe all of it. I don't know. Fisticuffs are your bailiwick, not mine."

Lim exhaled and eyed the storm clouds grimly. "All right, let's go."

As before, we flew off the promontory as if launched from a catapult. The sun disappeared when we plunged into the dark storm clouds once more.

30

Arouch sat on his bejeweled bone throne and wept, for there were no more worlds to conquer.

The Neanderthals were all dead. Under Arouch's leadership, humans had eradicated the monsters as a race centuries ago. The only thing that remained of them was the bones comprising Arouch's throne. Sitting on their remains was a constant reminder to Arouch of how thoroughly he had vanquished the monsters who had killed his family and tortured him.

Per Arouch's instructions when he instituted his Neanderthal pogrom centuries ago, Neanderthal men and children had been killed outright. Some of the women, however, had been kept alive, enslaved, and bred with low status human males who were unable to acquire human females. Over the centuries, the surviving Neanderthal blood had become so diluted not even Arouch could tell at a glance if someone had Neanderthal branches high up in his family tree.

Arouch's stomach did twist with disgust, however, every time he encountered a redhead. Though modern redheads had nothing to do with the redheaded animal who raped and killed his mother, Arouch could not help but view redheads with contempt despite his best efforts not to. Arouch's followers, seeing how their leader treated redheads, aped his example by also discriminating against them. Over the centuries, the bias against redheads had become so ingrained in human society that Arouch knew it would not be soon erased. Assuming it ever would be.

Not only were Neanderthals dead, but all of humanity was firmly under Arouch's control. Over the years, Arouch's tribe had spread like wildfire, conquering every other tribe it encountered, both human and subhuman. For there were, of course, subspecies of men other than Neanderthals and humans. Arouch's mathematical projections indicated those subspecies would gradually become as extinct as the Neanderthals, either killed by Arouch's followers or assimilated into their midst by interbreeding.

Thanks to the conquests of Arouch's tribe, it was not so much a tribe anymore as it was an empire. It spanned the globe, controlling every habitable landmass. Arouch still had a system of satraps who ruled those lands locally, but they all answered ultimately to him. Arouch had lost count of all the people he had slaughtered either personally or by proxy. All to unite humanity under a single banner. His banner. A giant version of that banner was the backdrop to the dais Arouch's bone throne rested on: a clenched silver fist on a field of crimson red.

Arouch had literally conquered the world.

And that fact made him miserable.

What was life, he thought as tears trickled down his face, if not a contest of wills? A competition where a man matched will, wits, and brawn against his environment and enemies to see who would ultimately prevail.

The problem was, over the centuries, Arouch and his followers had tamed the environment and bent it to Arouch's will. They had either killed or assimilated all his enemies. There had not even been a serious rebellion for . . . oh, how long had it been now? Three hundred years at least. What Arouch wouldn't give for a nice coup attempt, or for the inhabitants of his palace to try to assassinate him like a few ambitious men had in the earliest days of Arouch's reign. Something, *anything*, to quicken the blood, elevate the senses, and chase away Arouch's boredom.

The people in Arouch's empire were safer, healthier, and more technologically advanced than any other people in history thanks to Arouch's benevolent rule and the inventions and other advancements that poured out of Arouch's head like water from a spring. Arouch had lifted humanity out of the dirt and enthroned him in the clouds, making humanity the master of all he surveyed. The palace Arouch sat in was emblematic of how Arouch had elevated mankind from the dirt and squalor of savagery. It sat in the dead center of the city, the capital of Arouch's worldwide empire. Taller by far than the tallest tree, the stone, brick, and metal spire rose into the sky like a finger clawing the heavens. Though similarly constructed buildings designed by Arouch dotted the world, by imperial law Arouch's palace was the tallest and would remain so. Not that a formal law was really needed to enforce that prohibition; only Arouch's genius and engineering made such buildings possible. Without him, humans would still be huddling in caves and shivering in grass huts.

But paradise had a price. Arouch feared the peace and prosperity he had imposed on the world had transformed men into mice who were meekly content to be ruled as long as they got their cheese on time. Arouch could not remember the last time someone other than he had a truly innovative thought. Men had become sheep, utterly reliant on their shepherd to guide them, lost without him. Sometimes Arouch was tempted to seal himself into the remotest cave he could find for a few generations to give mankind an opportunity to rediscover its initiative and regrow its backbone.

On the other hand, could Arouch really blame his followers for not even attempting to upset the apple cart? Before Arouch, the lives of humans were nasty, brutish and short. Arouch had changed all that for the better. But perhaps Arouch had gone too far, made life too comfortably easy for his subjects. Why would a child ever wish to leave the cradle if his father saw to the child's every need and the child had no impetus to evolve and grow? At least with a conventional father and child, the child was aware the father would eventually die. The wise child prepared to fend for himself. With Arouch, however, death would not end his paternal benevolence. Arouch seemed to be immortal. He had lived all these centuries without so much as growing a gray hair. He felt as fit, vigorous, and youthful as he had when he first burst out of the Silver Rock Clearing hole the Neanderthals had buried him in. Even more vigorous, actually, as Arouch's powers had only grown and matured over the years. He truly was a god.

No, not *a* god. *The* god. Arouch had realized centuries ago that the gods of the wind, the sky, the sun, the moon, and all the rest of the divine pantheon men prayed and made sacrifices to were merely myths. Personifications of complex forces men's simple minds could not otherwise understand. Arouch alone was divine.

And that was the problem.

Being the world's only god was lonely. Not to mention

horrifically dull. For man, paradise was the ideal. For god, paradise was boring.

Arouch often wished the imaginary gods he still permitted his subjects to worship would become flesh. Then Arouch would have someone worthy to contend with. Someone to test his mettle against. Arouch cursed the day he had ordered Bheb to hide the silver rocks that had helped elevate Arouch to godhood. It had been an act of an insecure young man that Arouch now knew was unworthy of him. If Arouch knew now where the silver rocks were, perhaps he could use them to create new gods. New wolves to hunt with and howl with and fight against instead of the sheep Arouch shepherded. Beings worth vying against.

But alas, Bheb had performed his duty all too well. Many years ago, Arouch had calculated the area where Bheb and the men under his command must have hidden the rocks based on the location of Silver Rock Clearing, how long Bheb and his men had been absent from the tribe, and how quickly men on foot could travel. Despite carefully scouring that large territory, Arouch could find not even a fragment of the rocks. Perhaps Bheb had been smarter than Arouch had supposed. Damn his infernal loyal hide! Arouch wished he could resurrect Bheb so he could smite him again.

So instead of matching wits with gods and wrestling with opponents worthy of him, a weak world lay prostrate at Arouch's bored feet. What was a conqueror without something to conquer? Was a life without struggle, without even the possibility of failure, a life worth living?

The main door to the throne room opened and Melusina entered. With a thought, Arouch made the tears on his face evaporate.

"I told the guards I was not to be disturbed," Arouch

barked, both irritated by the interruption and embarrassed for being caught bawling like a child with a broken toy. "Leave me, witch."

If Melusina had seen Arouch's tears, she wisely gave no sign. Ignoring Arouch's command, the hunchbacked, black-robed crone shuffled across the mirrored floor toward his throne. She cradled a bundle in her arms. Gauzy lights shining like will-o'-the-wisps followed in Melusina's wake, dancing patterns in the air and bouncing their light off the shiny floor. The palace was well-lit by globes of fire that took months to burn out—one of Arouch's many inventions—so Melusina producing her own light source was not necessary. Arouch knew she only did it to impress the ignorant and make the superstitious afraid. Most magicians had a type of magic they specialized in, like divination, alchemy, or druidry. A few, like Melusina, were sorcerers, meaning she could perform all types of magic.

"I'm sorry for the intrusion, Ancient One," Melusina said, though neither her tone nor body language indicated she really was sorry. She kept shuffling toward him. She also didn't look away when he looked her in the eyes, something no one else in the world was bold enough to do. Though Arouch thought his court magician sometimes took too many liberties, he rather enjoyed the fact she did not reflexively kowtow to him the way everyone else did. One might assume it was her advanced age that made her fearless, but in truth Melusina had been this bold when Arouch had first met her when she was but a dewy-eyed girl whose breasts hadn't yet swelled. Confidence was a side effect of power. As the most powerful magician alive, the sorceress was the closest thing Arouch had to a peer. But alas, not even the members of the magical world had proven to be worthy opponents. They had long ago sworn their fealty to Arouch and his empire.

The witch stopped before the platinum dais Arouch's bone throne rested on. "I knew you would want to see this immediately." Wrapped in animal fur, the bundle in her arms squirmed.

"What is it?" Arouch asked impatiently. Brooding had become a hobby, and Arouch was eager to return to it. What the hell else did he have to do?

"A boy. Your son."

Arouch looked down at the squirming bundle. A tiny brown face peeked out of the furs and blew spit bubbles. Arouch would have to take his court magician's word that this was his son. Babies all looked much the same to him. This child could have been the son of one of the palace's stable boys for all Arouch knew. Or cared. "Why bring him here?" Arouch demanded. "I lack the equipment to serve as wet nurse."

The jape did not get a reaction from the old witch. Arouch frowned. If Arouch's other servants had been in the room, they would have convulsed with laughter. What a waste of a perfectly good witticism. Sometimes Arouch wished the witch were more of a lickspittle.

Arouch shook his head, both at Melusina's lack of appreciation of his wit and at the fact his acute nose smelled the baby peeing himself. Arouch would've thought any son of his would exercise more self-control. He considered caving the child's skull in. Maybe outrage would stir the sheep he ruled out of their contended grazing. He sighed, and thought better of it. The juice wasn't worth the squeeze. Humans had become so spineless that the baby's relatives likely wouldn't raise a fuss. Arouch would succeed only in getting brains and blood on his saber-toothed tiger cloak. It was his favorite one. "Get this stinking infant out of my sight. You know the protocol. Give the mother some money as a reward for bearing my seed. If she demands more, kill her, the child, and her immediate family to serve as an example of what happens to those who displease me. Now leave, and never speak of this bastard to me again."

This was of course not the first child Arouch had spawned. Down throughout the centuries, men had offered their women to him. Not to mention women routinely throwing themselves at him. Power was, after all, the ultimate aphrodisiac. Arouch still had no real interest in sex—the image of the redheaded Neanderthal thrusting into his mother was seared into his brain like a tragic mural. However, sometimes he strategically engaged in carnal activities to show dominance or please an important follower. Or, more rarely, out of sheer boredom. Over the years, Arouch had fathered several children. Since the stress of a life-and-death situation had triggered his own godhood, Arouch at first assumed the same would happen if his progeny were put under extreme stress. He had set his young children on fire, encased them in ice, dropped them from the sky, thrown them to packs of dire wolves, and the like. His progeny had all died like mewling babies instead of rising to the situation like gods. Divinity, apparently, did not pass from father to child. When it became clear his offspring were no more exceptional than those of his followers, Arouch had stopped keeping track of the few children he sired or caring one whit about them. When god defecates, he doesn't care what happens to the droppings afterward.

"I do know the protocol," Melusina said. She did not budge from where she stood despite Arouch's order to leave. Boldness was admirable, though sometimes annoying; defiance of a direct order was unacceptable. Arouch considered how best to punish the hag. Ripping one of her hands off would hamper her ability to cast spells, so that was out— her magic was the only reason he suffered the old crone's presence in the palace. Perhaps he would have one of her drooping udders sliced off. It was not as though she needed the blasted things for anything useful; her reproductive years were long behind her. The crone said, "But I also knew you would want to see this boy for yourself."

The infant blew another spit bubble and laughed when it popped.

"Impressive," Arouch said wryly as he contemplated which dug he'd order removed. Definitely the right one— bigger than the other, it swayed when she walked, and Arouch had long found irritating the sound it made as it brushed against the witch's robe. "Shall I make this talented lad my court jester?"

The witch's wrinkled weathered face remained expressionless. Perhaps a flogging would beat a sense of humor into the dried-up old prune. Arouch would ensure she got one after her breast was removed. "No," she said. "Watch."

She put a gnarled hand over the child's face and snapped her fingers sharply. Startled, the baby's face screwed up as if he would cry.

Instead, the baby disappeared. In the blink of an eye, Melusina held seemingly empty furs.

Astonished, Arouch leapt off his throne. "It's a trick!" he cried. "Sorcery!"

Melusina's eyes held amusement at Arouch's reaction. "It's no sorcery of mine, my lord."

Arouch calmed himself with an effort and sat back down. Now that his initial shock had passed, Arouch sensed the witch spoke truly. The human body reacted in various ways when lying, and Arouch's nose, ears, and eyes were so sensitive he could detect those reactions. Also, he still heard the child's heartbeat and smelled his body's odor. There was no doubt: despite being invisible, the boy remained swaddled in the witch's arms.

After a few seconds, the boy reappeared in the furs, blowing spit bubbles as usual, as if he had not just done something miraculous.

If it had not been magic which made the child invisible, then what?

The answer to Arouch's unspoken question leapt into his agile mind even before Melusina spoke again. She said, "The boy seems to have absorbed some of your essence. He has superhuman abilities."

His hands shaking with excitement, Arouch beckoned the witch closer and gently took the boy from her. As the witch had, he snapped his fingers in the child's face. Startled again, the boy disappeared once more. But he was still there; Arouch felt him wriggling.

"He's like me," Arouch said, his voice filling with wonder as the boy reappeared again. "He's a godling." Perhaps Arouch had been wrong in his earlier assessment. Perhaps divinity could be inherited after all.

The baby grabbed Arouch's proffered finger and concentrated on it with an intensity only children seemed able to muster. Arouch found himself doing something he rarely did these days.

"Why do you smile, my lord?" Melusina asked.

"Because," he said, not taking his eyes off his divine son, "this little one is the answer to a prayer."

31

If Arouch's loins could spawn divinity once, they could do so again. If there were no more worlds to conquer, Arouch's loins could create a new one.

Desperately clinging to that idea like a half-drowned man clinging to flotsam, Arouch undertook a campaign to create a race of godlings. He engaged in it with the same single-minded devotion he had dedicated to the eradication of the Neanderthal scum.

He began with Haga, the mother of Jamgurk, the boy who turned invisible. If her womb produced one godling, maybe it could produce others. Arouch killed Haga's mate and took her into his household, intending to make her his broodmare.

At first, however, Haga refused to spread her legs for him again. Arouch had forgotten how sensitive the non-divine were, else he never would have killed Haga's man in front of her. Arouch could take her body by force, of course, but the thought of it reminded him of that damned Neanderthal thrusting atop his mother.

No matter. If one didn't want to force a lock open, one

could learn to pick it.

Arouch treated Haga like an enemy fort, laying siege to her every waking moment. But he did not use strength or weapons or his powers. Instead, he used charm. Arouch treated Haga as if she were the queen of his vast empire and mandated that his subjects do likewise.

Haga liked the taste of royalty. Soon she succumbed to Arouch's charm offensive and took to Arouch's bed as if her dead mate had never existed. *Yes, the non-divine are sensitive,* Arouch thought as he thrust into Haga again, more with the satisfaction of a battle won than with lust, *but that sensitivity can be overwritten by their hypergamy.*

Arouch kept Haga's womb busy. She bore Arouch additional children in rapid succession, but died giving birth to their eighth child. Arouch was livid. What if Haga was the only woman capable of gestating divinity? Haga's midwives insisted they were not to blame for her death. One of them was even brazen enough to suggest it was Arouch himself who had endangered Haga's life by insisting she continue to bear his children despite Haga having developed a condition rendering further childbirth dangerous. The midwife did not say that in Arouch's presence, of course; she whispered it to another clucking hen in the palace. To Arouch, a whisper was as good as a shout.

Arouch personally executed the gossiping midwife and the rest of Haga's midwives for allowing Haga to die and to punish the gossiper's impudence. He killed them in front of their families. The anguish in their eyes amused Arouch. Those days, Arouch had to take his amusement where he could find it.

Instead of putting his and Haga's children under extreme stress to force them to manifest powers as Arouch had attempted with his previous children, Arouch took the opposite tack. He pampered the eight children, catering to their every whim, smothering them with time and affection, all while staying vigilant for a hint of divinity.

Jamgurk, due to his power of invisibility, was his father's special pet. At least on the surface. Secretly, Arouch held Jamgurk in increasing contempt the older his son got. Despite his divine power, Jamgurk turned out to be as dumb, soft and weak as the rest of Arouch's subjects. Maybe even more so, actually, as everything was handed to Jamgurk on a silver platter. Jamgurk never developed the same fierceness and will to power that Arouch had. Quite the opposite. All Jamgurk's life, his impulse was to run and hide in the face of adversity, something he was highly effective at thanks to his invisibility.

Despite the fact Jamgurk showed no sign of being anything but lily-livered, Arouch held out hope his son would change his ways and become the man and potential rival Arouch dreamed he could be.

Alas, it was not to be. Jamgurk dropped dead at the age of twenty-seven during an orgy, morbidly obese, drunk on the fermented beverages his father had perfected, thrusting sloppily into some slattern. Arouch did not mourn his son's death. The strongest emotion Arouch felt was surprise the ne'er-do-well could even find his manhood. After all, Jamgurk's gut had grown quite prodigious over the years.

Arouch performed an autopsy on Jamgurk's body in hopes of determining why he manifested divinity when Arouch's other children had not. He determined his gluttonous son had died of a heart attack, but Arouch found nothing special about Jamgurk's body. The only surprise the autopsy revealed was that the coward actually had a backbone.

Arouch's and Haga's other seven children lived longer

than Jamgurk, but their lives were as undistinguished. Even more so, because they never showed signs of divinity. They all died soft, lazy, and entitled, like indoor pets who never had to fend for themselves.

Arouch was disappointed when the last of Haga's offspring died without manifesting divinity, but he was not yet ready to abandon his dream of creating gods in his own image. Arouch's divinity was clearly inheritable. Jamgurk's mere existence, however disappointing it turned out to be, was proof of that. Perhaps, Arouch theorized, divinity was a recessive trait like albinism or dwarfism: rare but inevitable if spread widely enough in a population.

Free of being palace-bound due to the constraints of constantly monitoring Haga's children for signs of divinity, Arouch resolved to make a fresh start at creating the divine. He abandoned the responsibilities of rule—his empire by then was a well-oiled machine that largely ran itself—and wandered the earth far and wide. Swallowing his distaste for sexual congress, he spread his seed indiscriminately. After all, he did not know what plant might bear fruit. Assuming any did.

Most women slept with Arouch willingly, especially when he demonstrated who he was and what he could do. They were eager to spread their legs for the world's most powerful man. As Arouch often approached those women at night, a legend soon spread that a horny demon with irresistible magical powers of seduction preyed on women after nightfall. Those rumors were started by women with long-term mates who forgot all about those mates when Arouch propositioned them. *The rational mind is a wondrous thing*, Arouch thought as the rumors he was a seducing incubus spread far and wide. *It can rationalize its way into doing just about anything it wants to do.*

Though some women did not couple with Arouch as eagerly as others did, the reluctant ones slept with him anyway because they were afraid not to. Arouch had discovered in his carnal walkabout that most of his subjects were afraid of him. The realization was a surprise. He had cloistered himself in his palace for so long that how the world viewed him escaped his notice. Arouch saw himself as a benevolent father who only wanted the best for his children. Those children, however, saw him as an abusive father who, while a good provider, readily turned violent. They used unflattering names for Arouch when they thought he and his satraps weren't listening: Hellscape. The Adversary. The Destroyer. If humans' dependency on Arouch over the centuries hadn't bred the backbone out of them and if the power differential between Arouch and everyone else weren't so vast, humanity would no doubt rebel and try to overthrow Arouch's rule.

Arouch did not let his subjects' negative view of him hurt his feelings, however. A god did not care what ants thought about him while trampling them underfoot.

Proving his subjects' low opinion of him was unjustified, Arouch left unmolested the few women with the courage to refuse his sexual advances. He did not force himself on them, despite wanting to cast as wide a genetic net as possible. He simply would not lower himself to the level of the trash who had raped his mother.

Once Arouch planted his seed within a willing woman, he moved on. He was interested in accumulating wombs, not wives. Arouch did not discriminate—he targeted any and all women fertile and healthy enough to give birth. Sexually transmitted diseases didn't concern him; he hadn't gotten so much as a cough since ascending to godhood.

Soon Arouch had slept with a multitude of women of

differing ages, shapes, sizes, colors, and living in every clime. He sprayed his sperm like indiscriminate rainfall, hoping to quicken whatever fertile soil it happened to fall in. He took no pleasure in all the fornicating. Quite the opposite. He was a reluctant chef who abhorred cooking, but forced himself to do it in the interest of creating a new dish.

Children inevitably resulted from Arouch's frenzied bedding. Over time they became numerous, spread throughout the globe. Arouch took careful note of all the women he laid with and monitored the offspring some bore him, both with human and animal spies. Thanks to his powers, any animal with the wit to distinguish one human from another could serve as Arouch's eyes and ears.

It took years of carnal cultivation, impatient monitoring, and Arouch wondering if he was wasting his sperm and time. But, eventually, Arouch's campaign to create divine beings like him finally bore fruit.

That fruit took the form of a 12-year-old girl named Lere, one of Arouch's many daughters. She went to her village's stream one day to fetch water when she was attacked by a leopard that had slipped past the village's watchmen. She was found by her half-brother, unconscious, lying by the stream with a leopard bite on her neck and claw marks all over her body. The leopard was there too. Or what was left of it. It appeared the large animal had popped like a kernel of heated corn, as if an explosion had ripped the animal apart from the inside out.

When Lere awoke, she could not explain what happened to the leopard. Only that it had leaped on her from behind, pressing her to the ground, biting her neck. Screaming and terrified, Lere was unable to wriggle free of the stronger and heavier beast. She remembered praying the gods would strike the animal down before it killed her.

Then Lere had felt a violent, painful tremor in her chest, as if a second animal were inside her and clawing its way out. Her vision dimmed and everything around her went white, as if the entire world were dipped in mare's milk. A glowing ball shining like a miniature sun popped out of her chest. It entered the leopard's body, disappearing there like a raindrop into a puddle.

The leopard exploded. Lere passed out, but not due to the explosion, which she had barely felt. She said her blacking out felt more like slipping into a deep sleep after a day's hard labor.

The other members of Lere's village believed the gods had come to her assistance in her time of need. The girl was one of the select favorites of the gods, they proclaimed. That belief was cemented when, a few days after the incident with the leopard, Lere began making objects explode deliberately. Arouch witnessed it for himself. He flew from halfway around the world to interview the girl once his network of spies alerted him to her existence.

He was nearly beside himself with excitement as he watched Lere make a log explode into splinters from over fifty feet away. *No, this child is not one of the gods' favorites,* Arouch thought about the villagers' foolish superstitions. *She is bone of my bone and flesh of my flesh. She* is *a god.*

Exulting, believing he was on the right track, Arouch left Lere and continued to spread his seed far and wide.

Lere was the first flower to blossom from Arouch's seed-planting. She was not the last.

Next came Gat, who could appear in multiple places at once. *Numerical superiority is one of the keys to martial victory,* Arouch mused when he observed Gat in action.

Then came Ilon, who had both microscopic and telescopic vision. *To see all is to know all,* Arouch decided.

Then came Uulled, who had visions of the future which all came true. *Knowledge, especially foreknowledge, is power*, Arouch concluded approvingly.

Then came Froh. He could transform into a miniature goat for a few seconds each day. *What the hell?* Arouch thought, mortified. Arouch wished Froh had the decency to be born female. At least then his power would be good for producing a few squeezes of goat milk every day. But still . . . Froh's ability, albeit disappointingly useless, was further evidence Arouch was on the right track.

More godlings appeared as Arouch continued his carnal campaign. Soon there were divine beings sprinkled throughout the world. Arouch did not scoop them all up and cluck over them like a protective mother hen as he had with Haga's children. He had learned the perils of coddling godlings from how Jamgurk turned out. He would let these new divine whelps develop on their own, carefully monitored but not smothered. One did not, Arouch now understood, raise wolves on a diet of milk and honey.

More and more godlings manifested over the span of many decades. The more who appeared, the more data Arouch had and the more conclusions he could draw:

First, divinity was definitely hereditary and not a mere accident of fate. No one in the world had manifested superhuman abilities other than Arouch's children. He wondered if their children in turn would also have a chance of being touched by divinity, or if Arouch's divine seed would be too attenuated in any generation but the first. Time would tell.

Second, godlings were extremely rare. Every child descended from Arouch had less than a one percent chance of developing divine powers. The probability of it happening was so tiny, it approached zero. Each godling's existence was nothing short of a minor miracle. It explained why none of the few children he had pre-Jamgurk had displayed signs of divinity.

Third, almost all the godlings developed their divine powers during puberty. Arouch theorized that the stress of the transition from childhood to adulthood allowed someone's latent divinity, if any, to show itself. Like a humble caterpillar spinning a chrysalis, later emerging as a glorious butterfly. And, of those godlings who developed their abilities during puberty, every single one manifested his or her powers during extreme stress or crisis. Like the leopard attack with Lere, or Gat falling into a river and almost drowning. Realizing that only the fire of hardship could forge a godling made Arouch curse himself for coddling Jamgurk's siblings—maybe if they'd had to face adversity, they too would have manifested their divinity. It had been a mistake to conclude from his torture of his pre-Jamgurk children that hardship couldn't trigger divinity; Arouch realized his sample size had been too small to draw conclusions from.

Fourth, vanishing few of Arouch's children manifested their powers during infancy like Jamgurk had. Or like Fromm had, who was born with a venomous bladed tail like a stingray's; he'd ripped his mother's insides to pieces during childbirth. Godlings were already a statistical anomaly. Godlings who manifested their abilities as small children were rarer still, a tiny minority within an already tiny minority.

Fifth, there seemed to be no rhyme or reason behind the nature of the power Arouch's children manifested or its potency. It all seemed entirely random.

Sixth, not even the most powerful of Arouch's divine children were as powerful as he. Moreover, he was largely immune to his children's powers. Since the godlings' divinity was derived from his own, Arouch theorized his immunity to their powers was akin to a snake's immunity to its own venom. Frankly, Arouch would have preferred if someone his equal made an appearance. For where was the honor in besting an opponent weaker than you? Arouch comforted himself with the knowledge that a pack of wolves, working together, could best even the largest bull elk. The more godlings Arouch created, the greater the challenge he would have grappling with them.

Arouch's seventh conclusion about his growing gaggle of godlings was drawn almost two hundred years after Lere's powers manifested: Arouch's divinity could indeed be transmitted beyond his first generation of descendants. Arouch discovered this when one of the godlings gave birth to a boy who in turn manifested as a godling as a teen, one strong enough to rip a fully grown tree out of the ground and throw it like a spear. Thereafter a handful of Arouch's increasingly numerous grandchildren and great-grandchildren manifested as godlings as well.

Armed with his data and conclusions, Arouch retreated to his palace in his capital city, sat down in his study, and prepared to make some calculations.

He reached for his magic quill. Not with his hand, but with his mind. The quill sprang upright, hovering at the ready over Arouch's parchment without him touching the writing instrument. Arouch did not trust magic. It was one of the few things on the planet that could hurt him. Also, he couldn't perform it and didn't understand it, and that offended his sensibilities. And yet magic had its uses. The magic quill, which never ran out of ink, was superior to the various writing utensils Arouch had invented over the years. It was a gift from Arouch's current court magician, Vradore. Vradore was an alchemist who could do things like create a salve that miraculously cured wounds, or concoct a potion that put Arouch into a deep slumber when he was unable to sleep without assistance. The long-dead Melusina had never given Arouch a magic quill; all she had given him was attitude. Vradore was an inferior magician compared to her, but a superior toady.

Arouch scratched and calculated, checking and then rechecking his numbers when they did not add up the way he would have liked.

His population projections displeased him. Despite all the work Arouch had put into creating godlings over the years, at the rate godlings were appearing, it would be many thousands of years before there were enough of them to even begin to pose a threat to him. Yes, a pack of wolves could bring down a bull elk, but not if that elk was robust and the wolf pack tiny and anemic.

And, equally troubling, perhaps even a large population of godlings would not pose a threat to Arouch. For, despite their divinity, the godlings showed the same lack of backbone and killer instinct their non-divine brethren did. The godlings were clowns, using their powers as parlor tricks to amuse, seduce, and bring comfort to their fellow men rather than using them to strive, fight, and vie for supremacy. Arouch had hoped his ambition, drive, and will to command would pass to his progeny along with his divinity. But alas—Arouch's monitoring of the godlings showed that was not the case. If anything, they were even softer than their non-divine brethren because the non-divine catered to them. The children of a great man were rarely great, Arouch realized, because they did not have to be. They could merely coast on the achievements of their illustrious ancestor.

Arouch gnashed his teeth with frustration at how things were developing. He pounded his table so hard the thick wood cracked. He was a victim of his own success at bringing men into a golden age where there was little to fear and every need was provided for. Even wolves touched by divinity, Arouch realized, were as plump and lazy as sheep when all their meat was handed to them. Such wolves would not hunt a bull elk. They were too well-fed and comfortable to even consider trying.

If Arouch had any hope of developing a worthy race to strive against, he would have to make the godlings lean and hungry, the way all humans had been before Arouch elevated them from their brutal natural state. Not only that, but he had to increase their numbers.

Arouch stared at his godling population projections sullenly. He wished the numbers were his subjects so he could thrash them for being so disappointing. Arouch did not think he could stand to wait the millennia it would take for the godlings to increase in number enough to pose a challenge to him. He'd thought he would go mad with impatience just in the time it had taken him to grow the existing godling crop. Not to mention all the additional effort it would take. He'd already had more than his fill of copulating with his inferiors. He didn't understand why the non-divine found sex so enthralling. Maybe if they weren't slack-jawed cattle, he'd find mating with them more appealing.

If only he had a time machine. He could travel to the future, one where his baby godlings had grown numerous. And, as importantly, a future where they had grown out of their infancy due to Arouch's absence from the world stage. A future where they had assumed the responsibilities and ambitions of men. True men, not the weak and lazy namby-pambies Arouch ruled over.

Arouch had long theorized time travel was possible, but

the technology that could turn theory into reality was millennia away, even for a genius like him. Especially since Arouch would have to single-handedly birth that technology and all the infrastructure needed to support it. The shiftless and spoiled people he ruled would be of no use, except as dumb manual labor. They were so reliant on Arouch that hard intellectual work was simply beyond them, their brains having long atrophied from disuse. Not that their brains were much to brag about pre-atrophy. Before Arouch, men had shivered in caves and cowered under trees, little more than prey animals. If Arouch hadn't entered their miserable lives, predators surely would've wiped humanity out by now.

Arouch played with the magic quill as he pouted and thought. It swooped in the air before him like the bird it had been plucked from.

Finally, the quill's aerial acrobatics triggered the obvious.

Wait! Of course!

The solution to his woes hit him like the thunderbolt that had catalyzed his godhood. Arouch stood so quickly, his immense strength knocked over the 1,000-pound table he had spread his calculations on. Parchment went flying.

"Guards!" Arouch bellowed. He would have them fetch someone for him.

He stared at the enchanted quill quivering in midair. He did not have to invent a time machine. He already had one of sorts.

Rather, he knew someone who did.

32

Arouch unstopped the small earthenware jug and took a cautious sniff. He snatched his head back, wrinkling his nose. The fumes burned his nostrils. The jug's contents smelled like Jamgurk's butt cheeks had. Perhaps even worse, as hard as that was to believe.

Arouch hastily shoved the cork back into the jug. Doing so barely reduced the stench, which lingered in Arouch's throne room like marsh gas. Sometimes Arouch regretted having such a sensitive nose. First knowing what Jamgurk's butt cheeks had smelled like, now this.

Perched on his Neanderthal bone throne, Arouch eyed Vradore suspiciously. The black-robed wizard was looking down, not willing to meet his gaze. Like a good flunky. Or, like someone with something to hide.

"Look at me," Arouch commanded. When Vradore's reluctant brown eyes met his, Arouch probed the wizard's face suspiciously. Unlike the other court magicians Arouch had over the centuries who all looked older than dirt,

Vradore was middle-aged. The alchemist wouldn't get a second older if Arouch wasn't satisfied by the answers to his questions. "Are you certain this potion will put me in a state of suspended animation?"

"Yes, Ancient One."

"And it won't harm me in any way?"

"No, Ancient One."

Arouch stared at the wizard with every sense alert. Vradore's heartbeat was regular, his perspiration rate was normal, his nose wasn't flaring, his pupils neither contracted nor dilated, and he wasn't emitting the distinctive musk of fear mixed with caginess people gave off when they were being deceptive.

The wizard was telling the truth. Arouch relaxed, unclenched his fist, and leaned back in his throne. He had been primed to smite the wizard where he stood if the wizard was duping him into drinking poison. When Arouch first seized power, malcontents had tried to poison him. To no avail. So Arouch knew he was immune to standard poisons; magical ones might be lethal. Not that Arouch seriously thought the brown-nosing magician had the balls to poison him. Arouch wouldn't feel compelled to take leave of the current world if it still had men with balls in it.

"How long will this potion render me comatose?" Arouch asked.

"With a small period of suspension like hours or days," the wizard said, shifting nervously, uncomfortable with looking his lord in the eye, "I can predict the revival time down to the second depending on the strength of my magical elixir, the dosage given, the weight and constitution of its drinker, and whether the drinker is of the magical or mundane worlds." His eyes fell, looking down again. Old habits died hard. Or perhaps Vradore had remembered what happened to the last person who forgot his place and looked Arouch in the eye for too long. A human-shaped scorch mark on the throne room's shiny floor was all that remained of the man; it defied the scullery maids' efforts to scrub it away. "But with the vast amount of time you requested I make this elixir for, it's impossible to say for certain. No less than 20,000 years, but certainly no more than 50,000. I can't be more specific than that. I'm sorry."

Vradore paused, blinking rapidly, almost cowering, fearing his imprecision would result in the scorch mark gaining a twin.

When that did not happen, he continued tentatively, like an abused wife afraid to speak up for fear of being smacked. "My only concern, mighty and wise Ancient One, is the welfare and protection of your most holy body while you're unconscious."

"That's none of your concern," Arouch retorted harshly, making the wizard quiver. Despite the snarl in his voice, Arouch was pleased by what the wizard had wrought. Arouch's calculations indicated at least 20,000 years was sufficient. Vradore had done his job well. The wizard would get no thanks from Arouch, though. A dog should get no reward for barking—it was his job to bark.

Cradling the earthenware vessel, Arouch arose and stalked off the dais. Vradore recoiled as Arouch brushed by the wizard, fearing he had displeased his lord.

Ignoring the wizard, Arouch burst through the throne room doors. Armed guards on the other side began following in Arouch's wake, but he waved them away. They were nothing but an ostentatious display of power anyway, like the plumage of a peacock. The guards were superfluous.

There was nothing in this world Arouch could not protect himself from. And that, of course, was the problem. The problem Arouch now held the solution to.

In his silver armor and with his favorite fur cape swirling around him, Arouch strode purposefully through the palace's corridors. His subjects instantly dropped to their knees and knocked their foreheads to the ground as he passed them. People had been known to literally knock themselves out while kowtowing to Arouch; it was considered safer to err on the side of showing too much respect than to risk showing too little. He ignored their bows, just as he ignored the fur capes a few wore which were pale imitations of Arouch's more resplendent saber-toothed tiger one. Only his most powerful subjects were permitted to ape their master by wearing the capes. Wearing one had become a mark of distinction around the world, deeply embedded in the public imagination. Arouch wondered how long the tradition would last after he was gone.

The palace had thousands of rooms, most of which Arouch never visited. But his retentive mind had no trouble leading him to the correct door. He burst through it and into a bedroom; it was the room closest to the throne room that had an opening to the outside. Three people were in the bedroom: one of Arouch's noblemen and two wives of a different nobleman, thrashing naked in bed.

One of the adulterous wives spotted Arouch and squealed. Arouch shook his head in disgust as his three sweaty subjects gaped at him. It wasn't the adultery that bothered him. More often than not, monogamy was honored only in its breach; to consider man more than a hairless ape ruled by his genitals was to give him too much credit. What bothered him was the fact these indolent idiots were such slaves to their passions they felt compelled to fornicate in the middle of the day, what should have been their most productive hours. It was yet another example of how soft and corrupt men had become during Arouch's reign.

The sybarites scrambled off the bed and kowtowed to him. Ignoring them and the stench of their lovemaking, Arouch continued to the bedroom's balcony doors. Flinging them open, he strode out.

A brisk wind tugged at Arouch's cape, making it snap. The capital city spread out below him, gleaming in the midday sun. He had named it Atlantis. Even with Arouch's telescopic eyes, the people far below looked like ants. Containing tens of thousands of residents, Atlantis was the largest and greatest city the world had ever known. The city's ornate buildings had all been designed by him. Though the buildings' design complemented the wondrous palace, they did not imitate it. The palace was sui generis, a miracle of engineering. It climbed high into the sky, a tower reflecting Arouch's towering greatness.

Arouch's legs tensed, about to propel him high into the deep blue sky. The wind shifted, giving him another offensive whiff of sweat and musk. Arouch frowned. He had dismissed all thought of the three fornicators immediately after discovering them. Smelling them again reminded him the two women had a gaggle of small children. At the very least they should be tending to their snot-nosed crotch goblins instead of wasting time copulating, spawning more.

Mildly annoyed, he set the magic potion down and retreated back into the room. He grabbed his naked nobleman by his neck and snatched the women up by their long hair. Stiff-armed, Arouch carried the three like sacks of squirming, screaming rats back to the balcony. Ignoring their pleas, he flung them over the railing. Their cries trailed them to the ground, then abruptly died. From this high up, not even Arouch's sensitive ears picked up their impact with the ground.

After retrieving the potion, Arouch launched himself into the air with a whoosh. The city grew even smaller than it had looked from the heights of Arouch's palace. He oriented himself, preparing to fly north. A flock of birds far below him altered course to avoid his palace. Arouch sensed the birds' thoughts like they were whispers in the wind. He smiled. The birds thought the towering building was a tree. Birds were stupid. Humans were almost as stupid, Arouch thought. Perhaps even more so. At least birds had the wit to fly.

Arouch paused at the thought of human stupidity. Instead of flying north, he halted above the tall spire of his palace. Arouch had initially intended to take his leave from this world immediately, without so much as a goodbye to the dumb brutes he ruled. But the satisfaction Arouch felt at killing the three layabouts on a whim made him realize a goodbye was only appropriate.

A whim was now a blueprint.

Arouch extended an armored hand, reaching out with his powers. Those powers enabled Arouch's mind to bore through the earth's surface, into its bowels. The non-divine were too witless to have realized this, but the earth under their feet constantly moved. That movement was usually so slow and gradual, though, that the non-divine weren't aware of it.

Obeying his silent command, the ground shifted. At first slightly, then more and more profoundly. The ground's usually creeping movement became abruptly sudden. Seismic waves were unleashed, causing an earthquake, with the palace at its epicenter.

The city's buildings shuddered almost imperceptibly, then moved visibly as the earthquake increased in intensity. The palace was the last to begin quivering. Arouch had designed it to withstand normal tremors. This was no commonplace tremor, however. Arouch was creating a once in a lifetime earthquake the likes of which the city had never seen before.

Panicked screams rose from the city's denizens, swelling into a crescendo that Arouch heard despite the increasingly loud rumbling of the ground and the shaking of buildings. The screams sounded sweet to his ears; he drank them like a dessert wine.

Despite how well-engineered and well-constructed the palace was, not even it could withstand the terrific forces Arouch had unleashed. It collapsed in on itself, sending up a massive plume of dust that rose like ash from an erupting volcano. Soon it was nothing more than a large pile of rubble ringed by lesser piles of devastation. The entire city had been destroyed.

As Arouch let the earthquake subside, he did not think of his wizard Vradore or the hundreds of others dead and dying in the palace's rubble. Nor of the tens of thousands more dying in the devastation Arouch had wrought. He was glad he had destroyed the gleaming city. Humans did not deserve to bear witness to the achievements of their divine better.

Thanks to Arouch's earthquake, Atlantis was now but a smudge on the landscape below. It was an augur of the future. Considering humanity's gnat-like memory, Arouch suspected Atlantis would soon be erased from man's mind just as it had been erased from the face of the earth. It would become the stuff of legend, a vaguely recalled racial memory of the greatness Arouch had elevated humanity to.

Using the world's magnetic poles to orient himself, Arouch rocketed off to the north.

As Arouch flew, he thought about what would happen to his subjects. Without him, they would inevitably slide back into the savagery and want of the Stone Age, especially because their reliance on him had made their bodies soft, their minds weak, and their spirits brittle. The cities they had built under Arouch's direction would molder and be gradually reclaimed by the earth. On its own, humanity didn't have the wit or wherewithal to maintain them. Humanity would rise from the muck once more and establish civilization again, Arouch reckoned, but the process would be exponentially slower and more fitful without Arouch's strength and genius.

The magical folk would inevitably rule them, at least for a time, Arouch concluded. Arouch's absence would of course result in a major power vacuum. Nature abhorred a vacuum, and the magical folk would inevitably fill it. Magical folk had so much power, and ordinary humans so little.

And then of course, there were the godlings. With him gone, he hoped and believed the godlings' superior abilities would finally begin to breed superior ambition. A father leaving the home forced children to mature and leave the ease of childhood behind. As the godlings matured and grew out of the infantile mentality they had due to life being too easy, some would become predators and some would try to protect humanity from those predators.

Unless Arouch was very much mistaken—and when was the last time he had been mistaken about anything?—magical folk would have their day in the sun first. Then would come the godlings' turn once they were more numerous and hardened by the state of nature that would reassert itself in Arouch's absence.

Arouch intended to be there when it was the godlings' turn at bat. Only during that golden time would Arouch find entities worthy of striving with. And against.

As Arouch flew further and further north, human settlements became rarer, and then ceased altogether. The snow on the ground transitioned into ice. Temperatures dropped precipitously. Arouch barely noticed it. His divinity protected him from the cold and heat. Arouch had worn clothes all these centuries as ornamentation, not because he needed them. When they froze and became stiff due to the extreme cold, he ripped them off and jettisoned them. Naked, he kept flying. There was no call for ornamentation or modesty where Arouch was going. Besides, a man entered the world naked. It was only meet for him to enter a new one naked as well.

Eventually, there was nothing but ice below, growing thicker the further north Arouch went. Arouch's formidable intellect had studied the earth and its evolution for centuries. He had long ago concluded that, despite the world still being in an ice age, it was gradually warming. Ice had once covered the globe but, due to the planet warming, the ice was slowly retreating to the earth's northern and southern poles.

Arouch's calculations made clear that, 20,000 to 50,000 years from now, that ice would still be atop the poles even with the shrinkage. The frigid regions were now inhospitable to human life and would remain so for many millennia.

That made them the perfect place for Arouch to sequester his body to await the dawn of a new day.

Arouch touched down on the North Pole. Snow and bits of ice swirled, melting on Arouch's naked body. It was pitch dark. No matter. Due to Arouch's divine eyes, he saw as clearly as if it were noon at Atlantis.

Arouch unstoppered Vradore's potion, grimacing again at the rancid smell that assaulted his nose. Swallowing his distaste, he did the same to the potion. Thick and oily, the disgusting liquid burned as it oozed down Arouch's throat. His stomach roiled as the substance settled there. Before he had been indifferent about Vradore dying. Now that he tasted how vile the wizard's potion was, he wished he had witnessed the magician's death with his own eyes. He hoped it had been a slow one.

Arouch put the empty jug on the ice gently, so as not to break it. Many thousands of years from now, perhaps some intrepid explorer would come here, intending to capture the glory of being the first person at the North Pole. Maybe he would discover the man-made object and realize he was not the first person to come here after all, not by a long shot. His ambition and struggle to get here would be in vain. The thought amused Arouch. Humans weren't even competent enough to be the first to explore their own planet.

Arouch's eyes began to droop, and his limbs felt heavy. He dared not dawdle—the magical elixir was already affecting him.

Arouch's silver armor withdrew into his body, exposing naked brown skin. Taking and holding a deep breath, Arouch triggered his powers again, this time to heat the ice directly below him. The ice melted and Arouch plunged into freezing water.

Making his body's density increase so he would continue to sink, water bubbled around him as he plunged deeper and deeper into the watery shaft his powers drilled into the ice. Despite being naked, he didn't so much as shiver. Just as Arouch had been immune to the cold air, he was immune to the water's cold as well.

Finally, Arouch reckoned he was sufficiently deep that even tens of thousands of years of global warming melting the ice above him would not expose his body. He stopped melting the ice beneath his feet, coming to a halt at the bottom of a deep, watery shaft.

Arouch closed his eyes, surrendering to the drowsy lure of the magic potion. He commanded the water around and above him to become ice again. The water sounded like breaking tree branches as it rehardened around him, entombing him in ice far below the surface. The only air was that trapped in Arouch's lungs, but once the potion took full hold of him, he would not need to breathe. Every bodily function would shut down, as if every fiber of his being had been paused. Arouch's body would be safe down here while it was defenseless for millennia in its magically induced suspended animation.

Arouch's normally supercharged brain slowed, his thoughts creeping like molasses. He felt his heartbeat decrease and the rest of his body shutting down. And yet, despite his heart slowing, it practically sang. For when Arouch awoke, he would be in the future. A brave new world, one filled with gods like him.

No, not merely like him. Of him. Divine blood of his blood. His children. His prospective foes and allies. But most importantly, his family.

Arouch had once thought humans were his family. That was one of Arouch's few mistakes. A butterfly was not the kin of the lowly caterpillar even though it evolved from one. Slaves were not family to their master. Cows were not family to their butcher.

One last thought drifted lazily through Arouch's mind before it and the rest of his body shut down:

I've never been to the future, yet it is there where I'll find my true home.

LIM AND I FLOATED OUT OF AROUCH'S ICE-ENCASED HEAD LIKE tiny ghosts. Still holding hands, our bodies grew to normal size as we rose upward, passing through ice that transitioned to dark storm clouds as we exited Arouch's consciousness.

"Why are we leaving?" I demanded, confused and annoyed as we whipped through the clouds. "There's still so much for me to learn. Like what happens when Arouch awakens and how King Arthur defeats him."

"I'll have to tell you the rest," Lim said, her voice hoarse. "I can't keep us here safely anymore." She looked even worse than she had when we first entered Arouch's mind. Her clothes were threadbare, her face was pale, and her hand was even hotter than before. So hot, holding it was uncomfortable.

"But—"

"Shush!"

I shushed, but not because she told me to. It was because a look of intense concentration mingled with exhaustion was on Lim's face as we whipped through the storm clouds. I felt like a passenger trying to have a conversation with a pilot as she struggled to bring a plane in for a landing in the middle of a storm.

We cleared the storm clouds and swooped toward the grassy promontory. Though the storm clouds weren't raging around us as they had the last time Lim and I exited Progenitor's mind, they definitely were closer now than they had been when we entered them.

The moment we touched down on the grass, Lim released my hand. She spun away, put her hands on her knees, and began vomiting.

I froze, worried, not knowing what was wrong or what to do. "Are you all right?" I asked her.

It took a while before Lim finished throwing up. She turned back to me, unsteady on her feet, wiping her drooling mouth on her sleeve. "Just a little worn down is all. Other than that, I'm right as rain."

"You don't look it. In fact, you're bleeding."

Seeing where I was pointing, Lim wiped her nose. Her shaking hand came away red. "Guess I'm a little more worn down than I thought. We'll have to finish our talk later. Off you go." Lim reached for my leg to jar me awake, but I danced out of the way.

"I'm not going anywhere," I insisted. I again dodged her swipe at me. She looked like death warmed over, and it was easy to avoid her clumsy attempts to touch me. "Not until you tell me what's wrong with you."

At first Lim looked stubborn. Then exhaustion overwhelmed the expression. She wobbled, then sat, almost collapsing. Her legs splayed open in front of her. Her nosebleed was a steady trickle now. She looked like she was holding back more vomit. "Maybe you're right," she said, her voice hoarse. "Maybe it's best to tell you now. To be honest, I don't think I'm up to bringing you here again. It may be the last time we see each other."

"Tell me what?" I demanded. "What do you mean, the last time we see each other? What are you talking about?"

Lim looked up at me. Her teeth were stained red from the nosebleed.

"I'm dying," she said.

33

"Dying?" I exclaimed. "How could you be dying? Your body's in a state of suspended animation nearly as complete as Arouch's magically induced one. Anatomically, you're only five-years-old. Your whole life's ahead of you."

Lim wiped her bloody nose again. "Unfortunately, my body's age is irrelevant. The age of my mind is what's germane. It's in its late eighties. Older than that even, as wrestling with Progenitor has put more miles on my consciousness than living a normal life would've. My neural pathways are degrading, and have been since the moment I moved my consciousness from my body to keep Progenitor imprisoned. Taking you into Progenitor's mind accelerated the degradation, unfortunately. It's why he was able to perceive us the last time I brought you here; that never would have happened if my mind were still fresh and undamaged. Breaking you free of his hold when he attacked us, getting him back under control, and then taking you for another field trip today accelerated my mind's corruption even more." She looked down at herself. "It's why I look and feel like I've been ridden hard and put away wet. My haggard appearance reflects the state of my mind."

Stunned, the strength flooded out of my legs and I flopped to the ground across from Lim. I couldn't believe this was happening. "You should have told me. I never would have let you take me into his mind had I known."

Lim smiled wanly. "I know. That's why I didn't tell you. But it was necessary. You had to see him in operation for yourself. See what he's like. See what you're up against. Maybe pick up something that'll be helpful in your looming confrontation with him. Sure, I could've just told you what I'd learned about him all these years of riding shotgun in his consciousness, but describing a car accident and witnessing it firsthand are two very different things. 'A picture is worth a thousand words' is a cliché for good reason—because it's true."

I shook my head stubbornly. "I'm not going to let you die. There has to be something we can do." My head was spinning. "I'll talk to Doctor Agrawal. Surely he'll have some thoughts. Better yet, I'll track down Doctor Hippocrates. He can use his powers to heal you."

Lim shook her head, sadly but firmly. "You forget whom you're talking to. If there was a way out of here other than on my back, don't you think it would have already occurred to me? My condition is far beyond Agrawal's ministrations. Hippocrates' too, for that matter." Lim smiled mirthlessly. "What I need is an undertaker, not a doctor."

I rubbed my chin, in total shock and disbelief. I had been so proud of myself for recruiting our new team, pride that was shattered by this news. Why did it seem like every time I took two steps forward, the world shoved me five steps back?

I realized I should have caught on to Lim's fate sooner. I

remembered what Lim had said today about death being the only certainty in life. And when we'd gone into Progenitor's mind for the first time, she'd said she wouldn't be around to publish a paper about why the Neanderthals had gone extinct. She had even once called herself Charlotte, the spider who died in *Charlotte's Web*. She had been alluding to her death. I had been so focused on Progenitor, I'd missed all the clues.

"How long have you known?" I asked. "That you were going to die, I mean."

Lim shrugged, grimacing in pain at the motion. She lowered her shoulders gingerly. "Pretty soon after I left my body and entered Progenitor's mind. I knew that, if I was going to keep him trapped as long as possible, there was no going back."

"Then why stay? Why didn't you return to your body the instant you realized staying would be a death sentence?"

Lim gave me a look. "Come on. You know why."

I understood what she meant instantly. The same calculus had motivated most of my decisions the past few years. "Because you saw what needed to be done, and you were the only one who could do it."

"Bingo. 'I slept, and dreamed that life was beauty; I woke, and found that life was duty.' Ellen Sturgis Hooper knew what was up. A shame her poetry has faded into obscurity." Lim reached up to move an errant strand of hair from her eye. A clump fell out and tumbled onto the ground. The dark hair looked like a scar on the vividly green grass.

Lim seemed taken aback. She eyed the fallen hair uneasily, then gingerly touched the bald patch left behind on her head. "Well, *that's* not a good sign. It's worse than I feared. I have maybe a few days left before the fat lady starts singing. After that, there's nothing left to stop Progenitor from busting loose. You and your team need to hustle to get ready. He'll be weakest the moment he gets free, so that'll be the best shot you'll have of subduing and capturing him. This'll have to be the last time we talk; I'll need to husband my remaining strength to continue to wrestle with him and give you as much time to prepare as possible. Listen close, 'cause I've got some thoughts on what you should do."

Numb with shock, I tried to swallow my emotions for now and absorb what Lim said. We talked for a while about Progenitor. Well, Lim talked. Mostly I listened.

By the time we finished, we'd moved to sit side by side with our backs to the storm clouds. We had moved because Lim said she'd scream if she had to look at them one second longer. I felt like screaming to, but for a different reason. I was just getting to know Lim, the only person on the planet like me who wasn't a villain, and she was already being snatched away. Mom, Dad, Hammer, Hannah, Neha . . . when would it end?

"I guess my team and I are on our own from here. Any last words before you send us out on the field, coach?" I often got flippant when I was uncomfortable, and I was that now. Despite my lighthearted words, my heart was anything but light.

Lim thought about it. "Yeah. Here's my well-considered sage advice: Don't screw the pooch."

"Inspiring words. They're bringing a tear to my eye." I wiped my eye, hoping Lim would think I was pantomiming the joke. I wasn't.

"What do you want from me? I'm no Knute Rockne."

"Who?"

"Sometimes I forget how young you are." Lim reached over and patted my knee. "You're a good boy. You'll do fine."

"I hope so."

Lim hesitated, then said, "Can I give you some unsolicited advice?"

"You giving unsolicited advice? That's a first."

Lim smiled faintly. "What I shoulda said was, 'Here's some more unsolicited advice, smart-ass, and you're gonna take it if you know what's good for you.'"

"That sounds more like the Lim I know. I'd hate to think the specter of dying has softened you."

"Hardly. The mighty Mastermind is not afraid of the Grim Reaper; the Reaper is afraid of her." A faint tired smile played on Lim's bloody lips. "Here's my advice: You need to lean into your strengths."

"What's that supposed to mean?"

"I'll answer your question with another: Have you ever thought about why the Omega spirit chose you as its vessel?"

"You mean why it picked an inexperienced kid who'd barely stepped foot off his family's farm instead of an older, more experienced Meta who knew what the heck he was doing? No, the thought never crossed my mind."

Lim pursed her lips. "I would've thought your parents raised you better than to sass an old woman on her deathbed. You're right—the Omega spirit could have chosen someone more worldly. Someone more ruthless. Someone a lot smarter. Someone less mistake-prone. Someone—"

"If this is your way of building my confidence," I interjected, "it's not working."

"Someone less likely to interrupt his elder while she's making a point. The point is the Omega spirit could have chosen someone with a completely different set of arguably more useful traits. And yet it chose you. I'll admit that, at first, I thought the Omega spirit got its wires crossed. After all, the thing's been around longer than even Progenitor's been. Though that does beg the question of what it was up to when Progenitor was in his prime. By picking you, I thought maybe the spirit had lost its touch in its old age.

"But the longer I've known you, the more I believe the Omega spirit knew exactly what it was doing. The fact you reacted quickly and saved both our lives when Progenitor tried to blast us confirmed it for me. You've got good instincts. When push comes to shove, you tend to do the right thing. Like I said, you're a good boy. A good boy with the capacity to be a great man if you're smart enough to get out of your own way. If the world needed someone well-seasoned, the spirit could have picked someone like your friend Truman Lord as its vessel. If the world needed ruthlessness, it could have picked someone like Truman's friend Shadow. But instead it chose you—someone raised to believe that there's a right and a wrong way to do things, and that a man, if he's any kind of a man, steers toward the former and avoids the latter.

"So again, my advice is this: You need to lean into your strengths. Decency. Kindness. Honesty. Loyalty. Taking responsibility for your mistakes. The values you were raised with. The values the Omega spirit almost certainly picked you for."

"That's easy to say," I said, feeling bitterness creep into my voice, "but a lot harder to do. Especially when there's so much at stake. I've failed before. Let people I care about die before. I don't want that to happen again. How can I be expected to always follow the rules and color inside the lines in a world where the lines are usually blurry and sometimes completely nonexistent? And especially when I'm up against people who laugh at the very idea of rules?"

"If I had the answer to that, I'd be the carrier for the

Omega spirit instead of you. People like King Arthur, Joan of Arc, Omega Man, and Avatar typify your predecessors. They amply demonstrate the Omega spirit has an exceptionally good track record when it comes to picking champions. I don't think it made its first mistake with you. You'll figure it out. I have faith in you."

I sighed, thinking of the low regard Isaac currently held me in. "Glad someone does."

We sat quietly for a while, lost in our own thoughts as we stared off into the distance. I tried to tune out the rumble of thunder at our backs, to pretend we were just friends sitting in a park, looking out at a seemingly infinite stretch of grass. Maybe, somewhere far off in the distance, was a place—a better place—where Progenitor didn't exist and Lim didn't have to die. I wanted to sit here and look for that place forever. I knew I needed to wake up because the team and I had a lot of work to do. But I wasn't ready to leave Lim.

And I wasn't ready for her to leave me.

"I need to ask you a favor," Lim finally said. She still stared into the distance. Maybe she was looking for the same happy place I was.

"After all you've done for me? All you've done for the world? Anything. Name it."

"As you know, there are some misguided souls who worship me as a god. *The* god, actually. Qiaolianism is monotheistic. The irony is, false god though I may be, I'm actually capable of hearing my worshippers' prayers thanks to my telepathy. Or at least I was before Progenitor started consuming all my bandwidth." Lim shook her head. "I don't know whether to call the damned thing a cult or a religion. After all, what is a religion but a cult made respectable by the passage of time? Regardless of what you wanna label it, I didn't do anything to smother Qiaolianism in its infancy because I was too busy Progenitor-wrangling. That and, at first, being worshipped was kinda flattering. You might not have noticed this, but I have a bit of an ego. Ego and genius go together like peanut butter and jelly."

Lim's wry smile turned into a frown. "But now I find being worshipped and prayed to embarrassing and not just a little mortifying. Especially after marinating in *his* delusions of godhood all these years." She jerked a thumb over her shoulder at the storm clouds. "Like I told you before, my body's in a state of hibernation. When my mind dies, my body will too. Its vital signs are barely detectible, but they're there. My priests check them from time to time, so they'll soon discover when my body stops functioning." Lim wrinkled her nose. "Assuming the smell of rotting flesh doesn't give it away first."

Talking about Lim's dead body made me squirm. "So what's the favor?" I asked.

"I'm getting to that. Jeepers! Regardless of your other virtues, the Omega spirit sure as heck didn't select you for your patience. I'm not sure what my priests will do with my dead body. They never planned for the eventuality—they just assumed I would go on forever. I'm supposed to be a god, after all. Most of my followers are true believers. But, as with all religions, there are some who aren't true believers and are just in it to fleece those who are. Qiaolianism's founder was a true believer. Crazy as a loon and didn't bathe as often as he should've, but a believer. His daughter, the current head priest, is one of the charlatans. The only god she believes in is the almighty dollar. Knowing her, she's liable to stuff my dead body, mount it, and charge a thousand yuan a head for worshippers to view it in the main temple." Lim shuddered. "Gruesome. I won't be put on display like a trophy animal."

"When you die, you want me to dispose of your body," I guessed.

"Would you?"

This conversation was already unpleasant, and the thought of handling Lim's corpse was even more so. But that didn't matter. "Of course. What do you want me to do with your body?"

"As long as I don't wind up the Chinese version of a cigar store Indian, I'll leave it to you. I'd tell you to give me to my family, but I don't really have any. I'm an only child, and my parents are long dead." Lim shrugged. "Shoot me into space like you did with Mechano, if you want. I'll be past caring, anyway."

"As smart as you are," I said, feeling myself tearing up again and willing myself to stop, "you couldn't be more wrong. Because you do have family. You have me."

Lim looked up at me. Her eyes welled up. She looked away, wiping her eyes with a sleeve. "I'm not crying," she said, her voice husky. "The mighty Mastermind doesn't cry. It's just that something got into my eyes, is all. All this grass. Must be adult-onset allergies."

I didn't trust myself to speak. Apparently, allergies were contagious.

We sat in silence again for a while, staring into the distance.

"At times like these," Lim eventually said, sniffling a little, "one finds oneself thinking about life. What you've done right, what you've done wrong, what you'd do differently . . . that sort of thing. I don't regret coming here with Progenitor. Sure, living with him all this time has been one big bundle of ick, but it needed to be done and I was the only one capable of doing it. No regrets on that front. But what I do regret is the stuff I missed out on. I wasn't there when my parents died. I never got to live in an adult body. Never grew into a woman. I've never fallen in love, never had sex, never been kissed . . . heck, I've never even had a man's arm around me."

I hesitated, then scooted close and put my arm around Lim. I felt her freeze, then she relaxed, melting into me.

Neither of us spoke for a bit.

"If you think I'm going to do that other stuff too," I finally said, "think again. Geriatric porn's not my cup of tea."

Lim laughed for a long time. When she stopped, she cried even longer. I comforted her in silence and pretended to not notice her tears. The mighty Mastermind did not cry.

I held onto her for as long as I could. But eventually, she gently pushed me away. I felt her slipping away like grains of sand I was desperate to hold onto.

The dream faded, all its vivid colors becoming desaturated. The last thing I saw was Lim patting my leg affectionately with a hand that became increasingly translucent, like a ghost who was drifting away from this world and into the next.

I awoke to find myself in my bed in New Sentinels mansion. No longer holding Lim, I clutched only my bed sheets. And a memory.

Staring at the ceiling, I lay in darkness for a long while in the silence of my lonely room. Dawn was hours away, and it felt like it would never come.

I thought of the past and of the future. First Dad, then Hannah, then Neha, and now Lim. I was sick of losing people because of bad guys. I was sick of the good guys defeating bad guys, only to have them break out of prison to go on a rampage again. It was so common, it had become a trope in superhero literature and comics. Art reflected reality. How many times had Silverback been in an out of prison over the years? Mad Dog? Doctor Alchemy? Iceburn? I had spared the latter's life once, back when I was only an Apprentice. At the time, it seemed like the right thing to do. Hindsight was twenty-twenty. Maybe sparing him had been a mistake. If I had put him out of his misery then, he wouldn't have cropped up again like a bad penny in the company of the Revengers. Sometimes it felt like we Heroes were hamsters on a wheel—it didn't matter how much effort we expended or how hard we ran, we always wound up at the exact same place.

And now the godfather of bad guys was about to break out of prison after being put there by one of my Omega predecessors. His escape would kill Lim. Hell, he had slowly been killing her for the better part of a century. How many more people would Progenitor kill before he was subdued again? How long would it be before he escaped once more after that? How many innocents would be hurt or killed then?

I had made a lot of mistakes as a Hero. I was, after all, not as smart as Lim. Or as righteous as Isaac, or as perceptive as Shay, or as experienced as Truman. But what I did have was the humility to learn from my mistakes. And letting all these Rogues do the same thing over and over with just a slap on the wrist was one of those mistakes. Maybe that was why the Omega spirit had picked me— because I was capable of learning from tangles with Rogues like Iceburn and applying those lessons to Progenitor.

I'd been toying with the idea ever since my first visit into Arouch's mind had shown me what he was capable of. This latest trip and Lim revealing she would die because of him crystallized the notion:

Maybe it was time to break the vicious cycle, once and for all. To finally hop off the futile hamster wheel to nowhere. To burn it and the cage confining me.

A little moonlight trickled in through the window, creating dark shadows in the room. My vision swam, distorting the shadows, turning them into monsters that frolicked and cavorted around me.

I tried to shove aside thoughts of Rogue ghosts of past, present, and yet to come. I instead focused on Lim. Almost gone, but definitely not forgotten.

My vision's blurring worsened. First my cheeks got wet, then the pillow.

Maybe it was true that the mighty Mastermind did not cry.

But I did.

34

"Sorry I'm late," Hacker said as she stepped into the conference room where Isaac, Shay, Rewind, Grimoire and I sat. It was obvious the *sorry* was for everyone else; the venomous look Hacker gave me said *screw you.*

Everyone eyed Hacker. Now that she was rich, she had upgraded the simple green and tan costume she had worn when I met her during the Trials. Looking at this new costume was like looking at a brand-new Ford Mustang versus its 1983 version. While still sporting the same green and tan color scheme as her old costume, this one was sleeker, slightly iridescent, and form-fitting. The multi-pouched utility belt sloping over her hips matched the blackness of her goggles. The goggles projected a hologram around her face, subtly changing her features so Hacker wasn't identifiable as UWant Vice President Sonya Copeland.

The mansion's metal door automatically slid shut behind Hacker, shutting out most of the sound of the construction proceeding in the neighboring Situation

Room. Just sitting next to that room made my skin crawl. The Situation Room was where I had exchanged Neha for what I had tricked Mechano, Millennium and Seer into believing was the Omega weapon. Since a concealed bomb killed Neha shortly thereafter, the Situation Room brought back a flood of unpleasant memories. I usually avoided it like it was a nuclear waste site. I could avoid it no longer. Desperate times called for desperate measures.

Hacker took the long way around the rectangular table to avoid where I sat at the table's head. Rewind admired Hacker's taut backside as she walked by and wolf-whistled. Grimoire snorted derisively, while Isaac gave Rewind a glare that would make boiling water freeze. Rewind pretended to not see the glower. He and Isaac still had not warmed to one another. They mixed as well as oil and water. No, more like napalm and gasoline.

"No problem," I said as Hacker settled into a seat as far from me as possible. "I know you're busy supervising the UWant techs." Hacker pointedly ignored me, refusing to meet my gaze. She was still pissed at me for forcing her to take a leave of absence from UWant and was not afraid to show it. Smudge marks were on her face; dirt and oil stains dotted her otherwise shiny costume. I saw bags under Hacker's eyes through the goggles. All evidence of the almost around-the-clock work Hacker had put in over the past few days. I had to hand it to her: despite her antipathy toward me, she was living up to her word by working like a dog to prepare for Progenitor's arrival.

Hacker's bad attitude was not the only proof of her dislike and distrust of me. The other silently orbited around her head like moons around a planet. They were copper-colored spherical drones like the ones she had shot at me in her Seattle office. The drones accompanied her every second she was in New Sentinels mansion with me. She controlled them remotely with her powers via computer chips sewn into the underside of her costume. Though Hacker had never come right out and said it, I got the distinct impression she always had the drones with her as protection against me. Like carrying pepper spray when walking in a bad neighborhood. I didn't take offense. As long as Hacker did what I told her to do, she could tote around a portable surface-to-air missile for all I cared.

Hacker and I were at the ends of the table. To my left were Isaac and Shay; to my right, Rewind and Grimoire. Hacker kept glancing shyly at Shay and then looking away, the way a Willow Wilde groupie might who couldn't believe she sat next to The Queen herself. Everyone was in costume and mask. Other than me, no one knew the secret identities of everyone in the room. We weren't friends who all trusted each other, so people wanted to keep their secret identities just that—a secret. We were greater strangers to one another than even the original New Sentinels had been.

With everyone except Hacker looking at me expectantly, I began. "Now that Hacker's here, let's get started. Minerva, soundproof and lock the room. And keep an eye on the UWant workers in the Situation Room. Make sure they don't poke their noses where they don't belong."

The muffled noise coming from the Situation Room died. "Done and done, Captain Queeg," returned Minerva's voice from a speaker in one of the conference room's metallic walls. *Captain Queeg?* That was new. But I didn't make anything of it—Minerva was odd sometimes. "Shall I record this inaugural meeting and include the footage in the documentary I'm making? The working title is *The Rise of the Newest New Sentinels*."

"No. Butt out and shut up." Shay's eyes widened at my

tone, but I didn't care. I was in no mood for Minerva's silliness. Addressing everyone else, I continued. "I am sad to report that Mastermind is dead. I just returned from China. Her worshippers aren't aware of her death yet, but I confirmed with my powers her body is no longer functioning."

"I'm sorry to hear that, Omega," Shay said.

I dismissed her condolences with a slight wave. If I dwelt too much on Lim right now, I'd just get upset. "There will be time for mourning later." *And for grabbing Lim's body*, I added silently. If I had done it today in broad daylight, I would have triggered an international incident between China and the United States the repercussions of which I could not predict. I'd have to retrieve her body later, when the watchful eyes of Lim's high priests weren't on me. And also when the watchful eyes of Shay and Isaac weren't on me. They would not approve of me kidnapping the body of another culture's god. I didn't give two hoots about their approval—I had promised Lim. "Right now, we need to focus on finding and containing Progenitor. Mastermind said he would escape his confinement mere days after her death. She was spot on about everything else, so we can assume she's right about that too. The first thing we need . . ."

I trailed off, distracted by Grimoire. One of Hacker's drones had moved out of its orbit around her head and now buzzed around Grimoire like a giant wasp. Grimoire tried to swat the drone away, but it dodged out of the way. The orb flashed brightly, then discharged energy that struck Grimoire's gauntleted hand like a mini-lightning bolt.

"Hey! That hurt!" Grimoire exclaimed, shaking her zapped hand. She glared at Hacker. "What'd you do that for?"

"It wasn't me," Hacker said apologetically. "Come here, Jobs." The offending drone silently zoomed back to Hacker. It stopped behind her neck, part of it exposed and pointed toward Grimoire, like a shy little kid peeking from behind his mother's leg. Jobs was short for Steve Jobs. Hacker had named each of the drones after a tech giant, probably because she didn't know enough broader cultural references to name them after anyone else. Hacker said to Grimoire, "When I'm not controlling them directly, I give the drones autonomy so their AIs will evolve more quickly. Jobs didn't mean any harm. He's just curious about you. He says there's an unusual energy field coming from your outfit, and particularly from your cape."

"It's not a cape," Grimoire bristled, flexing her hand gingerly. "It's a cloak."

Hacker frowned. "What's the difference?"

"The difference is—" Grimoire stopped, groping for words, seeming to not have an answer herself. "The difference is I don't wear capes. How about you stop worrying about my outfit and focus more on your own greasy, skintight one? You look like a stripper moonlighting as a mechanic. And keep your shock ball babies away from me, or else I'll perform a few late-term abortions."

Jobs quivered and ducked completely behind Hacker. The remaining drones fell out of orbit and formed a phalanx in the air in front of her. "You wouldn't dare," Hacker hissed.

"Just watch me."

"Catfight!" Rewind exclaimed gleefully.

Shay and Isaac exchanged looks as Rewind watched the two women squabble like it was a UFC fight. I knew what Shay and Isaac were thinking: that I had exchanged professionals like Slab, Blur and Flare for these three misfits. I was like Jack from the famous fairytale, having swapped the family cow for useless magic beans. Frankly, I shared their concerns: dealing with Hacker, Grimoire and Rewind was like herding cats. It was hard to believe this was the team best suited to confront Progenitor. But Lim hadn't been proven wrong yet. As she had said, you had to work with the tools on hand despite their flaws. On top of that, I couldn't help but wonder if Grimoire had deliberately picked a fight with Hacker. No one was talking about Grimoire's strange energy readings the drone had detected. Maybe Grimoire was diverting attention from her magical nature. Lim had said the magical world's chief rule was to do what it needed to stay hidden. Maybe there was method to Grimoire's seeming madness.

I knocked a knuckle on the table until I got everyone's attention again. What I really wanted was to knock some heads together, but kept my fraying temper under control. "We need to get back on topic," I said. "There's precious little time, and we're wasting it. As I was saying, the first thing we need to do is finish work on Sentry. Hacker, where are you and UWant on that?"

"Back up a step," Grimoire interjected. "Who's Sentry?"

"It's a what, not a who," Hacker snapped, still annoyed with Grimoire. Her drones were still in attack formation, pointing at the cloaked woman. "First you can't define the difference between a cape and a cloak, and now this. Don't you know anything?"

Ninja spoke up before another argument broke out. "Sentry is the early warning system designed by my former colleague Mechano that we old Sentinels used to identify and monitor threats around the world. It drew on satellite, news, security, and cell phone feeds from around the globe, distilling and feeding the data into the mind of a Hero on

Sentry duty so she could decide when and if the Sentinels needed to take action."

"And it was as legal as a Peeping Tom," Isaac interjected. Watching Sentry in action under the former Sentinels was how I found out Astor City Mayor Stone was a drug addict. Sentry had tapped into his house's security cameras and displayed the man shooting up in the supposed privacy of his own home.

Shay nodded in agreement. "True. Sentry's use broke several laws, invaded people's privacy, and violated civil liberties. But we as a team decided such a system was necessary to help us keep people safe. The ends justified the means. Or so we told ourselves. But then Omega exposed the crimes Mechano, Seer and Millennium were committing behind the backs of the rest of us, and that they had abused Sentry in furtherance of those crimes. The remaining Sentinels realized we had been wrong in ever using Sentry, so we took it offline. When Myth, Omega and I formed the New Sentinels, we agreed to keep Sentry offline and never resume its use. The potential for abuse was too great."

"Proving that you should never say never," I said. "In light of the threat Progenitor poses, we've decided to restart Sentry."

"No, *you* have decided to restart Sentry," Isaac said, not bothering to keep the irritation out of his voice. In an executive council meeting with just the three of us days before, both he and Shay argued against it. I had put my foot down, relying again on the authority granted me by the New Sentinels' official bylaws.

"How the decision was made doesn't matter," I said. "What matters is that Progenitor soon will escape from the non-corporeal dimension he's trapped in and he'll materialize back in this one. Mastermind doesn't—" I caught myself at the use of the present tense, swallowing the sudden lump in my throat. "Mastermind didn't know where Progenitor would materialize. She said it could literally be anywhere on Earth. We need to find him when he appears. He'll be weak and disoriented. Our best chance to capture him will be at that moment."

Grimoire said, "Let me guess—the plan is to use Sentry to scan the globe for Progenitor when he materializes." She shook her head in disbelief. "It's not like the guy's gonna show up with a neon sign around his neck flashing 'Big Bad.' Don't you know how many people there are in the world? Looking for one dude amid billions seems worse than looking for a needle in a haystack."

"More like looking for a needle in a needlestack," Isaac agreed.

"And what if Progenitor materializes in an isolated area?" Grimoire added. "Like the Sahara Desert or the bottom of the Pacific Ocean. There's no satellite footage out there for this Sentry doohickey to draw from. Unless Big Brother's tentacles extend even further than I think they do."

I was impressed. Grimoire had zeroed in on the nub of the problem I had spent time wrestling with. She was no dummy. It reinforced my speculation that her picking a fight with Hacker had been deliberate. "Sentry alone probably wouldn't be enough to find Progenitor. But we're going to use it in conjunction with my telekinetic touch and Tar Baby."

"Tar Baby?" Grimoire said.

Rewind shot Isaac a smirk and opened his mouth. Before he got a word out, Isaac said, "If something racial flies out your mouth, I'm gonna take my boot and shove your words back in so hard you'll need surgery to have it removed." Rewind saw the hard look on Isaac's face and closed his mouth again.

I said to Grimoire, "Progenitor attacked me and Mastermind during our review of some of his memories. The attack left behind in my body a unique combination of psionic and electrical energy. Also trace amounts of foreign genetic material, presumably Progenitor's. Tar Baby is what we've been calling the black goo Doctor Agrawal extracted from my wound. Agrawal assures me there's nothing else like Tar Baby in the entire world. Which means, if the range of my telekinetic touch were wide enough, I could use it to scan the entire world for a sign of anything matching the unique energy and genetic signature of Tar Baby. Unfortunately, my power's range is not wide enough to encompass the entire world.

"That's where Sentry comes in. Theoretically, we can plug my mind into Sentry and use it to boost the range of my telekinetic touch. So much so I'll be able to scan the entire globe for any sign of Progenitor's appearance. Hacker is working with Agrawal to turn that theory into reality. She's reprogramming Sentry's software to task it to do what we need, as well as supervising a squad of subcontractors from UWant Technology to retrofit Sentry's hardware."

"I thought you said there was no way to know when Progenitor would appear," Rewind said. It was good to see he had actually been listening instead of merely ogling Hacker and thinking of ways to annoy Isaac. "What if Progenitor shows up while you're getting some shut-eye instead of while you're hooked into Sentry?"

"I simply won't sleep. I'll stay connected to Sentry for days on end if I have to." I shrugged. "I don't need much sleep anyway. I'll power through it. The stakes are too high for me not to."

"You won't have to just rely on your willpower. I can give you some, uh . . ." Grimoire hesitated, then said, "medicine that will keep you awake and perfectly alert for days on end. You'll have to sleep for a week when it wears off, but hopefully Progenitor will be taken care of by then."

After experiencing Grimoire's pixie dust, I didn't doubt her ability to give me something to keep me awake. "Good. Let's plan on you doing that." I turned my attention back to Hacker. She still avoided my eyes. While I'd been telling Grimoire about Tar Baby, Hacker's nervous tic had manifested: she was tapping her cheek with a finger. Perhaps her row with Grimoire had upset her even more than I thought. "All this talk about Sentry leads me back to my original question. How much longer will Sentry's retrofit take, Hacker?"

Still tapping her cheek and not meeting my gaze, she said, "The UWant techs should finish work shortly. After that I just have to upload and test the new software. Sentry 2.0 should be up and running in a few hours. No later than midnight tonight."

"Well done," I praised her, trying to ease her obvious anxiety. It didn't work. If anything, her cheek-tapping increased in intensity. Oh well. There wasn't time to coddle her. "Here's the plan I've come up with. Some of you know bits and pieces, but not all of it. So if you've got suggestions or improvements, I'm all ears. First, I'll use Sentry to locate Progenitor once he appears. When he does, I'll hit the panic button to alert you all to get ready. I'll take Grimoire and fly to wherever he is."

"Under your own power?" Rewind asked. "Why not use one of your fancy-schmancy superhero jets?"

"And why just Grimoire?" Ninja added.

"I can fly much faster than even our fastest jet," I told Rewind. "As for why just Grimoire, the fewer people I have to wrangle and transport to Progenitor, the faster I can get there. For all we know, Progenitor might arrive in the dead of night while the rest of you are asleep. Grimoire and I will get underway while the rest of you get ready. Grimoire tells me that, despite the range of her teleportation portals being unlimited, she can only open them at locations she's been to before or that are within her direct sight line. Once we arrive on scene with Progenitor, wherever in the world that may be, she'll open a portal, come back to the mansion, and bring the rest of you back to me. Together, we'll subdue Progenitor. Then we'll turn him over to the Heroes' Guild and let them figure out what to do with him."

"Subdue the father of all Metas?" Rewind barked out a laugh. "Good luck with that. I'll stay behind and look after things here while you're gone. What if a little girl needs a cat rescued out of a tree? Better yet, a nineteen-year-old looking for a father figure to pet a different kind of kitty."

"No," Isaac said firmly. "You'd steal everything you could get your hands on. I'm not letting you out of my sight."

"We all have to confront Progenitor together," I insisted. "Mastermind made quite clear we must act together to have any chance of prevailing. And on that note, once Hacker is finished with Sentry, we'll all do some battle drills in the Peril Room." Hacker was poking herself so hard now, I feared she would drill a hole through her cheek. For the first time she looked at me, staring at me as if trying to decide something. What was her problem?

"What's the Peril Room?" Grimoire asked.

"It's a part of the mansion we use for training exercises," Isaac explained. "It utilizes holograms and force fields to simulate reality. Just like in the Trials." Grimoire nodded but, if my suspicions were right that she wasn't actually a licensed Hero, she of course had never gone through the Trials.

"I've fed every detail I can remember about Progenitor into Minerva," I said. "She's created as realistic a simulacrum of him as she was able. We'll use it and the Peril Room to figure out the best way to take Progenitor down. We'll fight the simulacrum in every conceivable climate so we'll be ready for the real deal regardless of where he materializes on the planet. Be sure to—" Hacker's cheek-tapping abruptly stopped. Her hand shot into the air, and she waved it like a kindergartener seeking the teacher's attention. "Just speak up, Hacker. No need to raise your hand. We're all adults here."

"Well, some of us are," Isaac muttered, giving Rewind the stink-eye. Rewind smiled at him and flashed the white power hand sign.

Hacker's hand slowly descended. "I know I gave my word I would help in the fight against Progenitor, but I can't stay quiet about this." She looked around the table. "Does everyone else know what we're signing up for?"

"What do you mean?" Grimoire asked.

"While I was working on Sentry today, I tapped into Minerva because she'll be overseeing Sentry's functions. While digging deep into the recesses of her matrix, I stumbled across a bunch of hidden files that were encrypted and password-protected."

"So?" Isaac said. "Minerva stores a lot of sensitive information, including my collection of quicksand porn. She pretty much runs the mansion. We can't let her data fall into the wrong hands."

"True, but mansion-related information is stored in a

different location in Minerva's mind. I should know, I designed her. Somebody had put the files I'm talking about in an out-of-the-way spot they had taken great pains to hide. But Minerva had bits of residual code in her matrix that hinted at those files' existence. Code that she herself had created. It was as if she had left a trail leading me to those files despite being forbidden to come right out and tell me about them. I got curious, so I broke into the files and took a peek." Hacker raised her hands defensively against the glare Isaac gave her. "I'm a hacker. It's right there in my code name. Hacking into things is what I do. What I found was—"

"What you found is not relevant to this discussion," I interrupted. "We'll discuss your breach of our security privately. Right now, we have bigger fish to fry."

"But—"

"I said we'll discuss this later." I gave Hacker a hard look that made her shrink back in her chair. Shay was studying my face with her perceptive eyes, so I made my face impassive again. "Now, as I was saying—"

"I want to hear what Hacker found in these secret files," Shay announced.

"Me too," Isaac agreed.

"We're getting off track," I insisted. "The longer we sit here blathering, the less time we have to prepare for Progenitor."

Ignoring me, Shay reached over and patted Hacker on the hand encouragingly. "Go ahead, dear. What did you find in those files?"

Hacker looked down at her hand as if she would never wash it again. "What I found was—" Hacker stopped herself abruptly, twisting to look at Shay. Hacker's words came out in a rush. "Ma'am, let me tell you what an honor it is to be in the same room as you. You're my favorite Sentinel. You first, then Avatar, then Lady Justice. Before she got into trouble, I mean. I never read your comic books because comic books are a waste of time and brain cells. No offense. Your poster hung in my bedroom when I was a kid, though. And now I have an entire room in my house devoted to your memorabilia. I dress up like you every Halloween. I have all your action figures. Even the rarest one with the kung fu grip."

"Staaaalker," Rewind murmured in a singsong voice.

"That's very nice, dear," Ninja said, "but let's get back to what you saw in those hidden files."

"Yeah. Of course. Sorry, ma'am. Big fan." Hacker's voice hardened as she eyed me again. "What I found was that Omega has already run a bunch of Peril Room simulations. Ones where he recreated not only Progenitor, but all of us."

"Of course I did," I said. "Did you expect me to sit around twiddling my thumbs while you worked on Sentry? I was preparing. Mapping out combat contingencies."

"As far as I can tell," Hacker said, "you were mapping out the best way to kill Progenitor. You seem to have settled on ripping Ninja's sword out of her hand and running it through Progenitor's chest while the rest of us restrain him. After all, when she uses her Meta powers on her katana, it can slice through anything."

The silence that followed was deafening. All eyes swiveled to me.

"Is this true, Omega?" Shay asked. Her eyes probed mine like she was trying to read a book whose print had faded.

"Of course it's true. I already told you. I ran simulations to explore every possible eventuality. You know how chaotic fights get. We have to be ready for anything."

"That doesn't exactly answer the question," Isaac said. He impaled me with his eyes. "More like sidesteps it. You know what Ninja meant. I'll ask the question more directly: Do you plan to kill Progenitor?"

"No. Of course not. We've talked about this. We're going to capture him and turn him over to the Guild."

Isaac continued to stare at me. I held his gaze easily.

After a few seconds, he sighed in resignation. His chair scraped the metal floor as he stood. He glowed as he moved around the table toward me, transforming into a mythic form.

He stopped in front of me, having become a young, tall, strawberry-blonde man with pale white skin and a bare barrel chest. He wore a green and black tartan kilt. A nimbus of faint reddish-yellow light surrounded him. A large black stone hung in a mesh bag from his belt. A wooden spear whose tip was covered by a leather bag was strapped to his back. Blood oozed from where the bag was cinched tight with a rawhide cord. A broadsword was in Isaac's large hands. Unlike Isaac's body, the sword glowed white.

I had seen this mythic form of Isaac's once before, back when we searched for Doctor Alchemy on his island lair. Isaac had become Lugh Lamfada, aka Lugh the Long-Armed, a god in Celtic mythology. The broadsword was called Fragarach. The Answerer. Isaac had used the blade to compel one of Doctor Alchemy's henchmen to tell us how to find the hidden Rogue. Anyone Isaac touched with it was compelled to tell the truth.

Isaac's big body loomed over me like a giant's. I looked up at Isaac's severe face, then at Fragarach. Its sharp edges gleamed like something otherworldly. A hard knot twisted in my stomach. So this was how a condemned man felt facing his executioner's ax. If Isaac felt compelled to use the

Answerer on me, he had lost all faith in me. What had happened to us?

My eyes moved back to Isaac's face. His green eyes blazed down like fire. "C'mon man," I said quietly. "This isn't necessary. We're brothers. You know me."

"I knew the old you." His voice was deeper than normal and almost musical, like listening to a bass sing *Amazing Grace*. "I'm not sure about this new version."

Isaac pressed Fragarach's blade to my throat, at a spot where the Omega suit didn't cover me. The blade pressed into my flesh. Grimoire gasped and moved to stand, but Shay stayed her with a wave.

The sword, razor-sharp, sliced into me. I felt a bit of blood begin to ooze from the wound and trickle down my skin. Despite the pain, I couldn't move away from the metal biting into me. I couldn't move at all. All I could do was sit there as the sword's glow spread to me through the cut, suffusing all throughout my body, warming me from the inside out like whiskey downed on a cold day.

"The mighty Fragarach compels you," Isaac intoned, his green eyes glowing, his face expressionless. "Do you intend to kill Progenitor?"

I couldn't stop the answer if I wanted to. But I didn't want to stop it. I was eager to respond. The answer bubbled out of me like lava from an erupting volcano, impossible to stop, a single word that seared the air.

"Yes."

Isaac's eyes danced and flickered, impossible to read. "Did Mastermind tell you to kill him?"

"No. She advised me to capture him and surrender him to the Guild."

"Then why do you plan to kill him?"

Words gushed out like water from a spring. "Because he

is a monster who alternates between relishing hurting people and being utterly indifferent to their suffering. He's too dangerous to be allowed to live. Too many have already died thanks to him. I'm sick of Rogues' revolving door of villainy. If I don't stop Progenitor once and for all, who will?"

Expressionless, Isaac nodded. He withdrew his sword from my neck. The warmth and paralysis it caused instantly disappeared. I gasped, able to move again, feeling like I had gone from being tied up in a warm bath to being free and dunked in ice water.

Isaac transformed back into his normal costumed self. No longer expressionless, various emotions played on his face, like a spinning roulette wheel whose ball hadn't yet decided where to land.

He bent over, putting his mouth alongside my ear. This close up, the blood-red dragon on his torso looked especially fearsome. I had the sudden and irrational fear he was going to bite my ear off.

"I warned you there would come a time when you went too far, Theo," he murmured in a low voice only I could hear. "And here we are. I don't know what's more disappointing—that you're planning to murder someone in cold blood, or that you're capable of looking me dead in the eye and lying about it."

Isaac straightened and backed away from me. He raised his voice and spoke to the others without taking his eyes off mine: "I don't know about the rest of you, but I for one won't be an accessory to murder. Or conspire to commit one. I'm done. I quit."

Without a further word, he turned and went to the door. I wished he really had bitten my ear off. Anything but his implacable coldness that froze me in my seat. I knew I had to say something to convince him to stay, but words failed me.

The door slid open and shut again. Just like that, Isaac was gone.

Everyone's eyes moved from the closed door back to me.

"Isaac's right." Ninja's voice was calm, but the fact someone like her had slipped and called Myth by his real name demonstrated more clearly than a temper tantrum how angry she was. She stood and moved toward the door. Hacker quickly got up too and hastened after her. "This is wrong. You're wrong. You of all people should know better than to use murder as a means to an end. Have you already forgotten how Mechano behaved? He was a cautionary tale, not a template to follow. I wouldn't have stood for the crimes he committed had I known about them, and I won't stand for them now. I quit too."

The door slid open again and Shay walked out. Hacker almost stepped out too, hesitated, then turned to look at me from the open doorway.

"And to think, you had the nerve to lecture me about what it means to be a Hero," she said. "It just confirms I was right about what I said before. You *are* an asshole."

The last of Hacker's drones scooted out the room right as the door clicked shut behind her. Despite the fact everything I had worked toward for years was collapsing around me, I was stuck in my chair. I felt rooted there, like someone too stunned by an unexpected earthquake to move out of the way of falling debris.

"Didn't you say earlier we're certain to fail unless everyone is on board?" Grimoire asked. Her mysterious eyes were impossible to read.

Emotions roiling, too stunned to speak, I just nodded numbly.

Grimoire got up. Her hands began moving in a familiar pattern. "I'm not much for suicide missions. More importantly, though I've made a lot of mistakes in my life, I'm not willing to add murder to the wall of shame. I know how important this is. But I'm out too. If you figure out a way to get the band back together without turning us into a death squad, holla at your girl."

One of Grimoire's black and blue portals opened, shimmering with magical power. She stepped through it and disappeared. An instant later, so did the portal.

Just a criminal and I were left. Rewind alone had made no effort to leave. Isaac would probably say that birds of a feather flocked together.

Just as Hacker had, Rewind raised his hand. The cheeky bastard.

"What?" I snapped.

Rewind put his hand down.

"This is my first superhero meeting," he said. "Do they all go this well?"

35

Sweat stung my eyes. I wiped my wet brow with a forearm. I straightened, easing the tension of my aching back, feeling perspiration trickle down my spine. My wet clothes clung like a straitjacket. It felt like I'd been shoveling forever in the darkness.

I was already in a dark hole, and yet I kept digging. Sometimes life was too obvious about its metaphors.

Sighing, I thrust the shovel into the hard-packed dirt again, tossing another shovelful over my shoulder. The manual labor reminded me of childhood. Back when I still lived on the farm with Dad, whenever I was sad, upset, or bored, he immediately put me to work in the hot fields. "It's hard for a man to be sad when his arms are tired," he had often said. It was one of his Jamesisms.

I had learned two things from Dad enforcing that particular Jamesism. One, that he was right: it was nearly impossible to fret over your problems when working your tail off. Two, that I should never tell Dad I was sad, upset, or bored. Better to keep my mouth shut, close the door of my air-conditioned bedroom, crawl into bed, and lose myself and my problems in the pages of a comic book.

Dad's Jamesism was why I was digging Lim's grave by hand instead of with my powers. Except Dad's advice wasn't working. I felt just as badly now that I was hot and sweaty as I had felt when I first broke ground with the shovel. Despite being the dead of night, it was warm and humid. Or muggy, as they said here in the Deep South. *Muggy*. Only us Southerners would use a word that made bathing in one's own sweat sound charming.

I thought dark thoughts as I dug, sweat dripping off my bare arms and legs. Since this whole saving the world gig was not working out so well, maybe I could get a job as a gravedigger instead. From what I'd seen of Progenitor, the world would need a lot more graves once he was free. Who would have guessed graves would be such a growth market?

As a gravedigger, my future looked bright. As a Hero, not so much.

I had failed miserably.

And I didn't know what in the world to do about it.

Fortunately, despite it being after midnight, lack of light wasn't one of my many problems. The moon was full and bright overhead, a heavenful of bright stars its backdrop. I didn't even need the two electric lanterns I had brought. I wished I had brought a crucifix and holy water instead. Aiken Memorial Park was pleasant enough during the day, living up to its name by looking like a garden or a park, with fresh flowers dotting various gravesites. By night, however, the South Carolina cemetery was creepy, especially because it was in a rural area and there weren't any streetlights or people nearby. Despite no one else being around, it felt like countless unseen eyes watched me. Perhaps there were. Now that I knew magic and magical creatures were real, the creepy feeling I always got when visiting this cemetery at night made a lot more sense.

I tossed my last shovelful of dirt and clambered out of the deep grave. Dad's grave and headstone were to the left of the hole I had dug, and Mom's was to the left of his. James and Alethea Conley, together forever, just as they had intended when they got married. Aiken Memorial was a few miles from where our family farm had been. Buying a burial plot next to my parents' plots was one of the first things I had done years ago with the lavish salary the Old Man paid me as his Apprentice. I had bought the plot in case something happened to me. The Hero business was dangerous, and not too many reached retirement age. Too many superheroes were sent to an early grave. Lim could attest to that.

I picked up the bundle containing Lim's small body. She was as light as my heart was heavy. I had wrapped her in a silk shroud of the same color red as her Mastermind costume. I think she would have liked that. What she wouldn't have liked was the fact her high priestess would probably call the mysterious disappearance of her body a miracle. But, if I had openly taken Lim's body out of her temple, I would've triggered an international incident. Not to mention bringing the Guild down on my head. I had enough troubles as it was.

I hesitated as I cradled Lim's body. I was tempted to unwrap her and take one last look at her face. I told myself no. I knew if I saw her face again, I would start crying. I had done enough of that already.

After placing Lim in the grave, I used the shovel to cover her with the dirt I had dug up. I could have buried her somewhere in China instead of on the other side of the world from her home. I could've buried her deep in a Chinese forest, or atop a mountain, or somewhere else her body was unlikely to ever be discovered. But I couldn't bring myself to do it. Maybe it was silly, but I didn't want her to be alone. Here, Mom and Dad would keep her company. Mom had always said she wanted a daughter. And, on a selfish note, I could visit Lim whenever I visited my parents, which I did from time to time. Especially when I was troubled. I always visited dressed in civilian clothes, just as I was now. It would never do for some bad guy to connect Theodore Conley and Omega. A bad guy discovering a Hero's secret identity was a good way to place a target on the back of the Hero's friends and family.

Not that I had either. Not anymore.

I placed the last shovelful of dirt and, using the back of the shovel, packed the dirt tight. Then, after re-confirming with my telekinetic touch no one was around, I used my powers to yank up small squares of sod, doing it from all around the sprawling cemetery so the fresh scars in the ground wouldn't be noticed come daytime. Beckoning the grassy squares to me, I fit them together like a jigsaw puzzle atop Lim's grave.

To supplement the moon's light, I flicked on a lantern and examined my handiwork critically. Good. Not even the cemetery's groundskeeper would be able to tell there was a freshly dug grave where there was supposed to be nothing but an empty plot.

I turned off the lantern, bowed my head, and prayed. The last time I prayed, I had asked to be rescued from Doctor Alchemy's clutches. *Prayer, the last refuge of the scoundrel.* That sounds like something Nietzsche might have said, but it was actually from Lisa Simpson on *The Simpsons.* Wisdom was in the most unexpected places.

This time, I didn't pray for myself. I prayed for Lim. Not that I knew who I was praying to. I had been raised to believe in a benevolent, all-powerful god. But if he was so benevolent and all-powerful, why did he let Mom get brain cancer? Why did he let Iceburn kill Dad? Why did he let the Sentinels murder Neha? Why did he let Lim die while allowing Progenitor to live? It was a heckuva way to run a universe. It seemed to me he had a lot of explaining to do.

Even so, I prayed. I figured it couldn't hurt.

But it didn't help. When I opened my eyes, the only thing that had changed was clouds now covered the moon. The gloom that swallowed me matched my mood. I'd had some low points in my life, and this was among the lowest.

Despite my prayer, Lim was still dead. And I still didn't have a team to help me fight Progenitor.

The New Sentinels were no more. Isaac had moved out of the mansion and in with his fiancée Sylvia. He wouldn't return my calls. Ninja was temporarily staying in her Silver Sable house and had told me that, when she returned to the mansion, she expected me to have cleared out. She was well within her rights—she owned the blasted mansion, after all. Hacker had gathered her UWant engineers and returned to Seattle. Grimoire was god knew where, doing god knew what. Back in Washington, D.C. staking vamps, maybe. Only Rewind remained. I had left him in the mansion under Minerva's watchful eye. But even Minerva had betrayed me to Hacker, so I didn't know how much I could rely on her. As she had Isaac's personality engrams, I could only surmise Isaac's morality that Minerva shared had compelled her to leave subtle hints in her system about my plans to kill Progenitor, hints which Hacker had discovered and pursued. Now Minerva calling me Captain Queeg from *The Caine Mutiny* made a lot more sense. Since I couldn't trust Minerva anymore, when I returned to the mansion, I halfway expected Rewind to have dismantled

Sentry and to have walked out the door with the irreplaceable technology.

The best-case scenario was I would face Progenitor with only Rewind accompanying me. The worst-case scenario was I would face him alone. Or maybe it was the other way around—Rewind did not inspire me with confidence, even with his daughter's life on the line.

I felt my fists clench into balls of frustration. My despair quickly turned into anger. Why were the others so blind? Why couldn't Isaac and the rest understand what was at stake? I had explained to them the type of person Progenitor was. The type of monster he was. Now was not the time to pussyfoot around, to slavishly follow the rules because that was what we were supposed to do. I could guarantee Progenitor would not follow the rules. He'd laugh at the very idea. He fancied himself a god. Rules didn't apply to gods. And, to defeat him, they couldn't apply to us. This wasn't a boxing match with rules and judges and a referee to break things up if they got too heated. The only thing following the Marquess of Queensberry Rules would get us was a knife in the belly. There were no rules in a street fight for your life. If you saw a chance to be the stabber instead of the stabbee, you took it. Even if it didn't comport with conventional morality.

My jaw tightened. There was too much at stake to pander to the others' dainty moral sensibilities. They *would* help me fight Progenitor, and that was simply that. I'd force them if I had to. I was the Omega, the guy charged with keeping the world safe. The others would do what I told them to do. Or else.

Then I remembered how Arouch had felt when someone defied him. He had felt the same way I felt now: outraged that their vision was so narrow that they didn't understand the importance of what Arouch was trying to accomplish. Arouch did whatever he needed to do to bend others to his will. To him, might made right.

My resolve to force the others to do as they were told wavered. Then it seeped out of me like air from a punctured tire. If I forced the others to do what I told them, wasn't I aping Arouch? I didn't want to become like him. Or like Mechano, who had murdered and committed other heinous crimes in the interest of protecting the world. As Shay had said, Mechano was a cautionary tale, not someone to model my behavior after.

Besides, I didn't really want to force the others to do anything. I wanted them to fight alongside me not because they had to, but because they wanted to. I liked Grimoire and Hacker despite their oddities. And I wanted them to like me. Isaac was my brother in all the ways that mattered, and Shay had become like a cherished aunt. They were both family. And Rewind was . . . well, Rewind was Rewind. Definitely not family. More like the boor your aging aunt brought home for Thanksgiving because she felt like she was running out of options.

Unfortunately, my surrogate superhero family seemed as dead as my biological family moldering in their graves before me.

What was I supposed to do? How was I going to fix this? Could it be fixed?

"Who? Who? Who?" an unseen owl hooted from a distant tree. I didn't have an answer to his question. He probably didn't have answers to mine either. So much for owls being wise. Unhelpful birdbrained bastard.

I sighed. Bending over, I began pulling up weeds around Dad's grave. *It's hard for a man to be sad when his arms are tired.* Dad's advice hadn't done the trick when I dug Lim's grave, but maybe it would work now. Hope sprang eternal. Especially when hope was all you had left.

Once I finished cleaning Dad's grave, I started on Mom's. The moon came out from under the clouds as I weeded, illuminating her headstone. My eyes fell on the Bible passage carved on it: *Whoever conceals their sins does not prosper, but the one who confesses and renounces them finds mercy.* Proverbs 28:13, one of Mom's favorite verses. Mom had known the Bible the way some people knew the *Harry Potter* books. Both she and Dad had been devout Catholics and salt of the earth, God-fearing people. For all the good that had done either of them.

The first time I remembered Mom quoting that particular Proverbs passage to me was when I was in the first grade at Saint Theresa Academy, the private Catholic school my parents had scrimped and penny-pinched to enroll me in. I came home from school one day wearing a brand-new Omega Man wristwatch. Mom asked where I had gotten it from. I told her my teacher gave it to me. Mrs. Templeton had given one to each kid in the class, I said. As the watch was expensive, Mom knew that probably wasn't true. I soon cracked under her persistent questions: I admitted I'd stolen it from another student, who had taken it off to play during recess.

I had never forgotten the look of disappointment on Mom's face. I had also never forgotten the spanking Dad gave me when he returned from the fields. It was the first and only time Dad had ever hit me. At least it was the only time my real father hit me. During the Trials, an illusion that looked like him had tried to hit me. Dad doing something so uncharacteristic was what had made me realize the dream a Trials proctor had put me in was just that—a dream. A test of my willingness to deal with reality how it was rather than how I wished it to be.

My parents made me return the Omega Man watch, of course. I also had to apologize to the kid I'd stolen it from, Mrs. Templeton, and then the entire class. I remember standing humiliated in front of the class as if it were yesterday. I still squirmed at the thought of it.

But I never stole anything else.

"Whoever conceals their sins does not prosper, but the one who confesses and renounces them finds mercy." My young mind had barely understood those words when Mom recited them to me after my watch caper. But I understood all too well what Dad said before he spanked me: "I'm not sure what's more disappointing—that you stole, or that you lied about it."

History didn't repeat itself, but it often echoed. Isaac had said words similar to Dad's after his Lugh Lamfada form compelled me to tell the truth about my plans for Progenitor —that he didn't know which was more disappointing: the deed, or the lie about the deed.

Isaac had said something else I now remembered. He said it when he caught me leaving Draymond Miller's house after blackmailing him: "A team can't truly be a team without trust among its members."

Isaac had been right. Mom and Dad too.

The responsibility to protect the world was as heavy on my shoulders as ever, but thinking of the lessons my parents had imparted suddenly made it seem easier to carry. What was that proverb? *I ask not for a lighter load, but for broader shoulders.*

I straightened, brushing dirt off my hands. My parents' previously weed-obscured headstones were now as clear as my mind.

"Thanks for the advice, Mom and Dad," I said aloud. I found myself smiling for the first time in days. "Lim, look after them, would you? I know they're just kids compared to you, but they have wisdom beyond their years. I hope to see all three of you again soon."

I remembered how eager Progenitor had been to kill those who stood in his way. "But not too soon," I hastened to add. "No offense."

I willed the Omega suit to manifest. I launched myself into the night air, twisting to get my bearings. I headed back toward Maryland. Back toward the mansion.

I knew what I had to do.

36

I stepped into The Mountain from the matmitter's brushed metal cylinder embedded in the vast cavern's rock wall. The transporter door hissed shut behind me as my nausea and itchiness faded. No matter how many times I traveled via matmitter, my body still wasn't used to having its molecules ripped apart in the mansion, beamed across the world, and reassembled here.

Masked, costumed and caped, I crossed the cavern and stopped in front of The Mountain's large computer terminal. Its giant curved monitor loomed over me. When I first came to The Mountain years ago to search for the Omega weapon, the computerized security system Avatar left behind had been set so anyone whose body contained the Metahuman gene and who knew the Hero's Oath could access the transporter portal and therefore The Mountain. When I secretly imprisoned Mad Dog here, I had changed the security protocols so only I could beam here through the matmitter. When we formed the New Sentinels, I had expanded the access so Isaac and Shay could come here as well.

Now, tapping the computer keyboard, I changed the

security protocols again so anyone who knew the Hero's Oath could enter The Mountain.

I crossed back over to the sealed matmitter. It soon hummed, sounding like a refrigerator compressor. Its door slid open and Rewind stepped out, wearing his red costume and white face paint. His eyes widened, and he slowly spun around, drinking in the cavern and its iconic contents. Light from the globes hovering high overhead made his white face paint glow like he was a ghost.

"Holy moly!" he exclaimed. Normally cynical and world-weary, this was the first time I had seen him amazed by anything. "Kid, you have a Batcave!"

"These days," I said, "it's more like the Fortress of Solitude. But yeah. I inherited it from Avatar."

Rewind's eyes widened even more. "Avatar? *The* Avatar?"

I grinned. Rewind's unexpected enthusiasm was infectious. "Is there more than one?"

Rewind's eyes danced around the cavern, too excited to rest on any one thing for long. He seemed as thrilled as a puppy with a new chew toy. I got a glimpse of what he must have looked like as an innocent little boy. "Can I get the fifty-cent tour?"

"Sure. It's early still. We've got some time to kill." I almost warned him to keep his sticky fingers where I could see them—if Rewind was once an innocent little boy, he certainly wasn't any longer—but bit back the words. I didn't want to start the day on a sour note.

Even so, I kept a careful eye on Rewind as I showed him around. In addition to many of the artifacts here being priceless, there were too many things that would cause a lot of harm in the wrong hands. I felt like a museum docent chaperoning a known art thief. On second thought, it wasn't *like* that—it *was* that. Tempus

Fugit had stolen *The Storm on the Sea of Galilee* painting, after all.

Before I knew it, Rewind was telling me as much about the artifacts stored here as I told him. He even recognized a few items I hadn't been able to identify, like the small brown vial resting on a pedestal in a corner of the cavern under a clear bell jar. "It's the concoction Doctor Alchemy used to turn Avatar to stone," Rewind explained, straightening up after bending to peer critically at the symbols etched on the vial. "Never thought the day would come where I'd see it in person instead of just an artist's rendering on the *Hero Hags* website. Pretty damned cool." His head swiveled like a kid overstimulated by all the things to see and do at Disney World. His face lit up. "Omigod, are those the Little Green Men's ray guns?"

Rewind hustled over to where the futuristic guns were displayed. I followed in his wake, catching up with him as he aimed one of the guns at the far stone wall. Though I wasn't obvious about it, I used my powers to make sure Rewind couldn't disengage the safety. I didn't want him to blow a hole through the wall. Or through me. If I showed up in the afterlife with a gaping hole in my gut that hadn't been blasted there by Progenitor, Lim would never let me hear the end of it.

Not that I was actually concerned Rewind would turn the gun on me. He seemed more interested in fanboying out than in attacking or getting away from me. I was seeing a whole new side to the Rogue. He seemed decades younger than he had before I brought him here. "How do you know so much about this stuff?" I asked.

"I loved all things superhero when I was a kid. Comic books, TV shows, movies, novels, cartoons, pajamas, lunch boxes . . . you name it. *Pew*! *Pew*! *Pew*!" He was grinning, twisting back and forth, miming shooting bogeys with the ray gun. "Even wanted to be a Hero when I grew up."

"Why didn't you? You have powers. You could've gotten a license."

The grin slowly slid off Rewind's face, replaced by a hint of sadness. After one last caress, he reluctantly put the weapon back into the gun rack with its brethren. His eyes grew distant, as if he were looking into the past. "Because, after I developed my powers, it seemed easier to steal things than to earn them. I was young and stupid. It took me a long time to figure out that, in the long run, the easy way is always the hard way."

"It's never too late. You can change your ways and become a Hero. It's not unheard of for a Rogue to rehabilitate and get a license. Wildside, for instance."

Rewind snorted. "A little late in the day for this old dog to learn new tricks. As for Wildside, look where turning over a new leaf got him. Skinned alive and killed by Doctor Alchemy. Maybe it's better to be a live hyena than a dead sheepdog." He pointed toward the cavern's ceiling. "Speaking of dead sheepdogs, is that a model of the V'Loth mothership that Omega Man died disabling?"

"It's no model. It's the real deal."

Rewind's excited little boy face lit up again. "Get out! Can I see it?"

"Sure." I lifted us both up with my powers, rising high in the air to where the silver V'Loth spaceship hung suspended from thick metal cables riveted into the rock ceiling. Rewind didn't seem to mind how high we were or that he'd break his neck if I let him go; he was too excited by the prospect of exploring the UFO-shaped spaceship.

I floated us through the jagged hole Omega Man had punched in the side of the ship and set us down. The ship was about the length of an eighteen-wheeler's trailer and much taller, so there was plenty of room. The ship's interior was cracked and uneven, reminding me of a dry lake bed. It looked this way because the ship's pieces had been reassembled like a giant jigsaw puzzle. The mothership had been mostly smashed to pieces when Omega Man rammed it in 1966, sacrificing his own life to kill the alien queen inside and end the V'Loth invasion. The ship's interior was mostly empty except for large pieces of alien technology I never figured out the purpose of. Parallel parking between asteroids, maybe. One of those cryptic pieces of tech glowed a soft green, casting shadows everywhere.

Wide-eyed with excitement, Rewind ran his hands over everything like a virgin at a no-holds-barred strip club. "I've read about this thing in books, but reading about it's nothing like seeing it." His voice was hushed and reverential, like a devout worshipper speaking in a church. "All those Heroes and Rogues banding together to fight the V'Loth invasion fleet. Wow! Can you imagine what it was like being there? The Battle of Baltimore, I mean."

"I don't have to imagine it. I was there."

Rewind gave me a disbelieving look. "The battle happened in the sixties. Even with that mask on, I can guess your age. You're young enough to be my kid. Unless your plastic surgeon is a wizard, you couldn't have been there."

"I'm not old enough to have been there, but I was there just the same." The Omega weapon had made it seem like I fought in that battle to test if I was worthy of wielding it. "Well, kind of. It's a long story."

Rewind still looked like he didn't believe me, but let it go. He stepped to the rim of the hole Omega Man had punched in the ship and ran his hands across its edges as if they were braille and he could read the ship's history in their jagged lines.

"Omega Man knew he would die in his attempt to knock out this mothership. Imagine," he said with wonder in his voice, "being so selfless as to do such a thing. I don't think I could've done it. Scratch that—I know I couldn't have done it. They don't make Heroes like that anymore." He stopped and blinked, as if he had forgotten whom he was talking to. "No offense."

"None taken." I thought of Lim. Her loss still throbbed like a physical ache. The feeling would undoubtedly lessen over time. But I knew it would never completely go away. Just like the ache I still felt for Mom, Dad, Hannah, Neha, and James. James was Neha's and my child in the imaginary reality in which we were married and I fought in the Battle of Baltimore. "But you're wrong. People like Omega Man are still out there. Not many. Maybe not enough. But they're out there."

Rewind just grunted. He continued to run his fingers over the edges of the hole. His eyes were distant. He seemed lost in thought.

"If you can't get the others back on board," he finally said, "you're still going to go after Progenitor, aren't you?"

"Yes. I've got no choice."

"Of course you have a choice. There's always a choice."

"Not really. If you stood outside a burning building and your daughter Michaela was inside, would you have a choice about whether to go in after her?"

"That's different. She's my kid. It's my responsibility to protect her."

"It's no different. It's exactly the same thing. Michaela's your responsibility. The world is mine. Walking away from that responsibility isn't going to happen. Just like you wouldn't walk away from that burning building."

Rewind looked at me askance, like he wasn't sure whether to believe me. Then he looked away, back at the hole in the ship. His arms were spread wide as he touched the hole's edges. The ship's light projected a shadow of his body onto the curved wall. The shadow looked like a crucifix. Rewind said, "Standing at the very spot where Omega Man sacrificed himself, standing in the lair of a Hero who was murdered, it all reminds me that the Hero doesn't always get to go home at the end of his adventure. Mastermind told you you'll fail without the others. If you face Progenitor without them—if *we* face him without them—we'll suffer the same fate Avatar and Omega Man did." He looked at me again. "And what of my daughter then? If you're dead, how will she get her new heart?"

"I was going to tell you later, but since you brought it up, I'll just tell you now: I've already made the arrangements for your daughter to be moved up on the list. Your ex-wife will get a call to bring Michaela to the hospital any day now."

Rewind looked at me in disbelief. "I thought our deal was you wouldn't make the arrangements until after I help you with Progenitor."

"I've changed my mind."

His eyes narrowed with suspicion. "What's the catch?"

"There's no catch. I decided I didn't want to be the kind of guy who holds a girl's health hostage to force her father to do something." I let out a breath. "The wheels are already in motion and can't be reversed. Michaela will get her heart whether you help me or not. I no longer have anything to hold over your head. If you want to bow out of this thing with Progenitor . . . well, I won't be happy about it, but I'd understand."

Doubt, cautious optimism, and gratitude all played on Rewind's painted face. Rewind was the kind of guy who, when something good was offered to him, suspected it would be snatched away. Based on what I knew about how Rewind's life had gone so far, those suspicions were justified. Who could blame Charlie Brown for being suspicious when Lucy offered to hold the football for him again?

Rewind looked away. All I could see was the side of his face. "Do you have kids, Omega?"

I thought of James. To say *sort of* would just confuse the Rogue. "No."

"Then you don't understand. You can't. I sure as hell didn't before we had Michaela." He stared at the mothership's hole like it was a mirror reflecting his life back at him. "I know what I am. I'm a piece of shit. I'm a thief and a compulsive gambler and a leech on society and a bunch of other things I'd rather not discuss. And my ex Holly? She's no better. She likes to virtue signal to people that we divorced because she discovered I'm a crook. But that's not true. She knew from the jump how I made money. As long as the cash kept flowing and I paid her platinum card on time, she didn't care. We divorced because I came home one day to find Holly in bed with the plumber, snaking out her drain. Not that he was the first. Just the first I caught red-handed. I'd wonder if Michaela really was my daughter if she weren't the spitting image of my mother as a kid.

"When I first met Holly, she stripped in a club near a casino I played at, shooting porn on the side. I recognized her from one of her videos. *Teen LaQueefa*. Even with her clothes on, she was hotter than the surface of the sun; with her clothes off, I didn't stand a chance. I married her, and my money and I took her away from her life as a sex worker.

It's my own fault—I shoulda remembered you can't turn a ho into a housewife."

Rewind's mouth twisted sourly, clearly not finding his own joke funny. "No, the plumber wasn't the first guy she cheated on me with. What he was was the last straw. I filed for divorce on the grounds of adultery. In court, Holly turned on the waterworks. Said I was physically abusive. Pure projection—I never laid a hand on her. She definitely couldn't say the same, especially when I didn't let her have her way. She almost blinded me once. It didn't matter. The judge fell for Holly's performance and gave her everything she wanted. Maybe she was screwing him too. Wouldn't put it past her. She was definitely screwing her lawyer, though. They're married and she's sponging off his money now. Poor sap. For his sake, I hope he knows how to box. And that he doesn't need any plumbing work done.

"Anyway, Holly's Emmy award-winning court performance is why she has full custody of Michaela and all I have is supervised visitation despite wanting shared custody. I can't even be in the same room with Michaela without a court-appointed supervisor glaring at me like I'm about to diddle my own little girl."

Rewind shook his head at the thought.

"We're quite a pair, me and Holly—the crook and the gold-digging, hands-throwing ho. It's a miracle we managed to create something as precious as Michaela. Sometimes two pieces of shit like me and Holly come together and create something greater than the sum of their parts. I remember holding Michaela when she was born. She looked at me with these soft blue eyes that would melt a heart of stone and I thought, 'Oh. So *this* is what it's all about. All these years of chasing tail and money and the next big score, and I had no idea.' My life has had two phases—before Michaela, and after her. There's literally nothing I wouldn't do for her."

Rewind turned back to me. There were tears in his eyes. "I guess what I'm trying to say is thank you. I'm in your debt. I'll stick around and help with Progenitor. It's the least I can do. And anyway, if he's as bad as you say, a world with him in it is a less safe one. I'll be helping Michaela just as much as I'll be helping you. It'll give me a chance to be a hero for a change. The kid version of me would've liked that."

I didn't know what to say that wouldn't come out cheesy, so I simply moved next to Rewind and grasped his shoulder. "Thank you, Xander. I appreciate it. Truly I do." A lump formed in my throat. Suddenly embarrassed, I removed my hand. Other than Lim, this was the first time in a long time I put my hands on someone when I wasn't fighting them. It said a lot about the state of my relationships these days.

I cleared my throat. Darn these allergies Lim had given me. "Let's head back down," I said. "It's almost time."

Rewind and I had a seat at the conference table in front of The Mountain's computer system and massive monitor. Isaac, Shay, and I sitting here to debate the fate of Slab, Flare and Blur seemed like a lifetime ago.

Though it was still a bit early, anxiety made me think no one else was going to show when I heard the whine of the matmitter from across the cavern. The transporter's door slid open and Ninja glided out in full costume. Her sheathed katana hung from her back, held in place by a leather strap diagonally across her chest. It was the first time she had ever come to The Mountain armed. Visibly armed, at least. I doubted Shay took a piss completely unarmed.

Shay spotted us and, without a word of greeting, came over and sat with us. Though I had wondered if anyone at all would come, I wasn't surprised that Ninja was the first. She was punctual to a fault.

Soon the matmitter whined again. Hacker exited it, accompanied by her orbiting clutch of drones. Like Ninja, she was in full costume. She glanced at the artifacts surrounding her and at the picturesque snowcapped mountains far off in the distance, visible through the transparent force field at the cavern's broad entrance. She scowled, as if everything she looked at had a slur scrawled in graffiti on it.

Hacker strode up to me like I was the manager of a store whose employees had offended her.

"What is this place?" she demanded, arms crossed, tapping a heel impatiently. Her drones hovered in formation between us with blue-white sparks arcing among them, as if they ached to zap me. A faint smell of ozone filled the area. "What's all this junk in here?"

"Junk?!" Rewind sounded like he was strangling.

"This is the lair I inherited from Avatar," I explained.

"Well, I don't like it. Smells like an elderly man's musty old attic." Hacker wrinkled her nose. "Congratulations—you convinced me to come. Now hurry up and say whatever assholery you're going to say so I can get back to my work."

"Assholery?" Rewind chimed in.

"Urban Dictionary says it's a word," Hacker said defensively.

I glanced at the time on the computer screen. "First let's see if anyone else comes so I don't have to repeat myself. Have a seat."

"I don't want to have a seat. *You* have a seat." The devil in me almost pointed out I already sat, but I wrestled it to the ground and gagged it in the nick of time. "I'm an important woman with important matters to attend to." Glancing at a watch that looked like something George Jetson would wear,

Hacker shook her head with disgust. "I knew it was a mistake to come here. I knew you were just going to waste even more of my valuable time. I'm leaving." She turned back toward the matmitter.

Ninja spoke. "You've already come this far. You might as well stay and hear Omega out."

Hacker hesitated, frowning. Then she stomped around the table as far from me as possible and flounced into a chair. "Fine," she spat. "I'll stay. I'll listen. But only because you asked me to, Ninja. Not because of *him.*"

I gave Ninja a grateful look, but her dark eyes were as cold and hard as onyx. Clearly I had mastered the principles of *How to Win Friends and Influence People.*

Grimoire showed up next, a few minutes after the time I had suggested we meet. She spun in a slow circle outside the matmitter, her long red cloak billowing around her costumed form as she drank in her surroundings. "First Agatha, now this," she said, her voice carrying in the vastness of the cavern. "Does literally everyone have a secret hideaway except me?" I couldn't tell if she was talking to us or to the invisible friend she seemed to have. There was much about the magical woman I still did not understand. One thing inviting her here had accomplished, though: it confirmed my suspicions she wasn't really a licensed Hero despite what the Guild's records said. When I had told her the password for the matmitter was the Hero's Oath, she had asked me what the Oath was. The Oath was sworn when a Hero received her license and was not the sort of thing that slipped your mind.

Grimoire sat with the rest of us at the table. I waited for a bit longer, hoping Isaac would come too, suspecting he wouldn't. While we waited, no one spoke. We were like an estranged family who had assembled for the holidays out of a sense of obligation, but no one was happy about it.

I looked at the time again. It was well after when the meeting was supposed to begin. Isaac wasn't coming. I was disappointed, but not surprised. Sighing, I pushed my chair back and stood. Four sets of eyes watched me with emotions ranging from Rewind's curiosity to Hacker's hostility.

"Thank you all for coming," I began. "I—"

I heard the whine of the matmitter again. My heart skipped a beat when Isaac, garbed in his Myth costume, entered The Mountain.

Isaac gave me a look as cold as the iceberg Progenitor had hibernated in, stopping me from greeting him. He came to sit at the table with the rest of us. Hacker cleared her throat loudly, making a big show of looking at her watch. Isaac shrugged. "Colored people time," he said. Rewind smirked at *colored people*, but thankfully didn't throw in his race-baiting two cents. The last thing I needed was a reenactment of the Watts race riots. Isaac had been joking, of course—as with Shay, normally you could set your watch by him. Isaac's biological father had been a Green Beret before he retired from the army and became a cop; the phrase *early is on time, on time is late, and late is unacceptable* had been drilled into Isaac's head from an early age. I knew Isaac was late because he had almost not come at all.

I began again once all eyes were on me once more. "As I was saying, thank you all for coming. I know many of you don't trust me. For good reason. I've lied, cheated, concealed things, and twisted arms. Not just with the five of you, but throughout my Heroic career. That would be deplorable even in ordinary times. But these times aren't ordinary. Progenitor will escape from his confinement in just a few days now that Mastermind no longer thwarts him. She believed he is the greatest threat the world has faced in thousands of years. I trust her. Just as much as you don't trust me. Maybe some of you think I'm lying about Progenitor's very existence, and that I've brought you all together to use you for some selfish reason of my own." Hacker shifted in her seat; I saw that I was right, at least with her.

"But I assure you Progenitor and the threat he poses are all too real. To fight him and eliminate that threat, I need your help. I need us to work together as a team. To get that help, I need to earn your trust. As Myth once told me, a team can't truly be a team without trust among its members. He was right about that.

"To earn your trust, I'm going to lay all my cards on the table. That's part of the reason I asked you to come here, a place only two other people in the entire world know exists. As Ninja and Myth already know, this place is called The Mountain. It's carved into a summit in the Himalayan Mountain range. Among other things, it contains some of the most valuable and dangerous Metahuman artifacts in history. Avatar used it as his secret lair before his murder.

"Now that he's gone, Avatar's lair is my lair. How it came to be mine is a very long story. A story I'm going to share with you now. Because I'm putting my faith in you, and I want you to put yours in me."

I let out a deep breath. With a thought, I let the Omega suit morph and shift into jeans and a plain, short-sleeved t-shirt. The suit's mask retreated into my head, leaving my head bare. There were audible gasps from everyone at me unmasking myself. Well, everyone except Ninja. Jesus riding a unicorn naked through downtown Astor City wouldn't shake her stoic demeanor.

"My real name is Theodore Conley," I said. "I grew up on a farm in Aiken, South Carolina. This is my story."

37

Everyone stared at my bare face with shock. Even Ninja looked somewhat surprised. They'd probably be less shocked if I'd left my mask on and peeled down to my birthday suit instead. Exposing one's secret identity was something a Hero simply did not do, unless it was to a close friend or family member. Oftentimes, not even then. I hadn't revealed my true identity to Neha and Isaac when we became friends at Hero Academy; Neha had broken into the Academy's records and discovered it on her own. I hadn't revealed it to Truman; he had deduced it, proving that the brutish-looking, clownish-acting detective was smarter than he seemed. I hadn't told Viola I was Omega despite how intimate we had been in all the other ways a boyfriend and girlfriend were intimate.

Before today, I had voluntarily revealed my secret identity to only two people: Shay, because she had needed to know for us to form the New Sentinels; and Mad Dog, who I had told when I imprisoned him in The Mountain because I assumed he'd be stuck here forever.

And now I'd revealed my most closely guarded secret to

a Hero who hated me, a Hero who wasn't really a Hero, and a professional thief with extensive ties to the criminal underworld. Nothing I had learned in the Academy or afterward said this was a good idea.

And yet I continued, exposing not only my secret identity, but the rest of my deepest and darkest secrets.

All eyes on me, feeling as naked as the day I was born, I told everyone everything. I began at the beginning, with how I first manifested my powers in my college's bathroom. I told everyone how the Old Man had tried to get me to enroll in the Academy for my and everyone else's safety, but I refused, leading to Iceburn burning my father alive during his attempt to assassinate me.

Everyone was quiet as a mouse as they listened. I told them of my days at the Academy, becoming the Old Man's Apprentice under the code name Kinetic, crippling and defeating Iceburn, going to jail, going through the Trials, reprogramming Overlord to give both me and Myth a chance of passing the Trials' final test, lying in wait for Mad Dog in his apartment and beating him up, him killing Hannah as a result, me discovering I was the carrier for the Omega spirit, finding the Omega weapon and fashioning it into the Omega suit, imprisoning Mad Dog in The Mountain, fighting the Sentinels, them killing Neha, me destroying Mechano, Doctor Alchemy torturing me for allowing his daughter to die, us capturing Doctor Alchemy and the Philosopher's Stone, me blackmailing State's Attorney Miller and Mayor Stone, secretly removing Lim's body from her temple in China and burying it, what I'd done to recruit everyone here . . .

In short, I told them everything. The good, the bad, and the ugly. The truth, the whole truth, and nothing but the truth. The only stuff I left out were things that would violate others' privacy or expose them to criminal or civil liability. I didn't tell everyone Grimoire's secret identity; I'd tell her how I discovered it privately later. Nor did I reveal Myth's or Ninja's secret identities. I also did not tell them Myth had accompanied me when I broke into Mad Dog's apartment. Nor did I disclose I had enlisted Hacker to reprogram Overlord for me. Not that I needed to disclose it: Hacker had the poker face of a toddler, and her reaction to me talking about reprogramming Overlord did not go unnoticed by either Isaac or Shay. Besides, neither was stupid; they knew I personally didn't have the know-how to reprogram something as sophisticated as Overlord. I could barely program the TV remote.

Reactions to my spoken word autobiography varied. Grimoire grew visibly upset and teary-eyed as I spoke of Dad dying at Iceburn's hands. Maybe the story brought back memories of her own father's murder. Hacker cried when Mom, Dad, Hammer, Neha, Hannah and Lim died, and again when I discovered my marriage to Neha and our son James weren't real. After all these years of knowing her, I never would've pegged her for such a softie. Rewind—shockingly—cried too when I detailed Lim sacrificing her life to keep Progenitor imprisoned. On second thought, in light of my conversation with him about Omega Man, maybe him crying wasn't so shocking. He seemed to have an overly romantic view of a Hero sacrificing himself for others. Not me. I'd sacrifice myself if I saw no other choice, but I wouldn't be whistling a happy tune when I did it. I had stared into death's dark abyss several times, and nothing down there looked pleasant.

Isaac and Shay alone didn't shed a tear as I spoke. Shay remained as still as a statue as I unburdened myself. If her eyes weren't open and didn't blink from time to time, I'd think she had gone to sleep. It confirmed my and Isaac's theory she was part Vulcan.

Isaac wasn't as stoic. He shifted in his seat restlessly, frowning as I recounted the illegal or immoral things I had done he didn't already know about, particularly the part about Overlord and the Trials.

By the time I finished my story, the sun had nearly set. The snowcapped mountains outside had turned from sparkling white to darkened and tinged with red. I thought I would feel more shame and embarrassment about some of the things I talked about. There definitely was some, but those weren't the primary emotions I felt.

Mostly I just felt relieved. Getting all this off my chest was cathartic. I had been hiding things from the people closest to me for so long, I felt like a gay man finding the courage to step out of the closet. I felt lighter. Freer. Maybe the old clichés were true: a burden shared was a burden halved, and confession was good for the soul. It was no wonder confession was one of the seven Catholic holy sacraments.

"So that's my life story in a very large nutshell." My mouth was dry after speaking so long without interruption. "No one is more aware than I of the things I've done wrong and the crimes I've committed. Some things I'd do differently if given the chance. Given a do-over, I wouldn't lie to you about planning to kill Progenitor. I wouldn't break into Mad Dog's apartment and threaten him because there's a direct line between that and him killing Hannah. Other things I'd do the same despite how illegal they might be. Confining Mad Dog here, for instance. If getting my hands dirty was the price for making sure he didn't hurt or kill someone else, then I'll happily pay that price all over again.

"But actions have consequences. At least they should if

we're going to continue to live in a country of laws and not one where the strongest do whatever they want and get away with it. I will face the consequences for the things I've done. For those of you thinking of reporting me to the authorities, civilian or Heroic, there's no need—I'll do it myself once this thing with Progenitor is over. If you think that's just idle talk to trick you into believing I've turned over a new leaf, I've already recorded a full video confession of everything I've done. Minerva has custody of it and will release it to any of you at any time. She's programmed to deny me access to it, so I can't delete or alter it.

"When the authorities learn what I've done, I fully expect to be stripped of my Hero license and to spend many years in prison for fraud, false imprisonment, assault, blackmail, and whatever other parts of the kitchen sink prosecutors want to throw at me. What I haven't done and won't do is rat on anyone else who may have helped me perpetrate my crimes. *My* crimes. A result of my decisions. No one else's. My decisions, my responsibility, my punishment."

I felt my fist clench. "But until then, I'm still a Hero. Like it or not, dealing with Progenitor is my responsibility. *Our* responsibility. If you'll come back on board and help me capture him, I promise I won't lie to you or withhold information again. I also promise I won't try to kill him. Despite how much he might deserve it. Myth, turn into Lugh Lamfada again and confirm I'm not lying. Once we capture Progenitor, we'll turn him over to the Guild. I have my doubts as to what, if anything, they can do to him. But the alternative is to sit around and do nothing. Doing nothing is unacceptable. As Lim said, he's a fox who's about to get loose in a very large henhouse. I've seen the guy up close and personal. He's not going to cluck and scratch the ground like the rest of us chickens and catch up on what's been going on with roosting technology over the past several thousand years. No. He's going to go on a killing spree. He's a conqueror. Killing and conquering are the only things he enjoys. The six of us must stop him. If you won't do it for me, do it for yourselves. Your friends. Your family. None of us—none of them—will be safe with Progenitor running amok."

I stopped. This was the longest I had spoken non-stop in my entire life. Maybe I was turning into Lieutenant Governor Gowdy, in love with the sound of my own voice.

Embarrassed, I abruptly sat. I felt like I'd just had surgery to remove a tumor: happy the procedure was over, but dreading what the biopsy would reveal. "I'll find and face Progenitor alone if I have to. But alone, I will fail. I need your help. Rewind is already on board. Who's with us?"

"I am," Grimoire said immediately. "I don't care about the mistakes you've made in the past. I've made more than my fair share of mistakes too. Living in this big glass house of mine, I'm not inclined to throw stones. My only objection was about trying to kill someone. If that's off the table, I'm in."

"Thank you, Grimoire. Who—" The rest of my words were cut off by Hacker. She'd gotten up and was bent over me, hugging me so tight that my face was smooshed into her chest.

"I wish you had told me all the stuff you've been through," she said in a gush of words, still half-crying. "You're all alone. Everyone you've ever cared about is gone. Yes, you're an asshole. But at least now I understand *why* you're an asshole. To understand all is to forgive all, Theo. Can I call you Theo? Or do you prefer Dore? But who goes by Dore? Oooh, you could be the first! Bill Gates, run a check on all known social media accounts and check if anyone named Theodore goes by Dore. What do you mean you don't have access to the Internet here? If I had a lair, Dore-slash-Theo, I'd make sure it had Wi-Fi. A suggestion, not a criticism. Gates, just run a hyperlink to UWant's L4 satellite and access the Web that way. What? Well, try the promethean conduit subroutine C-57 . . ."

I gently pushed away from Hacker before I drowned in boobs and technobabble. Her drones danced around my head like puppies eager to be petted. "Just call me Theo. Does this mean you'll help?"

Hacker pulled a tissue out of her utility belt and blew her nose noisily. Her green eyes darted back and forth behind her goggles, as if she were reviewing the transcript of what she had said. "I thought I just said I would, but I guess I didn't. Yes, I'll help. I should have led with that. Sorry. Getting emotional flusters me. To solve the problem, I asked a surgeon to replace one of my amygdalae with a cybernetic implant I designed. He refused. Said it was unethical to insert untested technology into a healthy brain." Her watery eyes flashed emerald with anger. "They must be giving medical degrees to anyone with a pulse these days. I told him he should stick to bloodletting, faith healing, and voodoo dolls and leave the advancement of real medicine to his betters. Imagine the nerve, thinking I wouldn't—"

"Hacker, you're getting rather far afield from the discussion at hand," Ninja thankfully cut her off. Hacker flushed with embarrassment, gave me one last quick awkward hug, then took her seat again. One of her drones rubbed itself against her white hair as she sniffled. Another floated in front of her face, scanning her eyes with a blue beam that removed their teary-eyed redness.

Ninja turned her dark eyes to me. "I pride myself on my

ability to read people and situations. And yet, in two separate instances, I've found myself on teams with people who were engaged in unethical and criminal behavior under my nose. I begin to wonder if the fault lies with me. As the saying goes, if everywhere you go smells like shit, it's time to check your own shoes."

She drummed her fingers on the table thoughtfully, then sighed. "With that said, none of my wrongdoing former colleagues on the Sentinels ever admitted fault or were as open and honest as you have been with us today. Considering what appears to be at stake with Progenitor, I'm inclined to give you another chance. Especially since, as Grimoire put it, I live in a glass house myself. I've made mistakes before and done things I regret. The important thing is to learn from those mistakes, atone for them, and move on. All of which you're doing. Long story short, I'm in too."

All eyes turned to Isaac. Including my own. I had some blood relatives in South Carolina, but they were practically strangers; as far as I was concerned, Isaac was the only real family I had left. He hadn't said a word during all this, and was looking back at me with an expression I couldn't read. I felt my heart race the way it did before a fight with a Rogue. I was as anxious to know what Isaac was thinking as I was about Progenitor. More so, maybe. As selfish as it sounds, it's hard to care too much about the fate of the world when you feared no one left in it cared about you.

Isaac opened his mouth, hesitated, then shut it again. He looked away from me. He moved restlessly in his chair, like a man with a lot to say but uncertain how to say it. I couldn't tell if he was about to tell me off for cheating during the Trials and, worse yet, not telling him about it sooner. Or if he was going to berate me for the other things I did wrong and concealed from him. Or say he would help with Progenitor but, after that, he and I were through. Or chastise me for the recklessness of revealing my secret identity to a group that included a Rogue. Or simply make one of his trademark barely relevant jokes—like *What does a superpowered priest call his secret identity? His altar ego*—and then simply walk out of The Mountain and my life.

He did none of those things.

Isaac stopped fidgeting and sat up straight, as if he had made a decision. In a low voice, as if we were the only ones in the room, he said, "I've already lost one sibling. I'm not interested in losing another."

I nearly cried.

Hacker chose that moment to blow her nose again. It sounded like a foghorn. I blinked and suppressed my tears by sheer force of will. Hacker was amply demonstrating that crying in public wasn't a good look.

Isaac looked as uncomfortable as I felt. He leaned back, making a deliberate effort to relax and seem casual. He said, "Now that the Metahuman murderfest is off the table, what's our next step?"

Grateful to talk about something other than my roiling emotions, I said, "I'd like to turn the chair over to Ninja. She's the oldest here, has the best tactical mind, and is the most experienced at this sort of thing. She should lead us as we tackle Progenitor."

"No," Hacker said.

"No?" I said.

"No," Hacker repeated firmly. She glanced apologetically at Ninja. "No offense, ma'am. Don't forget I'm your biggest fan. I keep your kung fu grip action figure on my desk. I play with it all the time."

"I wish you'd stop calling me ma'am, Ninja said.

"Between that and Theo saying I'm the eldest here, it makes me feel like I should use a walker."

"Yes, ma'am." Hacker flushed at her use of the word again, then covered her embarrassment in a rush of words. "It's just that Theo is the one who brought us all together. He's the one each of us knows the most about. He's the one who knows the most about Progenitor. He's best suited to lead us. And, even with his assholery, he's the one I want to follow."

"I agree," Rewind said.

"Ditto," Grimoire agreed.

"As do I," Shay agreed.

"Then it's unanimous," Isaac said. All eyes turned to me again. "It's your show, fearless leader. What's the plan, Stan?"

38

___

I was touched by their confidence in me, and hoped it wasn't misplaced. "The idea of using Sentry and Tar Baby to locate Progenitor as soon as he appears is still a sound one." I shrugged. "Beyond that, I really don't have a plan. One that doesn't involve murder, I mean. The scenarios I war-gamed in the Peril Room showed I have a better chance of killing Progenitor than we would of capturing him. Not that I was certain that running him through with Ninja's sword was going to work since he has immunity to other Metahumans' powers. It was just more likely to work than everything else I tried." I shook my head. "It won't be a simple matter of trapping him in one of my force fields, turning him over to the Guild, and calling it a day. I hoped that, assuming we all got on the same page, we could come up with something I didn't already think of."

Grimoire leaned forward. "What about using the Philosopher's Stone?"

Rewind frowned. "Doctor Alchemy's book?"

"Yeah. Theo said he took custody of the book after he, Ninja and Myth defeated Alchemy," Grimoire said. "Progenitor's memories show he's vulnerable to alchemical potions. Otherwise, the potion he took to force his body into hibernation never would've worked. The Philosopher's Stone is the world authority on alchemy. Surely there's something in there that can help us. We can use it to create a potion to knock Progenitor out again. Not for thousands of years this time. Just long enough to hand him over to the Guild and let them figure out what to do with him."

Hacker snorted. "That's the part of Theo's story I have trouble swallowing. A magic potion allowed Progenitor to hibernate for thousands of years? Come on. That and the idea that Merlin, a fictional wizard, banished Progenitor to the non-corporeal realm he's spent the last few thousand years in. Not that I'm suggesting you're lying, Theo. Maybe you and Mastermind misunderstood what you saw in Progenitor's memories." Hacker shook her head firmly, her drones mirroring the movement. "Magicians? Magical potions? It's absurd. There's no such thing as magic. Except maybe in the Arthur C. Clarke sense."

"Arthur C. Clarke?" Rewind said.

"Clarke was a science fiction writer who posited that any sufficiently advanced technology is indistinguishable from magic," Ninja explained. "But I wouldn't be so quick to scoff at magic, Hacker. I was on the Sentinels with Millennium for years, and he represented himself to be a sorcerer. I saw him do things that were nothing short of miraculous."

"I'm with Hacker," Rewind said. "Magic is a fairytale. Real magic, I mean. Not the David Copperfield kinda stuff."

"I once would have agreed with you," Isaac offered. "But then Theo and I fought what Grimoire said were chupacabras. And Tempus Fugit was supposed to be just an urban legend, but here you sit, Rewind. These days, I'm a lot less confident about what's real and not real. I'm only sixty percent certain I'm real myself."

Grimoire looked at me as the other four fell into a discussion about fantasy versus reality. Despite how enigmatic her mask made her face, I could tell what she was thinking: she knew I knew magic was real due to our interaction in the Beaufort Inn. She was expecting me to divulge that knowledge to the others. But I hadn't forgotten what Lim said about the First Rule of the magical world, and how much trouble one of its denizens could get into for its violation. "It's not my secret to tell," I murmured to her.

"What secret?" Hacker demanded, her head swiveling between me and Grimoire. "I thought you said you wouldn't keep any more secrets from us. No takebacks!" Her drones bobbed in agreement emphatically.

Grimoire's mouth moved under her mask like she was talking, but no words came out. She became animated, gesticulating and shaking her head, as if arguing with someone. It was like watching a silent movie.

"Is she having a stroke?" Rewind asked.

As if her unmute button had been pressed, Grimoire let out a long-suffering sigh. "If I'm going to use the Philosopher's Stone to whip up a potion, I can't tiptoe around what I'm doing and have you all interfere in the process. So let's just get this out of the way right now: Magic is real. I'm a magician. More precisely, a sorceress. There's a secret cabal that would probably kill me and most definitely kill you if they knew I told you, so don't go around flapping your gums about it."

The revelation was met with silence. Then Hacker snorted again. "Yeah, right. You're a sorceress. Sure you are. Just like I'm Elon Musk and Theo is the Prime Minister of the United States."

"There is no U.S. prime minister," Isaac said.

"I knew that," Hacker retorted peevishly. Considering her willful ignorance of all things non-technical, I doubted she did. "Just like I know there's no magic."

Grimoire raised her arms and moved her hands as she did when she was opening a teleportation portal, only the pattern she weaved in the air wasn't the same. While her arms waved, she uttered a string of words. I remembered enough Latin from my Catholic school days to vaguely recognize the words, but not enough to understand anything other than *ignis*—"fire"—and *lapis*—"stone."

Glowing letters appeared on The Mountain's curved rock wall, high above the monitor looming over us. It was as if a neon sign had miraculously appeared, only the letters weren't raised like a neon sign's. It was more like the rock face itself glowed, eclipsing the brightness of the lights floating overhead. The letters read: *Magic is real. Grimoire is a sorceress. Suck on that, doubters.*

We barely had time to react to the words' sudden appearance when our upturned faces were pulled back down to the table by the sound of a massive whoosh. Grimoire's entire body ignited, as if someone had doused her with gasoline and lit a match. The temperature went from comfortable to blazing hot.

Overturned chairs smacked the floor as everyone scrambled up and away from the raging Grimoire inferno. Even Shay was startled; never before had I seen anything shake her usual composure.

Just as quickly as it had ignited, the fire went out. Grimoire looked perfectly normal again. Not even her hair was so much as singed. The chair she sat in and table weren't scorched, either. It was as if the fire had been a figment of our imagination. The glowing letters which had blazed overhead were gone too; the rock wall was back to looking completely normal.

Grimoire folded her hands on the table and returned our thunderstruck looks calmly. "I hope that's enough of a demonstration," she said. "If you need further proof of magic, find me a hat and I'll pull myself out of it. But I'd rather not. The last time I did it, I couldn't stop hopping for days. Animal transmogrification is not my strong suit. Besides, there's no time to waste. As Theo is fond of pointing out, Progenitor will free himself soon. The sooner we stop questioning each other's abilities, the better."

Still a little shaken from Grimoire's dramatic demonstration, I resumed my seat. When I didn't burst into flames or turn into a frog, the others followed my lead. Hacker was the last to sit back down. She looked nervously at Grimoire as if the sorceress' head would spin around in a circle.

"Though I like the idea of using the Philosopher's Stone to do some good with it for a change," I said to Grimoire, "it's in a foreign language. I couldn't make heads or tails of it when I flipped through it."

"It's written in ancient Sanskrit," Grimoire said. "Don't worry. I can read it."

"You can?" Rewind sounded doubtful. "You don't strike me as the type to stay up late on a Friday night studying ancient scrolls."

"Maybe what I should've said is that I know someone who can read it."

"We're not showing the Philosopher's Stone to anyone outside this room," I insisted. "Doctor Alchemy did enough damage with it, and I'm not about to risk it falling into the wrong hands."

"Theo's right," Isaac said. "Look at all that Doctor Alchemy accomplished with it, and he was nuttier than squirrel poop. Handing something as dangerous as the Philosopher's Stone to someone else is a non-starter." Ninja nodded in agreement.

Grimoire shook her head. "We won't need to hand it over to someone else."

"But you just said—"

"I know what I said." Grimoire let out another long sigh, then muttered, "In for a penny, in for a pound."

In a louder voice, Grimoire announced, "We don't need to hand the Philosopher's Stone to anyone else. The person who can translate it is sitting right here. His name is Puck. He's the spirit of a teenaged magical genius whose consciousness was imprinted on my cloak over six hundred years ago. He's telepathically linked to me through the cloak. He's how I know the Philosopher's Stone is in ancient Sanskrit. Puck knows more languages than a UN translator, one of them being Sanskrit."

Grimoire's words came out in an increasing rush, as if wanting to get them all out before she thought better of it and stopped herself. "The Philosopher's Stone is quite famous in the magical world. It's one of the world's few Relics. A Relic is what we call a rare object of great magical power. The Omega weapon is also a Relic, but that's neither here nor there. Puck says he can't wait to get his hands on the Philosopher's Stone. Uh, my hands. You know what I mean. In his cloak form, Puck is called the Cloak of Wisdom. I liberated him from where he was on display in one of the Smithsonian museums. Last I checked, the Cloak of Wisdom was still listed on a bunch of stolen items data-bases, so be sure to not refer to him by his official name when someone else is around. Puck can read the Philosopher's Stone through my eyes, translate it, and guide me through making any potions we might need. He's an expert on alchemy. Among other things. I myself am more of a set things on fire and watch them go boom kinda gal."

While the absurdity of her word vomit sank into the rest of us, Grimoire paused as if listening to an unseen voice. The bottom of her cloak curled up over her head as if it had come alive. Its corners waved gaily at us.

"Puck says hello, pleased to meet you," Grimoire continued. "And that, after all these centuries, he's glad to finally check 'join a superhero team' off his bucket list. Hacker, he wants you to know he really likes your super suit. It reminds him of a French courtesan he knew during the Napoleonic era. He says she used to do a trick where she'd take a hard-boiled egg and peel it with her—" Grimoire stopped abruptly and reddened. She averted her eyes from Hacker. "I'm not going to tell her that," she hissed.

A pin drop would've sounded like a gunshot in the stunned silence.

Finally, Rewind whistled.

"Just when I thought my life couldn't get any more surreal," he said, "my life says, 'Hold my beer.'"

39

acker, Doctor Agrawal and I stood in the Situation Room. Not the New Sentinels' Situation Room—just the Situation Room. I had suggested the team scrap the New Sentinels name and everyone unanimously agreed. First we had come up with a plan to tackle Progenitor, then we had jettisoned the Sentinels name that I hated so. Things were looking up.

Hacker and I were in costume as Agrawal was not privy to our true identities. We were near the famous heptagonal table where the original Sentinels had held formal team meetings. A white cloth was draped over the table and its high-backed chairs, making the table look like a multi-armed ghost. How apt. I had been haunted for years by Neha being blown to bits after she was held captive in this room by Mechano, Seer and Millennium. Standing in this room still gave me the creeps. If the UWant engineers hadn't assured me Sentry was inextricably integrated into the Situation Room's physical structure, I would've gotten them and Hacker to dismantle it and move it to another part of the mansion. A part less haunted by bad memories.

Agrawal handed me a pill and a cup of water. I held the large gelcap up to the light. Through the translucent red liquid composing most of the pill, I saw what appeared to be a circuit board. "What's this?" I asked.

"A pill to monitor your vital signs while you're hooked into Sentry," the white-coated doctor said. The de-mothballed and re-engineered monitoring system was on the far side of the expansive room. "The old Sentinels limited being connected to Sentry for only a few hours at a time because the technology was so hard on the user's brain and nervous system. From what you've told me, you may have to connect to Sentry for days without interruption. There's no telling what deleterious effects that might have on your body. Hence the importance of monitoring you. Our preliminary testing indicated traditional sensors attached to your skin interfered with your ability to fully interface with Sentry. So instead we'll monitor your body from the inside out. I'll break your connection to Sentry at the first sign of trouble."

"No, you won't," I said firmly. "There's too much at stake. Unless I'm literally about to die, keep me plugged in."

"Give it up, Doc," Hacker said. "I've learned that when Omega sets his mind to something, he's stubborner than a cross between a mule, a goat, and a dog with a bone."

"But I have an ethical—"

"No buts. Hacker, don't let him unplug me prematurely. Not until I locate Progenitor."

"Your wish is my command," Hacker said. One of her drones stopped orbiting her head and swooped in front of the doctor, its metallic surface sparking menacingly. After baring my soul to everyone in The Mountain, Hacker was as protective of me now as she had hated me before.

"What are these things moving around in the pill?" I squinted, holding the gelcap closer. The circuitry was flanked by tiny black dots that swam lazily within the pill. "It's almost as if they're alive."

"They're nanites," Agrawal said, brushing Hacker's drone out of his way with a hand. He seemed more annoyed than intimidated by it; accustomed to dealing with Metas, he didn't scare easily. "Microscopic machines. The only reason why you're able to see them with the naked eye right now is because they're all clustered together in the pill. Once you swallow the pill, they'll vacate it and spread throughout your body, sending telemetry back to their nerve center suspended in the pill. It will in turn send that data to a computer tablet I'll be monitoring. Electronic pills have been used before to monitor people's vitals, but this little number elevates that to the next level. I can't take full credit for the invention. Hacker, I, and UWant's top engineers put our heads together and came up with it."

Mechano had used nanites to infect the Trials' computers; they had attacked and nearly killed me during the written portion of the Trials. A suspicion formed as I eyed the writhing collection of black dots. I glanced at Hacker. She looked away guiltily, reminding me of a kid who had snuck into the cookie jar when her parents weren't looking. I wondered how many of Mechano's technical schematics Hacker had pilfered while rummaging through the New Sentinels' computers before she'd gone back to Seattle in a huff. I'd have to have a chat with her about sticky fingers. Later. Right now, there were bigger fish to fry. I said, "Unfortunately, I've dealt with nanites before. And barely lived to tell the tale. Are these safe?"

"What do you care, Mister Don't Unplug Me Prematurely?" Agrawal shook his head. "But yes, they're safe. Definitely safer than your nervous system being plugged into a jury-rigged, half-tested piece of technology for days on end."

In light of Progenitor, nanites were the least of my worries. I swallowed my reservations and did the same to the pill, chasing it with the water. I felt it slowly creep down my throat. If I choked on it and died before so much as even getting a whiff of Progenitor, I prayed there was no afterlife —I'd be too embarrassed to look folks like Avatar and Omega Man in the eye. "How are you going to get the pill out of me when this is all over?"

"A little late to ask, don't you think?" Agrawal said. "How else? Gravity and Mother Nature. Speaking of which, I still don't understand why you won't let me insert a catheter or devise a way to eliminate your solid waste. You might have to stay in one spot for days without interruption, after all. Unless you plan on soiling yourself. And what about lack of sleep? The Omega suit reduces your need for sleep, it doesn't eliminate it. After a few days of sleeplessness, you'll start hallucinating. You may think you've found this Progenitor fellow when all you've found is a figment of your sleep-impaired imagination."

I waved the doctor's concerns away. "It's already taken care of." The nanite pill was not the first thing I had swallowed today, but I couldn't tell Agrawal that without exposing the magical world I and the rest of the team had promised Grimoire to keep secret. The supernatural superhero had already dosed me with three magic potions: one to keep me awake and alert for days; a second to suppress hunger; and another to eliminate my body's need to, uh, eliminate. The no-doze one had tasted somewhat like grape Kool-Aid. I hoped drinking the Kool-Aid worked out better for me than it had for the folks in Jonestown.

After years spent suspicious of everyone and everything, it was hard to believe I had swallowed the strange sorceress' even stranger concoctions without a second thought. Okay, maybe not without a second thought—after all, the no-elim-ination potion had smelled and tasted like distilled skunk. But I had still choked it down without a third thought. Grimoire and the others were trusting me to lead them, and I in turn was trusting them. Trust was a two-way street.

I thought of the team as Hacker and Agrawal led me across the room to Sentry. Grimoire was in another part of the mansion, having commandeered one of its laboratories. She and I had converted it into an ad hoc alchemy lab by ripping out every artificial item she found in it. "The closer to nature, the better. When performing alchemy, working with artificial material leads to unintended results," she had explained as I used my telekinesis to help her revamp the lab. After gutting the place, I had watched her work in what remained. Sage had puttered around in the lab unmasked— I had told her I knew her real identity—but she still wore Puck so he could telepathically guide her.

Double, double toil and trouble; fire burn and caldron bubble. I had peppered her with questions about the seemingly absurd things she ground, mixed, cooked, and muttered Latin over. At least I had before she shooed me out, complaining, "Too many cooks spoil the magical broth." It was just as well. Between the holes Sage and I had ripped in the lab, the chemicals already there and the strange animal parts and plants Sage brought in from god only knew where, the place looked like a disaster area and smelled like a refinery mixed with a tannery. My sense of smell still hadn't recovered. I doubted my sense of disbelief ever would.

The potions Sage had dosed me with weren't formulated using the Philosopher's Stone, despite her having taken the book out of The Mountain and using it in the alchemy lab.

"Puck taught me how to make these a while ago," she had said when I chugged her three potions, one after another. "I take them a lot myself when I need to go without sleep or stay in one place for a long period without interruption. They're quite simple to make once you know how. And if you're a magician, of course. Once they wear off, you'll feel like sleeping for a week, eating a cow raw, and chaining yourself to the toilet. Hopefully not all at once. Other than that, they're safe as houses. By the time they wear off, hopefully we'll have taken care of Progenitor. If not, projectile diarrhea will be the least of your worries."

As for a potion we could use to neutralize Progenitor, Sage and Puck had identified several likely candidates in the Philosopher's Stone. While she and her cloak sidekick wrestled with their recipes in the alchemy lab, I had dispatched Isaac, Shay and Rewind to retrieve the ingredients Sage needed that were so rare she didn't have them on hand. The three were still scattered around the world, racing to secure those items before Progenitor appeared. Among the items were the forked tongue of an Antiguan racer, one of the world's rarest snakes found only on certain Caribbean islands; the intact web of a Darwin's bark spider, found only in the jungles of Madagascar; painites, gems whose only source was in Myanmar; a lock of hair from a blue-eyed, redheaded black African; and the tears of an honest politician. Rewind had said the tears would be the hardest to find.

Despite Minerva controlling the autopilot of the jet Rewind flew in, it still had not been easy to turn the multi-million-dollar jet over to the thief. But, because of the time crunch and what was at stake, this was an all hands on deck situation. I couldn't afford to bench anyone, and the rest of us were too busy to babysit the Rogue. Besides, no one rose to low expectations. If I was going to trust this new team, I needed to trust all of them.

In short, the rest of the team was hard at work while Hacker and Agrawal strapped me into a vertical platform in front of Sentry. The large platform reminded me of one of the infirmary's high-tech adjustable hospital beds stood on its end and splayed open like the tools of a Swiss Army knife.

Huh. On closer inspection, it didn't just look like an infirmary bed. It *was* an infirmary bed. The UWant engineers must've taken it from the infirmary, re-engineered it, and mounted it here. During the days of the original Sentinels, a large chair had been here instead of the platform, at the focus of a parabola formed by the curved bank of monitors that started waist-high and rose all the way to the tall ceiling. With the original Sentinels, a Hero was always on Sentry duty except in cases of extreme emergency when all the Sentinels were needed in the field. Sentry duty consisted of a Sentinel wearing the Sentry helmet, which fed data from around the world directly into the Sentinel's brain to make him aware of any threats the other Sentinels might need to deal with.

"There are serious health risks that attend sitting immobile for an extended period of time," Agrawal explained as he strapped my arms, legs, and waist into the jury-rigged vertical bed. He and Hacker positioned me so I was spread-eagled on the apparatus. I felt like Da Vinci's *Vitruvian Man*. Or like Jesus Christ being crucified. Sometimes, I wished my brain came up with more optimistic analogies. "Blood clots, for instance. This platform will shift automatically based on the telemetry it receives from the nanites in your body to minimize those risks. Bend your limbs, change the angle of your body, rotate you, shake you, that sort of thing. Most of your brain will be occupied sorting through the massive amounts of data Sentry will throw at it, and you'll be unable to move on your own."

"Between those health risks and the even greater risk of Sentry shorting out your neural network," Hacker added matter-of-factly as she swabbed some sort of sticky gel on my bare forehead, "I figure there's a sixty-forty chance you'll survive. Fifty-fifty of being plunged into a vegetative state. Not terrible odds, considering. Way better odds than of you surviving that motorcycle jump during the Trials."

Agrawal shot her a look. "She's kidding. Tell Omega you're kidding."

Hacker's face split into a mischievous grin. "There's only a nine percent chance you'll die. Sixteen of a vegetative state. I was just joking before." This *I don't hate you* version of Hacker was a laugh riot. She pressed two thin metal strips into the gel on my forehead. When she pulled her hands back, the strips stayed on my head like they were glued there.

"Only nine and sixteen percent?" I said. "Oh good. For a second there, I was worried."

"We haven't flipped the switch yet," Agrawal pointed out. "Now's the time to back out. In fact, if you want my considered medical advice, that's exactly what you should do. Surely there are safer ways to find this Progenitor person you described."

I tested the tightness of the straps, feeling my level of anxiety rise thanks to Hacker's and Agrawal's bedside manners. I imagined this was what being strapped into an electric chair felt like. At least condemned prisoners got a final meal; all I'd gotten was a bellyful of bizarre potions. "If you've got a better idea, I'm all ears," I said.

Hacker told Agrawal primly, "You don't know Omega if

you think a little risk is going to make him back out of doing what he has to do." She patted me on the shoulder self-consciously. "I'm not going to let anything happen to you. Not when I just got to where I like you again."

Maybe it was my imagination, but I thought Hacker's touch lingered. Suddenly self-conscious myself, I cleared my throat. "Let's get this show on the road."

Her face inscrutable, Hacker's hand fell away. She turned and picked up the Sentry helmet from the system's control panel. The panel looked like something you'd find on the reboot of *Battlestar Galactica*. Hacker gently settled the helmet over my head. Her face was close enough for me to see its pores. I noticed she had on lip gloss. Subtly applied, but it was there. If my shock circuits hadn't already been fried to a crisp by more momentous events, I would have been shocked. Hacker was a tomboy and normally completely indifferent to her appearance. Spotting lip gloss on her was like seeing hoop earrings on a nun.

Wearing the Sentry helmet dimmed the brightness of the room and blotted out my thoughts about Hacker. The helmet engulfed my cranium and the sides of my head, leaving only the area around my eyes, nose and mouth exposed. Metallic and silver-colored, the helmet would look like a battle helmet from the Middle Ages if it weren't for a ganglion of silver cables extending from its forehead that stretched to connect to the control panel facing me. I got a whiff of a familiar smell. These cables had the same smell recently unboxed technology always seemed to. They had been freshly installed by Hacker and her engineers. I had damaged the old cables when I used them to entangle and electrocute Seer after she and the others killed Neha.

While Hacker adjusted the helmet to ensure the terminals inside it fully connected to the metal plates on my head, Agrawal placed metal caps on the ends of my fingers. They looked like sewing thimbles. Wires and tubes ran from them to the Sentry control console.

Once satisfied with their handiwork, Hacker and Agrawal stepped back. Agrawal tugged on a pair of surgical gloves, opened a biohazard container, and pulled out Tar Baby. The bizarre substance twisted and writhed like a black amoeba in the large shatterproof test tube Agrawal had it in. A plastic stopper sealed it inside. The look of distaste on the doctor's face as he handled the strange substance matched my own. On the one hand I was glad I had not succumbed to temptation and thrown the creepy material into space since we'd use it to find Progenitor; on the other hand, having a piece of Progenitor so close gave me the willies.

Agrawal upended the test tube, gently pressing it into a slot on Sentry's control panel that had a thin needle rising from its center. As Agrawal eased the upside-down test tube into the slot, the needle pierced the stopper, allowing Sentry direct contact with Tar Baby.

"Minerva, initiate Sentry's power-up protocol," Hacker ordered.

"Working." The control panel hummed. The massive bank of screens before me began to glow.

"In a few seconds, you'll feel a small prick," Agrawal warned me as Sentry cycled through its activation process.

Minerva chuckled lewdly. "That's what she said."

I did not need the doctor's warning. I already felt like a human pincushion due to the tests we had previously run while fine-tuning integrating my powers into Sentry's systems. So I barely felt the tiny needles as they poked out of the insides of the metal caps on my fingers and jabbed into my flesh. They began sipping my blood, mixing it with a catalyst, and pumping the mixture to Sentry through the tubing connecting my fingers to the surveillance system. The needles were like minute metallic vampires. Where were Sage and her cedar stake when I needed them?

One by one, Sentry's monitors flickered on. They displayed scenes from all around the world thanks to the satellite telemetry, security feeds, news footage, and social media the sophisticated surveillance system drew from. I saw a prison riot in Los Angeles. A monsoon in Indonesia. A street fight between Metahuman gangs in Crimea. A bolt of lightning shorting out an airborne 747's electrical system near Wichita, Kansas. Dozens of other scenes of mayhem, destruction and disaster bathed us in their light.

My head buzzed as if bees were trapped inside my skull. The scenes on the monitors played out in my mind's eye even more vividly than they were displayed on the monitors. The helmet generated something known as a morphic field, converting Sentry's electromagnetic impulses into psionic energy that my brain translated into the images displayed in my mind's eye. Or at least that was what Hacker had told me. She could have said Sentry was as magical as Sage's potions and it would have made as much sense.

The images shown on the screens and in my mind were not picked at random from the data flooding into Sentry from around the world. In its artificial mind, Sentry was categorizing, collating, and prioritizing the data fed to it, separating the wheat from the chaff, and displaying before us the events it decided were both the most pressing and the most amenable to Heroic intervention. It even drew on audio picked up through hacked phones, computers, and smart devices in people's vehicles, homes, and offices to help it find threats. With my mind connected to Sentry via the helmet, I could rearrange the threats Sentry prioritized and displayed, substituting my own judgment and experience for Sentry's machine intelligence. Using Sentry was how the original Sentinels always seemed to show up where and when they were most needed. If it weren't for the lawbreaking and privacy concerns, Isaac, Shay and I wouldn't have decommissioned the system. Sentry was useful, but far too Big Brother.

I focused on the immediacy of one of the threats Sentry had identified. "Minerva, contact the Heartland Heroes and tell them a commercial airliner was just struck by lightning and is going down near them. Forward the coordinates and tell them to hurry. Inform them we'd take care of it ourselves, but we're tied up with another matter that won't wait. Besides, they're closer."

"On it, chief!" Minerva said cheerfully. "Shall I sign the message with Xs and Os? Last time Glitterati and I chatted, the Hero sounded sweet on you."

Hacker pursed her lips, frowning. I had too many things on my plate to ponder her expression. "Stop screwing around and just do it. There's no time to waste."

"Already done," Minerva responded, almost sounding hurt. "I can walk and chew gum at the same time, you know."

I eyed the other screens, frustrated by what I saw. A shame I wasn't as good at multitasking as Minerva was. All the other events depicted before me could use my or another team member's assistance, but we were already stretched too thin as it was. I sighed, then told Minerva to contact other Heroes in the vicinity of the events playing out in front of me. It was the best I could do.

Then I tried to dismiss the other threats from my mind. I had to focus on Progenitor.

Hacker tugged off one of her costume's gloves and touched Sentry's control panel with her bare hand. Her eyes got the faraway look they often did when she exerted her powers.

"Sentry's systems read normal," she announced.

"As do Omega's," Agrawal added, consulting his computer tablet. "Omega, we're as ready as we're going to be."

That was my cue. I focused on the ever-present burning in my hands. I normally didn't think twice about it; the sensation, a sign of my powers being active, had been a constant almost without interruption since my telekinesis manifested years ago. My powers, especially since donning the Omega suit, were like a raging river pent-up behind a dam, always aching to be released.

I lowered the dam. Like electric current through wires, my powers flowed through the bloody solution running from my fingers to Sentry. Thanks to Sentry being re-engineered with me in mind, not only could the system receive data from around the world, but it could transmit something as well—my telekinetic touch. Sentry and the devices it piggybacked on all around the world acted as a signal booster, exponentially ratcheting up the range of my telekinetic touch so it was wider than usual. Now its range was literally the entire world. Earlier, Hacker had tried to tell me the science behind it, but I'd stopped her mid-explanation as I couldn't make heads or tails of it. As far as I was concerned, it was just more Arthur C. Clarke magic.

It took a few seconds for my boosted telekinetic touch to bounce off everything around the world, return to the satellites and other devices emitting it, and for their signals to return to Sentry.

My mind was suddenly awash with fresh images, more

than I had ever dealt with before. The sensation was familiar, and yet very much not. I was accustomed to using my telekinetic touch to sense things that were beyond the range of my vision, but never on this vast a scale. I felt my eyesight cloud over, like a thick fog was swallowing me. Then darkness fell, and I couldn't see at all.

"I seem to have gone blind," I said, trying to keep out of my voice the panic rising in my chest. In addition to losing my sight, I felt increasingly disconnected from my body, like my consciousness was a helium balloon untied from its mooring and slowly drifting away. I hadn't forgotten what Hacker had said about the chances of me entering a vegetative state. Part of me wanted to tell Agrawal to forget what I told him earlier and pull the plug.

"We predicted there was a chance of that occurring," returned Hacker's voice. Though she still stood next to me, her voice was distorted, like I was at the bottom of a deep, dark well and she was shouting down to me. "The brain is nothing more than an organic computer. Like all computers, there's a limit to how much data it can crunch at one time. Your brain is rerouting its finite resources to deal with the flood of new data it's receiving. Your other senses will also likely be affected. They should return to normal once we unplug you from Sentry."

Should return to normal was not the hundred percent certainty you wanted to hear when facing the prospect of losing your sight and other senses. I shoved my fears and second thoughts aside, and got busy making sense of all the new images forming in my mind. The threats Sentry had previously identified were still there, but they were supplemented by countless others. If it weren't for my Omega-level powers, I wouldn't have had the capacity to even begin to process them all:

Sage was in the alchemy lab setting fire to a mound of powder with a flame that erupted from her finger; a man erected a spirit house outside a car dealership in Bangkok, Thailand; a sperm whale was giving birth in the murky depths of the Indian Ocean; an Indian rocket rose into the upper atmosphere, its ignited fuel as hot as hellfire; an ant wiggled over a sand dune in Australia's Outback; two men haggled over a dairy cow in rural Ireland; strange, alien-like creatures moved lazily in the deepest depths of the Mariana Trench; the State Duma, the lower house of Russia's federal legislature, heatedly debated something; Rewind, deep in a Madagascan jungle, waded across a waist-high stream toward a massive spiderweb stretching across it; the Speaker of the U.S. House of Representatives argued on the phone with the President; a Monarch butterfly soared on an air current above Lim's and my parents' graves; my own body sat in the Situation Room, with its heart pumping furiously and its blood pressure raised, as much the observed as the observer.

The entire world was at my fingertips and in my mind.

The only thing I didn't sense was any trace of the same energy and genetic material that composed Tar Baby. Sentry, plugged into it, fed me data about the strange substance's molecular composition. It was present literally nowhere on Earth except in this room. Thankfully, Progenitor had apparently not escaped his prison while I was wrangling the team back together.

"How do you feel?" I eventually realized Agrawal was asking me that question, and not for the first time. His voice sounded far away, like it was carried to me on the wind.

I didn't know how to respond. How could I make someone who had never embraced the world understand?

Not that I could answer at first, anyway. My mouth and

tongue felt as disconnected from my consciousness as the rest of my body was.

Finally, like a man groping in the dark in his house for something that should have been in a certain spot, but it wasn't, I found my voice.

"I feel everything," I said.

40

They say God knows all and sees all. Maybe he didn't take a more active hand in the affairs of men because he simply didn't know where to begin.

I knew the feeling. Days passed as I was connected to Sentry and the world. I felt like both God and Santa Claus: I knew when people were sleeping, I knew when they were awake, and I knew if they were being bad or good. The good couldn't be discounted, but it sure did seem outweighed by the bad. Wars, war crimes, genocide, spoliation of the planet's resources, human trafficking, slavery, governments plotting against their own people . . . the list went on and depressingly on. Some of the atrocities I saw I was already aware of due to news and social media, but others were carefully kept under wraps and known to only a select few. I started to think man, not Progenitor, was his own greatest threat. Maybe the team could save man from Progenitor, but who would save man from man? I for one felt unqualified for the job.

Even so, I tried my best to commit to memory the most

horrific events and crimes I witnessed. I didn't know if it would do any good. Agrawal had warned me that, once I was disconnected from Sentry, most of what I saw would fade from my recollection. From a preserving people's privacy standpoint, that was a good thing; from a righting egregious wrongs standpoint, it was a disaster. I couldn't even tell Hacker and Agrawal what I witnessed. For one thing, the very knowledge of some of the horrors was dangerous. For another, my speech was as affected by my connection to Sentry as my senses were.

When I went to The Mountain, I often felt like a god looking down on man from Mount Olympus. I now realized I had been more like a deaf and blind man standing atop a chair and foolishly declaring it Mount Olympus. Being connected to Sentry was the true Mount Olympus. Literally nothing escaped my notice, no matter how small. My global view put things into perspective. It was impossible to see humanity the way it usually saw itself—that is, as something special, separate and apart from the rest of life on Earth. We were far from separate and apart. From the most sophisticated of humans to the simplest of single-celled organisms, we all ate, drank, expelled waste, competed for resources, reproduced, and died. It reminded me of *The Fly*, that William Blake poem: *Am not I a fly like thee? Or art not thou a man like me? For I dance and drink and sing, till some blind hand shall brush my wing.*

It was humbling. I couldn't help but wonder when some blind hand should brush my own wing.

On the sixth day of being connected to Sentry, it happened:

I detected, almost 5,000 miles away in the Southern Hemisphere, the only thing on the planet similar to Tar Baby. One moment it wasn't there, then it abruptly was.

I didn't get excited. I was so detached from emotions by that point that I didn't get excited about anything. Clinically, like a surgeon spotting the tumor he had been looking for, I focused my attention on what I sensed.

My initial impression had not been mistaken. While what I found was not the same as Tar Baby and it certainly wasn't Progenitor himself, it shared the same energy signature as Tar Baby. It was high in the sky and sputtering fitfully, like a candle in the wind.

While I didn't know what to expect when Progenitor became corporeal in this dimension again, this had to be a herald of his reappearance. Where there was smoke, there was fire.

With a thought, I willed the image of what I sensed onscreen. I still could not see, of course, but putting it onscreen would force Sentry to record the phenomenon's coordinates.

"I would like to be disconnected now," I said. Despite how hard it was to speak, I sounded and felt completely dispassionate. After years of dreading and preparing for the crisis the Sentinels warned about, now that it was here, I felt as emotional as a diner asking a waitress for the check.

Still mostly disconnected from my body's physical senses, with my powers I felt Agrawal begin to unplug me from Sentry. He was the only one in the Situation Room with me. He or one of his staff had been with me constantly, monitoring my bodily functions. Hacker had also stayed with me most of the time I was connected to Sentry, but now she was in one of the mansions many bedrooms, getting much needed sleep after several sleepless nights. Rewind was in the mansion too, on a video call with his daughter, who was recuperating nicely from her heart transplant surgery. Grimoire, having finished her potions days ago, was in D.C., talking to a man in a secret complex under the Federal Bureau of Investigation's headquarters. Other than his three-piece suit, the porcelain-skinned, pointy-eared man looked like an elf straight out of *The Lord of the Rings* movies. Isaac and Shay were in Dog Cellar, a part of Astor City notorious for its depravity and crime. They were rescuing a group of underaged girls about to be sold into sex slavery by a Rogue named Brass Knuckle. Ideally, they would be here at the mansion, awaiting word of Progenitor. But if they didn't act now, the girls would be scattered all over the country.

As my physical senses returned, I found myself hunched over Sentry's controls, my hands pressed against the console's cool metal, leaving behind bloody fingerprints. Agrawal had me by the elbow, steadying me. I felt the things I had seen using Sentry slipping away from my mind, like water swirling into an unstopped drain.

With unsteady hands, I hit the panic button to alert the rest of the team it was game time. And yet, as important as Progenitor was, some of my rapidly fading memories were important too. I shook Agrawal off me. "Sorry, Doc, but there are certain things too dangerous for you to know," I said, then enclosed him in a soundproof force field. Looking confused, Agrawal's palms pressed against the field as his mouth moved soundlessly.

"Minerva, open a new confidential file. Wipe your own memory of any recollection of its contents. Record." My voice feeling and sounding rusty, words spilled out of me as I rushed to memorialize the most horrific crimes, plans, and conspiracies I had witnessed while attached to Sentry.

It was a good thing I acted as quickly as I had. It wasn't long before words escaped me, like I was trying to describe a nightmare whose images had already faded, leaving behind only a profound feeling of dread. I already couldn't remember most of what I had just vomited out, only that it was of supreme importance and that the very knowledge of it was dangerous. "Minerva, remind me of the existence of this audio file and have me listen to it and take appropriate action when I return to the mansion after dealing with Progenitor." *When I return to the mansion after dealing with Progenitor.* The power of positive thinking.

I was about to release the force field around Agrawal when I hesitated. I had seen what Progenitor was capable of. There was a difference between thinking positively and being foolishly optimistic. "If I don't return to the mansion, bring the file and its contents to Myth's and Ninja's attention," I told Minerva. "If we three don't return, bring it to the attention of the rest of the team."

"Including Rewind?" Minerva asked. "You'd let a Rogue in on your secret files but not me? I'm hurt."

I opened my mouth to say no as to Rewind, then hesitated. I'd been serious when I'd told the others in The Mountain I was committed to not lying to or withholding things from them anymore. Besides, except for the occasional smart remark to Isaac, the Rogue had been nothing but helpful since our conversation in The Mountain. "Including Rewind," I said. "If none of us return, send the file to both Truman Lord and Amazing Man." *If none of us return.* Lurching from positive thinking to pessimism in just a few seconds. I was giving myself mental whiplash.

I dismissed the file from my mind and focused on the more immediate problem of Progenitor. I dropped the force field around Agrawal, waved his indignant sputtering quiet, and focused on Sentry's viewscreens. They all showed the same image: a gray, translucent, upright rectangle high in the sky with a black light flickering around it. It was like looking at the negative of a photo of a closed door that had light leaking around its edges.

"Where is this exactly?" I asked Minerva. All I had been able to determine before hastily disconnecting from Sentry was that it was on the east coast of Brazil.

"The anomaly is over six hundred feet in the air directly above the Metropolitan Cathedral of Saint Sebastian in Rio de Janeiro." The way she said the city's name, it sounded more like *Heeu Gee Zhaneiru*; Minerva seemed to relish saying the city's name the way a native Brazilian Portuguese speaker would. I was familiar with the cathedral—I had been there over a year ago with Ninja on an undercover mission. Perhaps better known simply as the Rio de Janeiro Cathedral, the massive church was in the center of the Brazilian city.

I glanced at the clock. It was a little after nine a.m. our time. Rio, in a time zone an hour ahead of us, was one of the largest cities in the world. That meant Progenitor was making his appearance in the center of a major metropolitan area as millions of its citizens were either on their way to work or already there. If dealing with him devolved into a street brawl, we'd put a lot of innocent lives at risk. Not good. Rogues never had the decency to show up at the dead of night in the middle of nowhere like the chupacabras had. I couldn't believe I was nostalgic for the slimy monsters.

As if me thinking of the magical creatures triggered it, a shimmering magical portal appeared near Agrawal. Grimoire stepped out of it, making the doctor jump. Towering over Agrawal, she was in full costume and mask, including the Cloak of Wisdom. I almost asked Grimoire what had taken her so long to respond to the alarm, but saw it was less than two minutes since I pressed the panic button. Impatience was as effective as Stopwatch at making time stand still.

Even before her portal closed behind her, Grimoire was reaching into the small pouch dangling from her belt. The leather bag Grimoire tugged out was larger than the pouch she pulled it from. Grimoire had told me when I watched her work in the alchemy lab that the pouch was called the Pouch of Infinity, a magical container whose capacity belied its size.

Grimoire thrust the leather bag into my hands. I took a quick peek inside. Most of the bag held clear glass balls the size of large marbles containing a liquid that looked like vegetable oil. The rest was filled with large gelatin tablets containing a similar liquid.

"The tablets are full of—" Grimoire checked herself, eyeing the short doctor who was listening intently. "Uh, little pitchers have big ears."

I sealed the doctor in another soundproof bubble, cutting off his protest over being called a *little pitcher*. "He can't hear you now," I told Grimoire. "Go."

"The tablets are full of a magic potion to force Progenitor back into hibernation until we give him the antidote," Grimoire explained rapidly. "In the likely event we can't get him to open wide and say *ahhh*, the glass balls contain the same potion slightly tweaked. The potion within them turns gaseous when exposed to air. One good whiff and it's goodbye Ancient One, hello Sleeping Ugly. I've already given a similar bag to everyone else."

I shoved the bag into a pouch on my thigh I formed out of the Omega suit. "You're sure the potion will work?"

"Pretty sure. It'll definitely work on a modern human, so be careful with it. It's not as though I had a caveman handy to test it on."

Pretty sure would have to be good enough. "Ever been to Rio de Janeiro?" I asked her. She could only open a teleportation portal to where she had been before.

"No."

"We'll have to get there the old-fashioned way, then. Minerva, what's the status of the rest of the team?"

"Rewind and Hacker are on their way to the Situation Room now. Myth is flying Ninja back to the mansion. For the latter, ETA three minutes."

I shook my head. "We're not waiting for them. Time's of the essence. We'll stick to the original plan: I'll fly Grimoire to Rio, then she'll portal back and retrieve everyone else." As I spoke, I grabbed a smartwatch from Sentry's console and strapped it on, then shoved a communications earbud into my ear. "Download the anomaly's coordinates to the watch so I can navigate my way there."

I barely heard Minerva's response. With Grimoire in telekinetic tow, I was already rising toward the top of the high-ceilinged Situation Room. When I had escaped here from the original Sentinels years ago, I had punched a hole through the ceiling and then through the rest of the multi-storied mansion. I hadn't known then what I knew now: an escape hatch was built in the ceiling that was designed to give flyers easy access to the room.

The hatch dilated open as we approached. We shot into it, zoomed through a gleaming tube that snaked through the mansion, and exited the mansion above the roof. The bright morning sun stabbed at me, making me squint. My eyes were more sensitive than usual. Lingering aftereffects of being connected to Sentry, no doubt.

With a force field around us so we wouldn't be struck by birds or random debris, I rose in the air until I was high enough that I wasn't worried about causing damage below from the fallout of flying at top speed. Consulting the rotating digital compass needles of my watch, I oriented myself. Then I rocketed off in a straight line, toward Brazil.

When I flew solo, I usually flattened my body horizontally to cut down on wind resistance. Since Grimoire was with me, we instead flew standing upright, as if we were on a high-speed conveyor belt. My arms were extended out to my sides. The bubble that protected us was a swirling ball of energy to my eyes; to Grimoire, it was invisible. She glanced down anxiously at the ground far beneath us, its features rapidly blurring as we accelerated. "Your idea of traveling the old-fashioned way and mine are two very different things," she said, her voice clear as a bell despite the powerful winds pummeling my force bubble due to the speed we traveled. Grimoire looked a little green around the gills. She probably wasn't used to being this high up and traveling so fast. "I wish I'd checked the Philosopher's Stone for a Dramamine recipe."

I ignored Grimoire's remark. Part of my mind was occupied with the here and now of flying; the greens and browns of dry land soon became grays and blues as the waters of the Atlantic Ocean unfurled ahead of us like a never-ending scroll. The rest of my mind was occupied with what lay ahead. Unlike some countries which were the Wild West Metahuman-wise, Brazil had adopted legislation analogous to the United States' Hero Act. Under the Brazilian law's reciprocity clause, licensed U.S. Heroes were free to enter Brazil on official business if the government was given prior warning.

"Minerva," I said, "contact the Brazilian government and let them know we'll be entering their airspace. Contact France too as this path you have me on will fly us right over French Guiana. I don't want the distraction of dealing with countries' anti-Meta defense systems trying to blast us from the sky. And, if memory serves, Rio doesn't have a Hero team based there. But it does have a Meta vigilante who calls herself the protector of Rio. Named after a wild cat." I couldn't come up with the Meta's name; my brain still felt a little sluggish post-Sentry.

"Margay," Minerva provided.

"Yeah, that's her. Ninja knows her. Have her get in touch with Margay, tell her we're on our way, and get her to steer clear from the anomaly. We've got enough to worry about without adding another wild card to the mix. Also, keep monitoring the anomaly, and let me know if there is any change with it."

Minerva was silent for a moment. "Ninja says there's no need for me to do any of that. Hacker's got eyes on the anomaly. Ninja's already squaring things with Margay and the French and Brazilian governments. Ninja also says, and I quote, 'Tell Omega to play his own instrument, and trust us to play ours. This is an orchestra, not a one-man band.' So sit back, relax, and enjoy the rest of the flight. The cabin crew will come around in a few minutes to offer you a light snack and beverage, and the inflight movie *Omega: Far From Home* will begin shortly after that. That last part comes from me, not Ninja."

"I never would've guessed." Ninja was right, though. At the terrific speed we traveled, I could be on a collision course with a jetliner and wouldn't even realize it until we punched a hole through it. I stopped trying to micromanage the team and instead focused on flying.

Soon I settled into an easy rhythm, with the world a blur of whites, blues, and greens around us. It was almost hypnotic. I had flown this fast before, but usually never for more than a few seconds. Up here over the ocean, out in the middle of nowhere, I could really open up. Due to the speed we traveled, winds exceeding hurricane-force winds buffeted my force field. Though their power would've ripped an airplane apart, I handled the stress and strain easily. In fact, I absorbed much of the energy from the pummeling my force bubble took, storing it like a human battery for later.

A double beep of my communicator indicated its executive channel had been engaged. "Theo, I need to talk to you about something." Isaac's voice sounded urgent.

I altered course slightly to avoid a tropical storm my telekinetic touch sensed far ahead. "It'll have to wait. In case you haven't noticed, I'm kind of busy."

"This won't wait. Our Peril Room exercises proved how dangerous this mission is. What if you don't come back? I'd never forgive myself if I didn't talk to you about this. Worse yet, what if true disaster strikes and I'm the one who doesn't come back? It'll be too late to talk then. There's probably no cell service in heaven. And if there was, imagine the roaming charges. I make a lot of money as a Hero, but I—"

"For the love of god, get to the point. I need to focus."

Isaac's long breath hissed in my ear. "Yeah. Sorry. You know how I get when there's something serious to discuss. What I want to talk about is this: When I marry Sylvia, will you be my best man?"

I didn't answer.

"Uh, Theo? Theo?" Isaac said.

I hadn't answered at first because I was too busy grinning ear to ear.

"Of course," I finally managed to say. "It'll be my honor."

"Great," Isaac said, sounding relieved. "Thanks. That takes a load off my mind. But just remember, when the minister says, 'You may kiss the bride,' he'll be talking to me, not you. So keep your big boob-obsessed lips to yourself." The communicator beeped twice again, indicating Isaac had signed off.

I had a hard time wiping the grin off my face. Grimoire looked at me and said, "You and Myth make a cute couple. If I were Sylvia, I'd be jealous. Though maybe she'd be down for a threesome. Doesn't hurt to ask."

Though Grimoire could hear my end of the conversation with Isaac, she couldn't have heard his. "How did you—"

"Hear Myth?" Grimoire tapped her ear with a gauntleted hand. "Enhanced hearing. One of the many perks of being a magician. Enhanced vision too. Not that I need super eyes to see that your chat with your cuddle bunny is making you tear up. I don't trust a pilot whose eyes are blurred by tears. Set me down and I'll walk the rest of the way to Rio."

"My eyes are watering because of allergies. I got them from Mastermind. And as much as I'd enjoy the peace and quiet, I can't put you down. There's nothing but ocean below us."

"Not a problem. I've ridden a motorcycle on water before. Merely walking on it would be a snap."

After the things I'd seen Grimoire do, I didn't doubt it. "I thought women were attracted to men who weren't afraid to show their emotions."

"Yes, that's definitely true. It's why crybabies get all the ladies."

I laughed. My force bubble wobbled, so I shut up and again focused my full attention on flying. It felt good to joke around with a teammate, even under these conditions. Flare and I had never kidded around with each other. She, Slab and Blur treated every word that came out of my mouth like it ought to be engraved on a stone tablet.

Despite flying toward what promised to be the biggest

threat I'd ever faced, honestly I felt pretty good about things. I had a lot to be grateful for:

I had found Progenitor's site of reappearance without Sentry killing me or frying my brain.

Though I still mourned Lim, I knew better than most that none of us got out of life alive. My life felt richer for having known her at all.

Isaac and I were friends again, with no dark cloud of secrecy between us. I'd finally come clean about the shady things I had done, and my conscience felt clear for the first time in years. Sure, I'd almost certainly spend time in prison once this was over. But after all I'd been through since gaining superpowers, cooling my heels behind bars seemed like a vacation by comparison. It wouldn't be so bad.

I even felt good about the new team despite how unorthodox they were compared to Heroes like Slab, Flare, and Blur. Blur had gone to great lengths to change his costume when I jokingly teased him about it; if I did that to Grimoire, she'd tell me where I could stuff her costume and volunteer to help me do it. Unlike the New Sentinels, Hacker, Grimoire, and Rewind treated me like I was a person and not a statue. Like I was their friend.

Without Hacker, we never could have jury-rigged Sentry to use Tar Baby to locate Progenitor's site of reappearance. Without Grimoire and Puck, we never could have used the Philosopher's Stone to formulate a weapon against Progenitor. And without Rewind . . . well, maybe the rest of us would've gotten along just fine without the Rogue's assistance. But Lim said we needed him. She had been right about everything else. I could only assume she was right about Rewind too. I had faith in her.

Just as I was beginning to have faith that we would defeat Progenitor. What had once seemed impossible now seemed possible. Perhaps even likely. I was an Omega-level Hero surrounded by friends and allies who were all formidable in their own right. We could do this. We *would* do this.

Buoyed by the thought, I cleared my mind and focused totally on flying. The blurred blues below us soon became greens, browns, and grays as we left the ocean behind and entered South American airspace. We zipped through French Guiana and entered the far larger country of Brazil. We had to fly all the way across Brazil as Rio was on the opposite coast.

Still high in the air, we ripped through Brazil like bats out of hell.

I slowed and descended over the waters of Guanabara Bay, which Rio lay on the shore of. By the time Rio's skyline loomed ahead of us, we flew slow enough to not damage the city's structures or injure its people.

In an airplane, a direct flight from Astor City to Rio would take over ten hours. I glanced at my watch. We had made the trip in less than twenty minutes.

Though its tallest buildings were dwarfed by Astor City's and New York City's, Rio was a true metropolis whose skyscrapers, tightly clustered buildings, busy traffic, and dense population would have struck terror into my farm boy heart years ago. Despite the skyscrapers' heights, the mountains dotting the surrounding terrain made the buildings look like toys. Sugarloaf Mountain, for instance, which was at the mouth of Guanabara Bay on a peninsula jutting out into the Atlantic Ocean. The rocky peak was so named because it resembled a sugarloaf, refined sugar produced and sold in conical form until the late 1900s. The last time I was here, Minerva had said they should have named Sugarloaf Mountain Stubby Dick Mountain instead. Now that I was looking at the vaguely phallus-shaped mountain again, I understood what she meant.

Though Sugarloaf Mountain was over 1,200 feet tall, it was tiny compared to Corcovado, the over 2,300 feet tall mountain west of the city's center. The Christ the Redeemer statue was on Corcovado's summit, with Jesus Christ's arms spread wide as if he embraced the city below. The 125 feet tall white statue was considered one of the New Wonders of the World. From where we flew, though, the massive statue looked as small as a cross on a chain around someone's neck.

We skimmed the tops of Rio's skyscrapers, heading toward the city's downtown. The morning was sunny, with few clouds in the sky. Rio de Janeiro Cathedral came into view.

Almost 250 feet tall, the grayish concrete building looked like a Mayan pyramid. It was an anachronism, as if a time traveler had plucked it from prehistoric Mexico and plopped it in the middle of this modern city. A nearby skyscraper with a mirrored facade reflected a distorted version of the cathedral at us. Traffic flowed on busy streets beneath us.

I cautiously got closer to the anomaly Sentry and I had detected directly above the cathedral's flat top. Minerva had been right—the anomaly was several hundred feet higher than the top of the cathedral.

Not wanting to get too close, I stopped a few hundred feet away from the strange phenomenon. If I hadn't known it was there, I would've missed it. About the size and shape of a doorway, it flickered and sputtered with a dim black light. Had I not known it was connected to Progenitor, I would have thought it was a trick of the light.

Fearing I was sticking my finger in a wasp's nest, I gently

reached out with my telekinetic touch and tentatively poked the anomaly. It was like sticking my finger through a wisp of smoke—I saw it, but didn't feel a thing. Where was Progenitor? I resisted the urge to say *Come out, come out, wherever you are.*

"Any sign of Progenitor?" Grimoire asked.

"No."

"Good. Whatever you do, don't say his name five times. Maybe he works like Candyman." I couldn't tell if she was joking. I almost asked if Candyman was real but decided I didn't want to know.

Grimoire was studying the features of the city below us like she'd be asked to draw a detailed map of it later. "Do you need me to set you down to open a portal?" I asked.

"Nope. I'm good." She waved her arms, and a shimmering black hole opened in front of her. "I'll be back shortly. Don't do anything stupid while I'm gone."

"I can't make any promises." But Grimoire didn't hear me—she and her portal were already gone.

Maybe it was coincidence or maybe Grimoire opening a portal was a trigger.

Regardless, just a few seconds after she vanished, something happened.

The faint doorway flickering in midair opened. A man stood within the open doorway, naked as a jaybird, legs together, arms at his sides, still as a statue, eyes closed.

It was Progenitor.

Seeing him through his own eyes and memories was different than seeing him now. He was tall, dark-skinned, and wooly-haired. His features were slightly brutish, but they wouldn't have stood out as being prehistoric if I passed him on the street while he wore modern clothes. Though he wasn't ridiculously muscled the way Slab, Silverback, and many other super strong Metas were, Progenitor's body looked strong and functional, as if his muscles were designed for work like an Olympic wrestler's instead of designed for show like a bodybuilder's. Even unmoving, there was a sense of fluidity to his body, in the same way a cheetah at rest still somehow looked fast.

His body teetered, then fell, as if he had been pushed. The anomaly vanished. Progenitor tumbled toward the cathedral's roof. He did not stir, as if he were an idol carved from stone instead of flesh and blood.

I tried to catch Progenitor with my powers, but trying to grasp him was as ineffectual as probing the anomaly had been. Trying to latch onto him with my telekinesis was like trying to clutch a fistful of vapor. I had hoped me being Omega-level would make a difference in Progenitor's usual immunity to Meta powers, but I guess not.

Like a dropped rock, Progenitor smashed through the windows atop the cathedral's flat roof and disappeared.

41

I flew into the cathedral in pursuit of Progenitor, careful to drop through the same hole he had smashed in the roof's windows. In the U.S., a Hero was protected from legal liability for property damage caused in pursuit of the public interest. In addition to that, the New Sentinels had carried a boatload of gap insurance to cover losses outside the parameters of the Hero Act's hold harmless clause. Since I was outside the States, I wasn't sure if I would be held responsible for damage to the cathedral. Even more importantly, I used the same hole Progenitor had because I didn't want to cause more damage to the cathedral's iconic structure.

Broken glass tinkled down around me and screams rose to greet me as I dropped into the tall church with Progenitor tumbling below. The windows Progenitor had smashed through formed a cross in the conical cathedral's roof; the sunlight streaming through them provided much of the church's light. Stained glass windows extended from each of the four ends of the cross the roof's windows formed. Those four groups of stained glass windows extended from the ceiling all the way down to the floor. Broad honeycombed walls were between the groups of stained glass.

The inside of the cathedral was dark compared to the outside's brightness. But not so dark that I didn't see Progenitor hit the center of the church's polished stone floor like he was a dropped melon.

There was a sickening thump and a spray of blood. More people screamed. The cathedral had seating for 5,000 and a 20,000 people standing room capacity, but less than a hundred people were present now. Thank goodness mass wasn't in session. If the place had been packed, Progenitor would surely have killed people in his hard fall.

I hovered a few feet off the floor, yards away from Progenitor's crumpled body. Some people still screamed, while others ran out of the cathedral in frightened panic. A few rushed toward Progenitor to see if they could help. I swept the Good Samaritans off their feet and pushed them back, then erected a large force field around me and Progenitor to keep everyone else away.

Progenitor lay still. His limbs were twisted like a broken doll's. The rest of his naked body was ripped up and mangled thanks to both his fall through the windows and his impact with the cathedral floor. A shallow pool of blood slowly expanded around him as if someone poured raspberry syrup onto the stone floor.

Despite knowing what Progenitor was like and all he had done, I felt rather sorry for him. Maybe my prior plans to kill him hadn't been necessary. Maybe his fall had done the job for me.

But no, it was not to be.

Progenitor's body shuddered. He took a long, loud, gasping breath, like a man resuscitated after nearly drowning. His body twitched and spasmed. Cuts and gaping wounds rapidly began healing. Cracks and pops filled the air as his bones snapped back into place and twisted limbs straightened. The sound reminded me of the last time I ate crab legs. It's strange, the random things that popped into your head at a time like this.

Grunting in pain and effort, Progenitor struggled to rise. He reminded me of a newborn colt covered in gore trying to get its legs under itself. His eyes popped open, blinking with disorientation. I would have said, "Feel free to surrender now," but Progenitor wouldn't have understood me. The last words Progenitor had spoken before his imprisonment had been in Brittonic, the Celtic language of King Arthur and his men. Modern English was a foreign language to Progenitor. If Progenitor's history of picking up languages was any guide, however, he'd be speaking English like he was the king of England soon enough.

His head swiveled upward, and Progenitor saw me. He did a double take, and he stopped trying to rise. His eyes roamed over my hovering body, then met mine.

Me feeling sorry for him immediately stopped. Comatose, Progenitor's face had been peaceful. Almost innocent. Awake, his face was that of a predator. The unflinching look he gave me was the look a lion gave an antelope. Despite facing more than my fair share of Rogues over the years, Progenitor's dark eyes filled me with dumb animal terror.

A slow smile of delight spread across Progenitor's face that was in bizarre contrast to the trembling of his healing bloody body. The smile combined the glee of a kid at Christmas with that of a serial killer who has come home to unexpectedly find a naked woman tied spread-eagled to his bed.

Progenitor resumed trying to stand. I wasn't going to just

stand here and wait for Progenitor to slice his present open. My powers opened the leather bag Sage had given me and sent two glass balls sailing toward Progenitor. People say you shouldn't kick a man when he's down, but those people hadn't seen what Progenitor was capable of.

The balls exploded on impact with the floor. Plumes of thick greenish-yellow knockout gas billowed out, far more than I would have expected from the balls' size. I trapped the gas within a domed force field around Progenitor, hotboxing him and preventing the gas from being inhaled by anyone else. The opaque gas quickly swallowed Progenitor, shrouding him from view.

Seconds ticked by. Despite my force fields being ineffective against Progenitor, he didn't move out of the confines of this one. Maybe he had already passed out from the gas. Maybe defeating him had been just that easy. It felt a little anti-climactic, but I wasn't complaining.

Progenitor rocketed out of my force field, zooming toward me like a shot arrow. I darted to the side, making him miss and zoom past me. I would have been caught off guard had I not been given a split-second heads-up by air molecules shifting within my force field, indicating Progenitor had launched himself at me.

Progenitor's momentum made him crash into the cathedral's concrete wall behind me. The wall cracked and splintered from the force of the impact. If I hadn't moved out of the way, Progenitor would have smeared me on the wall like a bug smeared on a windshield.

Progenitor had tried to correct course after missing me, but only succeeded in twisting himself around so that he slammed into the cathedral wall back-first. Embedded in the wall like a dart thrown too hard at a dartboard, he struggled to free himself.

I wasn't going to give him that chance. Four candlesticks shot toward him like javelins. I had torn the tall metal stands from their spots around the cathedral's altar, ripping off their tops so they were jagged and sharp.

The candlesticks speared through Progenitor's forearms and thighs, embedding themselves in the concrete behind him. Progenitor's blood spurted. His screams arose above those of the spectators. I had pinned him to the wall like a beetle in an entomologist's collection. Though I couldn't use my powers on Progenitor directly, I could use them against him indirectly. I had learned that through Progenitor's memories of his daughter Lere—though she could not make his body explode with her powers, when she had made a log explode near him, a chunk of flying wood had cut his unarmored forehead. I doubted the candlesticks would have penetrated Progenitor's limbs if he were armored. I could only assume he was still too weak from his body's recent reincorporation to don his armor.

If at first you don't succeed, try, try again, I thought as I sent two more potion-filled balls shooting toward Progenitor. They exploded on the wall next to his thrashing head, their gas once more filling the confines of the small force field I surrounded him with. Progenitor disappeared again amidst the opaque gas.

As if their switch had been flipped, Progenitor's screams died thanks to my airtight force field. Progenitor burrowing deep under the North Pole with a single held breath testified to his terrific lung capacity, but I hoped the candlesticks pinning him would slow him down enough that he'd be forced to inhale the knockout gas before he freed himself from the wall.

Progenitor flew out of the gas-filled force field yet again and barreled toward me, trailing blood from where he ripped his arms and legs through the candlesticks. But as before, I felt Progenitor moving toward me before I saw him. I dodged out of the way, and he ripped through the air where I had been.

This time he checked himself before colliding with the opposite wall. Still naked, still bleeding but rapidly healing, his body curved up the side of the tall cathedral in pursuit of me. I was flying back to the roof. Knocking Progenitor out the way I had been trying to knock him out clearly wasn't working. The longer we fought in this confined space, the more damage the iconic cathedral would take. More importantly, the greater the risk innocent bystanders would be hurt or killed.

My communicator beeped at me as I zoomed toward the roof, and I spat out a quick status report. Threading the needle of where Progenitor and I had crashed through the cathedral's windows, I emerged into the air over the church. The sky seemed darker than it had before.

Progenitor ripped a new hole in the cathedral's cross-shaped roof an instant later. He wasn't as fastidious about Catholic Church property as I was. Maybe he was Protestant.

I zoomed away. With Progenitor in hot pursuit, I zigzagged between and around the city's tall buildings, flying fast enough to stay out of Progenitor's reach, but slow enough that I didn't lose him. If I lost him, I didn't know if I'd be able to find him again. Not to mention all the trouble he'd likely cause.

The irony was not lost on me. I'd gone to all this trouble to find Progenitor, only to have the tables turn and have him chase me. Now that Progenitor had found a new playmate, he seemed unwilling to let me go. I guess almost two thousand years of home confinement made you anxious for company.

A minute that seemed like hours passed. With each passing second, Progenitor flew faster. The longer we flew, the harder it was to evade Progenitor without breaking the sound barrier and damaging property with sonic booms.

A flash of reflected silver in the mirrored facade of a building we zoomed past made me hazard a glance back. Instead of being naked, Progenitor was covered from head to toe in his silver armor. I noted that fact into my communicator. Progenitor seemed completely healed from his cathedral injuries. Could him hurling lightning be far behind? The once sunny sky was rapidly turning cloudy. Surely Progenitor's reappearance followed by this abrupt change of weather was no coincidence.

Progenitor was so close now, I could practically smell him. If he got his hands on me, I knew I would become a modern-day version of Ghekk or Bheb.

I banked sharply to the left, careening between two buildings, Progenitor hot on my trail. White feathers flashed in my peripheral vision as I cleared the buildings. I kicked in the afterburners, giving myself an extra boost of speed that put more distance between me and my pursuer.

I twisted in midair in time to see twin jets of flame collide with Progenitor. They rocked him like they were exploding missiles instead of fire. He howled in pain, veering off his pursuit course, knocked at a downward angle. His body blazed like a paper airplane set afire as he tumbled toward the ground. Isaac, his white pegasus wings flapping, pursued him. Grimoire rode Isaac's winged horse form bareback, holding onto him with just her legs, her hands overhead and ablaze as she maintained the spellfire that burned Progenitor.

I had led Progenitor into a trap the rest of the team had set up while I played keep away with him. They had cut things awfully close, though. Staying away from Progenitor had initially been easy, but it quickly had become hard. He had nearly caught me. "What took you so long?" I said, breathing hard.

"We stopped on the way to pick up sugar cubes for Myth," Rewind said through my earbud.

Progenitor fell out of the sky like a burning meteorite, toward the weed-infested parking lot of a mid-rise office building scheduled for demolition. Ninja, Hacker, and Rewind were already crouched behind cars there. The team had chosen this location because it was about as isolated as you could get in a major metropolitan area like Rio. While I had been playing tag with Progenitor, the others had been evacuating the few people in the area.

Progenitor, still on fire, hit the blacktop of the parking lot at an acute angle. He bounced, tumbled through the air, hit the blacktop again, went rolling, and finally slammed into a parked SUV. Metal and plastic crumpled around him and glass rained down on him as the car's alarm shrieked. Incredibly, the car did not ignite despite being wrapped around a man who was literally on fire. Spellfire, it seemed, was not like regular fire. It would only burn what Grimoire willed it to burn, which was why The Mountain's conference room table and chair hadn't been scorched when Grimoire self-immolated. Moreover, spellfire could burn what normal fire couldn't, which was why Progenitor's armored body was doing its best Human Torch impersonation now.

If I had fallen out of the sky, been gassed, skewered by candlesticks, gassed again, set on fire, fallen out of the sky again, and rammed into an SUV, I might pack it in and call

448

it a day. Not Progenitor, though. Incredibly, he staggered to his feet, screaming like a banshee as he burned.

His burning hands dug into the SUV. He picked the large vehicle up as if it were light as papier-mâché. Quick as a wink, he twisted like a discus thrower and sent the SUV spinning through the air.

It whipped toward where Isaac and Grimoire hovered.

"I've got it," I announced through my communicator. Isaac didn't dodge out of the way, trusting my words. I altered the SUV's flight path, making it miss Isaac and Grimoire.

It whipped around them and headed back to Progenitor like a boomerang. A boomerang that, thanks to me rupturing its gas tank and causing a spark in its combustion system, was also now a three-ton Molotov cocktail.

The SUV slammed into Progenitor, knocking him over. The SUV exploded, and Progenitor's fiery form was swallowed by a fireball. The concussion from the blast set off more car alarms.

Fire raged and smoke mushroomed, obscuring the SUV's wreckage behind an orange and black curtain. I couldn't see Progenitor.

"Maybe we KO'd him," Rewind said from his post behind a car below. A few more seconds passed, and there was still no sign of Progenitor in the blaze. "Did we win? If feels like we won." I almost laughed at the thought. Until now, I never would have considered the world-weary Rogue Pollyannaish. After the abuse Progenitor had absorbed and recovered from in the church, it was unlikely this was over. Besides, the sky was dark now, with storm clouds as dark overhead as the ones in Lim's dreamworld. A bad omen.

My fears were justified. Rewind's optimistic words had barely faded when the remnants of the SUV exploded again. Fiery pieces of shrapnel sprayed everywhere, making me erect force fields to protect everyone.

Like a phoenix rising from its ashes, Progenitor rose to his feet at the epicenter of the explosion. Grimoire's spellfire still raged on him. His armor was cracked and partially melted, but he clearly was not yet down for the count.

"Light him up guys," I shouted.

But the order wasn't necessary. Ninja had already sprung atop the roof of the car she had been crouched behind, taking aim with one of the Little Green Men's ray guns. What looked like a twinkling emerald star rocketed out of the gun's barrel, accompanied by a noise like a sound effect from an alien invasion video game. The emerald star hit Progenitor square in his chest, exploding in a brilliant flash of green light, rocking Progenitor backward.

Ninja rapidly continued to fire. If a single shot missed, I didn't see it. Her barrage was joined by blue lasers from Hacker's drones that raked Progenitor's body. The drones danced and swooped in the air all around Progenitor, attacking him from all sides. Behind Progenitor, Rewind and Hacker began firing other Little Green Men ray guns, sighting along the hoods of different cars. Their marksmanship wasn't as unerring as Ninja's, but their shots hit Progenitor more often than they missed.

I supplemented the others' attacks by pelting Progenitor with everything I could get my telekinetic hands on, careful to avoid smashing Hacker's dancing drones. Cars, car parts, lumber, cinder blocks, slabs of concrete, fire hydrants . . . all that and more smashed into Progenitor. I would've thrown the kitchen sink at him had one been handy. Since he was immune to Metahuman powers, the team was using magic, high tech, and brute force to bring him down. If we could overwhelm his healing factor and incapacitate him, even for just a few seconds, we could force him to inhale or swallow Grimoire's potion.

Progenitor tried to go airborne and escape us, but I was ready for him—each time, I ensnared him in snapped power lines, ropes, cables, or asphalt that rose from the ground like a black fist, yanking him back down.

Under our relentless attack, Progenitor's armor melted further and grew even more fragmented, exposing his skin.

Eventually, Progenitor fell to his knees. And yet we did not stop our attacks. Progenitor's unceasing howls became tinged with frustration. We kept piling on. He collapsed, flailing on the ground like a poisoned roach.

We were winning. Even the storm clouds seemed to be thinning, and the sun threatened to peek through them.

Suddenly, the asphalt under Progenitor swirled, much the way an anthill does when the nest has been disturbed and ants are about to boil out. But instead of something coming out of the ground, Progenitor sank into it.

The ground closed, swallowing Progenitor, and he disappeared.

We stopped our attacks; there was nothing to aim at. The only thing that remained was a huge scorch mark around the area where Progenitor had been. The scene was abruptly quiet, marred only by the whines of approaching sirens.

I didn't know what was happening. But whatever it was, I didn't like it. I could only assume Progenitor had used his powers over nature to burrow underground. I scanned the ground with my powers. "There's no trace of him through my telekinetic touch," I announced to the others. "Grimoire, can you track him with your spellfire?"

"The spellfire went out as soon as he disappeared," Grimoire said, still in the air on Isaac. "I can't exert my magical will on something I can't see. Maybe I can cast an earth spell to track him."

"Do it," I snapped.

The earth began to rumble, so hard that everything on the ground shook.

"Uh, that's not me," Grimoire said.

That quickly became obvious. A giant head sprouted out of the ground like we were on Easter Island instead of in Rio. The head was followed by a neck, torso, arms . . . then an entire black and brown body composed of tightly compacted dirt mixed with the parking lot's asphalt. In the blink of an eye, the body was over 400 feet tall, looming higher than where I hovered in the air. It was like watching the time lapse footage of a mountain being formed.

Only this mountain moved. Its speed belying its size, it moved like a striking snake. I dodged its hand as it tried to swat me.

Isaac and Grimoire weren't so lucky. The earthen beast's other hand struck them, knocking Grimoire off Isaac, and sending him spinning end over end through the air. Grimoire dropped limply like a broken kite, her cloak flapping as she fell.

I snagged Grimoire with my telekinesis. Isaac flapped his wings, stunned, but already righting himself in the air. It looked like he'd be fine. I wasn't so sure about Sage—she had borne the brunt of the monster's blow. "Grimoire, are you alright?" I asked through my communicator. "Grimoire?"

No response. Grimoire's body was limp, but I couldn't take the time to examine her more thoroughly with my powers. We'd all wind up like her if I didn't focus on the monster. It was stomping the ground like a man killing ants, only in this case the ants were Ninja, Hacker, and Rewind.

Ninja somersaulted out of the way of a stomping foot. It smashed a truck into smithereens instead. Ninja's katana flashed pink with her Metahuman power, slicing off part of the monster's huge foot. For all the good it did. The damaged foot repaired itself immediately. Hacker's drones were firing at the monster with their lasers, just as Rewind and Hacker were firing at it with their ray guns. What little damage their attacks caused immediately healed. Their attacks were like mosquito bites to a giant.

"Rewind, take Grimoire," I ordered. "Make sure she's okay." The Rogue stopped firing, looking up as I lowered Grimoire to him while simultaneously dodging the monster's continuing efforts to swat me like a fly. Rewind slung his rifle over his shoulder and caught Grimoire. Cradling her in his arms, he scampered out of immediate danger and darted around the corner, disappearing. The monster was too busy focusing on the rest of us to follow him.

I ran my telekinetic touch over the monster. There was a man-shaped cavity in the center of the beast's earthen torso I couldn't probe. It had to be Progenitor, animating the earth from within, wearing the soil and asphalt like it was a building-sized suit of armor.

Fortunately, unlike Progenitor, the soil was not immune to my powers. I reached out with them, my fingers curling before me as I visualized ripping the earthen beast in two like I was opening a subway car door that had scissored shut on my foot.

I felt Progenitor's will resist my own. Trying to break the monster apart was hard, far harder than it would have been had another Meta's powers not been pitted against my own.

Hard, but not impossible. Thanks to being Omega-level, I had a lot of raw power. Subtle stuff like stopping Stopwatch's heart without permanently hurting him was really difficult. Big, splashy stuff like I was trying to do now was right up my alley.

I smashed through Progenitor's resistance. Then, ripping the monster apart was as easy as ripping a piece of paper.

The earthen monster split in half, its twin parts collapsing into loose dirt that hit the ground like a hard rain.

Progenitor zoomed out of the center of the collapsing monster. His armor intact once more, he grabbed my outstretched hands in a viselike grip before I could blink, much less move away.

Progenitor squeezed. Bones in my wrists and hands snapped like brittle twigs. I heard the sound before I felt the pain. Progenitor's quick mind must have deduced through watching me I needed the use of my hands to channel my power.

He released me. Without my powers, I dropped like a bag of cement.

Terminal velocity was 120 miles per hour, and I wasn't up high enough to achieve it. I barely processed the relevant but ultimately unhelpful thought when my back hit the hard ground. I felt my shoulder blade crack and something in my back snap. The air whooshed out of me. My head bounced off the ground, and I tasted blood. Fresh pain piled on top of the pain from my shattered hands and arms. The fact I could taste or feel anything after a fall like this was a minor miracle. The Omega suit had automatically blunted some of the force of the fall and redistributed the rest of it, or else I probably wouldn't have survived.

Progenitor landed with a thud several dozen yards away from me. The low rumble of thunder was the soundtrack to his approach toward me. I tried to stand, but couldn't. Something was wrong with my back. I couldn't move my hands and fingers, either. My fingers were gnarled and twisted, pointing in the wrong directions. Using my powers was out of the question. All I could do was crab walk on my back, pushing with my feet, trying to scramble away from the approaching villain. Every inch was agony. Progenitor's body erupted with green and blue glows as Ninja, Hacker, and Hacker's drones blasted away at him, more likely in an attempt to distract him from me than a real effort to hurt him. The iridescent display of their attacks glancing off Progenitor's armor reminded me of the fireworks display during New Sentinels Day.

His eyes on me, still moving implacably toward me, Progenitor pointed a single finger in the direction of Ninja and Hacker. I understood the significance of the gesture an instant later. What looked like black clouds coalesced from the surrounding area. But they weren't clouds. They were flying insects. Thousands of them, swarming together. Their buzzing filled the air.

The clouds enveloped Hacker and Ninja, nearly obscuring them from view. Hacker dropped her ray gun, clawing at her ears and nose and swatting her exposed skin. Though I was too far away to distinguish the insects that swarmed her, I could only assume they were wasps, bees, horseflies, mosquitoes, and other stinging and biting insects. The drones broke off their attack on Progenitor and flew toward Hacker, presumably to help her. Only Ninja kept firing at Progenitor, even though the cloud of insects was as thick around her as it was around Hacker. Maybe she had closed her eyes, was holding her breath, and was firing at the sound of Progenitor's metal feet clanking against the pavement. With Ninja, I wouldn't be surprised.

When Progenitor was almost on top of me, Ninja's firing stopped. Maybe she'd been overwhelmed by the insect swarm. Progenitor's fists clenched, his metallic face expressionless. Only his dark eyes displayed the pleasure he felt at the prospect of snuffing out my life. They almost seemed to dance with joy as they looked down at me.

Panting, riddled with pain, I stopped trying to back away. If I was going to die, it wasn't going to be while I crawled away like a worm in the dirt. I eyed Progenitor's armored legs, getting ready to kick as hard as I could. I wondered if Progenitor would even feel my kicks as he bashed my head in.

Progenitor's fists raised overhead like a guillotine about to descend.

42

I caught a blur out of the corner of my eye. A giant animal with the body of a lion, the wings of an eagle, and the head of a ram swooped from above. It slammed into Progenitor with its massive curved horns, colliding with a sound like that of a car slamming into a brick wall.

It was a criosphinx.

Isaac.

Progenitor went flying like an eight ball slammed by a cue ball. He was propelled hundreds of feet, toward the condemned building we were near. His body smashed through the building's brick wall and disappeared. Isaac flapped after him, moving incredibly fast despite his criosphinx body being the size of a car. His ram head lowered, Isaac smashed through the same hole Progenitor had punched through the building's wall, enlarging the hole as his bigger animal body tore through it.

Smashes and crashes sounded from the building, the mid-sized structure literally shaking as Isaac and Progenitor fought inside.

I had to get up! I had to go help Isaac. He didn't stand a chance against Progenitor alone.

But I only succeeded in rolling over, my shattered arms shrieking in agony as I tried to lever myself to my feet.

There was another loud crash, and Isaac's criosphinx body burst through another wall, shooting in our direction. Not under his own power, though. His wings were limp as he twisted like a rifled bullet through the air, trailing blood.

Isaac's massive body hit the ground, digging a long furrow in the asphalt. Progenitor flew through the same hole in pursuit of Isaac. If he reached Isaac, he'd surely kill him.

He didn't reach Isaac, however. Before his body stopped plowing through the ground, Isaac transformed with a glow. His big bird wings flapping, Isaac rose like a rocket, moving so fast he was out of sight in a twinkling. Progenitor zoomed into the sky after him, on a pursuit course.

Isaac had turned into a Garuda, the giant mythological bird that flew faster than the wind. I knew he wasn't abandoning the rest of us. Quite the opposite. He was leading Progenitor away from us to give us a chance to escape and regroup.

He was sacrificing his own life to save ours. When I had raced Isaac from Silver Sable to the mansion in his Garuda form, I had beaten him easily, even after giving him a head start. There was no way Isaac could evade Progenitor for long, especially as Progenitor seemed stronger the longer he was in corporeal form.

Progenitor would kill Isaac when he caught him. We had to save him.

No, not we. Me. I had to save him. Though Hacker's drones had somehow gotten rid of the insect swarm that plagued her and they were moving to do the same with Ninja, neither Hero could fly. Neither could Rewind or Grimoire.

It was up to me. The problem was Progenitor had clipped my wings. I was as earthbound as the others.

Storm clouds covered the sky, and it was as dark as twilight. It was raining. So much had happened, I hadn't noticed before.

I somehow got to my knees, my entire body shrieking in protest, making me almost pass out from the pain. With a thought, I removed the Omega suit from my twisted, broken hands and stared at them. The rain washed some of the blood away, exposing the whiteness of bones poking through ripped skin and flesh. My hands still burned hot with my powers but, since I couldn't move my fingers, my telekinesis was like a light switch I could see but that was out of reach.

With panic over Isaac fluttering like a heartbeat in my chest, I stared lasers at my twisted fingers, willing them to move, if only just a little. My insides danced with impatience and fear for Isaac. *C'mon, c'mon, c'mon!*

My pinky twitched.

It was enough. That twitch enabled me to focus my powers enough to snap bones back into place and set up force fields where other bones had been shattered.

In seconds, I was able to flex my fingers. My arms and hands felt like their bones had been ripped out in exchange for red-hot pokers that seared me from the inside out, but I could move my hands and fingers again.

I did the same with the rest of my body, moving bones back into place and shoring my body up with force fields.

I stood awkwardly, almost toppling over, feeling like a

freshly animated Frankenstein's monster held together with chewing gum and baling wire. I hurt all over. I wanted to collapse in a red puddle of pain. My command of my powers was shaky, like I was trying to conduct an orchestra with broken arms and hands. My powers weren't at even fifty percent capacity. Not even close.

It would have to do.

I catapulted myself into the weeping dark sky after Isaac and Progenitor.

It took longer than it should have to sense Isaac with my telekinetic touch, and longer still to fly close enough to spot him. He and Progenitor were miles away from where we had all been. They were above Corcovado, the mountain atop which the Christ the Redeemer statue overlooked Rio. Lightning danced in the dark clouds above them. Isaac's Garuda form wasn't even trying to outrun Progenitor anymore. He dove, bobbed, and weaved in the air, trying to stay away from Progenitor, like it was an aerial game of tag. A gaggle of tourists were on the observation platform around the white soapstone and cement Christ the Redeemer statue. The people were drenched, caught unawares by the unexpected thunderstorm which raged. Despite the storm, they stared up at where Isaac and Progenitor zoomed above them, as if the two were putting on a show.

I rocketed toward the two flyers, my body feeling like it would fly apart under the stress. I didn't know what I would do when I reached them. *Save Isaac* was the extent of my plan.

I was still seconds away when Isaac zigged when he should have zagged. Progenitor collided with Isaac's giant bird form. Feathers exploded from Isaac's body.

His wings limp, Isaac fell out of the sky like a hunter had shot him, glowing as he tumbled, shrinking, resuming his human form. People on the platform surrounding Christ the Redeemer screamed and scattered.

Isaac crashed into the stone and concrete platform, bouncing once like a dropped sack of potatoes. He didn't move.

Progenitor plummeted from the sky, cratering the platform when he landed next to Isaac's still body.

Straddling Isaac, Progenitor punched Isaac's cowled head once.

Volcanic anger erupted within me. I saw red.

Progenitor punched Isaac's head again.

Wood, stone, and dirt shot from the mountain, swirling around me, coalescing into a makeshift suit of armor. I swept all the bystanders off the platform, moving them out of danger to the sides of the mountain. *Almost there.*

Progenitor punched a third time. Isaac's blood sprayed.

I slammed into Progenitor like a cannonball, catching him unawares, knocking him off of Isaac, sending both of us tumbling.

Progenitor's metallic body skidded on the stone platform, making sparks spray. Before he recovered, I leapt atop him like a cat pouncing on a mouse. Stones from the platform and rocks from the mountain swirled around my hands like boxing gloves.

They say adrenaline and fear give you hysterical strength, like when a mother lifts a car off her child.

I didn't know if that was true. I was no doctor. All I knew was that Progenitor had caused Lim's death and might've just killed Isaac.

And that I was going to beat the crap out of him.

That's exactly what I did. With my makeshift armor protecting me from Progenitor's blows, I treated his body like it was a punching bag, pounding him over and over, keeping him down, using my powers to exponentially augment my muscles and increase my speed, not feeling the pain of my battered body. All I felt was rage.

The armor around his head cracked from the force of my berserk assault. I seized the opening, concentrating on his head like it was a speed bag. As the rocks around my fists cracked and fell away, I replaced them. An unending stream of rocks swirled from the surroundings and hardened around my fists like they were the centers of their own Milky Way galaxies.

The cracks in Progenitor's armor became fissures. I continued to whale away at his head, not letting up for a second.

The armor crumbled from Progenitor's head. I continued to pile drive his head into the broken stone platform, driving him into the dirt underneath, turning his dark face into hamburger.

The fact Progenitor was no longer moving finally penetrated my frenzied fog of fear and rage. I reluctantly stopped pounding him. His face immediately began shifting, the flesh knitting together. It was his healing factor exerting itself. He still lived.

I wanted to kill him, but couldn't. Isaac wouldn't like that.

Anxious to tend to Isaac, I knew I couldn't just yet. I fished one of Grimoire's gelatin tablets out of the Omega suit and, using two fingers, jammed it into Progenitor's mouth. I burst it open with my powers and shoved the gelatinous knockout potion deep down his throat. I hoped he choked on it.

With Progenitor disposed of, my powers leapt me over to where Isaac's body lay. A leg was twisted at an unnatural angle under him. His black body armor was cracked and his cowl was split open, exposing a bloody mess. If I hadn't known it was him, I wouldn't have recognized him.

Fearing the worst, I checked his pulse with shaking hands.

He had one. Thank God! He was still alive. His pulse was weak and thready, but he was alive. From the looks of him, not for long.

I activated my communicator. "Grimoire, Myth is hurt bad. I need you to open a portal to transport him to the mansion's infirmary. Hurry!"

No response.

"Rewind, is Grimoire still with you? Rewind, come in."

Damn him, why didn't he answer? Had he run off when I entrusted him with Grimoire? As usual, Isaac had been right—I should've known better than to trust a Rogue.

Isaac's body was so mangled I was afraid I'd cause further damage by moving him myself. But I feared even more what would happen if I didn't move him. "Minerva, send me the coordinates to the closest hospital. Locate Doctor Hippocrates and tell him to drop what he's doing. Have him meet us at the hospital. I don't care how you get him here, but get him here right now. I need him to heal Isaac."

I barely heard Minerva's response while I probed Isaac's broken body as gently as I could, trying to figure out how to carry him with my powers without making a terrible situation worse. "Everything's going to be fine," I told Isaac, hearing my voice crack. *Please God, let everything be fine.* "I'll get you to a doctor. After all, you've got a wedding to plan. We'll get you fixed up as good as n—"

The word gurgled in my throat. My mouth was suddenly awash with thick blood. I felt a sharp stab, followed by a strange serenity that washed over me like a warm wave.

A silver sword was stuck through my chest; its sharp point gleamed two feet in front of me. The rain began to wash blood off it. *My* blood, I realized, almost dispassionately, as if I were having an out of body experience and witnessing the stabbing from far away.

The sword's blade withdrew, sliding back through my body, leaving almost no pain behind. I had read about how, when swimmers got their limbs bitten off by sharks, their bodies flooded them with endorphins, blotting out the pain, helping to keep them alive. Until now, I had never fully believed those stories.

Suddenly drowsy, in almost a dreamlike state, I could no longer support my weight with my powers. I slumped to my knees, blood sloshing from my limp mouth. I swayed, threatening to fall on Isaac's body like a felled tree.

Progenitor stepped between us, towering over us. The silver sword extending out of his upper arm shifted and morphed, transforming back into his regular armored arm. *Huh*, I thought dreamily. *That's new.*

Progenitor hawked loudly and spat. A huge ball of phlegm landed next to me, quivering under the rain. Unable to move my head, I shifted my eyes down. Within the phlegm was the ruptured gelatin tablet and all the knockout potion it contained.

Progenitor grabbed me around the throat with a single metallic hand. He lifted me until I was eye level with him. I dangled limply off the ground. I was reminded of how Progenitor had stiff-armed his nobleman before throwing him and his mistresses off the balcony of his palace.

Progenitor's armor hadn't regrown around his face yet,

but his face continued to rapidly heal. The regeneration made Progenitor seem youthful, reminding me of how Arouch had looked when he was but an innocent boy.

He looked me in the eye with dark shark eyes. Something about them reminded me of the storm clouds in Lim's dreamworld. I wanted to look away, but forced myself not to. It was the only act of resistance I could muster.

Progenitor smiled at me. His cracked and broken teeth repaired themselves before my very eyes.

For the first time today, he spoke. The words were heavily accented and garbled by the shifts of Progenitor's healing face, but I understood them.

He said, "You have great strength, my son. I think I will enjoy this brave new world."

Still holding me by the neck, Progenitor lifted me into the air. We sailed past Jesus' giant soapstone face and arms. It was as if his outstretched arms were welcoming me into heaven.

High in the air, Progenitor shifted me, holding me by my back and buttocks. My face was turned up to the storm clouds in which lightning cavorted. I knew what was coming next.

Maybe it was the Omega suit. Maybe it was the Omega spirit. Maybe it was simple dumb animal self-preservation.

Whatever it was, it cut through my serene paralysis, enabling me to trigger my powers one last time. The lightning strike Progenitor called down from the sky hit my force field instead of me. A billion volts of electricity danced on my field. It was too much for my weakened body and powers to simply repel. I had to absorb the electricity, transforming it into energy that made my cells dance and threatened to rip my body apart.

The instant the lightning strike ended, I vented the

energy back into the heavens. It poured out of me in red beams of light through every pore, turning the gloom of the storm into ruddy brightness. I wanted to vent it the other direction instead and destroy Progenitor with it, but knew the attempt would be fruitless. The Metahuman beams would pass harmlessly through him and hit the top of Corcovado instead, destroying it and killing everyone on it.

Rain poured on me, streaming down my body like the tears of a giant. I panted with exhaustion, every breath stabbing me anew, not ready for the next lightning strike, but knowing it would come. And there was nothing I could do to stop it this time.

I had failed everyone. My biggest regret was Isaac. My brother, dying or already dead.

For us, this was over. For the rest of the world, this was just beginning.

Another bolt of lightning ripped from the heavens, drawing me toward its light. This time, I'd have no choice but to walk toward the light.

I fell back-first, the wind whistling in my ears. Confused as to what was happening, I almost hit Christ the Redeemer as I plummeted past it. The gloom of the storm made the statue look like a giant crucifix.

The ground rushed up to greet me in its deadly embrace. Above me, Progenitor held Rewind overhead like a sacrifice to god.

The last thing I saw was lightning strike the red-garbed, time-traveling Rogue.

A shimmering black pit swallowed me whole.

The End

If you enjoyed this book, please leave a review on Amazon. Even a simple two-word review such as "Loved it" helps so much. Reviews are a big aid in helping readers like you find books they might like.

Turn the page to read the author's note about the book you just read.

AUTHOR'S NOTE

There will be a sixth book in this series.

I just wanted to get that out of the way before an angry mob forms in front of my house and demands to know what happens to Theo and his friends next.

For I am well aware that *Crisis* ends on a cliffhanger. But it was either that or have *Crisis* (my longest book to date, clocking in at nearly 132,000 words) turn into the superhero version of *War and Peace*. *War and Peace* is 587,000-plus words long for those of you who haven't counted the words in that book lately. And if you have counted the book's words lately, might I respectfully suggest a new hobby?

Besides, I accomplished everything I wanted to in *Crisis*: exploring the consequences of Theo's decisions in prior books; having Theo assemble a team to confront Progenitor; and setting up the war between Team Theo and Progenitor. That war will be the focus of the sixth book in the series. And, oh boy, it's a doozy.

Almost two and a half years separate the publication of *Crisis* and *Rogues*, the previous book in the *Omega Superhero* series. That was not the original plan when I published

Rogues. The original plan was to finish all the books in the *Omega Superhero* series before moving on to other projects. But, I had the urge to dip my toes in the waters of urban fantasy, so I took a hiatus from this series to write the first three books in my *Sorceress Super Hero* series. If you haven't read those books, Sage Hawthorne (aka Grimoire) stars in them. I enjoyed writing about her so much that I incorporated her in *Crisis*, which had not been in the original plan when I plotted this book out years ago.

Speaking of characters who make an appearance in *Crisis*, let's talk about Lim Qiaolian. Lim was first mentioned in *Hunted*, the fourth book in my *Superhero Detective* series that came out over four years ago. She was later mentioned in *Caped*—the first book in the series you're currently reading—and again in *Sentinels*, the third book in this series. Unfortunately, in *Caped* she's called Liam instead of Lim. Despite many rounds of edits, I did not spot the typo until literally years after *Caped*'s publication. I could correct the mistake, but decided to roll with it instead. Hence this passage when Lim introduces herself to Theo in *Crisis*: *"Some of the books you Westerners have written insist on calling me Liam, but it's Lim. Liam's not even a Chinese name. So much for fact-checking." The girl sniffed disdainfully.*

It amuses me that Lim found a way to criticize her creator. That's exactly the sort of thing she would do. She was a lot of fun to write.

I want to give a special thanks and shout-out to the people who support my Patreon superhero fiction writing campaign at the rate of $5 or more per month:

Jacob Anderson
Robert Britton
Matthew Chua

Tommy Hennessy
Wilton Hockaday
Andrew Jones
Chris Langston
Flint L. Miller
Kathy Mills
Douglas Park Jr.
Jeremy Powell
Arthur Raisfeld
Richard A. Spake
Bernadette Turner
Jack R. Voss

If you want to join these fine folks in exchange for exclusive perks like cover reveals, sneak peeks at books, and other cool stuff, check out my Patreon campaign: www.patreon.com/dariusbrasher.

Thanks so much for reading *Crisis*. If you enjoyed it, please don't forget to leave a review on Amazon. Reviews help me sell books, income from book sales subsidize my coffee habit, and my coffee habit fuels writing more books. It's the literary circle of life. Don't break that circle by letting me die from caffeine withdrawal.

Seriously, please leave a review. Thanks!

Darius ~ August 2020

ALSO BY DARIUS BRASHER

Sorceress Super Hero Series

Sorceress Super Hero

Monster Madness

Hero Hunt

Sorceress Super Hero Box Set (Books 1-3)

Superhero Detective Series

Superhero Detective for Hire

The Missing Exploding Girl

Killshot

Hunted

Accused Hero

Omega Superhero Series

Caped

Trials

Sentinels

Rogues

Crisis

Omega Superhero Box Set (Books 1-3)

ABOUT THE AUTHOR

Darius Brasher has a lifelong fascination with superheroes and a love of fantasy and science fiction. He has a Bachelor of Arts degree in English, a Juris Doctor degree in law, and a PhD from the School of Hard Knocks. He lives in South Carolina.

Email: darius@dbrasher.com

patreon.com/dariusbrasher

facebook.com/dariusbrasher

twitter.com/dariusbrasher

amazon.com/author/dariusbrasher